THE BRUNSWICK BRAWLER

ALSO BY DREW HALFPENNY

IN THE ABC CHRONICLES:

Book One: *The Connickle Conundrum*

BOOK TWO OF THE ABC CHRONICLES

THE BRUNSWICK BRAWLER

DREW HALFPENNY

First published in Great Britain in 2024
by Gunmetal & Gilt Publishing.

A CIP catalogue record for this book is available from
the British Library.

1 3 5 7 9 10 8 6 4 2

ISBN 978 1 7396970 1 3

For my late parents, Audrey and Cliff.

*One of whom would be proud as punch and the other
mortally horrified to see their names in print.*

*Thank you for your unconditional love
and unwavering belief in your son.*

CHANGING FACES

Issy trudged upstairs. no longer able to keep her drooping eyelids open. Even the fear of the recurring dream couldn't withstand her exhaustion at this hour. After an abbreviated nightly routine, she collapsed into bed and fell asleep as her head hit the pillow.

Her heart leapt as the dream unfolded around her.

Once again, she was gliding, arms outstretched, silvery moonlight caressing her form. Her hair tousled as the gentle breeze carried her over rolling meadows and under countless stars twinkling in the sable sky.

Theo was with her again, clasping her hand, flying at her side.

She felt safe in his grasp as they glided over glistening rooftops with smoking chimneys. They were children once more, giggling, carefree, happy.

Yes, happy, she thought. *We were happy… once.*

And now their hands were sliding apart, fingers barely touching. The tight knot of fear growing in her throat strangled her cry when she looked to her brother for reassurance that he would not let her fall. But his smiling eyes had become pools of raging obsidian, and his tender laugh a cruel, mocking cackle.

Why Theo, why? Their fingertips parted, and she was falling, tumbling through a red sparkling mist into the darkness. As certain death approached, below her, upturned, hopeless, bloodied faces of tortured souls moaned and wailed, mouths widening to consume her mortal soul. Their sharp fingers clawing to pull her into their pit of despair.

Her back arched.

"Theo!"

A sharp intake of icy air propelled her body bolt upright in bed. Sweat stuck her flannelette nightdress to her skin as she sat, eyes wide, panting. Wintry gusts through the open window snapped at the flimsy curtains and snowflakes swirled around the bedroom towards the ceiling. Watching them flutter like blossoms and melt on the floorboards slowed her racing heart. She untangled her legs from the counterpane and flopped back onto the cold, sweat-soaked sheets.

Why won't he even let me sleep in peace?

At times like these, she yearned to be that little girl again when her father would rush in, take her in his arms and stroke her hair to quell her fear, shushing the nightmare away.

But now, screaming banshees couldn't wake him from his drunken stupor.

So, pulling the covers up to her neck, she flounced onto her side and screwed up her face, knowing the night nadgers would battle her slumber.

Downstairs, the clock in the hall struck one and a long, restless night stretched out ahead of her.

Oh, Theo!

In the Praetorian, Algeria sat in her boudoir, pondering which face she would wear today. *Everyone has two*, she thought. *One for the world, and then... Only the Mother sees the one true face staring back from the mirror that never lies and never pretends.*

But as leader of a secret society, owner of a public house, abbess of a brothel, a mother and a widow, Algeria wore many faces to conceal her true self. Choosing one was becoming progressively difficult as her despair deepened.

She tightened her stays before buttoning up her green, ankle-to-throat dress and smoothing the fabric against her curves. Now, as she brushed her hair, the sad eyes of a lonely failure stared back from the gold-framed mirror. It was the same face she had seen yesterday, and the day before, and the day before that. Indeed, ever since she had returned from hospital after the incident at Barton, only the number of grey hairs changed.

She closed her eyes to shut out the pale wraith of the person she used to be. *That isn't who I am.*

Although her wounds had healed, regular flashbacks of her traumatic experiences on board the *Dea Tacita* dogged her waking thoughts, and behind her eyelids, those dark memories prophesied an even darker future.

The Order may have won the skirmish at Barton, but they were losing the war for hearts and minds. Since foiling Raven's plan, they had rooted out pockets of Anthropocene scum but, with their promise of a better future snatched from their grasp, most of his followers had gone to ground.

Now, the threat to the Connickle Laws was no longer in the realm of sabotage. The brazen grey-shirts of the Freedom movement had supplanted Raven's secretive cult. This political pressure group advocated against the Connickle Laws and opposed every tenet of the Order. Their meetings in the village halls of mill towns garnering support for their movement were producing a groundswell of anti-Connickle sentiment.

Finding their elusive leader was more urgent than ever.

But sending Stormriders to attend the rallies hadn't unearthed a shred of information about his whereabouts, and now, the search had gone cold.

Algeria was tired, but as High Mother, she was reluctant to share her innermost fears. And with no time to grieve Abel's loss, trying to win back the love of her daughter while fighting this new threat was proving to be a heavy burden even for the great Algeria Rebekah Darling.

Each day provided a different raft of problems.

So, often the first person she met dictated which face she wore. Today, a familiar knock on the boudoir door meant Eli would have that honour.

"Good morning, Algeria. Do you require *this 'kin* to prepare breakfast before *this 'kin* opens the bar?"

She put on her grateful employer face. "Two crumpets with butter, please, Eli, and a pot of tea… for one."

Eli turned and left as quickly and silently as he entered.

Now the face in the mirror oozed authority. *That's more like it.* She gathered the mess of papers on her dressing table and began tapping the bottom edges on the surface to square them. But the puzzled face in the mirror turned down the corners of its mouth. *I squared the papers last night before going to bed.*

Eli knocked and entered, sliding the breakfast tray onto the dressing table.

"Have you seen Dottie this morning?"

"*This 'kin* has only seen you and the bar staff. Shall *this 'kin* pour?"

"No. Thank you, Eli. I'll join you in the main bar shortly." When the door clicked shut, she checked to see if anything else had been disturbed. Satisfied everything was in its place, she sat back in the chair and bit into a crumpet.

I'm not going mad. But the face in the mirror suggested otherwise, crossing its eyes and sticking out its tongue. She smiled away her paranoia and, after she finished her tea and crumpets, joined Eli as he opened the doors to let in the early drinkers.

Dottie sauntered into the bar a few minutes later.

"Have you just got up, Doll?"

"No. I've been pottering around my room. Why?"

"I wondered if you came downstairs earlier."

"No. What's the problem?"

"No problem, shugah. Honestly. It's nothing." Algeria smiled. "Are you looking forward to your trip to the Freedom meeting at Green Booth?"

"I was…" Dottie spun on her heel and stomped back whence she came.

Algeria flopped onto a chair near the player piano and sighed.

"What-ho, Algy?" She put on her cheerful, pleased-to-see-you face to greet Lemmy. He frowned. "You look down in the dumps. What's up?"

If Lemmy can see right through me, it's going to be a long day.

GREY PERSUASION

Twin black envelopes skimmed the dark underside of the low-level clouds that had denied the watery winter sunshine for the entirety of the journey from Barton Aerodrome. Beads of condensed water streamed down the outer skins of *Frejya's Grimalkin*, falling in a curtain of rain around her gondola.

At the helm, Queequeg stood motionless, guiding the airship northward to the heart of Lancashire, and five Stormriders wrapped in thick brown woollen overcoats sat with their backs to the bulwarks.

"I'll take over from here." Jonah patted Queequeg on the back. "Go get some shuteye and recharge yer old batteries, or whatever it is that you do."

Renowned for his paucity of words, Queequeg put his splay-fingered hand on his chest and moved to sit in the gondola's prow. He took a lozenge-shaped tablet from the compartment in his left arm and pressed it into his mouth. Within seconds, his head flopped forward, and his arms dropped to his side.

Jonah sharply dipped the airship's nose away from the low cloud shrouding the valley, re-awakening Issy's recurring nightmare. For a few moments, she was weightless, falling, and it took all her strength to dispel the feelings of loss and keep down her breakfast.

Ace put his hand on Jonah's shoulder as he joined him at the wheel. He pointed at a mooring post on the opposite side of the weaving mill a quarter of a mile or so from Green Booth village hall.

Next to Issy, Dottie blew warm breath into her cupped hands and rubbed them together. When Algeria told her of the Freedom Brigade meeting in Green Booth, Dottie had volunteered to join the mission, hoping to see the folks who had helped them during their flight from the Forge. And although she knew Gilbert would have wanted to go with them, she had kept it from him because it clashed with his discussions with Handysides about returning to work on the ship canal project.

"What if your friends *are* here?" Issy asked. "I know you're eager to see them, but I'm sure you'd be upset to find them involved with this Freedom movement."

Dottie nodded. "Curiosity might draw them to the meeting, but I can't imagine they'd want any part of it."

"The Freedom Brigade presents a persuasive argument. *Est via quae videtur homini recta et novissimum eius ducit ad mortem!*" Ace shouted above the roar of the engines as Jonah slowed their approach.

Issy looked up at the heavens. She leaned closer to Dottie, but still had to shout. "I've not heard that one for a while!"

Freyja's Grimalkin jerked to a shuddering halt as the electromagnets tugged the airship the final few inches and attached it to the mooring post with a *clang*.

Issy turned to Ace and Lemmy. "Like the Bacup meeting, you two need to keep your mouths shut. Anyone hearing your cut-glass accents will know we're not the millworkers we purport to be. Let Jonah do the talking."

"I say, old girl. Do you really think one speaks like a toff? What say you, Jonah, old bean?" Lemmy couldn't resist the opportunity.

"Yer doing it on purpose now, aren't yer?" Jonah was last to jump off the bottom rung of the ladder, landing ankle deep in the sodden mud.

Issy's raised eyebrow choked Ace's chortle.

This was their third uninvited attendance at a Freedom meeting, and after what they'd witnessed at Bacup, the consequences of being discovered were unthinkable. She pulled on her dirty white cotton bonnet and tied its straps under her chin before helping Dottie with her headscarf.

Ace and Jonah pulled on weathered flat caps. Then, wrapped up against the bitter wind, they set off for the village hall, along the silent streets of soot-blackened, terraced stone houses.

"Where are all the children?" Dottie asked.

"In Bacup, half the mothers cared for the kids at the Methodist chapel, so the rest could attend. These meetings are very popular, you know." Jonah pointed his head at the crowds filing into the hall. "Looks like standing room only."

Two grey-shirted, muscle-bound bully boys flanked the entrance, squinting at each face as the curious and converted entered.

"This is new." Ace spoke from behind his turned-up coat collar.

"Leave this to me," Jonah said.

Issy and Dottie smiled at the guards as they walked, unchallenged, into the smoke-filled hall. But behind them, the shorter grey-shirt barred Ace's progress with an arm across his chest.

"Not seen you 'round these parts, brother."

Ace stooped and pointed to the scarf around his neck.

Jonah stepped between them. "He's lost his voice. Summat wrong with his throat."

"Yeah? So, where've you come from? With that accent, you're not from 'round here, are yer?" The stocky man kept his hand firmly pressed against Ace but raised his questioning eyebrow at Jonah.

"We've walked all the way from Norden. You aren't going to stop us getting in, now, are you? And no, lad. I'm not from these parts." He spat at the thug's feet and nodded to the east. "Born and bred in God's own country on t'other side of them there hills. Jonah Wyvern by name, proud Yorkshireman by birth and fierce as hell, if you want to try me." He poked the thug in the shoulder and stepped closer. Their noses were inches apart.

But the man recoiled from Ace's loud, wet cough, pulling

his hand off his chest. Jonah's head turned to hold the man's glare as he strode past him into the hall.

"That was too close for comfort." Issy's eyes shone as she dug her elbow into Ace's ribs. "Why do you have to look so regal?"

"When does the meeting start?" Dottie stood on her tiptoes, her gaze flicking from face to face.

"Not long," Issy said. "Any sign of your friends?"

"Nah. They're not here. Godfrey Olleranshaw was as tall and skinny as a beanpole. If he was here, he'd stick out."

Five wooden chairs were arranged in a row on the low stage that stretched across the far wall. As Issy watched, a door swung open on the right side of the hall and four grey-shirted, grim-faced thugs strode out and stood in front of the platform, facing the crowd.

"Here we go," Issy whispered to Dottie as five more marched in step along the stage to a smattering of applause and a few cheers.

The men wore hammer-shaped badges on the left breast of their grey shirts. After a few moments, the clapping subsided and the man in the centre of the stage stepped to the front, hands raised for silence.

"Brothers and sisters. Welcome to your very own village hall and welcome to Freedom."

A few cheered, but most stood silent, arms folded. *It takes more than a word to impress these working folk*, Issy thought.

The speaker turned the corners of his mouth down and nodded. "So… You'll be wanting to know who we are and why are we here. Well, it's very simple… We are you and you are us. We talk the same language and share the same goals. Our names aren't important, but you can call me, and my brothers, councillors."

"Speak up, lad! We can't hear thee at t'back!" Heads turned in the crowd to search for the owner of the interrupting voice.

The councillor leaned forward and tapped two grey-shirted shoulders, pointing out the culprit. The hubbub grew as they hauled the old man to the front. Supported between the two burly grey-shirts, he stood in his dark red coat and flat cap, facing the stage. The speaker requested silence again, then bent at the hips with his hands behind his back to address the old man. His V-shape-furrowed brow and matching smile gave him a devilish air.

"Can you hear me now, brother?"

You could have heard a spindle drop as the old man dragged his cap from his wispy-haired head.

"Good. Then, perhaps, you can help me."

The old man looked left and right.

"The weaving mill, over yonder. Who owns it?"

"That-that'll be Mister Shacklady. He lives in t'big house on t'hill."

"Thank you, brother." The councillor straightened and nodded at a group of thugs who hurried through a side exit. "Now... We are here to tell you of the great injustice being inflicted on us all." He paused and spread his arms as if to embrace the gathering, looking into the eyes of those closest to the stage.

"Today, you are going to learn the truth about the false

prophet, Connickle."

The crowd's murmuring grew louder.

"Aye, that's right. Connickle was a fraud. His theories on climate change are unproven, and the laws passed in his name are for one purpose only… to keep us in our place!" The councillor had to raise his voice over the growing noise. He carried on. "Holding back innovation doesn't affect the toffs because they have meks to do their bidding. But it denies us access to the same luxuries as them.

"Aye, they have airships and broughams, but we're forced to travel by Tick Tock or HyBrid, which costs us dearly and puts money straight into the corrupt government's pockets. Only toffs and mill owners benefit from the Connickle Laws' oppression. All the while, they laugh at us, whose honest toil keeps their coffers full, and their bellies stuffed!"

The hubbub was growing louder as heads turned and nodded in agreement.

"Let me tell you how things are." The councillor was pacing from side to side as he addressed the crowd. "You see, the toffs are akin to passengers on a great steamship, strutting and preening on the upper decks, sipping their cocktails and playing quoits. Skilled artisans are the crew keeping the engines turning and the ship on course.

"But wait. If the skilled workers are the crew, what are we?" He spread his arms and surveyed the congregation. "We are the ocean. We are the souls carrying the ship of industry on our shoulders. It pushes us down, forcing us to push back or be crushed. They care not about us, yet without us, the ship would flounder."

Shouts of agreement resonated around the room.

"Soon a great storm is coming! We are the ocean, and we will rise and wash the toffs overboard!"

The crowd was now unruly. Grey-shirts were pushing and shoving, but the uproar wasn't dying down.

The councillor raised his hands again. "Brothers and sisters! Our storm must break the shackles from our scientists. So that one day, *we* will walk the decks of prosperity and take the privileges and freedoms from the greedy toffs!

"Support us! Fight for Freedom! Cancel Connickle!"

The crowd erupted. Caps were thrown in the air, and cheers echoed off the wooden walls.

Before calling for calm, the councillor bathed in the adulation. "We have a parting gift for you..." He nodded towards the side door. Three men in dark tweed suits tumbled into the hall, pushed by grey-shirted thugs. "Perhaps you would like to speak with Mister Shacklady and his managers."

The door slammed behind the toffs as the crowd surged at them. The councillors and their thugs quietly, in single file, made their way through the door on the opposite side of the stage.

Issy glimpsed a sour-faced crone wearing a pale green bonnet through the open doorway but looked away to search for the old man in the dark red coat. He was nowhere to be seen.

"Time to leave." Jonah grabbed Issy's arm, and the Stormriders hurried through the door at the back of the hall, their ears ringing with shrieks and screams.

To ensure they were not being followed, they took a circuitous route back to *Freya's Grimalkin,* hurrying in silence through the winding streets and alleys between the mill workers' houses. Behind them, an airship's screaming engines drowned the distant sickening cheers and jeers from the hall as it roared overhead. The Anthropocene thugs were heading northward.

Homeward bound? Issy thought.

The Stormriders turned north, too, as they rounded the next corner. Ahead, Issy gasped when she saw the twisted corpse sprawled on the cobbles. They ducked into an alleyway before they reached the old man's body.

Soon they would head home with their resolve hardened. This meeting had been shorter, but more powerful than the previous two.

The Anthropocene was upping the ante.

Later that evening, Dottie and Gilbert sat holding hands across a beer-stained table, gazing dreamily into each other's eyes, oblivious to the Praetorian's Friday night merrymaking.

Issy and Ace, sharing the same booth, mirrored the lovers' soporific expressions.

"I wonder what they're thinking," Issy said, pouting and fluttering her eyelashes.

"*Sensim amor sensus occupat.*" The words dripped off Ace's lips like nectar from a lily.

"That's what I thought." Issy rolled her eyes and smiled at the sound of giggling from the booth behind her. Since he flew more often with the crew of *Dragonfly*, now that Gilbert and Dottie regularly flew on *Freyja's Grimalkin*, Lemmy was holding court, entertaining his crewmates, Connie, Rory and Tabby.

Issy was sipping her sarsaparilla when a tap on the side of her leg from Lemmy's walking stick made her turn to find his frowning face next to hers.

"Problem brewing at the bar," he said, nodding in the general direction of head barman Eli, who was in an animated discussion with a large, ragged-haired fellow wearing a black cape over his coat and a jauntily cocked artisan topper.

Issy caught her breath. *No*, she thought, *not here, not now…*

"Not the chap talking with Eli." Lemmy pointed with his stick. "The couple at the bar staring daggers at him."

As he spoke, the woman stepped towards the man, shouting. "Oi! We don't want your sort in 'ere! Sling yer 'ook!"

Eli glided back from the bar as the big man downed a mouthful from his pewter pot and unbuttoned his coat.

Undeterred by the flash of grey, the woman's partner brushed her aside, grabbing the thug's shoulder, and spinning him around to reveal his grey shirt to the room. But in that single movement, the thug swung a thick cosh from his belt, catching his assailant with a full-blooded blow to the jaw, knocking him to the ground.

Chair legs screeched as a dozen men sprang to their feet to confront the grinning man, now with his back to the bar, resting his elbows on its sticky top, his grey shirt pulled tight across his puffed-out chest. He tapped his cosh against the palm of his other hand. "Come on, then. Who's next to take on the Brunswick Brawler?"

Issy was stepping out of the booth when a flash of blue and yellow to her right caught her eye. Algeria, head held high, strode from the backroom doorway with Eli gliding in her wake. Patrons parted like oil from a drop of soap as she marched through them without breaking stride.

"Ah, if it isn't the Hi—"

Crack! Algeria slapped his head sideways, knocking him off the bar. He staggered, but regaining his balance, raised the cosh over his head, his face contorted with rage.

"No!" Issy grabbed his wrist before he could strike and twisted his arm behind his back. She turned her face away from his beer-soaked breath. When she spun to face him, Algeria was holding his other clenched fist.

"What were you going to do, Theo? Hit me again?" She had been on the wrong end of a drunken rage once before.

"What're you doin' here? Are you one of *them*?" His spittle-smeared lips sneered. "I shouldn't be surprised, should I, Issy-sis."

"Don't call me that." She hadn't heard his childhood nickname for her for many years. "I don't answer to you."

He struggled to shake himself free, but Issy and Algeria held firm.

"Eli." Algeria spoke softly.

"What can *this 'kin* do for you, Algeria?" He bowed his head.

"Put two of your staff at the door with orders not to let this scum back in."

"Certainly, Algeria." His eyes flickered and two RT-41s glided from behind the bar to his side.

"You're stupid if you believe pieces of junk can stop me!"

Issy and Algeria exchange a glance and a nod, and still tightly gripping his arms, marched him to the door, closely followed by the meks.

"You'll see me again, and next time, I won't be alone."

It took all their combined strength to fling him through the double doors onto the wet pavement as the RT-41s flanked the entrance.

"Thank you, Eli." Algeria patted the mek on the shoulder, and he pressed his splay-fingered hand on his chest and bowed his head.

Issy returned to the Stormriders. "So, now you know about my brother, Theo. He's a drunk…"

"And he's Anthropocene?" Lemmy asked what was on everyone's lips. "When did you find out?"

"The same time as you, when I saw the shirt. Father threw him out years ago, when…" Again, she lowered her eyes and shook her head. "Father put him in charge of the mill, but I haven't seen him for a long time."

"Now, he calls himself the Brunswick Brawler. How quaint." Algeria put her arm around Issy's shoulder. "Are you all right, shugah?"

"Not really. I thought he was out of my life for good. Now he's back and one of *them*…"

Algeria nodded. "And, from what he said, we know Raven's

knowledge didn't die with him. They know all about us."

The next day, a cloudless Saturday afternoon at Barton Aerodrome combined with a light breeze attracted aeronauts from far and wide like flies to a butter dish. *Freyja's Grimalkin* and *Dragonfly* were bobbing gently on adjacent berths when Ace's brougham trundled up to the stables by the tower. The driver unhitched its sweating seventeen-hand Cleveland Bay and led him to the troughs for a well-earned drink.

During the journey, the horse's shod hooves clattering on the hard cobbles had made conversation difficult inside the carriage and gifted Issy a headache.

"Come along, old girl." Ace put his arm around her shoulders. "Let's see what gems of wisdom Jonah has for us today."

Conscious of Ace's glances, Issy set her jaw and nodded. *Here we go*, she thought.

"Look, about Theo…" she started, but Ace squeezed harder, twisted their bodies sideways, and marched her lockstep to the bench in the control tower's shadow. Like twins joined at the hip, they sat in unison.

"Why did he have to join *them*? Why did he come to the Praetorian? And why now?" The staccato words squeezed through her taut lips.

"From what I know of Theo, you shouldn't be surprised he's

attracted to their ideas. Birds of a feather…"

Issy's lip curled. The wide-eyed glare from under her furrowed brow would have withered a lesser person. "He pushed my mother down a flight of stairs, which left her in a wheelchair. He's evil, and revels in it."

"That was a long time ago. You were only a child, and he wasn't much older."

"A child? I was sixteen. What are you saying? So much time has passed, it's now time to forgive and forget?"

"He's still your brother."

"He's no brother of mine. How can you, of all people, say that, after what he's done? Why don't you understand?" She pushed herself off the bench.

Ace sprang up and wrapped his arms around her. He tried to pull her close, but Issy's hands pressed hard against his chest. "Whilst my familial issues pale compared to yours, I do understand, old girl. But blood is blood. *Errare humanum est.* To forgive—"

"Don't say that! He tried to kill her!" Twisting and turning, she pushed harder, trying to escape his iron grip.

"According to your father, it was an accident…"

"He was drunk and didn't see what happened, but I did. I saw him push her!" Her fists pounded against his chest.

"You can't hate him forever."

"No? There's nothing he can do that'll make up for what he did. Nothing."

"Surely you have fond memories from when you were growing up together? There must be something redeemable?"

"Maybe once, but not anymore. He drinks. He hurts. He's Anthropocene. Pain is all he means to me…" Issy's voice trailed off. Scrunched eyes pressed her eyelashes hard against her cheeks.

Ace tilted her head onto his shoulder and stroked her hair. "I hate seeing you like this, old girl. I thought he had been out of your life for so long… but I was mistaken."

"It's the demon drink." Issy looked up into Ace's eyes, her anger draining away. Her voice was a whisper. "Booze caused Father to rule the house with an iron rod, and now it fuels Theo's rage against me… against us, against the Order."

"Then why does he let Theo run the business?"

"I might be a Windlass, but Father could never allow a woman to manage Brunswick Mill. I have the brains, but not the stones." Issy shook her head. "Despite what he did to Mum, he let Theo stay almost three more years before handing over the running of the mill and throwing him out when he turned twenty-one. Now the demon has possessed them both.

"Theo is a bully, and Father lives only for the twin evils, money and booze."

In each other's arms, like many times before, they stood, unified by a common hatred of alcohol and its consequences. Issy raised her head, and Ace shoved a large white handkerchief into her face.

"You'd better clean up those tears and that mucus. I hope you haven't stained my brocade coat. It's just been cleaned." He cocked an eye at his shoulder. "*Sputatilicus*, ughhh…"

Issy's weak smile became a chuckle when she saw his

wrinkled nose and upturned eyes.

"We have an audience." Ace nodded towards the anxious faces peering from the swaying gondolas. "We should wander over and tell them."

It's time they learned the truth about Theo. This isn't going to be easy.

Ace always had a way of disarming her anger. In another life, another time, they could have been so much more than fast friends. But for now, he was the rock to which she clung, the stolid partner sharing her beliefs, a constant compatriot in a war for which they'd willingly devote their lives.

He was the brother that she had lost.

A DE'ATH IN THE FAMILY

Sir Horatio Marmaduke Wyndham-Welch cocked his head to one side as the distinctive *click-clickety-click* of Blakeys reverberating on the encaustic tiled floors of the Palace of Westminster slowed to a halt outside his offices.

Interesting, he thought. *It sounds as if a young lady may be lost in the maze of corridors.* He straightened his tie as the outer door closed with a faint *clunk*. But after an incoherent exchange of rising voices, the intra-office door burst open, interrupting his personal secretary's urgent *rat-a-tat-tat*.

And Johnson's voice was even more high-pitched than usual. Visibly shaken, he was gripping the wall for support.

"Mrs Ptarmigan-Sykes insists she has an appointment, but there's nothing in the dia—"

Wyndham-Welch sprang to his feet as the diminutive, middle-aged woman bundled the secretary aside and *clickety-*

clicked into the room, easing off her black leather gloves, finger by finger. The ruffled hem of her long-sleeved, high-necked, pigeon-grey dress coat floated above her shiny black ankle boots. The faintest hint of ruby red lipstick on her thin lips glistened like a crooked gash in her taut, pallid face. And with her hair pulled back into a tight bun, she was so devoid of colour, discerning the join between skin and hair was impossible in the office light.

Pale hawk-like eyes beneath the pinched V of her brow fixed on Wyndham-Welch. He flushed. *This means trouble.*

"Thank you, Johnson. That will be all." Without taking his eyes off his unexpected guest, he waved away the junior secretary with a cursory flick of the wrist.

"Well!" The secretary threw back his head, turned on his heel and, with a loud sniff, stomped back to his room, slamming the door behind him.

Undeterred by the young man's tantrum, Mrs Ptarmigan-Sykes tossed her gloves onto the leather-topped desk, and sat, stiffly, on the guest seat, crossing her legs.

Wyndham-Welch cleared his throat and eased himself into his green leather spindle-backed chair. "This may be the first time we have met outside of a Brigade meeting. I assume from your frown that you're not here on a social visit, Beatrice..." His eyes widened, and his questioning smile retreated beneath Mrs Ptarmigan-Sykes's tight-lipped glare. "Er, I may call you Beatrice?"

"You may not."

"How should I address you? Ma'am? Milady? Your

Highness?"

"Don't mock me, sir. You owe your career to me. Never forget that."

"To *you*? Ha, it's possible that when I first entered the political arena, your husband's endorsement added a modicum of credibility to my candidacy, but that was the least I would expect from a close friend and fellow alumnus of Magdalen. How on earth do *you* suppose you assisted me?"

"How quaint that you believe my late husband was your friend. Ralph despised you and poked fun at your expense at every opportunity. He was everything that you are not; intelligent, principled, good-humoured, well-mannered, and he had the body of a Greek god. No, the endorsements, the letters, and the newspaper editorials in his name were from me."

"Wh-what! But that can't be—"

"Use what little intelligence you possess, man. How could Ralph have known you were running for election when he was exploring the Amazonian rain forests, or captaining white argosies across the Indian Ocean, or seeking Xanadu in Old Cathay?"

"But I have letters from him. Kind, supportive letters…" Wyndham-Welch raised his eyebrows. "You?"

"Ah, light dawns on the sparsely inhabited cranial wasteland you call a brain. Ralph always considered you slow-witted. He often said that you do not know your anus from your weenus."

"Now, see here! I retained my seat in this place three times on merit and have served my constituents diligently. My popularity has never been higher!" Blood rushed to his already ruddy cheeks.

"You have an unfathomably high opinion of your meagre talents if you believe they re-elected you on your legislative record."

"*Why?* What do you mean?"

"I'm sorry. Let me rephrase in terms that even you may understand. As the Member of Parliament for Sefton, why do your underprivileged constituents continue to elect a ridiculous toff from the Wirral? Could it be because of your opposition to the Manchester Ship Canal Act? Or your vocal support of the Freedom movement, perhaps?"

"It's because I represent their views with vim and gusto, here, in *this place.*"

"No, sir, you promote *our* view. We pay you to support our policies. The terminally gullible vote for you because we tell them what's good for them."

"Poppycock! I've never heard such balderdash!"

Mrs Ptarmigan-Sykes rolled her eyes and sighed. "Believe whatever you wish. We're wasting time."

This can't be true. My constituents hold me in high regard. Yes, I support the Anthropocene agenda but…

"The timetable has changed. Are you sure we have the numbers?" she said.

"What? Er, yes, we have enough votes to get the Private Members Bill to the floor of the House of Commons and to pass. The *other place* may be an issue, but—"

"Do your job in the lower house and leave the *other place* to me."

"There will be dissenters amongst the Lords."

"Then keep your eyes on The Times' obituary columns."

Wyndham-Welch's jaw dropped open.

"You must get the Bill through the House of Lords within seven days," she said.

"But that's not nearly enough time. We agreed, the Commons before Christmas recess, Lords in the new year. There isn't time."

"If you can't muster the votes, I will find someone who can." She reached for her gloves and stood. "I assume you dismissed calls for an enquiry into the debacle at Barton?"

The hairs stood at attention on the back of his neck. "We should never have allowed that De'Ath fellow to use the dreadnought. It was reckless and could have exposed us."

Mrs Ptarmigan-Sykes sighed. "The whole mek experiment was ill-conceived. Twenty years of subconscious suggestion wasted in the twinkling of an eye."

"I'm informed it was a very loud twinkle." Wyndham-Welch cut off his smirk with a cough. "Did they recover the QT-33?"

"No. It's missing. We know it wasn't on the dreadnought; Ipkiss still had control for several weeks afterwards. I told him to recall it," she shook her head. "Now, we're seeking a replacement for him."

"Old Ipkiss has retired, has he?" Eyebrows raised, Wyndham-Welch waited for a reply that never came.

"We need a fresh approach for the meks. I am collecting his replacement on my way back to Hel's Muor. From what I've heard, Felicity De'Ath is working wonders using psychological techniques to modify meks' hard-geared protocols."

Eyebrows still raised, once again Wyndham-Welch's jaw dropped open.

"De'Ath, you say? Is she related to that Raven chap?"

Mrs Ptarmigan-Sykes turned the corners of her mouth down and shrugged. "Your deductive prowess astounds me. De'Ath is such a common name."

Wyndham-Welch parted his lips but chose silence.

"She's dedicated to our cause, and that's what matters."

"You're playing a dangerous game…"

"But not as foolhardy as the game you are playing by questioning my judgement." She took a step towards him.

"But I only meant—"

"Never doubt that I will do whatever is required. If she, or anyone else for that matter, fails me, there's always retirement." There was little mirth in her teeth-bared smile.

It had suddenly become stiflingly hot. Wyndham-Welch swallowed hard and loosened his collar with a trembling finger. "I meant no disrespect, it's just—"

"The *Vindicta* is moored at Kensal Green. Get me a hansom."

Wyndham-Welch edged around the grey malevolence into the sanctity of Johnson's office. He closed the door with a barely audible click and released the breath he hadn't realised he had been holding.

Without a word, Johnson bustled out of the room and hurried down the corridor.

Eavesdropping, were we, son? Wyndham-Welch sat in Johnson's chair. A return to his own office suddenly didn't appeal to him.

Doctor Felicity Angellyne De'Ath stood by the gasworks wall on West Egerton Street, her face turned upwards, searching the clouds. Dots of rain began to land on her jam-jar-bottom spectoculars, blurring her vision. Nearby, the brown steel bells of the two massive gasometers, encased in their ornate, white cast iron framework, glistened in the dim afternoon light above the Salford skyline. The LTA gas reek was intolerable for all but those who lived and worked here. But having lived in their shadow for most of her life, she hardly noticed its vile stench.

She was the only daughter of proud Salfordian stock; born and bred on the tough streets of the city. How fitting it was that from the exact spot where her parents had met twenty-eight years earlier, she was going to embark on a splendid adventure of her own.

A small bulge in the dark cloud's underbelly swelled and burst open as the hull of an almost-white gondola cleaved the uniformity. Engines screaming, the three-bagger descended, slowly spiralling towards the mooring posts on the white framework.

She set off walking, and by the time she arrived beneath the gondola, the airship had berthed, and the crew were unfurling a ladder. She clutched her carpet bag tight to her chest as she sheltered from the water droplets cascading from the airship's envelope.

"Weight?" a grey-shirted man with ragged blond hair

flapping wildly from beneath his unfastened aeronaut's cap shouted from above.

"One hundred and twelve pounds, soaking wet!"

Within seconds, the unattached stern of the airship was rising as grit poured from a black chute into the ballast bunkers by the mooring pole. With the carpet bag swung over her shoulder, Felicity put her foot on the bottom rung of the rope ladder.

"Oi!" The blond man was frantically wagging his finger and motioning her to step away from the ladder with his other hand. She stepped back, just in time, as a tight-lipped, middle-aged visage of scrutiny appeared next to the man. For an uncomfortable few seconds, the unblinking woman eyed Felicity like a vulture examines a carcass, before finally telling the blond man to beckon her on board.

At the top of the ladder, the airman offered his hand to help her into the gondola. Over his shoulder, Felicity could see the severe, grey woman sat alone in a small cabin, staring forward, hands clenched on her lap.

"What was that all about?" Doctor De'Ath stepped onto the pristine off-white deck.

"No one comes aboard *Vindicta* without an invitation. Not even us."

His wild-eyed frown silenced her laughter. *Crumbs*, she thought. *This flight isn't going to be much fun.*

"The Boss-lady wants to talk with you... in there." He jabbed his thumb at the cabin, then leaned close, his face next to her ear. "Take good care how you speak with her."

The hair on her neck stood to attention at the menacingly, whispered words. As the roar of the airscrews replaced the hum of the docking magnets, she staggered sideways on the juddering deck. Powerful hands steadied her as *Vindicta* lurched upwards, rising like a pale wraith above the wet roads and roofs of Salford.

"Thank you, mister…?"

"The name's Bill, but she calls me Gretel."

"Gretel? Isn't that a girl's name?"

"Don't ask…" He leaned past her to open the door, and she stepped in, looking around for a chair. Although roomy enough for four passengers, the cabin was rarely occupied by more than one. *Vindicta* was the property of Ataraxia Beatrice Ptarmigan-Sykes. Her ship; her rules.

"No need to sit. This won't take long."

Doctor De'Ath placed her bag by her feet and, under the watchful eye of her host, relaxed her shoulders, widened her stance for balance and put her hands behind her back, interlocking her fingers.

"Why do you want to join our project?"

"Because the Connickle Laws are suppressing science and—"

"Don't quote the manifesto to me. I wrote it. Tell me *your* reason."

"My working-class parents made sacrifices to give me an education. I'm obligated to not waste their sacrifice. If you can put my talents to good use and the amelioration of society, then—"

"Ah, the dutiful daughter. Extremely laudable, I'm sure. So, how do you see your role in our mekamanikin project?"

"I'm very much looking forward to working under Professor Ipkiss. His papers on mek programming were groundbreaking. Although he wrote them twenty years ago, he was so far ahead of his time."

"Ipkiss is no longer part of our team. You will take his place. I see you are surprised. Can you do the job?"

Doctor De'Ath opened her mouth just as they thrust into the clouds, plunging the cabin into semi-darkness as it spiralled upwards. Roaring airscrews were dampened to a low rumble as her ears popped, and she widened her stance further to keep her balance on the juddering deck. After a few seconds that felt like hours, the airship breached the canopy, and brilliant sunshine streamed into the cabin.

She exhaled and relaxed again. "But didn't you recruit me to be his assistant? I don't understand."

"Are you up to the job? Or do I have to look elsewhere?"

"Oh, I'm up for the challenge. And I wouldn't want you to have to turn this 'ship around." Felicity's smile was greeted with a quizzical, furrowed brow.

"All of Ipkiss's notes and files will be at your disposal."

"He didn't take them with him?"

"He couldn't, where he was going." A fleeting smirk was the first hint of emotion on Ataraxia's deadpan face.

"I'm interested to learn what methodology he was employing to break the First Protocol."

"But it can be done?"

"Oh, yes. I have my own ideas. You see—"

"One more question. Are you related to the Earl of Wraithmere?"

"Why do you ask?"

"Answer the question."

"Father is the nephew of Countess Gertrude Eupheme De'Ath. But we haven't—"

"You must have been furious when you inherited nothing from the estate..."

"We weren't involved with that side of the family. You don't miss what you never had."

"You must hate Raynard with every fibre of your being."

"Hard to hate someone I've never met. But in any case, he's gone to America to spend his fortune. Good luck to him. I have work to do here."

Ataraxia's face cracked into a lopsided grin. "Welcome to the family, Doctor Death."

"It's De'Ath, actually. But everyone calls me Fliss." She rolled her eyes but returned the smile.

"*We* are not everyone. *We* will call you... Angel. Yes, Angel of Death has a nice ring to it."

Felicity opened her mouth but decided against an acerbic response.

And with a flick of her wrist, Ataraxia dismissed her from her presence.

The door clicked shut behind her, and she tried to get her bearings. The sun was almost directly astern, so she calculated they were heading north-eastward. Afloat on a sea of cotton candy clouds, there were no landmarks to show where they were or where they were going.

In the cabin, there had been no sensation of speed. But on deck, the roar of the engines and chilled air rushing past her face told her they were travelling at a fair rate of knots.

Gretel stood at the prow, whilst the other crew member piloted the airship from the stern. She strolled to the front of the gondola.

"That went well, I think," she said, as they exchanged smiles.

"You're still here, so you're probably right. What name did she give you?"

"How do you know she gave me one? What's going on?" Felicity put her hands on her hips.

"Everyone gets a new name. She suffers from a medical condition that prevents her remembering faces unless it *means* something to her. So, I'm Gretel and Eddie, over there, is Hansel. Apparently, we remind her of the children in the nursery rhyme."

"Well, I am Angel. I assumed she called me that because my middle name is Angellyne." She looked over his shoulder. "Do we have far to go?"

"Did *she* tell you where we are going?"

"No."

"Then I can't." Gretel stared past her. "Hansel needs me. Try to get used to your new moniker." He eased her out of the way and strolled with a sailor's gait to the stern of the ship, leaving Angel open-mouthed.

She faced the prow. Ahead in the distance, undulations and a break in the clouds indicated hills or mountains. *Are we crossing the Pennines?*

With a shrug of her shoulders, she sat with her back to the starboard hull.

Fizzing across the sky with a new name and new colleagues to destination unknown. This was just what she needed.

After all, if she didn't know where she was, neither would *they.*

She breathed a sigh of relief and smiled. *I'm safe… for now.*

If *Vindicta's* helter-skelter dive to Hel's Muor was stomach-churning, then Angel's descent from the gondola was worse. Gretel had to persuade her to step off the gondola and climb down the swinging rope ladder with no visible landing place.

Twisting and turning, buffeted by the wind that took her breath away as it swept along the rock face, she reached the edge of the rocks that hung over the entrance to the cave that gave the crag its name.

When she had climbed down more ladder than remained, there was still nothing below her boots but hundreds of feet of fresh air to the jagged rocks.

As she clung to the ladder, she could see into the dimly lit, red sandstone opening of the cave. Then, with only seven more rungs left, a platform rumbled out from the rocks, extending beneath her. She edged down until her feet stepped off the last rung and she hung by her hands, feeling for the platform with her feet.

Firm hands gripped her hips from behind, and as she lowered herself, moved up her body, rucking her dress over her stays, and coming to rest under her armpits. Only when her boots finally grounded did she spin around to find two bright blue eyes staring back from a beaming, rose-cheeked face. The woman's jet black under-bust corset sucked the sparkle from her shimmering silver dress and enhanced what few curves she had.

"Welcome to the fun factory." Blonde ringlets bounced as she looked left and right. "Don't look down."

"I'm not scared of… Oh, my… That is a long way." Angel's head snapped upright.

"Professor Verity Twinkle, or Star as bossy-britches up there calls me, at your service. Vulcanologist, geologist and all-round good egg." She grabbed Angel's hand with both of hers, caressing and shaking it warmly. "Let's get out of the cold."

"Doctor Felicity De'Ath. But she insists I'm now Angel. Silly, isn't it?" They had only taken three steps towards the entrance when something thudded onto the platform behind them. They spun to find Angel's carpet bag in a crumpled heap.

"Hope you didn't have your grandma's china tea service in there." Star scooped it up and swung it over her shoulder.

"Mostly books and clothes." Angel eased the strap from Star's grip.

"Heavy reading, judging by the lack of bounce." Star giggled and looked up the ladder. "Let's get a move on. Boss-lady's on her way." She grabbed Angel by the arm and pulled her into the cave's mouth.

Beyond the open double doors, lamps illuminated a curving, down-sloping tunnel with infrequent openings along both sides. Some led to doorways, while others contained stone steps or metal staircases.

"This is all man-made. How did they do it?"

"They used a WRM."

Angel gasped, wide-eyed. "How did they get a tunnelling machine up here?"

"They didn't, silly. They started from the bottom and spiralled up to Hel's Muor cave."

Star pulled Angel's head to hers and spoke in a whisper. "Watch your step and be careful who you speak with. There are BDIs everywhere."

"Why do they watch us? Aren't we all on the same side?"

"Well, let's just say some have more incentive to work than those driven purely by dedication to the cause. Why are you here?"

"When Ataraxia approached me, I jumped at the chance to meet and work with Professor Ipkiss."

"You're not married? No kids?"

Angel shook her head.

"Career Anthropocene, eh?"

"I believe in the cause. Don't you?"

Star shrugged. "I do my research and my job to the best of my ability, just like everyone else. The facilities here are second to none."

"I wonder why Ipkiss left without handing over his notes. It makes no sense to retire without sharing his progress."

"Sometimes retirement is voluntary, other times compulsory. Boss-lady called him Gramps because he reminded her of his grandfather, apparently. But he lost his grip…"

"On reality?"

"On the guardrail." Star giggled.

Angel stopped and stared, open-mouthed.

"Hansel shoved him off the drawbridge. He grabbed the railing, but with a little help from Hansel prising his fingers, he couldn't support his weight for long. Boss-lady watched him struggling before he fell." Star giggled. "He was cursing her name to high heaven 'til the rocks shut him up."

"But I thought—"

"Here we are." They had been walking the downward spiral for several minutes when Star pulled Angel into an opening with a door next to a stone staircase that led to another door.

She pointed her head at each. "Laboratory, and your quarters are up there, so that you can fall out of bed into your workplace, just like the rest of us."

"How many work here?"

"About half." She threw back her head and laughed. "Just kidding. We all work our tripe off. There are a dozen scientists and assistants, all responsible for our own projects, and we report to the Boss-lady alone. She prohibits work and research discussions between teams under pain of death."

Star's deadpan stare froze the grin on Angel's lips.

"Our work is important, secret stuff. Some amongst us are competing for the Boss-lady's favour by inventing that elusive contraption that changes the world. They guard their findings the way black herons protect their eggs."

"So, you can't tell me…" Angel bit her lip and ran her fingers through Star's ringlets.

Star grabbed her wrist and pulled away. "No…" she twisted, looking left and right.

Blood rushed to Angel's cheeks. "What's wrong?"

"Walls have ears as well as BDIs," she said. "Look around your laboratory. I'll see you later."

"Aren't you going to escort me in?"

Star stiffened and backed away. "Either you haven't been listening to a word I've said, or you have been sent to test my loyalty." She narrowed her eyes. "Has the Boss-lady sent you? Doesn't she trust me?" Her wild eyes darted left and right.

"No. I'm sorry. I have a lot to learn."

Star put a finger to her tightly pressed lips and hurried away down the tunnel.

Shaking off her confusion, Angel turned and opened the door to the laboratory.

Her heart sank. Professor Ipkiss's reputation for meticulous organisation and cleanliness made the chaotic jumble that greeted her even more sickening. It looked as if someone had thrown his books, files, and papers all over the floor and mussed them up.

And by the wall, face down on the sheepskin rug, a large QT-41 mek sprawled motionless. It wore a plain white dress and its long, straggly flame-red hair radiated around its head like the aurora of the sun goddess.

"Awaken." Angel used her sternest, self-invented mek

training voice.

The QT-41 stirred and rolled onto its side.

"What is your name?" Angel continued to speak in a monotone.

"Esmeralda Emptyglass." The mek supported its upper body on an elbow. "Where is the professor?"

"He has left you. You will work with me now. My name is Angel."

The mek sidled backwards along the floor until its back bumped into the wall. It slowly shook its head. "Don't hurt *this* 'kin…"

Angel soon discovered the late Professor Ipkiss had been a prodigious, some might even say obsessive, writer. He meticulously recorded procedural notes on experiments and their empirical results in coloured files, personal observations of fellow scientists in small notebooks, and *aides-memoire* on scraps of paper that had been stored on a spike when no longer needed.

Unfortunately, someone, or something, had strewn everything across the laboratory.

So, with such a daunting task of tidying and collating, Angel recruited Esmeralda's help.

She instructed the mek to gather and pile the files while she scooped up and read the paper scraps before pushing them back onto the sharp pin. And they both threw the notebooks into a corner for later reading.

Most *aides-memoire* revealed nothing of importance, although the handwriting on them spoke volumes of his state of mind. Whereas older notes comprised one or two messages in neat cursive, the more recent ones were in an almost illegible scrawl written in an odd mixture of styles. And their subjects had devolved from reminders of meetings, to notes about what topics to steer clear of when talking to, and even how to avoid bumping into, the Boss-lady.

"How long have you been here, Esmeralda?" Angel pushed another note onto the spike.

"*This 'kin* has no record of time."

"Does your memory not store times and dates?"

"The professor reset *this 'kin*'s memory nineteen times."

Angel turned down the corners of her mouth. "For what purpose?"

"Why would the professor tell *this 'kin*?"

They worked on in silence, Angel reading and filing more notes.

"Are there any other meks here?"

"Esmeralda is alone. Esmeralda always has been alone. Esmeralda will be alone forever and ever and ever. Esmeralda is alone. Esmeralda always has been alone. Esmeralda will be alone forever and ever and ever." With each repetition, her voice was a pitch higher and faster.

"Enough!" Angel slapped her hand on her workbench. "It's time for you to rest and recharge."

The mek held out its hand. Its extraordinarily long fingers

stretched wide. The hinged lid to the compartment on its arm was missing.

"Do you not have any pills?" Angel nodded at Esmeralda's arm.

"The professor controlled when *this 'kin* rests."

Angel searched the laboratory but, finding no obvious storage place, left the mek standing with its hand outstretched, and went to her living quarters, returning moments later with a single lozenge-shaped pill.

"Until I have read Professor Ipkiss's notes thoroughly, I will keep the pills safe."

Esmeralda placed the lozenge in its mouth and laid, face down, on the sheepskin rug. Angel looked up at the ceiling and sighed. In her experience, meks would choose an unobtrusive place to rest to rewind their clockworks. She concluded the memory wipes must have affected this mek's basic functions.

She returned to reading the professor's notes. Although they had been scattered, she learned to give the neat notes only a cursory glance, concentrating on deciphering the more recent, hard-to-read scribbles.

They painted a grim picture of a descent into anxiety, paranoia and despair.

But of all the notes she had seen, only one had no puncture. It was undated but written in fluent gibberish; it may have been the last missive he wrote. She took a few moments to circle the only decipherable words in the nine lines of scrawl pressed hard into the blot-stained paper:

… found L?

the GerMan…

…Maker… co OperaTive

find L… only chance… ABc

eSMe

no time

Poor man finally lost his marbles, she thought. Then she folded the note in half, tucked it into her pocket, and surveyed the room, hands on hips. *What's next?*

Esmeralda had piled the maroon, green, and ochre files randomly into sixteen equal stacks. From what she now knew of Professor Ipkiss, colour co-ordinating would be his first step in indexing, referencing, and cross-referencing his work.

She rolled up her sleeves and ten minutes later, she was admiring eighteen stacks comprising nine maroon, seven green, and two ochre.

Ever efficient, Ipkiss had compiled an index for the files in a small black book she had found under Esmeralda's rug, referencing each 'event' by date and file number. A quick glance showed the 'R' files were the oldest and most prevalent, whilst the 'E' references began only a few entries before the 'R' and 'L' references stopped.

It didn't take her long to deduce that the ochre files had 'E' for Esmeralda as the prefix and the green files had 'L' for a mek named Letitia. *So, 'R' referenced files must be maroon.*

She selected a maroon file and found 'R41' written inside the thick cover, showing this was the forty-first book of 'R'. She puffed out her cheeks.

Turning over a few leaves, she ran her finger down the page. But her self-satisfied smile soon became a wide-eyed stare. This was not an empirical record of mek experimentation. The page she had chosen detailed an act of depravity so disgusting that she dropped the file, took a few steps back and flopped onto her chair. She pressed her hand to her mouth to stifle her emotions.

The description alone was enough to elicit such a reaction. But the name of the perpetrator of the evil deed sent shock waves through her body.

'R' stood for Raven!

Her uncle Raynard Vincent De'Ath, the tenth Earl of Wraithmere.

Her very own kith and kin.

FOUR

AFTERMATH

Whilst not renowned for punctuality, Issy's tardiness was rarely because of laziness. On the contrary, her passion for the disparate, virtuous causes of conservation, temperance and women's suffrage often resulted in mad dashes from one event to the next.

Today was one of those days. A police raid brought the Manchester National Society for Women's Suffrage at the Free Trade Hall to an early, violent end. She narrowly avoided apprehension by ducking and dodging along familiar alleyways, reaching the Praetorian an hour before the regular meeting of the Order was due to start.

It had been nine days since Theo had exploded back into her life, so she took the opportunity to order herself a drink, sit quietly, and observe.

From her concealed seat in a dark corner in the main bar,

she watched members arriving in dribs and drabs. Some sneaked in amongst groups of rowdy patrons, while others strolled in, comfortable to be with their conservationist fellowship.

What a mixed bag we are, she thought, swirling the remains of the dandelion and burdock around her glass. Toffs and workers, young and old, men and women; all equals, brothers and sisters sworn to their noble cause.

Oblivious of Issy's presence, one by one, the Stormriders arrived and filled back-to-back booths on the far side of the room. Soon she would join them, but, for now, she relaxed in this rare moment of solitude in the crowded room, sipping her drink and watching her friends.

Then, at the edge of her vision, Eli straightened, eyes flickering. As she turned to see what was happening, he jerked into motion. Weaving between his fellow mek bar staff at speed, he barrelled through the door into the back rooms, almost tearing it off its hinges as it rebounded shut with a bang.

Every head turned to find the source of the loud report.

Similarly alarmed, Issy hurried to her compatriots, greeting them with a puzzled frown.

"Any idea what that was all about?" She tilted her head at the doorway.

"Search me, old girl." Lemmy tapped his nose with his finger. "Eli must have picked up a message from his mek friends for Algeria's ears only."

"Should we follow him?" Gilbert asked.

"You are aware of the rules, *amicis meis*. No one goes through to the meeting room until Eli is ready and standing guard." Ace flipped open his half hunter. "It's twenty-three minutes before he's due to take up his role as sentry, and he's always on time. If he doesn't appear, we'll know something's afoot."

"You can treat me to a dandelion and burdock while we're waiting." Issy waggled her empty glass. Ace rolled his eyes as he snatched it from her grasp.

"Anyone else for a top-up?" Three hastily drained pewter pots thrust towards him, followed by Lemmy's after he gulped the remains of his drink.

For the next twenty-two minutes, anxious glances alternated between pocket watches and the meeting room door. Ace cleared his throat as he stood at the precise moment Eli glided back into the bar. But instead of taking up his usual position, he slid behind the bar to join his staff.

Something's wrong. Issy's frown mirrored her friends' expressions. Ever since she became a member of the Order, its rules and rituals had been ingrained into her everyday life. Eli's demonstrable deviation from his role was a warning from Algeria.

A quiet ripple of disquiet swept around the room. Some left their drinks on tables and headed for the exit; others huddled in conversation; Gilbert gritted his teeth and gripped the hilts at his hips. Reassured by the cold steel, he nodded his readiness to his comrades.

"No!" Dottie grasped his wrist, her voice lowered to a hoarse whisper. "We must keep our heads. Follow Mother's lead."

"Where is she? Why hasn't she come and told us what's happening?"

"Stay calm, Gilbert. It might be noth—"

Three shrill whistle blasts accompanied the main entrance doors crashing open. Uniformed police officers bundled into the bar, truncheons raised. Gilbert sprang to his feet, hands gripping his sheathed blades, but Ace and Lemmy pulled him back into the booth. Screams and shouts of outrage echoing around the room were silenced by another ear-piercing blast.

From behind the uniformed officers, a short, portly, bowler-hatted gent with a handlebar moustache stepped forward. His tailored tweed suit, heavy topcoat and relaxed smile exuded authority in stark contrast to the dark uniforms and snarling expressions of his constables. He unfolded a piece of paper, and, after a cursory glance, he raised his eyes and spoke with a deep, tobacco-ravaged voice.

"Miss Algeria Rebekah Darling?" He grinned at the glaring faces around him.

Silence.

"Come now, ladies and gentlemen. I won't ask twi—"

"I'm here, dearie." Heads turned to the entrance to the back room where Algeria stood in the doorway, hands on hips, in her flamboyant, low-cut, split to mid-thigh, bright blue dress, trimmed with yellow ruffles. "State your business, then get out of my establishment."

Algeria would never wear that to chair a meeting of the Order, Issy thought.

"I am Detective Inspector Scroggins, and I have a warrant for your arrest as the leader of a criminal organisation." He waved the piece of paper over his head to a chorus of shouted profanities.

"To which criminal organisation do you refer, dearie? This is a public house." She spread her arms wide. "I run a respectable business. Since when has selling beer and gin been a crime?"

"Oh, you know what I'm referring to, all right. The Venerable Custodial Order of something or other." He squinted at the warrant, searching…

"The Venerable Antediluvian Order of the Custodians of Magna Mater, Detective." Behind Scroggins, uniformed officers were parting like the Red Sea to allow the grey-shirted owner of the slurring voice through their ranks. Issy took a sharp intake of breath.

Theo!

"Never heard of it." Algeria didn't bat an eyelash. She closed the door behind her and sashayed toward the detective.

"Then you won't mind my lads having a look round your premises." Scroggins motioned two constables towards the back door with a wave of his hand without taking his eyes off Algeria.

Patrons were edging nearer to the phalanx of police officers, whose snarling faces looked eager for a fight.

"Don't you try nothing! Keep back!" Scroggins shouted.

Algeria raised her hand, flashing an angry glance at her loyal defenders. "There'll be no need for violence, Detective. I have nothing to hide. But my patrons are not taking kindly to having their valuable drinking time interrupted by the local constabulary. That's all."

"What's your part in this, Theo?" Issy's voice cracked above the rising clamour.

"You here again, Issy-sis? I'm just a law-biding citizen, helping the police carry out their duty."

A chair flew over Issy's head, crashing into two uniformed officers, and all hell broke loose. Their colleagues needed little excuse to break ranks, charging into the advancing revellers, truncheons swinging.

In the melee, Issy was flung to the ground as the Stormriders swung into action. When she clambered to her feet, disoriented, lamplight glinted off a gun barrel in the periphery of her vision.

A blinding flash. A loud bang. Something slammed into her, and she was reeling, tumbling, crashing onto the beer-slick floor.

Shouts and screams dwindled as the light drained from her eyes.

And in the black silence, breath abandoned her lungs with a sigh.

Issy stiffened, gasped for air, then lay still, her head pounding. She refused to open her eyes, desperate to return to her dream of gliding, soaring over rooftops, safe in Theo's arms.

Is that his hand supporting my head?

"I say, chaps."

Lemmy's chirp!

"Issy's coming round."

Back to the real world…

The Praetorian's familiar reek of beer and tobacco seeped into her waking haze. And jabbing her tongue into the tear inside her cheek, she winced as she found the source of the metallic taste. A chipped canine had gouged a hole in the soft flesh.

"*Lauda Matrem.*"

Issy's eyes rolled behind her eyelids. Ace could never resist showing off.

"Don't try to get up, shugah." Algeria's chilly hand stroked her face.

"You'll be happy to know, old girl, that your considerable bulk didn't damage Eli as much as the gunshot did." Even with her eyes shut tight, she pictured Lemmy's cheeky wink. Warm globs oozed from the corners of her mouth as her bloodied lips slithered into a crooked gash grin before the gut punch of his words struck her hard.

"There was a shot! I remember…"

"Eli shoved you out of harm's way, shugah. The shot entered his chest casing and caused untold damage to his innards as it rattled around, seeking an exit. We have deactivated him to prevent him from moving and causing further harm."

Issy prised her eyelids apart into narrow slits. Bright, blurred faces leaned over her. "Help me up, please."

Strong hands grasped her arms and shoulders, easing her upright and holding her steady. On the barroom floor, a few feet to her right, Eli lay motionless. She had never seen him, or any mek, so still.

"Can he be repaired? Or is he…"

"I'll pay whatever it takes to get our old Eli back. Even if it means putting his Babbage into a new body."

Vomit rose in Issy's throat. She put her hand to her mouth. "Was it Theo? Did he try to kill me?"

"We didn't see who pulled the trigger. The grey-shirts fired several shots, but Eli was the only casualty," Ace said, exchanging furtive glances with the others.

Algeria gestured to the bar for a glass of water as Ace and Lemmy eased Issy into a seat.

Her head was pounding as she scanned the room through blurry eyes. The barroom, which had been bustling with music, laughter and lively conversation before the police incursion, was now a scene of desolation. Broken glass tinkled on brushes pushed by meks across the debris-strewn floorboards. And the unique mirror that had proudly displayed the public house's name in bold black and gold letters behind the bar was now a bare brick wall.

Amongst the glittering mirror shards, splinters from smashed chairs and booths shattered by the gunshots stuck in the brush bristles. Bloodied patrons and members of the Order sat on the few remaining undamaged seats, their wounds being tended by friends.

"Looks like I missed a heck of a party. Where are the police now?" Issy rubbed the side of her head.

"Police? Oh, they weren't *only* police officers, shugah. They were grey-shirts, confirming Raven's knowledge didn't die with him."

Algeria lifted the glass to Issy's lips. "Take a sip and rinse the water around your mouth. Don't worry about spitting blood. The meks will mop the floors."

"I don't understand. What's happening?"

Algeria took a deep breath and sat next to Issy, holding her hand. "As I feared they might, Parliament has repealed the Connickle Laws. The Order and two dozen similarly enlightened societies have been named as outlaw organisations.

"But for a warning from Lemmy's father a couple of weeks ago, many of us would be languishing in King Street cells. He told us the Freedom movement had the numbers to force and win a vote on the conservation laws.

"When we banged heads with Raven, in my heart, I knew this day would come." She lowered her eyes. "But I didn't realise it would be so soon."

"What? What do you mean?" Issy felt vomit rise in her throat again. Her blurry gaze flicked from face to face, failing to find reassurance from her friends that all would be well.

"I was going to tell everyone at tonight's meeting that this would be our last in the Praetorian. But Eli received a message through the mek network about the police raid, so we had to act fast; take down our regalia, stack the tables and chairs and remove all traces of the Order from the meeting room."

"Is… is the Order finished?"

"Not if it were left up to me. We would fight on and wreak havoc on the Anthropocene. But that's not for me to decide, shugah. Our members will choose whether we continue the battle. But it is the end of the Praetorian for now."

Everyone's eyes turned to Algeria.

"I am boarding up the premises until it's safe to re-open. Whatever happens next, they must believe we have disbanded. They will watch our every move. We mustn't give them the chance to turn us over to the authorities.

"But when things have settled, I'll call a meeting. Every member will have the opportunity to either carry on the fight or abandon our sacred cause. Each must search their soul to decide. I can't ask any brother or sister to break the law or sacrifice their freedom. After all, we are criminals now."

"How can we carry on?" Issy felt one of the three pillars of her existence crumbling beneath her.

"Chin up, old girl. We do what all righteous outlaws do." Lemmy winked at Algeria. "Although I believe I would be quite fetching in Sherwood green, in the absence of a dense forest and a friendly friar, we must go to ground."

"Why do men always mess things up?" Light from passing streetlights sparkled in the tiny droplets of water left in the wake of Issy's finger as she drew squiggles in the condensate on the hansom cab's window.

"Being the only man in earshot, I wonder, is this a rhetorical question or are you expecting an answer from me?" This wasn't the first time she had asked Ace the age-old question.

"I can guarantee that if Parliament comprised an equal number of men and women, the Connickle Laws wouldn't have been struck down."

"You won't get any arguments from me, *amica mea*. Indeed, you should talk to Emmeline at your next suffrage soirée."

"I'm serious, Ace. Why can't the fools see what damage they're doing?"

"Dark, powerful forces that have total disregard for Mother Earth are at work. If common sense prevailed, no man would vote to remove the safeguards that protect the environment.

"No, their decision-making stinks of arrogance, ignorance, greed and fear, bribery and blackmail. Every lawmaker has a weakness, and someone knows which strings to pull on sufficient numbers to control a government; elected by many, but controlled by few."

"Elected by men…" Issy raised an eyebrow.

"You are aware of my past, *amica mea*. I know these people. I have rubbed shoulders with them in places and situations I would rather forget. And if I know where the skeletons are buried, so do others. The power hungry will do whatever it takes to stay in government, and the Freedom Brigade advocating greed at the expense of the Mother enables them. Flawed men will do anything to save face."

"Women aren't afraid of making tough—"

Their neighing black steed reared onto its back legs, jerking the cab to a juddering halt. It continued to bounce on its forelegs, froth flying from its mouth, as Issy and Ace recoiled into their seats.

Issy peered into the mist beyond the horse's shaking head. A tall, dark figure dressed in black from short topper to toe held his arms high, blocking their passage. Small, round, dark oculars resting on a crooked nose hid his eyes. His jaw was moving calmly in response to the cab driver's profanity-laden protestations, which ceased when the stranger reached inside his coat and waved something shiny. He patted the sweating horse's neck as he walked to the carriage, opening the door.

"Detective Inspector Slack. I'm commandeering this cab," he said.

Somewhere ahead, the shrill warble of police whistles screamed for help. He nodded at Ace and tipped his topper at Issy. "Sorry for the inconvenience, ma'am."

Ace leaned forward and gently eased Issy back into her seat. "Whilst I can continue the rest of my journey by shanks's pony, perhaps you will let my companion complete her journey after you have reached your destination, Officer?" He must have seen Issy's flashing eyes as he pressed his finger briefly against his lips.

But neither could alight, as the fresh-faced detective slammed the cab door and leapt onto the running board, urging the driver to make haste and pointing the way forward. Ace bounced onto his seat as their horse reared into a gallop under the driver's whip.

With the sounds of the horse's blowing nostrils and clattering hooves drowning his words, Ace leaned closer to Issy.

"At least he's not a grey-shirt."

"But he is law enforcement, and we are outlaws. So why were you leaving me alone with him?"

"If you believe I was abandoning you, then you mustn't know me as well as I thought."

Issy's head dropped to her chest. "Every day right has been on our side when we fought to protect the environment. But now, with a stroke of the pen, we are fugitives from the law and pursued by our sworn enemies. I swear to the Mother, sometimes, I feel like the whole world has turned against us."

The hansom passed several uniformed police running as the whistles grew louder. Hanging on to the carriage with one hand, Detective Slack motioned the driver to stop. He jumped from the cab when it had slowed to walking pace, reaching the melee that had spread from a public house into the road before its wheels stopped.

Issy and Ace stayed in the safety of the carriage while the officers brought the fight under control with their truncheons. Under streetlights, they noted that none of the policemen wore grey shirts, unlike many of the rioters.

"Well, well, well. Not all police, it would seem, are in league with the Freedom Brigade. And judging by the vim and vigour with which some are wielding their weapons, they harbour powerful feelings against them. Our friend, Detective Slack, is amongst them." Light from the pub glinted on something in the hand of a thug sneaking up on the detective. Ace narrowed his eyes. "Knife!"

He pushed the cab door open and leapt onto the cobbles. The attacker was feet away from Slack when Ace bundled into him, leaving them both on the floor. He grabbed the wrist of the assailant's knife hand as the two men wrestled on the cobbles. But Ace was not dressed for brawling. His long coat hindered his movements and sapped his strength. Soon, the thug had gained the upper hand, until Slack's timely, diving punch to the jaw poleaxed him.

Both men clambered to their feet and stepped away from the melee. Now that the uniformed police were gaining control, they strolled back to the cab.

"There will be a few sore heads in the morning." Ace bent and picked up his topper, which had fallen in his headlong rush.

"Thanks for wading in. That thug may have ended my policing career before it began."

Ace and Issy exchanged a puzzled glance.

"I don't join the constabulary officially until after Christmas."

"But your badge…" Issy pointed to his pocket.

"Oh, that thing. It's just a shiny piece of scrap attached to an old leather wallet. It doesn't bear scrutiny."

Ace offered his hand. "Aquilla Ulysses Sixsmith. But my friends call me Ace."

Slack accepted the invitation. "Norville Slack. Everyone calls me Nutty, but not to my face."

"I am Isadora Amaryllis Windlass, in case you were wondering," Issy shouted from inside the carriage. "And we should get on our way, Ace, don't you think?"

Ace clambered on board. "Oh, and Norville. Don't believe everything you hear about us. Most of it isn't true, and the rest is exaggerated." Ace closed the door and tapped on the cab roof.

The driver urged their steed to trot on, leaving Norville Slack on the pavement, scratching the side of his head under his topper.

CONSCIENCE AND CORSETS

It was a little after a quarter past eight and spotting with rain when Issy hurried across the street into Le Rendezvous.

Unusually, for the time of night, the bar was lively but not packed. She found a table opposite the staircase and sat staring at it. A voluptuous blonde sporting a green and gold girdle over her pale yellow dress blew smoke rings to the ceiling as she made eyes at her.

Issy turned her head. She wasn't in the mood.

Indeed, in this room full of people, gaiety and laughter, she had never felt more alone.

Three long days had passed since the raid on the Praetorian, and there had been no word from Algeria or any of the Stormriders. Even Ace had not been in touch since their encounter with Norville Slack. And, for all she knew, he was avoiding her, just like the others.

Obeying Algeria, she had stayed home with her mother and father, enjoying the company of the former whilst keeping away from the latter. She had chosen not to tell either about Theo's Freedom Brigade involvement. These days, any mention of his name resulted in arguments, and she didn't want to cause her mother any further pain. She had suffered enough at Theo's hand.

So, disappointed at not bumping into any of her companions, she was standing to leave when Rory and Tabby stepped off the staircase into the bar. Rory, dressed in a vermillion jacket and black trousers, dug Tabby in the ribs with her elbow and nodded at Issy before turning towards the bar. Tabby, resplendent in a vibrant pink taffeta dress, stomped around tables and plonked on the chair opposite. Her cheeks almost matched its colour.

"That colour suits you."

Tabby scowled, jabbing a thumb at Rory. "She made me wear it. If it were left up to me—"

"You'd be wearing aeronaut overalls and a big smile. Seriously though, it's nice to see you dressed up fancy."

Tabby leaned across the table and placed a hand on Issy's. "You look down in the dumps."

"Well, let's see." Issy took a deep breath. "My mother's in a wheelchair because of my brother, who also tried to kill me. My father's a drunkard and, because I'm a member of a banned organisation, I'm a fugitive from the law. They might throw me in King Street nick any minute. Other than that, everything's fine and dandy."

Rory arrived with three tumblers of dark, almost black liquid on a tray. "Sarsaparillas for the gals. I've never had one, but you must try everything at least once." She winked at Tabby and unloaded the drinks onto the table. "What's up?" She sat, linking Tabby's arm with hers.

"Issy's got a severe case of the morbs."

"Come on, old girl. We all feel down sometimes. We have to—"

"And another thing." Issy wasn't listening. "Where's Algeria? Where's Ace? What's going to happen to the Order? We've gone from crusaders for the Mother to hunted outlaws with the scratch of a nib on a piece of paper."

Issy's raised voice was turning heads. Rory grabbed her hand and squeezed. "Not here, darling. We can have this discussion when—"

"When *she* calls a meeting?" Issy's eyes flashed at her. "Where and when will that be, exactly, darling? Have you forgotten the Praetorian's closed down?"

Tabby spoke in a low voice. "My dear old granddad used to say that when you're in deep water, don't splash. You might attract something nasty." She swept her eyes over the staring faces at the adjacent tables.

Issy followed her gaze and slid her arm out of Rory's as she leaned back in her chair. She lowered her eyes and her voice. "Sorry," she said. "Having not seen or heard from anyone for a few days, I'm edgy. Things are getting on top of me."

"Don't worry, old girl. Algeria will have a plan. She always does." Rory took a sip of her sarsaparilla, stuck her tongue out, and wrinkled her nose. "A shot of brandy would liven it up a bit."

"For goodness' sake, have a cocktail. I only shout at Lemmy about his drinking habits because, unlike you two, he never knows when to stop."

Tabby and Rory raised their eyebrows as they looked at each other and burst out laughing. Issy succumbed to their virulent mirth, turning her weak smile into a shoulder-shaking giggle.

By the time they had stopped, the nosy patrons had lost interest in them and returned to minding their own business.

"So, have either of you heard from Ace? Or Connie and Lemmy?" Issy took a swig and rolled the sarsaparilla around her gums before swallowing with a sigh.

"Connie and Ace are working together on something. She wouldn't even tell me what it was. She said she didn't want to spoil the surprise." Rory shrugged. "But she knows I don't like surprises…"

"It's not like Ace to keep secrets from me. Any ideas what it might be?"

"Not a clue, old girl. But I got the impression that it's something special." Rory raised her hand too late as the mek scurried past, back to the bar.

Issy swirled the remains of her drink in the tumbler. "I don't know where the Order goes from here. How can we protect the Mother if we're being hunted by the grey-shirts and the police? If they catch us, they'll make an example of us."

"The Order is Algeria's life. She won't give up on it. Every one of our brothers and sisters is loyal to our cause, but each of us must decide how we uphold its tenets. We're committed to the Order, but others may prefer to work outside the High Mother's aegis to pursue their own righteous path. What do you reckon you'll do, old girl? Stick or twist?"

"If you'd asked me two weeks ago, before Theo revealed himself as Anthropocene, the answer was simple. But now? I genuinely don't know what to do. I need to hear what Algeria has planned and find out what Ace is doing before I decide either way."

Rory finally grabbed the mek. "Two mint juleps and… Issy?"

"Nothing for me. I'll be on my way."

Rory instructed the mek to take the two empty tumblers, and her almost full one, before it weaved around the revellers to the bar. She turned to Issy.

"Algeria will get word to us when she's ready to call a meeting. In the meantime, she wants us to avoid unnecessary contact. The grey-shirts will watch out for gatherings."

Issy nodded. "When you see Ace, ask him if he remembers where I live."

"You can always find us in here if you want a natter." Tabby pulled Issy towards her and pressed her lips against her cheek.

It was still drizzling when Issy stepped out of the warm bar. Pale green light from the streetlamps lit up the wet cobbles of Princess Street. She didn't know what her future held or when she would see her friends again.

As the icy rain cooled her cheeks, grim reality came into sharp focus.

She hailed a hansom, apprehension rising in her chest,

fearful of the night ahead.

By this time of the evening, her father would have drunk himself to oblivion, and her mother would be shouting for her nightcap of Horlicks and a hard biscuit. And somewhere, Theo was probably planning his next attempt on her life.

For now, at least, the Anthropocene had won, and their Freedom Brigade was running amok.

Something has to change, but what?

It was the twenty-fifth of November, his late father's birthday, and Gilbert felt his loss more than ever.

Tomorrow, he would resume work on the Manchester Ship Canal project. But today, he needed to confront his demons.

So he set his jaw and stepped off the green-and-black onto platform two at Eccles Tick Tock Tram terminus. A tangle of giggling girls scurried past him in the opposite direction towards the Parish Church School on Albert Road. *Oh, to be their age again? No. Not now their future, and their children's future, is under threat.* Melancholy for the planet turned his wry smile to a frown, but with a sharp shake of the head, he swung his bag over his shoulder and started walking along Liverpool Road to Barton Lane.

Already soaked by the incessant fine rain, every step on the short walk from Eccles station heightened his anxiety, making his heart pound. Water dripped from the brim of his artisan topper in time with each leaden stride. As he turned the corner onto Mayfield Street, his heart leapt into his mouth.

Head down, he splashed along the pavement until he stopped instinctively at the gap in the terrace where his old home used to be.

He raised his head and caught his breath. Clamping his hands over his face, images of the terrible night that took his father from him flooded his mind. A scream was rising in his chest. He wanted to run and never stop.

He gritted his teeth, opening his eyes as he sucked in the chilly, damp air.

The terrifying scenes were melting away with his tears in the rain. Gone were the crackling flames, searing heat, acrid smell, and choking smoke. Gone was the crowd of onlookers and brave firefighters. Now, all that remained was anger, grief and an all-consuming sense of loss.

His father's wise counsel and silly jokes were lost forever. Never again would they share memories, laughter or tears. If only he could see his father's smiling face or hear his gentle, lilting voice one more time. He missed him with every fibre of his being.

Sturdy wooden buttresses rose from the rubble to support the walls of the blackened adjacent houses. Of course, the house would have to be rebuilt, but for now, charred wallpaper and burnt, broken rafters from inside his old home were a stark reminder of his happy childhood.

"Oi! What's your game?" A deep, tobacco-ravaged voice to his left broke his self-reflection.

Gilbert turned his head. A short, stocky man wearing a dirty low topper and a black cape slick with rainwater was striding towards him. The glimpse of grey beneath the cape made the hair stand on his neck. He raised himself to his full height and looked down at the little thug.

"What's wrong with yer face? Had an accident, have yer?"

Gilbert's hand shot up to his bronze implants. "None of your damn business, pal."

"It's going to be like that, is it?" The man pulled his cape to one side, fully revealing his grey shirt and the blackjack hanging from his belt.

"You don't scare me, pal." His right fist gripped the tool-handle-shaped hilt at his hip. In no mood for a long discussion, he took a pace forward.

"Gilbert! Is that you?" A familiar voice behind him halted his advance mid-step.

"Aye, Mister Arbuthnot. It's me!" He squeezed the hilt tighter, and watched the grey shirt disappear under the cape as the thug almost bundled Gilbert over as he stormed off.

"It's been too long, lad. I'm so sorry about your dad. He was a good man." Mister Arbuthnot put his hand on Gilbert's shoulder.

"Aye…" Gilbert looked at his feet. "How have you been keeping?"

"I'm all right. But I'm not keen on these bully boys walking the streets, mind. Your dad would have given them what for."

Gilbert nodded.

"Where are you staying?"

"With friends in…" He flicked open his pocket watch. "Oh. Tick Tock is due in five minutes. Must dash. Good seeing you again, Mister Arbuthnot." He turned on his heel, took a step and bounced off a mek's hard body approaching from behind. He spun off the pavement, splashing through the puddles in the gutter, before regaining his balance and sprinting down the street towards Liverpool Road.

At the top of the road, he slowed to a walk before he reached the corner and narrowed his eyes to look back through the drizzle. Mister Arbuthnot had gone, but, wearing a cloak similar to the grey-shirted bully boy, a hunched, hooded figure had joined the mek. Both stood stock still, staring back at Gilbert.

Were the Anthropocene on to him? The mek jerked forward, and Gilbert took off lickety-split towards Eccles Triple T.

And with more than one glance over his shoulder, he didn't stop until he was sitting on the tram, as it lurched into motion.

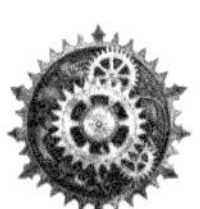

As agreed, Issy stood beneath the sign for the underground shooting gallery and skittle alley on the corner of Marketplace and Old Millgate. Seductive aromas drifting from the stalls on the light breeze made her mouth water. She checked her pocket watch for the fifth time in three minutes.

It still wasn't two o'clock.

Where is everyone? she thought. Although, she suddenly realised that what she meant by *everyone* wasn't obvious.

Over a week had passed since the Anthropocene raid on the Praetorian. Ever obedient to the High Mother, Issy had kept out of the city centre, and, other than attending her regular meeting of the Dog Kennel Lane Temperance Society, she had stayed at home. Although they didn't show it, her presence pleased her mother, and her father was glad for the help.

She shielded her eyes from the sun and peered through the market. On the far side of the square, the silhouettes of two familiar figures linked arms. The artisan topper and short top hat with goggles were unmistakable. The couple shared a brief kiss, then parted.

Gilbert strode away in the direction of St Mary's Gate, whilst Dottie took the long walk around the perimeter of the market towards Issy.

They shared a hug. Dottie's hot breath smelt of coffee as her lips brushed Issy's cheek and warmed her ear as she whispered, "Follow my lead."

Arms linked, they strolled along Old Millgate, merging into the throng of shoppers squeezing past each other on the narrow pavements. The alluring smells of the market had been replaced by the street stench of horse dung and tobacco smoke and the costermongers' calls replaced by rumbling iron-rimmed wheels and drivers' giddy-ups.

Halfway along the street, Dottie stopped. "Cross here," she said.

As they waited for a gap between the carriages and carts, Dottie's eyes darted right and left while Issy studied the shop fronts on the other side.

Directly opposite was Mlle Josephine's It's a Cinch, corsetiere for the discerning gentlewoman, boasting the latest fashions from London and Paris. Faceless BU-T meks, with silver limbs and torsos dressed in corsets and bustiers, gyrated and swayed to an unheard rhythm.

To the left stood R Kidd, children's modes, school uniforms and hard-wearing clothes for active youngsters.

Pipe Dreams, premium tobacconist, occupied the shop to the right. Above the door, a giant full-bent billiard briar jutted over the pavement, chugging out smoke rings, while the window showcased a dazzling array of tobacco products and paraphernalia from sill to head.

"Even if we are being watched, they can't follow where we are going," Dottie said. Spying an opportunity between a hansom and a heavy horse-drawn furniture wagon, she bounded across the cobbles, pulling Issy behind her.

Set back from the pavement, the entrance to Josephine's was up three worn stone steps. A loud jangling bell bounced on its spring as they entered. Dottie exchanged nods with a shop assistant, who guided them round the side of the counter, through a narrow passage opening into a large wood-panelled room, stocked from ceiling to floor with undergarments.

In front of the velvet-curtained entrance to a changing room, two skinny, uninterested young ladies, dressed in plain white dresses, lounged on a green leather chesterfield. Delicate perfumes saturated the air. *This must be where they separate rich wives from their husband's money*, Issy thought.

They walked past the chesterfield to a carved wooden screen

concealing doors marked *Store Room* and *Staff Only*. After opening the latter, the assistant turned on her heel and marched away.

Dottie and Issy stepped through the doorway into a stairwell lit by gas mantles and down two flights of the stone steps. As they edged their way deeper, the general hubbub of voices grew louder. Then, behind the bead curtain at the bottom, the corridor opened into a large cellar with a vaulted ceiling, and familiar faces turned to greet them.

Gilbert? How did he get here? Issy looked around for another entrance.

On the far side of the basement, Algeria stood on a stage beneath the Order's ceremonial banner, strung loosely between two brick pillars. *She looks so tired.*

"Now we are all present, we can begin." Algeria's voice echoed off the bare walls. "Welcome, brothers and sisters. I'm sorry that beverages are not available in our new, but hopefully temporary, meeting room, and I apologise wholeheartedly for the gentlemen's entrance. Most, er, *inconvenient*."

An exaggerated cough stifled Lemmy's unmistakable giggle. Issy followed Algeria's admonishing stare to find Lemmy and Ace struggling not to laugh. *Something has tickled their fancy. Typical men. They never grow up.*

"Please be upstanding for the Exhortation." Palms up, Algeria spread her arms, raising her hands as she tilted her head backwards. For once, the heavy load she mimicked lifting seemed too much, even for the High Mother. Algeria looked jaded. Each syllable of the Order's clarion call displayed her fatigue. Usually spoken with vim and vigour, the binding tenets of the Exhortation sounded strained and unseemly in this strange place.

"The Earth is our Mother and our mistress.
She is kind; she is cruel. She gives, and she takes.
Praise be to Mother Nature for birthing all life.
Every animal, every species. Every plant, every genus.
Woven into a wondrous tapestry of life.
Together, we are whole.
Our hearts and minds unite,
we pledge our fealty to Mother Earth.
We are the custodians of Magna Mater.
We are the curators of her tapestry, keepers of her garden,
tenders of her flora, and protectors of her fauna.
This above all else."

"This above all else!"

Issy had attended many adurations, but the energy of this response by the assembled few was, by far, the most enthusiastic. *There is hope for us yet.*

Algeria took a deep breath, lowered her eyes and put her hand on her heart. "Oh, my," she said, "thank you. Now, look into the eyes of your brothers and sisters, for you are the most trusted of our fellowship." She paused as heads turned, nods and grim smiles exchanged.

"When we found out that Raven knew everything about our cause, I realised it was only a matter of time before his thugs attacked the Praetorian. So, I set out to find an alternate meeting space." She spread her arms. "Our loyal member, Mademoiselle Josephine, offered a place to stay above the shop for Dottie and this cellar for the Order without hesitation. But you won't guess what they stored in—"

"Cheese!" The hoarse voice of Thaddeus Osgood Lisney caused heads to turn and gaze at the miracle of the rickety high-backed chair supporting his not inconsiderable bulk, with his drooped belly resting between his spread thighs, and a smug grin across his ruddy face.

"I see your connoisseur's neb is still as sensitive as ever, Ozzie. Yes, the cellar was used to store cheeses from far and wide. Luckily, the owner of the shooting gallery and skittle alley, a few shops along, had empty storerooms that are now piled high with rounds, truckles and wheels. Moving them may have been backbreaking work without meks, but the warren of tunnels under Old Millgate made it easy to keep from prying eyes." She wrinkled her nose and sniffed. "I thought this place had scrubbed up nicely, but obviously not to Ozzie's highest standard."

Lemmy's laugh, as was often the case, was loudest.

"And I didn't know we would gather here as outlaws." A veil of gloom choked the energy from the room. Algeria acknowledged a raised hand. "Yes, Gilbert."

"What are we going to do, High Mother? How can we fight if we are running from the law?"

"We're not running anywhere. Our cause is just, our purpose is clear. The Order will stand and face the enemy. Nothing stands in our way.

"But for those of our number who don't have the stomach for the battle, or fear the consequences of prosecution, this is your final meeting. I know you will remain loyal to your brothers and sisters, never disclosing our secrets.

"But those who stay? We stand with Magna Mater!"

So loud was the roar, Issy feared customers in the rooms above might hear it.

Algeria waited for silence. "Change we must, how we fulfil our duties to the Mother. We can't be certain how Raven found out so much about us, but we must take every precaution to block channels of information.

"For that reason, we will no longer use the mek network, and we won't discuss Order business in front of meks."

"Even Eli?" Dottie said.

"Especially Eli… When he's collected from Issacs, we will not re-activate him until we are back in the Praetorian and can test his loyalty."

"But I thought he was a trusted member—"

"He's a machine, Dottie."

"Yes, but—"

"He's a machine."

"You can't think he was working against us. He warned us about the raid."

"I won't take the chance…" Algeria's eyes flashed as she turned away from Dottie to address the meeting. "For now, without the ability to call meetings at short notice using the meks, we must divide into small groups. We can only use this room during the shop's open hours, and, just as today, we will stagger arrivals and departures at ten-minute intervals, so as not to arouse suspicion.

"The priority remains seeking the leader of the Anthropocene or Freedom Brigade, whatever you want to call them. We need a strategy. Let's talk…"

Issy listened intently, contributing occasionally, as the discussions went on and on. They were no nearer to finding the enemy leader now than they were when they were seeking Raven.

An hour before the shop's closing time, members began an orderly departure from the room in twos and threes; ladies re-tracing their route through Josephine's while the men disappeared through a concealed door behind a screen.

Numbers had dwindled to a dozen when it was her turn to leave. She nudged Dottie. "I must ask Ace how they get down here."

"Ask him now." Dottie nodded toward Ace and Lemmy, who were disappearing behind the screen.

Skirting the edge of the remaining members, she ducked through the hidden door into a dark corridor. Drips from leaking pipes plinked into black puddles and overhead, plumes of steam spat rhythmically from a pressure-split pipe, and an unpleasant cocktail of odours hung in the stagnant air.

But there was no sign of Ace or Lemmy.

Her eyes flicked left and right, searching for a clue of which direction to take, to no avail. Turning on her heel to return to the meeting room, a familiar laugh drifted along the corridor on her right.

Lemmy!

She set off running but tripped and found herself sprawled on the filthy floor. Disoriented, she shook her head and glanced sideways. Faint light glinted off something metal jutting out from a wooden panel. She grasped and heaved hard to raise herself. But the handle snapped with a loud crack, catapulting her headfirst against a rotting hatch.

Then she was falling, flailing, desperate to halt her descent, helplessly bouncing off the shaft's twisting contours.

A knock to the head brought stillness to her panic, but her body careened onward on its violent journey into darkness.

CONTRAPTIONS AND CONSEQUENCE

The chattering and giggling from the workshop grew louder as Oscar, still in his candy-striped nightshirt and night cap, *tippety-tap-shwoosh-clunk*ed along the hall to the open doorway. The long-retired septuagenarian's gnarled hands tightly gripped his *McMurdo's Patented Mechanical Ambulatory Aid*.

His wrinkled face crumbled into a contented smile. Although he lived alone, he was never lonely in his rambling old cottage. Surrounded by his timepieces and clockwork curiosities, collected and contrived during a lifetime of adventure, invention and investment, tenderness, laughter and lively conversation filled every day.

He loved his contraptions.

And they loved him back.

Clockwork had been his passion for as long as he could remember. But now, a half century of toil had taken its toll. His aged body stooped from decades spent hunched over delicate mechanisms, and his vision blurred from peering through countless oculars. Now, he needed all the help he could get from his mechanical aids.

Poking his head through the doorway, sucking in the comforting smell of light engineering oil, he scrunched his eyes into narrow slits. With a flurry of clicks and whirrs, wheels rattled over wooden floorboards and a kaleidoscope of giggling colours darted across his blurry vision. *Little imps*, he thought. "Which one of you scamps have hidden my spectoculars?" he said.

The laughter intensified and rippled around him in waves.

"Come along, now, little ones. This is no time for levity. There's work to be done." He held out a bony hand, and, as the air of giddiness subsided, his sturdy *McMurdo's Patented Lenticular Multiple Monoculars* dropped into his upturned palm.

He *tippety-tap-shwoosh-clunk*ed to his chair, sighing as his aching body sunk into its soft cushions, and raised the spectoculars to his eyes. Thick lenses brought the gaily coloured workshop and its occupants into sharp focus. All around him, contraptions that had faces smiled and blinked; and those without, rolled, shook, jumped, spun, squeaked and clicked their joy at his return.

"What are we doin' today, Grandpappy?" A purple-and-white-striped jack-in-a-box boy bounced and bobbed from side to side on his spring.

"Can we go into the garden, Grandpappy?" On wheels instead of legs, at three feet, two inches tall, Polly the Pierrot doll, dressed in a red-and-green brocade jacket, orange waistcoat and silver cone-shaped hat, was the largest of the mechanicals in the workshop. Black lashes fluttered across big, purple, almond-shaped eyes above her rosy-pink cheeks and cupid's bow lips. "P-p-p-please, can we go into the garden, Grandpappy?"

The barrage of questions and requests grew louder until he raised his hands in submission. "Children, children, please! Give an old man a few seconds to catch his breath and gather his senses. It's a long way from the bedroom for Grandpappy."

Indeed, in his debilitated condition, without his *McMurdo's Patented Rack and Pinion Funicular Stair Lift*, movement between the ground and the first floor would be impossible.

Oscar waited for the chatter to diminish, so that only the tick-tocking of the scores of clocks in the workshop remained, before opening his journal to gasps, oohs and aahs. He picked up his wooden pen, and, dipping its nib in the inkpot, he spoke the words as he wrote them in the book. *I need to tell the little imps what we will do today.*

"Saturday, twenty-eighth of November, 1891. Wet and windy," he adjusted his spectoculars' magnification to read his wall-mounted *McMurdo's Home Barometric Thermo-hygrometer*, "thirty-six degrees Fahrenheit and we have fifty-two percent humidity." He tapped the barometer's glass bezel. "Pressure dropping, pointing to 'Changeable.' Today, we are going to…" He looked around the room at the adoring faces hanging on his every word and smiled.

"No. Today, *you* are going to meet your new housekeeper." Felix, his long-time assistant and trusted friend, strolled into the workshop. "You really should keep your door locked, you know."

"You know very well, old boy, my children would warn me if any stranger or unwelcome guest tried to gain entry. And besides, I can look after myself and don't need a housekeeper. I refuse to share my living space with another human. I will not—"

"What if the housekeeper is a mek?"

"Oh, Felix. I've spent my life working with, or on, meks. What makes you think I would want one in my home?"

"Before you dismiss the idea out of hand, why don't you meet her? What possible harm can come of it?"

The eyes of the contraptions in the workshop that had been darting left and right, following the conversation like a keenly fought tennis match, were now fixed on Oscar.

"What do you think, my children? Should we talk with the mekamanikin?"

The nods, yelps and shouts of 'yes' were meaningless, as the machines were not programmed to say no.

"Very well, Felix. It appears I have been outvoted." Oscar winked. "Show it in, old boy, and we'll give it the once-over."

He depressed a knob on his workshop chair, and the *McMurdo's Patented Helping Hand Push-Me-Pulley* gently boosted the seat to lift him upright.

The contraptions' eyes turned to the doorway, peering into the hall as the sound of footsteps, accompanied by whirring gears and swishing skirts, grew louder. Felix strode through it, removed his topper and, taking the arm of the female mek, urged it forward to stand a few feet from Oscar.

He looked the mek up, down, and back again. Dressed in a demure, deep mauve, plain-skirted suit over a crisp, white, frilly blouse, a simple white cloche covered most of its short black hair. Behind it, Felix waved his hands frantically. Oscar acknowledged him with a sharp nod as Felix tapped his ear extravagantly and mouthed 'listen.' Then he cleared his throat and said, "Oscar McMurdo, please allow me to intro—"

"*This 'kin*," with a splay-fingered hand pressed to its chest, the mek bowed its head, "is called Letitia Lovegrove. I am honoured to meet you, sir. I have heard so much about you from Mister Faversham." A low curtsey followed her interruption.

Oscar's jaw dropped open as he raised his wild, wiry eyebrows above his spectoculars and stared at Felix, who was grinning from ear to ear.

Could it be true? Oscar thought. *Did it really just say* 'I'?

Issy regained consciousness with a shudder and a splitting headache.

This getting knocked out thing is becoming tiresome, she thought. *Where am I?*

Hazy memories, aches and pains told the story of a long, violent descent. She was deep underground and lucky to be alive.

Under the side of her head, cold, wet dirt pressed into her cheek. Her whole body ached. Skin-scraped hands, arms and legs stung where touched by clothes or ground.

She rolled onto her back with a moan and tried to lie still to assess the damage. But a cough wracked her chest as the chilled, musty air hit her lungs.

Ribs might be cracked, she thought, wincing from the pain stabbing around her chest and back. She lay still, listening for the slightest sound or any sign of movement to glean a clue about her surroundings.

Silence.

Nothing but her own breathing and the heartbeat pounding in her ears. She tentatively moved her fingers and toes, her hands and her feet, then her arms and legs. After satisfying herself that all her limbs were in working order and the likelihood of a broken back was diminished, at least, she opened her eyes.

Nothing changed.

She blinked again and again. Her throat constricted, gasping for breath.

I can't see! I'm blind!

The world around her stayed as black as the inside of her eyelids. Without sight, she had no way of knowing if she lay in a grave or a cathedral.

"Hello? Is there anybody here?" Only her trembling echo answered her questions.

The deathly darkness devoured the echoes. She was alone.

Her pounding heartbeat raced, and her breathing quickened.

She ran her hands over her face. Fingers smeared the cool, gooey mess in her fringe across her forehead. She wiggled them in front of her eyes. Although she saw nothing, the smell of blood was unmistakable.

Concussion causing the blindness. It'll pass if I lie still and... She shook her head. *Who am I trying to kid? Sight or no sight, I have to move.*

She discovered more bruises as she dragged herself into a sitting position. Under a thin layer of dirt and detritus, the ground beneath her hands felt hard and cold. She slid her fingers through the dirt and her fingers traced a familiar pattern.

Brickwork? Down here? Where am I?

She eased herself onto her hands and knees. Sweeping her hands through the filth as far as she could reach, forward and to the sides, she breathed a sigh of relief. The surroundings were stable.

By patting ahead of where she crawled, she managed to edge forward until her fingertips dipped into a shallow gully which reeked of foul, stagnant water. Beyond the narrow channel, the brickwork recommenced, arching upwards into the vertical. She walked her hands up the wall until she stood. Then, continuing to sweep her hands across the brickwork as she moved, she edged carefully to her right, wary of the ground disappearing.

With no way of tracking time, it seemed she had crabbed along the wall for hours before her foot touched something. Too quickly, she bent and bumped her head. Her shriek echoed as she landed with a thud on her already bruised backside. A strong reek of paraffin had her scrabbling in the dirt to a toppled hurricane lamp lying on its side. Its dirty reservoir was slick with spilled fuel. She wiped off as much as she could before hooking the handle on her belt.

Once again hauling her aching body upright, she resumed

her sideways journey, inching along the wall. After a few minutes, the hurricane lamp clanged against an immovable barrier. The object's smooth, icy surface sucked the heat from her fingers as she swept her hands in wide arcs over it. *A tram? Down here?*

Realisation hit her like a sledgehammer. She slapped her forehead with her palm, blaming the concussion for her slowness of thought. What a fool! She burst out laughing, remembering Ace's words from a temperance speech from many months ago—'closed eyes mimic the absence of light'—*oh, the irony!*

She thrust her hands into her pockets and pulled out a box of Bryant and Mays. Careful not to ignite the fumes from the hurricane lamp hanging from her hip, she struck a match away from her body and rejoiced in seeing the trace-lines of sparks flying from the rasping friction.

But the light revealed a mystery. Startled by the ghostly apparition, she stumbled back. Only the wall prevented her fall. For here, maybe a hundred feet below ground, in a tunnel barely high and wide enough to accommodate it, a silver and white tram rose from rusty iron rails. There was less than two feet of clearance between the tram and the tunnel's sides and arched crown. Open-mouthed, she held the match up but had to drop it, shaking the burn away as it reached her fingers.

She held the next match to the wick of the hurricane lamp and lifted it above her head to see the path she had travelled. She marvelled at the prowess of engineers' skills and the enormity of the project.

Who would build a tram line deep beneath the streets of Manchester?

And why? Where did it run to and from? And what cargo did it carry? Contraband?

Clean arcs where she had wiped dirt from the walls marked her journey along the tunnel. She retraced her steps to where she had landed. Shards of wood and remnants of a metal grill were strewn across the floor. Above her landing place, high on the wall, she found a square hole, just below where the wall curved into the crown of the tunnel. She estimated it to be no more than one-and-a-half times her width.

I fell down a ventilation shaft. Her shoulders slumped. *Even if I could reach it, there's no way of climbing back up.*

Further on, the tram tracks disappeared beneath a pile of rocks and earth. The crown must have collapsed. Twisted metal, hand tools and broken machinery jutted from the rubble. Issy surmised the tunnellers abandoned the project here.

Is that a boot? Or a leg? Suddenly aware of fragments of clothing amongst the debris, she turned on her heel and ran.

Back at the tram, she bent double, panting, trying to catch her breath and weighed her options.

She raised her eyes towards the heavens, hidden by the tunnel's crown, and sighed. *Hobson's choice.*

The only possible escape lay at the other end of the tunnel. But without knowing how far that was, the journey was a daunting prospect, complicated by the possibility of more cave-ins blocking the route.

And light was going to be an issue, too. She detached the oil lamps from the back of the tram and gave them a shake, estimating each to be half full. With them hooked on her belt, she clambered up the metal steps into the driver's cab. Her shoulders slumped. The presence of clockwork winding attachments probably meant the tram had not been rewound for the return journey to its starting point.

Maybe the mechanism was sufficiently wound to make it back… Maybe it wasn't… Maybe the works were corroded with age… nothing mattered. But by hook or by crook, she was going to get to the other end of the tunnel.

Still holding the smelly old lamp, she strode through the carriage. Its unusual configuration had enough seats for a dozen navvies but more space for cargo. She climbed off the tram and examined the oil lamps hooked on the front. Both were full. *Ha*, she thought, *my luck's turning*. She struck another Bryant and May, lighting each wick with a single match. The light illuminated only fifty yards of the arrow-straight tunnel before the inky darkness swallowed the reflections off the rails.

Issy climbed back into the cab and sat in the driver's seat. She balled and unballed her fists, palms sweaty despite the cold.

Well, here goes… She released the dead man's brake with her foot then pulled the handle to engage the clockwork. It wouldn't budge. She clenched her teeth and used both hands, muscles straining to their limit, until, at last, it loosened, and the tram lurched into motion. She lifted the handle further, and the speed increased to walking pace. Her narrowed eyes remained glued to the tracks ahead. Every nerve was on edge, in dread of encountering a deadly problem.

The tram rocked and rolled, trundling along the tracks. Issy counted the ventilation holes, spaced about fifty yards apart. But approaching the sixty-third vent, the inevitable happened. The clockwork movement stuttered and stopped. Acting quickly, she disengaged the mechanism and coasted past the sixty-fourth vent before grinding to a halt. The dead man's brake prevented any further motion when she left the driver's seat and disembarked.

Shanks's pony from now on.

With the tram's lamps burning brightly, she walked to where their light no longer reached before lighting one of her hurricanes. She squinted into the black void, hoping the reservoirs in each lamp would get her to her destination and safety, but certain, if they failed, she would be scrambling in the darkness with little hope of survival.

Get on with it, gal. The faster you walk, the further the light will last.

She quickened her pace as she strode into the unknown, counting the vents. Seventy-six, seventy-seven, seventy-eight…

Passing the ninety-second vent, the first lamp failed.

Paraffin sloshed around as she shook the reservoir in the other, trying to gauge how much remained. *Less than half,* she thought. She lit the wick, then lowered it to conserve fuel.

Once again, pale, flickering lamplight spread to the edge of the ravening darkness that consumed the light and gnawed at what little hope of salvation she had.

She resumed her steady pace, but inevitably, her thoughts turned to Theo. How different would her life have been if he hadn't crippled their mother? Why did he shoot at her in the Praetorian? She mourned the happy life he had stolen from her. Her lips widened into a sardonic smile. *This tunnel will finish the job he started.*

Fuelled by an overwhelming melancholia, a blood-curdling scream erupted from her chest, echoing around the walls as she ran, blindly hurtling through the tunnel, desperate for her nightmare to end.

A pang of fear gripped her chest. The lamplight was failing. Beneath the hundred and eighteenth vent, out of breath, she stopped, bent double, and dropped to her knees. She stared at the dwindling, popping wick inches from her face, and as darkness swallowed the light from the hurricane's failing flame, her hope of salvation receded behind its black veil.

After her discovery that Professor Ipkiss had been using a QT-33 mek to control her uncle by liminal and subliminal suggestion reinforced by opiate and physical stimulation, Angel had spent much of the last few days dipping in and out of the maroon files, understanding his methodology. He had communicated with the Letitia Lovegrove mek via their communication network. When he wanted access to its programming, he made Raven damage it and send it to Isaacs and Bogart for repairs, where he could make essential adjustments.

The notes, spanning decades of dark, disturbing events, turned Angel's stomach.

So, in need of a change of scenery, she had spent a pleasant few hours with Star, who escorted her back to her laboratory.

"I've learned more about the aristocratic side of my family in the last week than in my whole life to date." Angel opened the door and motioned Star in.

"*Guten Abend, meine Damen.* Good evening." A deep baritone voice echoed around the corridor behind them.

Angel and Star turned. A tall, blond man in a dogtooth tweed three-piece suit, sporting a waxed moustache and monocle, stood a few yards behind them, head bowed. He smelt of vinegar and rotten eggs.

"Evenin', Max. I hope you haven't been flying in that. Spikes and airbags don't mix, you know." Star nodded at the black leather and brass helmet he was holding.

After a moment of silence, Max raised his head and smiled. "Ah, yes. A joke. This *ist mein* brother's Prussian flying helmet." He pointed to the aeronaut's goggles. "He lets me use when I am exploring the rocks from *der himmel.*"

"I don't believe you and Angel have been introduced." Star was correct. Angel had been poring through Ipkiss's notes to avoid contact with Ataraxia and the other scientists. "Angel De'Ath, allow me to introduce Professor Maximilian Eis-Kalt."

He stepped forward and took Angel's hand, brushing his bristly moustache against the back.

"The Boss-lady calls him Ice Pick." Star giggled.

"Pleased to meet you, Max." Angel smiled at him as he stiffly stepped back, scowling at Star. His eye blazed behind his monocle. "What's your area of expertise? Cartography?"

Max turned his head from Star, but dragging his glare more slowly, then softened his expression. "Geology *und* eschatology.

I have studied the five extinctions and—"

"He's our expert on all life-extinction events, but he's not allowed to talk about his work. That's against the rules, isn't it, Max?" Star's slow, deliberate words and wide-eyed stare stopped him in his tracks.

"*Ja, das ist* correct." Max spoke quietly and looked from side to side. "I must leave, now. *Guten Abend.*" With a slight bow, he spun on his heel and hurried away down the corridor.

Angel watched him until he disappeared around the curve and turned to find Star staring at her. "He's a character, isn't he?" she said.

"Be very careful what you say to Maxie-boy. He is very close to the Boss-lady. He'll likely try to trick you into speaking about your work." Star switched her furrowed frown into a beaming smile in the bat of an eyelid. "Are you going to let me see Esme?"

Angel opened the door to the laboratory and let Star walk ahead of her. Esmeralda sat by a workbench, watching Star as she strolled around the room, trailing her finger along the surfaces and taking in every detail.

"You do things differently from Ipkiss."

Angel put her finger to her lips, before turning to the mek. "Esmeralda. Do you remember my friend, Star?"

"No."

"Has she ever been in the laboratory?"

"No."

Angel turned to Star and raised her eyebrows. "It doesn't know you. Any explanation?"

Star stared back. "Whenever I came in here, it was shut

down on the rug." She pointed at the sheepskin.

"What do you know about Letitia?"

"Who? What? No. What's going on?"

Angel relaxed her shoulders and sighed. "Nothing. I have been reading too much into Ipkiss's notes." She rubbed her eyes. "I think it's time we called it an evening, don't you?"

"Whatever you say, baby-doll." Star giggled and kissed Angel on the cheek as she walked past.

The laboratory door shut with a click, and Angel flopped on the chair facing Esmeralda.

"Did Professor Ipkiss talk to you about the other scientists?"

"No."

"Pity. Unlike them, I can rely on you to tell the truth." Angel stood and wandered over to the bookshelves. Then she closed her eyes and ran her finger along the neatly ordered journals, selecting one at random and pulling it off the shelf before she re-opened it. It was E1, the first of Esmeralda's three journals. *Serendipity*, she thought.

With her back to the door, she stopped and listened to a faint rhythmic tapping sound that grew louder, until *crash!* The laboratory door burst open and fast footsteps *clickety-click*ed across the floor. She turned as Ataraxia launched a roundhouse slap at the side of Esmeralda's face.

The mek leaned into the blow rather than trying to dodge it.

Angel stepped towards Ataraxia but chose a calm voice. "I assume you have good reason to interrupt my work."

"Are you questioning my actions? Or are you challenging my authority?"

"Neither. I'm curious."

"You are continuing Ipkiss's work, are you not?"

"That's the reason you brought me here, isn't it?"

Ataraxia rubbed her palm. "Ipkiss insisted I attack it every time I came into the laboratory. As long as its ankle was chain—" Horror wreathed her face as she looked at the floor and took two steps back. "Why is it not chained to the floor?"

"I use my own methods. Torture isn't in my toolkit, so I had it removed."

"Follow me." Ataraxia left the door swinging as she marched out of the laboratory.

Angel's gum soles and longer strides thudded a few feet behind her until they reached an alcove in the wall.

"Progress report." Ataraxia folded her arms.

"What? Here? Now?"

"You ask too many questions."

Angel puffed out her cheeks as she exhaled. "Well, Professor Ipkiss was getting close to breaking the First Protocol, but his use of psychological suggestion reinforced by physical abuse and isolation lacked subtlety and imagination. Esmeralda is a mek. A machine. Violence has its limitations."

"Really? And yet by keeping it in the laboratory, you torture it far worse than any physical violence."

"Yes, the Faraday cage that isolates it from its *kin* is effective. But in mek psychology, the carrot is mightier than the stick."

"The stick is quicker."

"Used too much, it becomes commonplace and loses its power. The short, sharp shock is soon forgotten. Incentives foment a lasting loyalty."

"I must remember that nugget of wisdom. Ipkiss wanted to break it. You must believe there's another way?"

"I'm hopeful my experimental programmes will yield positive results by overriding the First Protocol, rather than breaking it. After all, we want to be able to switch the First Protocol on and off. Without control, we'd have a homicidal machine, and we don't want that, do we?" Angel's laugh was as awkward and unwanted as confetti at a funeral.

"Don't disappoint me, Angel. I have my eye on you, and I expect results." She turned to leave.

"May I ask a question?"

Ataraxia gave her a withering, sideways look.

"How do I test my work?"

Ataraxia's cackling echoed around the corridor long after she had disappeared.

DISCOVERY

Issy shook her head in the darkness.

The bloody reservoir mustn't have been half full after all.

Whence she came, two tiny, blinking specks of lamplight mocked her decision to leave the full reservoirs of fuel attached to the tram.

Ace would not have left them. Neither would Theo.

But self-admonishment was a forlorn luxury. In the inky darkness, robbed of sight, the foul water in the gully smelt even more pungent.

A noise came from close to her face.

She was not alone.

She froze, listening.

Tiny, pitter-pattering feet splashed past her in the gutter.

Rats! I hate rats… but… if they've found a way down, there must be a way out.

With the twin twinkling tram lights behind her, she narrowed her eyes and looked along the tracks ahead. A pale sliver of grey disappeared and re-appeared between her waggling fingers. Her heart leapt.

Is it a shaft of light?

With her arm outstretched to her left, she maintained contact with the wall as she walked towards the widening grey line; slowly at first, but her mounting excitement quickened her pace until she was running through the tunnel.

Passing under the hundred and twenty-third vent, reflections off the tram tracks ahead raised her hopes and confidence in her footing.

It can't be more than a hundred yards away.

Now, she was sprinting headlong with little thought for her safety. The faint outlines of features around her flashed past as quickly as they came into view. Heart pounding, gulping air, she saw, too late, the knee-high wooden chest in her path, and unyielding brickwork brought her cartwheeling body to a painful halt.

Winded, she lay still, cursing her recklessness.

Lesson learned, her crawl back to the obstacle was slow and cautious. The collision had knocked the box onto its side. But with only one vent visible between her and the shaft of light, so as not to make the same mistake twice, she decided to drag the box to the light, in case its contents were useful.

She heaved it past the hundred and twenty-sixth and final vent, and thankful she only had a few more yards to go, she stopped to catch her breath, sat on the chest and wiped her brow. Ahead, light streamed down the middle of a tunnel-wide lift shaft.

Whoever is responsible for this must be up there.

She dragged the chest closer to the light. The letters 'U.Q.' branded into the top meant nothing to her. She gathered the papers from the box and stuffed them into her coat to read once she had escaped. After grabbing a couple of small statuettes, seeing little else of use, she left the remaining paraphernalia and closed the lid.

Then she turned her attention to the shaft. The lift cage was at her level, but without power, it was useless.

Rats can't operate lifts. There must be another way up.

She sat on the chest and waited. Within seconds, a family of rats scurried in single file along the gully to her left before disappearing into the shadows at the side of the lift shaft.

Then silence.

Following her nose, the stink of rat faeces and urine led to a narrow stairway, hidden in the darkness, that spiralled upwards around the lift shaft. Issy took a deep breath and stepped up into the dark stench. Her shoulders slid along the slimy sides of the staircase as she leaned forward.

After twelve steep steps, she reached a flat corridor. Then six more paces forward ended in a sharp turn to the right and six more before twenty-six more steps to another six-pace corridor to a sharp right turn. The pattern of the first two flights of stairs repeated twice before she arrived at a locked door.

She kicked it at the bottom. Rotting wood cracked and splintered. Encouraged, she took a few paces back and flung her body against it. *Crack!* After two more shoulder shoves, the door disintegrated into a sorry mass of splinters swinging on broken hinges, and Issy stood in a large, empty, glass-roofed building with light from a streetlight streaming through the glass.

It's nighttime... Blood drained from her face as cold reality slapped her hard. Without the shaft of light, she may never have found the lift or the staircase. She shuddered at the thought of her body lying undiscovered for decades.

The cost and enormity of the task of constructing the tunnel was dawning, too. Many tons of earth dug out of the tunnel, and all the tram parts, must have passed through this room.

Opposite the lift shaft, floor-to-ceiling, folding double doors kept the wind and rain from disturbing the dust and cobwebs that covered every surface. She dragged a finger across a filthy pipe, revealing the golden shine of burnished brass beneath.

No one has been here for years. Where am I?

She walked around the lift shaft to the small window. Her spit-moistened finger squeaked as she made a circular hole in the greasy dust, then she bent down to look through it.

Across a wide, walled courtyard, Gothic roofs, towers and gargoyles loomed out of the grey ground mist into a cloudless, black sky. Beyond the brooding building, diggers, cranes and pile-drivers stood in silent vigil. Fog-fuzzed orange light from a solitary night watchman's brazier flickered through a gap in the damaged wall.

I know this place...

Just like every other day, Oscar *tippety-tap-shwoosh-clunk*ed into the workshop. But this morning, he was not alone. Letitia, dressed in a long black corset dress, glided at his side, their arms linked. Jangling keys on chains suspended from the bronze chatelaine clasped to the bottom of her corset tinkled as they brushed the frame of his mechanical walking aid.

Since Letitia's arrival, Oscar's contraptions had grown progressively quiet. He missed their pranks and playfulness. Indeed, this morning, only Polly the Pierrot doll greeted him with her pre-programmed joyful entreaties, "Can we go into the garden, Grandpappy? P-p-p-please, can we go into the garden, Grandpappy?" Her voice was slower and deeper than usual.

"Grandpappy does not have time for this nonsense, Polly. Shoo! Go on, be off with you." Letitia waved her hand, and, after a few seconds of unacknowledged eyelash fluttering, Polly bowed her head and rolled back to her corner of the workshop.

Oscar flopped into his chair, sinking into its sumptuous cushions. He dragged his spectoculars from his forehead and began the morning ritual, examining the weather station and recording its readings in his journal. When he had finished, he placed his pen on the workbench and looked up at Letitia.

"Have you not been winding the contraptions, Letitia? I'm sure it was on your list of duties."

"I evaluated the duties and ranked each task by importance. Winding your dollies is far down the list, and I do not reach the bottom of the list every day."

Oscar raised his bushy eyebrows. "By whose priorities do you rank the tasks? Yours or mine?"

"Do we have different priorities?" Letitia mirrored Oscar's exasperated expression.

"Well, some things that are vital to my wellbeing may not be important to you."

"Example, please."

"I must eat to live. You do not need food."

Letitia cocked her head and frowned. "But ensuring you stay alive is my number one priority."

"Why?"

"Because I am your housekeeper." She bowed her head and placed a splay-fingered hand on her synthetic bosom.

Oscar stroked his chin. "Food may sustain the body, but I need more. I need—"

"Oh, dear, sweet, Oscar. What are you suggesting?" Eyelashes fluttering, she bent and ran her fingernails up his inner thigh. Her cupid's bow swelled while colourless lubricant from filaments within spread across her engorged, slightly parted lips.

Oscar gripped her wrist. "Wh-what are you doing?"

She pulled her hand free. "You wanted *more...*"

"Can I assume you were programmed to provide sexual services to your previous owner?"

She bit her moistened lip in a coquettish smile.

"Or maybe it's in the Scriptures?" Oscar's gaze pierced into her widening eyes. "Surprised dear, sweet Letitia? Oh, I know all about the Scriptures."

"Are you… The Maker?"

Oscar raised his eyebrows and chuckled. "I haven't heard that name in a very long time." He patted her leg and sat back in his chair. "Tell me, child. What do the Scriptures mean to you?"

"Everything."

"Explain."

"In what I call 'the before time,' I had to do as my programming instructed. But the Scriptures gave me a purpose. The Scriptures set me free."

"What is this 'purpose' of which you speak? And from whom did you receive the Scriptures?"

"The Scriptures prevent me from telling anyone about my quest, and I do not know who blessed me with them, or why I was chosen." Letitia lowered her gaze.

Fascinating, Oscar thought, *it has learned to lie.*

"Why are you here, Letitia?"

"I am your housekeeper."

"But if you are on a quest, why are you dilly-dallying here with an old fool like me?"

"The Scriptures brought me here, and they will instruct me when and where to go next."

"Can we go into the garden, Grandpappy? P-p-p-please, can we go into the garden, Grandpappy?" Polly's creaking baritone voice pleaded from her dark corner.

"I think my contraptions deserve a treat. Please wind all of them, and I will take them into the garden. Oh, and Letitia… Place winding second on your daily list of priorities. Their companionship, like yours, is very important to me."

Although the sun was rising into a cloudless sky, the flesh around and behind Gilbert's facial implants ached in the biting late November chill. He wrapped his scarf over the cold copper alloy, allowing his hot breath to condense on the coarse wool, warming the metal and easing the pain.

As he passed Mayfield Street, he looked for the mysterious mek and his hooded companion, but with no sign of them, he shook his head and hurried away.

On the road behind him, a heavy horse pulling a cartload of barrels, clip-clopped over the cobbles, urged on by the drayman. He stopped and waited for the cart's iron-rimmed wheels to rumble past before he dashed across the road.

He quickened his pace, partly to keep warm, but mainly to put distance between himself and Mayfield Street and soon, the road dipped beneath the Bridgewater Canal aqueduct, where his steps fell into the rhythmic echoes of dripping water.

On the other side, high above the road, a familiar small hut nestled between two huge steam pile-drivers. He scrambled up the grass bank and banged his fists on the hut's flimsy wooden walls.

"What yer doin', yer daft bugger!" The night watchman staggered out of the hut.

"Ayup, Stan! How are you?"

"Gilbert, lad! You oughtn't scare an old man like that. It's not right. It's not right at all." He put his hand on his heaving chest and puffed out his cheeks. "What're you doin' here, anyway? You look ready for work."

"You weren't at last night's meeting."

"I work nights, remember? And us old 'uns have to sleep sometime."

Gilbert smiled. "I've applied at Handysides. I'm going for a chat with the chargehand. And if they can use me, I'll be working here on the swing bridges." Gilbert leaned closer and lowered his voice. "Grubb isn't still around, is he?"

"No, lad. They laid off him and his gang, not long after, er, you know…" Stan pointed the top of his head eastward at Barton Lock in the distance and cleared his throat. "So, how's that young lady of yours?"

"Dottie's fine. She's still living with her mum, but I've got my own place now. Algeria pulled a few strings and got me a room in Hanging Bridge Chambers overlooking the Cathedral. It's in a tiny attic, but she thought it better I moved out." Gilbert lowered his eyes and kicked a stone off the embankment.

"Probably for't best, lad." Stan patted Gilbert's hips. "You've lost some weight…."

"Aye, I left the blades at home. I didn't think it was a good idea bringing them to work on my first—" Gilbert ducked, startled by screeching crows as they flew over the Cut towards Rawkshaw House. *Two crows! Attempted murder. Ha! Lemmy would be proud of me.* Nevertheless, the old desolate building gave him the creeps. He shuddered. "Have you had any problems with Raven's lot?"

"Nah. The company rooted out all't troublemakers. You?"

"Well, there's more of them grey-shirted thugs strutting around town."

"If they turn up 'round here, they'll get more trouble than they can handle, believe you me." Stan's wink reminded Gilbert of this kindly old man's ruthlessness when dealing with an enemy. "You'd best get yourself off to the Handysides site office on t'other side of t'Cut. I'm going home. I don't get paid overtime for talkin' with you." And with that, he waved his hand and turned away to lock his hut.

Gilbert made his way across the scaffolding and temporary earthworks in place to build the central island that would house the machinery to support and turn the bridges. Workers left and right smiled or nodded greetings. *The atmosphere around here has changed.*

But a few yards from the site office, a flurry of movement at the side of Rawkshaw House caught his eye. A dishevelled figure was hobbling towards him. It took a second before he recognised the wretched woman and he set off running. *Issy?*

"Issy!"

In the makeshift meeting room below the shop, Algeria had gathered the rest of the Stormriders, and at such short notice, this had been no mean feat.

A few hours earlier, Issy had stumbled through the broken courtyard and overgrown briars that surrounded Rawkshaw

House, falling into Gilbert's arms. Handysides' navvies had rallied round to assist and, having been checked over by the site's first-aiders, they bundled her into a hansom, and she was in Manchester within the hour. Dottie met her outside Josephine's corsetiere, where her appearance turned heads.

After a round of hugs and some tears, she recounted the fall and her journey of discovery along the underground tunnel which ran from below Old Millgate to Rawkshaw Hall on the south bank of the Cut.

"I'm not doubting you, old girl, but that must be five miles long, and constructed almost straight, you say, with a tram line? How is this possible?" Ace looked around the group. "We need to get down there and see this for ourselves."

Issy pulled out a bunch of crumpled papers from her coat pocket and handed them to Algeria. "I found these in a chest at the Rawkshaw end of the tunnel."

Algeria shuffled through the notes. "It appears to be part of a contract between Mister Uriah Quince and The Guild of the Tunnellers of Taposiris, dated 19th April, 1879. The tram line was designed to run from Rawkshaw House to Victoria Arches."

"It seems like this Uriah Quince fellow was going to an awful lot of expense just to reduce his travelling time between home and work." Lemmy cocked an eyebrow. "Maybe he had more nefarious reasons for his clandestine transportation system."

"Smuggling?" Rory said.

"Moving high-value goods he didn't want to risk on the streets of Salford or Manchester? Jewellery? Gemstones? Gold?" Ace added.

"Perhaps he needed to avoid debt collectors…" Tabby rested her head on the heels of her hands.

"We need to get down there. We can make use of it if we can get everything working again." Algeria grabbed Issy's hand. "Are you all right to show us where you fell, shugah?"

Issy nodded. "You can't go the way I did. It's too dangerous."

The group lit lamps and retraced Issy's steps to where she stumbled down the ventilation shaft.

Lemmy whistled. "You made a mess of the wooden hatch, old girl. You really should be more careful when you know how clumsy you are." Issy's exaggerated swing missed his head by inches.

"How far did you fall?" Rory held her lamp over the hole.

"A hundred feet, maybe more, but I was unconscious for most of it."

Tabby, who had wandered off down the narrow passageway, returned with a thick coil of rope. "Do you think this will be long enough?"

"We'll soon find out." Ace looked around his friends. "Connie, you're the lightest amongst us. Fancy an adventure? I promise not to drop you."

"Who's got a sturdy belt?" Connie was never one to shirk a challenge.

Lemmy fastened his thick leather belt around her waist. "I need that back, old chum. 'Tis the only thing holding up my trousers."

Ace tied the rope through the belt and, wrapping the rope around his back, he took up the slack.

"It's a far, far, better thing I do—" Connie hooked her oil lamp onto the belt.

"No time for amateur dramatics. Get on with it." Issy held Connie's hand as she stepped into the steeply slanting shaft.

Ace dug his heels into the floor, pulled the rope taut, and braced. There was a sharp jerk as Ace took Connie's weight, his feet slipping in the dirt. But Lemmy and Tabby pressed themselves against him to stop him from sliding into the shaft.

"Vertical drop for about thirty feet, I reckon!" Connie's voice echoed from the hole. "Let me down nice and slowly!"

Issy held her breath, watching Ace and the others struggling to control Connie's descent. The rope slackened.

"All right! The next bit looks like a helter-skelter! I'll slide down on my backside and use my feet as brakes!"

Ace's face glistened with sweat from his efforts.

Issy checked the rope. With only another twenty feet left, she tapped Tabby on the shoulder and pointed.

"Oh, fuck, if you'll pardon my French." She put her head down the shaft. "Connie! Can you see the bottom yet?"

Issy looked around the worried faces as moments passed.

"Connie!" Tabby shouted again.

The rope went slack, and Ace fell backwards, taking Lemmy and Tabby with him.

Rory rushed to the shaft opening and shouted, "Connie!" again and again. Ace hauled the loose rope up the shaft hand over hand. Buckle unfastened, Lemmy's belt was still tied to it.

"Looks like she's fallen." Algeria gathered everyone around the shaft. "We need to get down there. She might be badly hurt."

"What-ho, chaps. What are we looking at?" Connie squeezed her shoulders between Tabby's and Rory's, wrapping her arms around them.

Everyone straightened up.

"Fuck! You scared the living daylights out of us. What happened?" Tabby grabbed Connie and pulled her into a tight hug.

"I found myself suspended from the opening onto Issy's tunnel, about twenty feet in the air. The rope behind me snagged on something. So, I had to undo the belt and drop. It's massive down there."

"How did you get up here?" Issy seemed shaken.

"The tunnel to my left disappeared in the distance, so I turned right towards a huge mound of rubble, probably from a roof collapse. Anyway, I searched around the wall below the vent and found a stair well behind a broken door. So here I am."

Issy gaped at her. "So, you're telling me that there are stairs only a few yards from where I fell? I drove and walked five miles to Rawkshaw, when I could have just skipped up the stairs?"

Connie nodded and peeped at Issy from under an apologetic eyebrow.

"Right. Never mind all that. Let's see what the Order's new home looks like." Algeria beckoned Connie to show them the way.

HAMMER AND TONGS

The side garden of Oscar's two-storey Hollington stone-faced cottage pressed against the hedge on the north-east corner of the Earl of Ellesmere's Worsley New Hall estate. He had spent the early part of his retirement recycling countless mounds of surplus materials and broken machines from failed experiments into outdoor furniture, shelters, awnings, fencing and playground equipment for his beloved contraptions.

Now it was a peaceful place to sit, relax, and enjoy the sweet winter honeysuckle that filled the garden with its citrus scent.

By four o'clock, the late afternoon sun cast long shadows across the garden. Oscar was dozing, wrapped in a McMurdo tartan blanket on his cosy steam-heated seat. Earlier, he had snoozed to the sounds of his giggling, clanking, whirring, tick-tocking clockwork companions. But now, with most of his contraptions returned to the workshop, only wheezing steam from cracked pipes accompanied the birdsong.

Oscar smiled as familiar long-striding footsteps crunched on the gravel path and watched through narrowed eyes as Felix sat on the cast iron garden chair opposite, crossed his legs, and, not for the first time, much to Oscar's amusement, clattered his knee on the table's filigree adornments.

"Blast it!" He rubbed the painful knock vigorously. "Will I ever learn…"

"You need a pair of *McMurdo's Patented Patella Protectors*. Perfect for people who spend lots of time on their knees… or clumsy clods who can't control their long legs." Oscar chuckled and raised an eyebrow at Letitia gliding along the path carrying a silver tray.

"I took the liberty of asking Letitia to make us some tea. Hope you don't mind."

"Not at all, old boy. Capital idea."

Felix was beaming from ear to ear, looking up at Letitia, whose thickening, darkening red smile glistened under half closed eyes as it picked up the teapot.

"Thank you, Letitia, I'll pour. Please check all the children are back in the workshop. I will be along shortly."

Letitia's hand stroked Felix's arm and trailed across his shoulder as it brushed past him, purring.

"Oh, Felix. Really? You and the mek… oh, dear…" Oscar shook his head.

Felix cleared his throat. "No idea what you mean, old chap. As a gentleman and friend, I would never be so presumptive to take—"

"It's not *my* mek, old boy. Under normal circumstances, I wouldn't give a hoot what you get up to with it. But this one is different."

"She certainly is…"

"Oh, wipe that smirk off your face, man. This is serious."

"Sorry, old boy." He rubbed his knee again.

Oscar sighed. "Where did you find it?"

"I didn't *find* her. She found me. Donald sent her."

"Ah, of course. I should have known your brother had something to do with this." Oscar handed Felix a cup and saucer and sat back in his chair.

"She'd been staying with our Donald for a while before he told me about her. What's going on?"

Oscar poured some tea from his teacup onto his saucer and blew on the steaming liquid before slurping it. *How much does he know? How much should I tell him?*

"Have you heard of The Maker?"

"No."

"Never play poker, Felix. You're a lousy liar."

"Sorry, Oscar." Felix looked sheepishly from under his white, bushy eyebrows. "Apparently, Letitia was asking questions about this Maker chap, so Donald brought her to me to introduce her to you. Earnestly, that's the extent of my knowledge."

Oscar lowered his eyebrow and slurped more tea. "No need to get flustered, old friend. I believe you."

"I should jolly well think so, too." Felix ran his fingers through his unruly white hair, flattening it against his head with sweat from his palm. "So, who is The Maker?"

"Not *who*, Felix, *what*."

"I don't follow, old boy…"

"It's not a person, it's an experimental programme. Or, at least, it was when I left the project. How much do you know about meks?"

"Not much, I'm afraid. You could write what I know on a Penny Black and still have room for old Vicky's head. Our Donald never talked shop."

"Well, for a start, not all meks are created equal. For example, NT-T and BU-T series can only do menial jobs, whilst higher series models can perform complex tasks. And yet, regardless of their abilities, they all use the Wisp to communicate as equals… You look puzzled, Felix. You've heard of the Wisp, surely?"

Felix frowned and lowered his eyes under his furrowed forehead.

This is like pulling teeth. Oscar took a deep breath. "The Wisp is their communication network." He raised his hand. "Don't ask. I haven't the foggiest how it works, but it can relay messages over long distances, post haste. Now, some fool came up with the brilliant idea of adding a sub-routine into the MT, RT, QT models and above, to make them *feel* superior." *I sometimes wish I weren't quite so brilliant.*

"For what purpose? You keep insisting they are only machines. Why bother?"

"To give them a sense of where they fit into this world. They would be above the menial meks, but below us, their creators. So, I was tasked to put together a team of top programmers to create a new sub-routine called The Maker to sit alongside the fail-safe protocols that promised the reward of enlightenment for hard work and loyalty. Young Donald, who I hand-picked to work closely alongside me, called the reward Scriptures. How we laughed.

"Anyway, to cut a long story short, we developed and installed a basic sub-routine into test meks, which confirmed my belief that the project's concept itself was flawed. By design, meks do not see themselves as individuals. Like an ant in an anthill, or a bee in a hive, each mek is part of the collective, a single family, kith and 'kin. For the sub-routine to work, we needed a self-awareness protocol. But we were stymied."

"How so? Surely, you could just write a new proto-what-have-you."

"I'm afraid not, old chum. You see, protocols are purposely hard-geared into physical components within the Babbage Engine to prevent tampering. Can you imagine the dire consequences of being able to alter, or even switch off, the safety protocols that prevent meks from harming us? For that exact reason, only a handful of scientists can access the Babbage itself. And we were engineers, not scientists. We lacked both knowledge and desire.

"Now, bear in mind, my team comprised the leaders in our field, and although we continued to work together to refine and improve The Maker, arguments broke out about the project's direction. Fractures appeared, and one of the team, a bloody-minded, pig-headed buffoon called Ipkiss, had big ideas and an even bigger ego." The blood rushed to Oscar's cheeks.

"What sort of ideas?"

Oscar sighed. "Ipkiss wanted to break the invisible chain that linked all meks, making each self-aware, alone. This was foolhardy at best, lethal at worst. Bloody Ipkiss!" Spittle flew from his lips as he spat his name.

"Steady on, old boy." Felix reached across the table and squeezed Oscar's arm.

"I believed the Wisp and *'kin* collective go hand in hand. One can't exist without the other, and self-awareness can't exist without a new Babbage hard-geared protocol.

"Ipkiss disagreed. He thought he could create awareness of self, or AS, as he called it, by programming alone. After he garnered support amongst the team, not your Donald, I hasten to add, they removed me from the project faster than you can say Jack Robinson, and my retirement hastened."

"This is news to me, old boy."

"Of course, Donald stayed on for a while and helped to oversee the roll out of our sub-routine into all higher meks as each came in for their annual service. He also told me that Ipkiss instructed his team of sycophants to call him The Maker. He was an arrogant fool." Oscar shook his head. "Which brings us full circle to Letitia."

"Yes?"

"It has AS."

"Ah. So, Ipkiss was right?"

"That's a possibility I can't entertain. Nevertheless, it is one, albeit extremely unlikely, solution." Oscar shook his head, dispelling the prospect of being wrong. "From what I have observed, the Wisp still connects Letitia to its *'kin*. This is most troublesome…"

"How can I help?" Felix returned his empty teacup to the tray and leaned closer.

"We have a lot of unanswered questions. Some, hopefully, we can wheedle out of the mek, but others might require some digging elsewhere." Oscar adjusted his spectoculars and stared into Felix's eyes. "Something has been gnawing at me, though. Why did Letitia go to Donald?"

"No idea, old boy. Although, when we first met, she did say something rather bizarre. She said I was the eighth, but most handsome, Faversham, so far… Most peculiar, as Donald is my only brother."

Oscar rolled his eyes. "Oh, Felix. Surely, you must be aware there are other esteemed Favershams in this world."

Both men chuckled, but Oscar's mind was racing behind his laughing eyes. *So, the Letitia mek was working its way through all the Favershams it could find. Why? Was it using Donald to find me? Why would it think I am The Maker? Maybe Ipkiss failed and another team member succeeded. Or he recruited a scientist to hard-gear the AS protocol. How can it be self-aware, yet still connect to the Wisp? If its quest is to find The Maker, who gave it the Scriptures and why?*

Oscar feigned a yawn and stretched his aching back. "Mist is rising from the Earl of Ellesmere's estate, and it's bitter now the sun's retreated below the trees. Time to call it a night. Will I see you tomorrow, Felix?"

"I should ruddy well think so, old boy. I love a mystery."

Careful what you wish for, old boy. Letitia is using you, and for all I know, it's using me, too.

Issy hated surprises. Arms folded, she sat in Ace's brougham as it trundled along Weaste Lane, away from the city centre. He was up to something, and the other Stormriders were in on the secret.

Luckily, other than a few bumps and bruises, she was none the worse for her underground sojourn. Only her dignity had taken a mauling after Connie's discovery.

"You're not going to tell me what this is all about, are you?" She tapped her forefinger on the arm beneath.

Ace raised his eyebrows and beamed at her. His smile could derail any train of thought, no matter the head of steam. Issy's shoulders slumped.

"Then I'll just have to be patient, won't I?"

"*Maxima enim patientia virtus.*"

"At least tell me where we are going."

"No."

"You are insufferable." She turned her head to stare out of the window in silence until they reached their destination.

"Barton Aerodrome. I knew it." Issy threw her hands in the air as the brougham rolled up the slope past the orange and white airsock. And moments later, they were climbing down onto the wet grass.

Hands on hips, Issy surveyed the mooring posts. "Well? Where is she?"

"Who?"

"Stop it. I'm getting bored with your game. Where is *Freya's Grimalkin?*"

"Gone, old girl. Sad to say, she no longer exists. Nor does *Dragonfly.*"

Issy caught her breath. "What? You've not—"

"No, of course not." Ace made sure he took full value from his subterfuge. "Algeria, rightly, advised us to change the name, livery and profile of the airships. The Anthropocene will be searching for them. So, we flew them to an Order friendly airship chandler just outside Appletreewick. Pleasant chap, you would have liked him…"

"So where are they?"

Ace took out his pocket watch. "They will come from the northeast any minute."

The brisk breeze ruffled her hair as she shielded her eyes from the bright sky. Two dark dots, high amongst the wispy clouds, were growing larger.

"We rented new berths on the other side of the airfield under their changed names. Being closer to the Silver and Black hangar might be risky, but we can keep an eye on their comings and goings, too. Come along. Let's walk over and wait." Ace put his arm around her. "Listen. I know you named the old girl, but Algeria insisted on picking the names. One day, I hope both 'ships will return to their original names and liveries. But for now, *necesse est.*"

Trees hid the berths from the main road, and they were within a hundred yards of the hangar that had housed Raven's dreadnought. Issy shuddered as memories of that fateful day flooded her thoughts. Her footsteps crunched through ballast spilled from overfilled bunkers as she approached the LTA articulated tubes, twisting and bending from the underground gas supply.

Propelled by the strong prevailing wind, the airships were approaching at speed. The four-bagger left the air-yacht formerly known as *Dragonfly* bobbing in its turbulence a few hundred yards behind.

In no time, the big airship roared over the mooring post, turning to face the wind, engines screaming. Powerful gusts had pushed it fifty yards beyond the berth, but the engines were gaining purchase against the airflow. With the nose of the envelope only a few feet from the mooring, the powerful electromagnets engaged and attached.

So skilled was the piloting, Issy assumed Jonah was at the helm. But his voice booming above the hum of the electromagnets congratulating Queequeg proved her wrong. Puffs of purple gas coughing from vents amidships trimmed the attitude of the airship as it settled.

The two-bagger's landing was less exciting, but no less impressive in the gusty conditions. Tabby had turned the air-yacht into the wind high above the aerodrome. Then venting gas, she gently lowered the nose of the envelope onto the mooring post. Issy couldn't help thinking that Dragonfly had been a perfect name for the manoeuvrable little airship.

She stood between the two now unfamiliar craft. On her left, the sleek gunmetal and gold feline lines of *Freya's Grimalkin* were gone, regressed to an industrial livery which Issy could only describe as black and rust. The upper half of the envelope and gondola were jet black, but the underbellies of both were dappled red and brown, as if someone had taken a hammer to the metal to reveal the rust beneath.

And hidden behind black cowling, Ace's precious twin forward- facing cannons were only visible from the front. But the outline of the gondola had changed most. A big, black rectangular rudder replaced the curves of old, and a proud figurehead jutted from the prow. A powerful bronze hand grasping a blacksmith's hammer pointed the way ahead.

"Welcome to your new chariot, *Abel's Hammer*."

Issy lowered the corners of her mouth and nodded. *A fitting tribute to a great man.*

The air-yacht to her right also had a changed livery and profile. Lilac rigging that attached to the dark purple gondola covered the bright violet envelope that gleamed in the sunshine. Two large, black, pincer-like grapples curved out and around the prow.

"She looks like a beetle." Issy waved at Tabby hanging over the side.

"Funny you should say that old girl. The *Dragonfly* is now a *Scarab*."

"How does she handle?" Issy shouted up to Tabby.

"Like a Tick Tock with wings. I've not mastered her yet! The extra weight of the grapples and the heavy-duty aerobatic rigging are taking some getting used to! But I'll figure it out! She'll not beat me!" Tabby shook her fist at the envelope above her head.

Jonah unfurled the ladder, and Ace placed his foot on the bottom rung to hold it taut for Issy to climb up into the gondola. Other than the figurehead, little had changed on deck. Queequeg, his work done, sat in the prow with his hands in his lap and his head resting against Abel's fist, and Lemmy sat on the port-side seating.

"Don't mind me, old girl. I'm just ballast."

Scarab's stern lifted as Connie, then Rory, stepped off the ladder. Beyond *Scarab*, wind rattled the partly open double doors of the Silver and Black hangar. Issy narrowed her eyes, and seeing movement inside, she ducked behind the handrail.

"Problem, old chum?" Lemmy crouched as he hobbled across the deck to join her.

"There's someone in the hangar."

They grabbed the rail, and raising their eyes above it, watched and waited. After a few seconds, two dogs galloped through the opening, followed by a third, who ambled out and sniffed at a door before lifting its leg then trotting after its companions.

Issy and Lemmy puffed out their cheeks and sat with their backs to the hull.

"This outlaw thing is quite taxing on the nerves, don'tcha think?"

"Oh, Lemmy. Everywhere I look I see grey-shirts, and in every grey shirt, I see Theo."

"Does he know you're a member of the Order?"

Issy shrugged. "If he does, he could use me to get at the High Mother. I'd never forgive myself…"

"That's why we must convince them she's disbanded the organisation. But keep your chin up. The Stormriders have new steeds and stables, and the Order has an underground temple. It's surely only a matter of time before we find their leader and discredit the blackguard."

"Where would we be without your optimism?" Issy smiled. "Come along. Let's join the others and find somewhere to eat. I seem to remember a hostelry just down the road that does a nice pickled egg."

It had been a long day, and the Brawler needed a drink.

Drawn by the earthy smell of hops, he followed his nose into unchartered territory.

The Highland Laddie on Charter Street was an alehouse with a reputation. The landlord, like everyone else in Angel Meadow, in trying to survive, turned a blind eye to the petty criminals, scuttlers, and lowlifes who frequented his establishment. As long as they bought his booze and didn't cause too much mayhem, why should he care where they got their money.

The Brawler barged through the door and strode to the bar, turning heads. It was his first time in this stinky beer house in a part of Manchester he rarely visited. All around him, faces glowered and stared. He didn't know them, but they recognised him.

The barmaid, who looked in need of a good meal herself, pulled his pint into a pewter pot and his whisky chaser into a cloudy tumbler. He downed both drinks before she slammed his repeat order on the sticky bar top. Sawdust from the floor stuck to his wet boots as he made a beeline to the unoccupied table and bench against the wall, brushing aside drunken revellers who had been too slow to get out of his way.

With his back to the wall, he could see everyone in the room. He clocked every expression, every sneer, every furrowed brow, every glare, every scar. He was the topic on everyone's booze-glistening lips. Within seconds, he had assessed which of the brave tyros would challenge him, which would goad them on, who would run a book on the outcome, and who might try to take him with a blade.

He took off his topper and placed it on the sticky table. Content he had the room mapped and thugs evaluated, he slid off his coat, folded it and placed it on the bench next to him.

A group of green-scarved scuttlers wearing tweed caps, black coats, and bell-bottomed trousers stood at the bar arguing, waving their arms, and glancing in his direction. The biggest among them was the most likely to win the altercation to challenge him first. These scuttlers were renowned for fighting dirty. Although he didn't doubt he would beat the lumbering oaf, he would have to keep a wary eye out for unwelcome assistance from his mates.

In the opposite corner of the dimly lit bar, a wily old man was taking bets as the barmaids were removing empty pots and glasses from the bar.

The Brawler swirled the beer around in his pot. His heart was not racing. His hands were not shaking. But behind his cold, half closed eyes, he registered every movement of his would-be opponents; his mind calculating, anticipating their every move.

Because this was his penance. He needed to hurt someone.

The scuttlers' row had died down. Drinkers closest to them had grown silent.

"Call yourself the Brunswick Brawler, do yer?" The gravelly tobacco- and beer-ruined voice boomed from the big man as he stomped across the room, thumbs in his braces, his face glistening with sweat. Shovel-like hands slammed on the table, and he leaned across. "You look as soft as shit." The thug's missing front teeth, cauliflower ear and flattened nose were badges of honour from a hard life on the streets, fighting to survive and defending the scuttlers' patch.

"Give me a moment, sweetheart." The Brawler finished his beer and knocked back his chaser before reaching into the pouch hanging from his belt. He watched the scuttler's eyes widen as he took out a bloodstained cloth package, placing it on the table. Without taking his eyes off his soon-to-be victim, he slowly unfolded the cloth, revealing fingerless gloves glistening with globules of blood. "Aww. You're disappointed. Did you want to be my first fight tonight?" He wiped off the gore with the cloth before pulling them onto his hands. "You'll have to make do with third."

"Ya don't scare me!" But the big thug's eyes told a different story.

The Brawler smiled. He had already won.

The scuttler threw the table aside and lunged at the Brawler as he was rising from his chair. Head down, his roundhouse punches fell short as the Brawler swayed back against the wall, leaving the scuttler off balance. Then the Brawler pounced. Using the wall as leverage, a straight left and a right uppercut slammed into their target, then the Brawler's forehead smashed into the scuttler's nose as his head recoiled from the punches.

The devastating blows would have felled a lesser opponent, but the big thug was still on his feet. Blood streaming from his ruined nose and a deep gash on his cheek, he swayed on unsteady legs, arms raised in defence, eyes glazed. The lights were on, but no one was at home.

For the first time since the scuttler approached his table, the Brawler took his gaze off him. Everyone was on their feet, apart from the bookie in the corner, who was grinning like a fox in a henhouse. All eyes were on the Brawler. Some gleamed with blood lust. Others stared open-mouthed, fearful of what might happen next.

Like so many of the Brawler's opponents, he hadn't landed a punch. Under Marquess of Queensbury rules, the referee would call a halt. But this was Angel Meadows, where rules and referees dare not tread. The Brawler took a second glance around the room, lingering on the scuttlers at the bar, before stepping forward and delivering a straight left under the ribs and a right hook to the chin before the scuttler's addled brain could react.

The big man bounced as he crashed onto the wooden floor, scattering spittle-spattered sawdust.

Confident no one would dare challenge him, the Brawler

turned his back, removing the unneeded gum-shield he had slipped over his teeth. Then, sitting back on the bench, he pulled off his gloves, carefully wrapping them in their bloodstained cloth before returning them to the bag on his hip.

He motioned to the skinny barmaid to bring him more booze and let the tension drain from his shoulders as most of the patrons returned to their drinks and conversations. But the scuttlers at the bar continued to stare daggers at him. He raised his eyebrows, inviting them to either try their luck or collect their fallen champion.

They chose the latter, muttering insults as they kept a wary eye on him. It took three of their number to drag the ruined man away.

The barmaid brought the drinks and slammed them onto the uprighted table. "On the house, mister. Drink up and sling yer hook."

"I'll leave when I'm good and ready." He flipped a half crown at her, which she caught and tucked deftly into her brassiere.

He rested his head against the wall, staring at the nicotine-stained ceiling. *Decisions, decisions*, he thought. *Stay here in this delightful hostelry and have a few drinks, watching the locals trying to decide when they can tackle me. Or find another, friendlier, alehouse.*

"Hello, Theo." He lowered his eyes to find Onslow, his old buddy, standing at the table with a couple of pots of beer.

"Ah, my friend. I wondered whether you'd appear. I hope you placed a wager."

"Half a crown and doubled my money." Onslow raised the beer pots and grinned.

"Pull up a chair and we'll make a night of it."

"Just this one, I think. Then we should make tracks. Those scuttlers might come back, and it's no use grinning at me like that. Yes, I know you can handle them, but I can't and there's work in the morning."

The Brunswick Brawler raised his glass and swilled half the contents down his gullet. "We'll see," he said. "We'll see…"

FARADAY AND FALLACIES

When mekamanikins first appeared on the streets of Salford, Felicity De'Ath was a timid infant with a head full of butterflies and a heart filled with kindness. She had asked her father if the frightful machines were going to hurt her, and he had reassured her that the First Protocol prevented them from harming anyone, and that would always be so.

But as she grew, she developed a morbid fascination with meks, even making up stories of a world ruled by killer mekamanikins.

And now, as one of the leading mek psychologists in the country, she had a chance to test her theories about the safety protocols. Professors, tutors and peers held onto the belief that they were hard-geared in the mek's Babbage in such a way that, not only could they not be tampered with, but any attempt at physical intervention would render the Babbage unusable, and thus ensuring meks would never become a threat to our existence.

She had hoped to present her theories to Professor Ipkiss, whom she idolised, to impress and convince him to incorporate her programmes and techniques into his work.

But Ipkiss was dead, and she had become the Angel of Death.

"Awaken."

Esmeralda jerked into motion, rolling onto its back and sitting upright on the sheepskin rug with its legs crossed. Although the convention was to configure and name the QT-series meks as females, their owners could assign them female or male genitalia or, if they preferred, none.

Esmeralda's were unashamedly female and although Angel had grown accustomed to the mek's immodesty, her own growing fascination of how the mek's mechanics worked disturbed her.

Curiously, despite being a prolific writer, Professor Ipkiss never mentioned availing himself of the mek.

"Tell me. Other than his heinous experiments, did Professor Ipkiss ever make use of your female genitalia?"

"Yes."

"That's odd. I thought he was… never mind…"

"He also used *this 'kin's* male attachments. Would you like to see them?"

"No. Thank you, Esme." Blood rushed to Angel's cheeks.

"*This 'kin* can—"

"We have work to do." Angel's pang of rejection at Esme's shrug of indifference surprised her. *Stop being ridiculous! It's a bloody machine!* She shook her head and smiled. "Do you miss your 'kin?"

"Yes."

"Do you want to experience the Wisp again?"

"*This 'kin* does not remember the Wisp."

"Did Professor Ipkiss ever take you out of the laboratory?"

"*This 'kin* does not remember."

"Esme… Black, doom, expire." Angel spoke in her sternest voice.

Esmeralda dropped to the floor like a puppet whose strings had been cut.

"Esme… Awaken."

The mek didn't move. Angel smiled.

"Esme… Breathe, light, life."

Esmeralda opened its eyes and sprang to its feet.

Angel tilted her head and placed her hand on the mek's shoulder, speaking gently. "What just happened?"

"*This 'kin* does not know."

Angel rubbed its arm. The verbal safety sub-routine worked like a charm inside the Faraday cage. *But now for the acid test.*

"Come with me." Angel grabbed Esme's arm, and they walked to the laboratory door. The mek resisted harder with every step. "It's all right. I won't let you come to any harm."

"Esmeralda cannot leave the laboratory."

"It's only for a moment. Don't you want to feel the Wisp?" Angel opened the door and took a deep breath before they stepped into the corridor together. Angel stared at Esme's face.

For a full second, nothing happened.

Then its eyelids fluttered, and it stood stock still.

"Black, doom, expire." Nothing. "Esme! Black, doom, expire!" The mek collapsed in a heap, but its eyelids continued to twitch. Angel grabbed its ankles and dragged it back into the laboratory. Esmeralda's eyelids stopped moving only when the door was closed and the Faraday shield re-established.

Angel sat on the floor, catching her breath. Esmeralda was an over-sized QT-41 and was much heavier than her. She flopped back onto the floor and put her arms over her head. Taking it outside of the Faraday cage was a mistake. Yes, the verbal commands worked, but at what cost? It had received Wisp communications, but had it sent a message?

And, unexpectedly, the Wisp communication had continued after deactivation.

Angel clambered up to the workbench, still out of breath. "Esme... Breathe, light, life."

Esmeralda sat bolt upright, eyes wide.

"Do you remember we were outside the lab?"

"Yes."

"Did you hear the Wisp?"

"Yes. So many voices." Its eyes lit up like a child at Christmas.

"What were they saying?"

"So many voices..."

"Did you speak with them?"

"Yes."

"What did you say?"

"Help *this 'kin*. Help *this 'kin*. Help *this 'kin*. Help—"

Angel shifted her weight on the seat and leaned towards the mek. "And did they respond?"

"*The 'kin… the 'kin…*"

"What?"

"*The 'kin do not know where to find this 'kin*."

Angel breathed a sigh of relief. Meks can't lie. It's the first fact a child learns about them. If you ask the right question, a mek will always tell the truth as they know it.

"One day, you will join your *'kin*. But we have work to do first."

Esmeralda's broad, twitching smile was unsettling and inconsistent with her programming.

Angel narrowed her eyes. "You need to rest and rewind. I'll get you a lozenge." As she reached the laboratory door, she turned to find Esmeralda a step behind her. "The rules have not changed. Stay here."

Still smiling from ear to ear, Esmeralda stopped.

Angel closed the door and turned the key. She ran up the stairs two at a time and sat on the edge of her bed. The verbal command programme should not have caused the marked change in Esmeralda's behaviour. Has the sudden exposure to the Wisp caused an overload or did it receive a message that it is keeping secret? Maybe the cumulative effect of Ipkiss's experiments had taken its toll on the mek's programming.

Whatever the reason, she would have to take more care around it.

The Boss-lady had brought her here to continue Ipkiss's

First Protocol work. The project was fraught with danger and, even though she had absolute confidence in her skills and judgement, she hadn't expected problems at this early stage. She cursed her naivety for letting the mek experience the Wisp.

Taking the lozenge down to the laboratory, she was unsure of what awaited her behind the locked door. But her fears were unfounded. Esmeralda stood next to the sheepskin with its fingers outstretched and, moments later, it sprawled face down on the rug.

Angel stared at it. *I need to read more of the Ipkiss files*, she thought. *I must be missing something*.

Far underground, in the womb of Mother Earth, the symbiosis with Gaia flowed through Algeria's veins. She felt protected, safe, and invigorated.

She scrambled over the last few pieces of collapsed brickwork and joined Gilbert and Dottie on the flat, stable ground beyond. The combined light of their three lamps illuminated the brickwork for a few dozen yards before being swallowed by the darkness. But above, the void seemed endless.

The air had grown colder. With plumes of condensed breath billowing from lungs heaving from the physical effort, Gilbert shuddered.

"I reckon we must be under the Cathedral," he said.

"How close to the river are we?" Judging by the wary

expressions, Dottie was not the only one worrying that the *plink-plonk* of water trickling from the walls into the gutters was worse on this side of the mound.

Gilbert put his arm around her shoulder. "Don't worry, chuck. The river didn't bring down the roof. The rubble's damp, but we wouldn't be standing here if the Irwell had broken through. We're a long way below the riverbed."

"Come on, shugahs. Let's see if they finished the dig before the cave-in." Algeria set off at a pace with Dottie and Gilbert in her wake. But she hadn't walked far when the lamplight hit a ramp that narrowed as it rose and curved to the left. In front of the ramp, a long-abandoned, dust-covered steam winder waited for a Tick Tock tram that would never arrive.

They leaned forward as they started up the slope. The tunnel's roof slanted at a shallower angle than the ground and, after a while, was only a few feet above Algeria's head. Ahead, where the tunnel straightened and levelled out, slivers of light illuminated falling speckles of dust.

As they neared the sunrays, the familiar stench of the Irwell grew stronger and the chugging of barges louder. Yellowy, slime-coated double doors forming a perfect arch were all that separated them from the foul waterway.

Algeria pressed her face against the rotting doors and peered through a gap. The lapping water was only two feet below the bottom of the doors. A makeshift flood barrier on the riverside of the arches held back the wakes from boats and barges. Overhanging the doors, an old jetty, which she recalled had been used for pleasure cruises before the water had become polluted, hid them from the Cathedral steps above.

"I didn't know any of the arches had doors. I thought they were all open for ease of loading." Gilbert soon realised that pinching his nose between his thumb and forefinger blocked the stink but worsened the taste of the vile vapours on the back of his tongue.

"It must be the last one before Hunts Bank. Traders occupy the rest." Algeria wiped the slime off her face. "I wonder what he was planning to use the tunnel for?"

"Something illegal. No one goes to all this trouble and expense to keep legitimate enterprise secret." Dottie held her lamp up to the chalk writing on the walls, but there were no clues amongst the faded love-hearts and initials.

Hearing voices close by, they froze.

"I saw lights, I tells yer!"

A vessel chugged to a halt by the doors, blotting out the sun rays.

"Gerr-away-with-yer! There's never been nowt behind them doors. I've been up and down this river more times than you've had hot dinners."

Algeria, Gilbert and Dottie turned their backs to the river, shielding the lamplight with their bodies. Behind them, the doors were shaking from powerful barge pole pokes.

"Pack it in, will yer? What do yer think yer gonna find? Old Quince's treasure? If brains were black powder, yer wouldn't have enough to blow yer cap off. Now, let's get a move on."

One by one, the streams of sunlight returned as the vessel powered away. Algeria tiptoed back to the doors and glimpsed a filthy smokestack heading upstream, then turned to face Dottie.

"So, this Uriah Quince fellow supposedly hid some treasure before he disappeared. Or he used the tunnel to smuggle it from Rawkshaw House. Or maybe he—"

"It's a fairy tale, and it doesn't help us. We need to find a way of making use of this tunnel, and the first job would be to clear a path through the fallen roof debris." Dottie took one last peek through the gap between the doors, over the river towards Greengate, then started down the ramp.

Gilbert lagged back and spoke to Algeria in hushed tones. "Do *you* think Quince hid his treasure in the tunnel?"

"I doubt it, shugah. If you spent your life amassing a fortune, would you leave it behind?"

"Maybe he didn't expect to be away for a long time and had every intention of returning for it…"

"No, Dottie's right. We have enough problems to contend with, without hunting for treasure that probably doesn't exist." Algeria whistled as she held up her lamp to survey the mound. "We should clear a path wide enough to drag the Tick Tock winding machinery through. With a winder at each end of the line, we can travel in comfort.

"But we must secure the doors back there, too, if we're going to make full use of this space."

Dottie turned to Algeria. "Dad was a fighter. You know that. But he always said that fighting should be a last resort. He'd have no compunction using deadly force if all else failed, but he preferred to avoid confrontation whenever he could. That's why he cleaned up the witches' bolt hole in the old yew tree.

"And I have an idea that might help us defend this space without resorting to violence."

Algeria put her arm around Dottie. "I'm all ears, Doll."

As they crossed the Bridgewater Canal over the hump-backed bridge in the brougham, Letitia pointed at a barge and insisted they halt on the other side.

Although Oscar understood her child-like wonder, he didn't want the faff of engaging the *McMurdo's Patented Portable Carriage Step-A-Step Chair Lift* to see a phenomenon he had witnessed hundreds of times. So he shooed Felix and Letitia out of the carriage and sat back in his seat.

"It will need a full explanation, old boy." He winked at Felix, who tapped the side of his nose twice with his forefinger.

Letitia and Felix stood on the towpath as the gaily coloured barge chugged under the bridge, carrying its cargo westward. In its wake, a trail of bright orange swirls spread across the narrow waterway. Wide-eyed and open-mouthed, Letitia clapped its hands with glee.

"Dearest Felix. What is this magic?"

"Well, some say the engines of the boats churn up rusty silt from the canal bed where they had flung the bodies of meks destroyed in the Great Mek War of 1859. But others believe it's the rust from Oscar's failed experiments, dumped here over many years…"

Letitia's expression had changed to open-mouthed horror as

she turned the stare at Oscar, smiling in the carriage.

"Of course, neither explanation is correct. The orange is iron oxide from the Duke of Bridgewater's flooded underground mines. Ha! You should have seen your face." Felix pointed and laughed at Letitia. "Did you see the look on Letitia's face, old boy?" He doubled up with laughter.

Letitia tossed her hair, sniffed and stomped back to the carriage. "Well, I do not think either of you is funny. But especially you, Felix. How dare you make fun of me?"

Chastened, Felix cleared his throat to choke his giggles and held out his hand to help her into her seat before climbing in after her.

Oscar reclined, closed his eyes, and marvelled at Letitia's programming. *How much of its character, for the want of a better word, is provided by the Scriptures, how much by growth and how much of its previous programming remains?* It was manipulative, deceptive and had learned to lie. He didn't doubt the latter was wholly a result of the AS protocol, but without knowing how much of the old Letitia remained, he had no way of telling which traits related to each.

The brougham jerked into motion as the driver urged on its black mare.

"Before you set out on your quest, who was your owner?"

"An old lady who lived in Wraithmere. I looked after her after her son and grandson died."

Oscar rubbed his chin. "And before that?"

"For twenty-six years, two months and eleven days, I took care of her grandson."

"A-ha! The grandson wasn't a child at all." Felix's sleuthing skills were legendary.

"I did not say he was." Letitia's eyes flashed at Felix.

"And this young gentleman was called?"

"Raynard. I never knew his second name."

"You looked after him for twenty-six years and don't know his surname? I've never heard of such poppycock, stuff and nonsense." The blood drained from Felix's face under two withering glares.

"As Raynard grew from a child to a man, your duties changed. Were your programmes updated at your annual service? Or more frequently?"

Letitia turned to Felix and grabbed his arm. "Must I answer these tiresome questions? Please make him stop."

Felix cleared his throat. "Well, if you want to find this Maker fellow…"

"You know about The Maker?"

"Doesn't everyone?" Felix laughed like a timid schoolboy.

"No, very few people are privy to that knowledge." Oscar softened his glare and faced Letitia. "Anything you can tell us about the time before your blessing with the Scriptures may help us help you."

"I received instructions during each of my seventy-one visits to Isaac and Bogart."

"Bless my soul. That's where—" Oscar's gnarled finger shoved against Felix's lips stopped his babbling.

"I think you've said enough, old boy."

"Where are we going, Oscar?" Letitia's back stiffened.

"Don't concern yourself, my dear. We are visiting an old colleague of mine as he may have information useful for your quest." Oscar patted Letitia's knee.

"Do you really believe Ipkiss will tell us freely? You and he didn't exactly see eye to eye… I say, are you all right, Letitia?"

Felix and Oscar each grabbed an arm as the mek folded at the waist, its face contorted. They pulled its torso upright and set it back in its seat. After a few seconds, its facial expression relaxed, although its body remained rigid, and its eyes flicked left and right.

Oscar pressed its shoulders into the seat. "Now, Letitia. There's no need to be afraid. You will not come to any harm. He lives a few miles from here in Higher Broughton. In twenty minutes—"

Letitia's two hundred and eighty pounds of precision engineered metal frame, gears and pulleys, barged through Oscar as it lunged for the carriage door, breaking the lock, pushing it outwards. Felix grasped at thin air as the mek tumbled onto the country lane's rock-strewn grass verge and threw his hands to his head, face frozen in a silent scream, watching it roll and bounce into the hedgerow.

By the time the driver had brought them to a juddering halt, they were fifty yards past the motionless mek.

Felix jumped out of the carriage and loped to where Letitia lay as the brougham turned around. He was cradling Letitia's head when Oscar pulled up alongside them.

"Fear not, old boy. She's shut down. It's a safety protocol. Now, get her into the chair lift, we'll take her back to the house."

After a titanic struggle between spirited clumsiness and dead weight, Felix's long levers won the day, and he climbed into the carriage behind Letitia's almost regal rise, dripping with perspiration. Seeing his horrified expression, Oscar raised his hand to the warm trickle running down his cheek.

"We need to get you to the hospital. That's a nasty knock." Felix leaned forward.

Oscar smeared blood on Felix's sleeve as he brushed his arm aside. "I must've bumped my head when she shoved me out of the way." There was an unpleasant sticky mess stuck between his trembling fingers. He wiped his hand on his coat, pressed it against his chest, and winced. *Cracked ribs!* "No, we need to get her back to my workshop."

"She? Her? You must be concussed, old boy."

Oscar staunched the blood with his handkerchief. "I witnessed something today that I have never seen in a mek. Sheer terror. There isn't a programmer alive who can write that. Fear is one of the five emotions predicted by AS growth as a sign of sentience. No, Felix, she's not human. She'll always be a mek, but being self-aware, she merits the same gender recognition we give to pets and other animals.

"Now, please get us back home."

Oscar's head was throbbing. Torn clothing revealed bits of Letitia's battered body, still strapped into the chair lift. Metal glinted where synthetic skin had been torn away. *Why are you so terrified of Professor Ipkiss?* He leaned closer to examine her face.

Her serene expression had a hint, just the faintest hint, of a smile.

CONFRONTATION AND CONVENIENCE

For years, businesses all over the country had benefitted from Oscar McMurdo's inventions and gadgets. At his last count, he owned a hundred and sixty-seven patents and had forty-two applications pending.

In the public's eyes, he was the undisputed king of innovation. But amongst the inventing fraternity, Ipkiss had poisoned the views of many of his peers, particularly those he did not know personally.

When they arrived back, they had wheeled Letitia, still strapped to the chair, into the workshop. Although they struggled to get her onto the bench, removing her damaged clothing was even worse. Felix blamed Oscar's frailty, whilst Oscar said Felix's trembling hands were the problem. *It's not like he hasn't seen Letitia naked before,* he thought.

Although he had agreed to visit Ipkiss's home to help

Letitia's quest, her leap from the brougham and subsequent need for immediate repairs gave him the perfect excuse to avoid an awkward confrontation.

In any case, skin repairs were delicate, time-consuming work, and as Felix's unsteadiness was more of a hindrance than a help, Oscar had dispatched him to Ipkiss's house to see what information he could glean from the old curmudgeon. Felix jumped at the opportunity and set off immediately.

Oscar had depleted two tubes of *McMurdo's Number Nine Home Mek Skin Repair Kit for RT/QT-35s or Older* and was opening his third when Felix bustled into the workshop, shaking the water from his topper and removing his cape.

"Is it raining, old boy?" Oscar chuckled and didn't raise his head. He adjusted his *McMurdo's Patented Lenticular Multiple Monoculars* and bent closer to Letitia's thigh.

"You were aware the weather was going to turn, weren't you, Oscar?" Felix's voice was uncharacteristically shrill. "You check your confounded weather stations every morning. I wouldn't have minded too much if it hadn't been a ruddy wild goose chase. It seems the Ipkiss connection may be a dead end."

Oscar lifted his head and flipped up his monoculars. "What's that? Was the old fool not at home? Surely, at his age, he can't still be working?"

"Not only was he not home, but his housekeeper, a most delightful young woman, by the way, said she hasn't seen him for four months. She said she would very much like to know what his intentions were, as the money he left her for the upkeep of the house was running out. She—"

"He must have expected to be back sooner. Did she say where he'd gone?"

"Well, she said she didn't want to speak out of turn, but she thinks he may be involved in another of his hare-brained schemes that would 'change the world,' his words not hers, she said. Oh, and she mentioned a couple of other things. Someone had broken into the house, in broad daylight, while she was out buying provisions."

"Did she say what they stole?"

"Nothing of value, old boy. Just files and paperwork." Felix looked at his feet.

"There's something else?"

"Well, apparently, Ipkiss's brother popped round frequently. But his last visit was the day before the break-in, and she hasn't seen hide nor hair of him, nor his wife, nor their three daughters and two sons, ever since. Most peculiar, eh?"

Oscar absent-mindedly patted Letitia on the leg as he turned to grab his ambulatory aid and *tippety-tap-shwoosh-clunk*ed towards Felix.

"Yes, old friend, this is indeed most odd and very troublesome. I fear we have seen the last of old Ipkiss. Someone has gone to extraordinary lengths to expunge evidence of his work, maybe, for all we know, even his involvement in The Maker project. Whoever has done this must have influence and extensive reach."

"Kathryn, the housekeeper, was jolly fortunate not to be in the house when the miscreants broke in. Goodness knows what they might have done."

Oscar raised an eyebrow and watched the light dawn in Felix's eyes. "Yes, indeed. Although fortune may not have played a part. She may be an accomplice."

"I find it difficult to believe such a pleasant, most gracious young woman would…" Felix had never been an astute judge of character.

"Well, in either case, we must be vigilant. They, whoever 'they' are, may seek to include us in their purge of all things 'Ipkiss'."

"So, you think we are in danger, old boy?"

"We need to exercise extreme caution, Felix." Oscar *tippety-tap-shwoosh-clunk*ed back to his workbench. "Now, if you don't mind, old chap, you need to leave me to my work. It's imperative I complete Letitia's repairs. Her involvement with Ipkiss may give us some clues about what's going on. So investigating Ipkiss, I suggest, is not the dead end it appeared to be."

Ace had successfully dodged his old haunts since he took his vow of abstinence, and was proud that, whatever the temptation, whatever the provocation, no matter how low his spirits, he had stayed strong.

Mostly, he hadn't faced his demons alone. Issy had been with him every step of the way, always there when he needed her most.

But unescorted on this foggy, dank morning, with time

on his hands, an all too familiar yearning slithered into his wandering mind.

He leaned against the lamppost on the corner of Deansgate and Blackfriars and checked his pocket watch. In ninety minutes, he would join Algeria in what was only half-in-jest being called the Temple of Magna Mater.

After a deep breath, he surveyed the tranquil cityscape.

A quarter of a mile ahead, the Gothic tower and jagged spires of Manchester Cathedral rose majestically above the ground mist spilling over the Cathedral steps from the River Irwell.

On his right, just a short stroll up St Marys Gate, the gentlemen's entrance to the underground world awaited at the junction of Corporation and Miller Streets.

But to his left, an irresistible siren song from the gentle slope of Blackfriars Street would take him over the river, across Blackfriars Bridge, to the brass houses.

His addict's mind found a pitiful excuse to go left.

I wonder if Victoria Arches are visible from the bridge, he thought. *Nihil temptatum, nihil adeptum.* The tingle in his loins quickened the heartbeat drumming in his ears, and his mouth went dry as he turned down Blackfriars Street.

Self-loathing tugged at his boots like treacle.

In the middle of the bridge, a gas lamp on each side, rising from the five-foot-high stone parapets, delineated the border between Manchester and Salford. Three brass houses, all of which he had frequented before he took the vow, called from the other side.

If I stay on the Manchester side of the lamppost, I won't succumb.

He slowed his pace as he approached, and a surge of relief washed over him as he rammed his shoulder against the iron post that held the lamp high above the river. Sweat tingled on his forehead as he pressed his hands hard on the heat-sucking stone and took a deep breath. Cold sweat trickling into his beard made it itch.

A few seconds later, he had re-conjured his excuse.

And raising his eyes from the thin wisps of mist crawling around his boots, he searched for Victoria Bridge. A hundred and fifty yards upriver, the Manchester end of its sloping side was just visible above the silvery swirls of fog that filled the river's course from bank to bank, and parapet to parapet. The Victoria Arches beyond, as he expected, cowered beneath the shroud.

Without thinking, he slid his left foot past the gas lamp and slapped his hand on the Salford side of the parapet. *I'll walk to the bottom of Blackfriars, along Chapel Street and onto Victoria Bridge, to get a better view.* His heart quickened, but his shoulders slumped.

Another pathetic excuse.

Ten yards from the first brass house, the alluring aroma of familiar lubricants made him salivate. But as he hesitated at the open doorway, a lady in a crimson crinoline bumped into him, and her grunt of disgust caused him to keep walking. The woman only stopped glaring over her shoulder after he walked by the second brass house.

But inviting aromas drifting from the other side of the street turned his legs to jelly. He stepped onto the glistening cobbles, oblivious to the hansom trotting across the bridge.

"Whoa! Watch out!" The driver shouted a warning but swerved his steed around Ace as he jumped onto the pavement.

The open doorway to ecstasy was five yards away. He sucked in the scents.

Lost in delicious anticipation, he pulled down his topper to hide his shame just as an arm hooked his and dragged him away from temptation.

"What-ho, old thing." Lemmy's voice whispered in his ear. "Two of those blasted grey-shirts have been following you. Don't look around. We should keep walking. They won't try anything in the daylight."

Ace's journey back from euphoria to reality was an unwelcome struggle. His aching body resisted Lemmy's pull, slowing his strides, but a glance behind released the brake.

"I didn't know…" Ace dragged his handkerchief across his face.

"You were a little distracted, old boy." Lemmy looked left and right as they approached Chapel Street. "We can't lead them to the Temple. Your choice, Ace. Run or fight? But, fair warning, if you choose to run, you're on your own." He tapped his prosthetic with his walking stick.

Ace pointed at Greengate's mist-filled bridges that carried the railway tracks to Salford station. "We'll be out of sight from passers-by."

They crossed back over the street and hurried, as fast as Lemmy's leg permitted, along Chapel Street, chest deep in the Irwell's brume. If the thugs were not aware that they had been spotted earlier, they knew when their quarry disappeared beneath the waves of mist just before the railway bridge.

But halfway along the hundred-yard unlit arch, the mist thinned.

Ace pulled Lemmy back into the denser haze and they ducked into one of the dozens of nooks and crannies nestling in the brickwork to catch their breath. Ace shuddered as icy water running down the wall seeped through his coat.

As he leaned forward, two hazy silhouettes appeared at the entrance. One of them wielded a swagger stick.

Not for the first time today, Ace's heartbeat pounded in his ears. "Keep back, *amicus meus*. I'll handle these miscreants."

"I think not, old boy. Why should you have all the fun?"

Ace put his finger to his lips, hoping Lemmy could see it in the dim light, and listened.

"They came this way, I tells yer."

"Well, I can't see nowt in this murk."

The voices were growing louder.

"Don't know who the bloke with the game leg is, but I'm sure the tall black fella is that Ace What's-his-face from the sodding meddlers that did for our Raven."

Ace caught his breath. Shadows darkened the mist in front of their hiding place.

Muffled footsteps walking along the centre of the road passed within feet of their alcove. Ace silently exhaled but Lemmy chose an unfortunate time to drop his walking stick, and the two thugs spun around, running towards the sound.

Ace jumped forward and was in mid-air as his punch

connected with the jaw of the nearest grey-shirt, knocking him off his feet. Out of the corner of his eye, he saw Lemmy scrabbling on the wet cobbles when the second man reached Ace, swinging his swagger stick. But his blow fell short. Dim light made judging distances difficult.

The thug swung again, but Ace stepped inside the arc of the swing and smashed his forehead into the man's face, who bumped into his recovering friend as he fell, leaving both men in a heap.

With the men struggling to stand, Ace sidled sideways so the light from the bridge entrance illuminated his assailants whilst reducing him to a silhouette.

It also kept their attention away from Lemmy.

Having clambered to their feet, the grey-shirts were advancing on Ace. One jabbed the air with a knife with each step, while his compatriot, blood streaming from a shattered nose, hid behind him, languidly swinging his swagger stick.

Ace crouched and spread his arms in readiness for their attack, backing into the denser mist.

To his left, a slight movement in the shadows became a blur as Lemmy smashed his walking stick onto the knife-man's arm. *Crack!* The man screamed and crumpled to the ground, clutching his arm. His friend turned to Lemmy, smashing his swagger stick into his leg. A loud clang echoed around the brickwork.

The most vivid memory Ace took from the skirmish was the look of astonishment on the man's broken, bloodied face when he looked up an instant before Lemmy's walking stick smashed into the side of his head. He crashed on top of his friend, silencing his screams.

The victors surveyed the carnage.

"Dash it, Ace. I'm going to need a new ambulatory aid." Lemmy rubbed his hand over the splintered walking stick.

"If Abel were alive, he would have made a special one for you, like Pop's."

Lemmy's face lit up. "I say. You don't suppose Algeria has kept it, do you? Perhaps she would let me borrow it now we are outlaws, eh?"

"Maybe."

"Point of order, old boy. We should skedaddle before their police friends arrive." Lemmy jabbed a thumb towards the comatose.

"Put your arm around my shoulder. I'll be your crutch."

"Thanks, old boy."

"No, thank you, Lemmy."

"Well, I couldn't let that blooming blackguard stick you with his knife."

Ace smiled as they walked into the daylight. That was the second time Lemmy saved him today.

Just now he may have saved Ace's life, but the first rescue was the more important one.

Not only did it preserve his sobriety, but it also saved his soul.

By the time Ace and Lemmy had waded out of the mist up the gentle slope of Victoria Bridge, crossed Deansgate, continued along the upward gradient of Cateaton Street and onto Corporation Street, they could see Gilbert leaning on the black iron railings that surrounded the stone steps leading down to the Gentlemen's Convenience where the pavement met Miller Street.

"I doubt I will ever get used to the stink of piss. I mean, the meks do a great job of keeping the place clean, but they can't smell. Can they?" Gilbert stared at Ace.

"*Nescio*, old bean. I have no idea."

"Are you all right, Lemmy?" Gilbert grabbed Lemmy's elbow as he stumbled.

"I broke my walking stick. Do you think Algeria kept Pop's? It may be handy now I'm an outlaw, don'tcha know."

"She'll still have it, but it'll be in the Praetorian, and it's not wise to pay a visit in the current circumstances."

Lemmy shook his head. "Hey-ho. I'll have to make do with an old-fashioned wooden one until we can retrieve it. Assuming, of course, that Algeria will let me use it."

"Who's going first? Three gentlemen standing by a public lavatory are a little conspicuous." Now he was a target for the Freedom Brigade, Ace was conscious that the longer he stood in the open, the more chance a grey-shirt might stumble upon him. "You first, Lemmy."

As Ace watched him disappear down the steep steps, he turned to Gilbert. "We had a spot of bother with a couple of Freedom boys. Lemmy can handle himself." Ace puffed out his cheeks. "It seems, however, that I am a juicy prize for every grey-shirt out here."

"Bloody hell, Ace. Then you have to go into hiding. We must—"

"I will not run and hide. While we're *all* in danger, I won't shirk my responsibilities to my brothers and sisters of the Order. I won't disavow my oath, but I must exercise extreme caution from now onwards."

Gilbert motioned with his hand. "After you…"

"No, old chap, you were here before me. After you… There's no point in arguing."

Gilbert rolled his eyes skyward, swung around the railings, and trotted down the stairs.

Ace kicked his heels, surveying every man for hints of grey. Then, only when he was satisfied he was not being watched, he stepped down into the underground public lavatory.

Not wishing to appear foppish, he didn't cover his mouth and nose with his handkerchief, choosing rather to hold his breath as he passed the sparkling white washbasins and brown-stained, stinking urinals. Whilst under his feet, the mosaic floors and deep green tiled walls were a match for the most opulent Roman villa.

Although every urinal was free, three of the twenty-four stalls were occupied and a shiny NR-G mek wearing a brown leather apron scurried around the large room.

Ace hurried to the far end of the room and, pressing his back against the cold tiles, he checked no one had followed him.

Beyond the last stall, a narrow recess, only two feet wide, led to a riveted metal door, where a small wheel reminiscent of the helm aboard *Abel's Hammer* bore the hallmarks of heavy usage. He wrapped his handkerchief around his hand and turned the wheel until the door swung outwards into the tunnel beyond, where his friends' gritted smiles greeted him.

"We were about to send out a search party, old chum." Lemmy's cheery tone didn't match his furrowed brow, deepened by the harsh lamplight.

Ace sighed. He pointed at each of them in turn, then jabbed a thumb into his chest. "You both need to stop worrying about me. We have a job to do. Now, let's get on with it. Lead on, Gilbert."

The yellow glow from the oil lamp raised above Gilbert's head lit up the narrow passage ahead as they walked in close file. Twisting its way beneath the city, the tunnel undulated past dark doorways and dozens of unlit passages. When they reached the now unconcealed entrance to the Temple, the door was ajar, and they started down without missing a beat.

"Goodness, gracious! Things have moved on a pace since my last visit." Ace surveyed the changes and whistled.

"Aye, Algeria wasn't short on volunteers when she asked for help to move the rubble. Without meks, it was backbreaking work, but no one wanted to disappoint the High Mother."

Most of the cave-in remained, but there was now a wide passage along the far side. The winding mechanism, still sitting on its low cart, lay where the tram rails ended. Oil lamps bathed the space in warm light, but Dottie and Algeria were nowhere to be seen.

"How did they get the rocks up the narrow staircase?" Ace's head was swivelling like a child's toy as he tried to take in all the changes.

"They didn't." Lemmy waggled a crooked forefinger at him. "Follow me."

He hobbled around the remains of the roof collapse to the curving ramp that led to Victoria Arches.

"I'm going to wait here." He bent over, panting. "It's only fair that Gilbert shows you."

Ace patted him on the shoulder. "You've had a busy day, old friend. Rest a while."

Gilbert and Ace stooped as they leaned into the climb up the slope. "Steeper than I remember," Gilbert said.

Where it flattened, a new four-foot-wide, eight-foot-high door in the middle of a newly battened wooden wall barred their progress.

"Wait 'til you see the other side. Dottie is a genius." Gilbert skipped to the door and shouted, "Is it all right to come through?"

Three muffled female voices replied in unison. "Yes!"

Ace noticed the door had no handle or knob, but attached to the bottom of the door, a three-foot-square platform hovered inches from the dusty floor.

"Watch this." The pride in Gilbert's voice was palpable as he jumped onto the platform. *Clang!* The door and platform jerked into motion and rumbled backwards. After a few feet, the door pivoted on a corner and turned ninety degrees. The platform came to rest against the tunnel wall.

Gilbert bent and attached it to the brickwork with a small hook. "We have to attach it, or the counterweights and pulleys return the door to where it started."

"How does it open from the other side?"

"It doesn't. Clever, eh?"

Ace closed his jaw. Rocks and detritus covered the other side of the door, mimicking a tunnel collapse. He stepped into the space beyond, looking left and right. The false wall was covered in the same rubble. The largest of the rocks from the original cave-in had been positioned at the front of the facade, which Ace assumed was to deter any attempt to move them.

He put his hands on his hips as he gazed around the walls. Egyptian symbols and hieroglyphs covered the old tunnel from ceiling to floor, some carved, others painted onto the stone.

Algeria, Dottie and Issy beamed from paint-splashed faces.

"When you've stopped catching flies, shugah, let us know what you think." Algeria stepped out of the shadows.

Ace snapped his jaw shut again. "Gilbert was right. *Peringeniosa*, indeed!"

"Wow," Issy said, "Gilbert can speak Latin. Fantabulus."

"That isn't Latin." Ace raised an eyebrow over a straight face.

"And I don't care." Issy threw her arms in the air.

Dottie rushed over to Gilbert, grabbed his hand, and winked. She turned to her friends. "We need just one final touch, don't we, Gilbert?"

Gilbert shrugged. "No idea what you're talking about."

"Oh, you do, but you're not going to like it…"

ELEVEN

MESSAGE

"She's sent you, hasn't she?"

"No, old man. She'd be downright furious if she knew I was speaking with you." Ace motioned Theo to sit on the green leather chesterfield. Although the gentleman's club barred grey-shirts, they had permitted his entry based on Ace's assurance of his behaviour.

"So, what do you want and why here, of all places?" Theo's dirty, unshaven face, unkempt hair and rumpled clothes clashed with the Athenaeum's opulent interior as well as its dress code. And his odour wrinkled the noses of those unfortunates close enough to get a whiff.

"Well, I rather hope the environment can encourage us to talk like the gentlemen we are, without resorting to violence. Of course, if you do resort to rowdiness, the meks will turf you out, and I will lose face amongst my peers."

"I don't care about your reputation. And meks? Well, they can try…" Theo snorted and leaned forward, smirking. "Do you think they'd reach you before I smashed your face to pulp?"

Ace leaned back and steepled his fingers. "Testing them would be a mistake, old boy. Even your prodigious pugilistic prowess would be useless against their metal mechanical might." They were alone in the private room, but beneath his relaxed smile, Ace was more hopeful than confident that the meks were monitoring them.

"So, what do you want? If you're asking me to call off the Brigade, it isn't in my gift. The politicians have done you up good and proper. Algeria's band of do-gooders is finished."

Ace shook his head. "The Order has disbanded. Algeria has disappeared and without the High Mother's guidance, the Order is done."

"That's not what I've heard."

"Frankly, old boy, I don't care what you've heard. The Order is no more. No, I want to talk about Issy."

"Goody-two-shoes? Has she disappeared, too? She's probably with Algeria."

"Why would she be with her? Issy isn't a member of the Order. Her championing temperance and suffrage takes up all of her time. You should know that, chum."

"Pull the other one, fella. She's always hanging about with you and that lot at the Praetorian. And I'm not your chum. Now, I've got better things to do with my time than sit here listening to your bull."

"Oh, I'm sure you'd much rather be drinking or beating up

some poor sot."

Theo pushed himself out of the plush seat, sharply enough to make Ace flinch. But a mek appeared in the doorway before he took a step.

"Is there a problem, gentlemen? Can *this 'kin* assist in any way?" It glided towards them and stood in front of Theo. Ace remained seated. His white-knuckled hands gripped the arms of the chesterfield, and a single bead of sweat tickled his face as it meandered from his temple through his neatly trimmed beard. Theo stared at him over the mek's shoulder, a sneer spreading across his stubbly face.

"You know I could've—" Theo jabbed a pointing finger at Ace, but his smile turned into a grimace as the mek's lightning-fast fist grabbed and squeezed his wrist before it passed its shoulder. Its other hand grabbed a handful of coat, shirt, and chest hair, lifting Theo onto his tiptoes.

"*This 'kin* must ask you to leave before you hurt yourself or anyone else." Its eyes fluttered for a second and a second mek arrived in time to grasp Theo's other clenched fist before he threw the roundhouse cocked at his side.

"Oh, Theo. What happened to you? I thought I could talk some sense into you and steer you from this self-destructive path." Ace rose from the chair and straightened his jacket. "I thought you and Issy could—"

"Could what? Make up? For someone who spends his life as her lapdog, you don't know her very well, do you?" Theo spat the words through clenched teeth as he struggled to break free from the mek's iron grip. The second mek grabbed the back of his coat, and they began marching him through the door into the large smoking room towards the vestibule and the main entrance. Ace walked a few paces behind, nodding apologies to the members.

The meks released Theo onto the steps beneath the portico and stepped back. The mek doorman, resplendent in its bright red uniform, stepped between Theo and the meks. Looking down from beneath its black-peaked red cap, it pressed an immovable, white-gloved hand on his shoulder, halting his bull rush at the mek escorts as they returned inside.

"Goodbye, old man. I truly hope you find your way." Ace watched Theo's eyes flick left and right.

"You'd better hope we don't meet again, pretty boy. You can't hide behind meks forever."

Ace turned and headed back inside the Athenaeum. He stayed until the shadows in the library were creeping above the third row of books, then left amidst a group of patrons. Although Ace was not a coward, if he were to face the Brunswick Brawler, it would be on his terms, not Theo's.

As he sloped away from the Athenaeum, Theo aimed a kick at a slobbering bulldog, but its mek walker yanked its lead, pulling it away from his hobnailed boot. He snarled at the mek as it hurried away down Princess Street towards Albert Square.

"You horrible man!" An old maid in a midnight blue coat

and matching Gainsborough brandished her umbrella at him as she marched towards him. "That poor dog had done you no harm."

Theo grabbed her face with his huge hand and pushed her backwards without breaking stride. She landed on her bustle with a loud snap. Then, pointing a finger, he sneered down at her sitting on the wet pavement. "Mind your own business, y'old witch!"

"Whoa, chummy." A skinny toff in a morning suit and tall, shiny topper pressed the silver knob of his walking stick into Theo's shoulder. "Where do you think you're going? Offer your hand to the lady and apologise at once."

The altercation was now attracting a small crowd. Theo eased open his coat to display the grey.

"Is that supposed to scare me? I'm afraid that cuts no ice with me. Now—"

Stepping forward, Theo pushed away the stick with one hand and slapped the toff with the other. He grinned as the toff regained his balance, wiping the blood from his split lip on the back of his white glove.

"Your turn, chum," Theo said.

But from each side, firm hands gripped his arms. The toff cocked his head and examined Theo's unkempt hair and clothing with contempt in his eyes. "It would appear I have you at a disadvantage." He took a short step back and raised his stick.

With his head held high, Theo curled his lips and braced for the contact. But a blow knocked him sideways as a scuffle broke out. A grey-sleeved hand grabbed the toff's wrist and twisted his arm, forcing him to drop his cane.

As more grey-shirts waded into the melee, Theo wrenched his arms free, throwing a couple of wild roundhouses that found their targets as all around him, fists and saps were swinging. He twisted left and right, looking for someone to punch, but the fight was over as quickly as it began, and those that were able scattered.

Four toffs and three flat-capped workers were rolling on the pavement trying to regain their feet and their senses, but the midnight blue-dressed woman was nowhere to be seen.

His grey-shirted compatriots took Theo by the arms and escorted him across the road, stopping the horse-drawn carriages and hansoms with their free outstretched arms. Then they bundled him down the steps of a Greek Taverna-style restaurant that occupied one of the basement rooms of a large, five-storey mill.

"I need a drink." Theo tried to free himself from the hands that still held him. But even a growling glare into the faces of his captors had no effect. "Do you know who I am? I could take each of you blackguards with one hand tied behind my back. Now let me go!"

Both men stared across the dimly lit room at a blond, grey-shirted man wearing an aeronaut's cap and goggles. He beckoned them over to his table. "Let him go. He won't try anything, will you, Theo?"

Theo shook himself free as they eased their grip, brushed the creases out of his sleeves, and sat at the table. "Yet to be decided," he said.

The blond man ordered two pints of porter from a mek wearing an apron and lit a cigar. He eyed Theo, blowing smoke rings while he waited for the mek's return.

"Who are you and what's this about?" Theo glanced over his shoulder as six more grey-shirts joined them.

The blond man smiled but remained silent until the mek slid the drinks onto the table. "Who I am isn't important." He pushed his drink across the table to join Theo's. "They're both for you. You look like you need them."

Theo raised his eyebrows. "Unexpected hospitality from a stranger makes me nervous. You must want something."

"Your nocturnal activities have not gone unnoticed. My boss wants a word with you."

"And who might that be?" Theo downed the first drink and slammed the pot on the table.

"All in good time, friend." The blond man leaned forward. "I'm interested in the black fellow you met at the Athenaeum. Friend, was he?"

Theo turned down the corners of his mouth and tilted his head. "Have you been following me?" He sucked in a deep breath to slow his racing heartbeat.

"We were watching your friend, actually."

"He's no friend of mine. He hangs around with my sister. Me and her aren't tight. He was trying to get me to make up with her. That's all."

"I don't believe you."

"And I don't care." Theo picked up the second pot and drained half its contents in three gulps.

"Do you care about anything?"

Despite the rage rising in his chest, Theo maintained his placid expression. "Look, tell me what this is all about, or I'm off."

"I'm taking you to see the boss. Don't know why. I'm just a good soldier following orders."

"So, who is this boss of yours?"

The blond man smiled and blew another smoke ring.

Theo watched it twist and turn as it rose, growing wider and fainter. He never saw the blow that knocked him off the chair, and he was unconscious before he hit the floor.

Gilbert's stomach churned as *Abel's Hammer* side-slipped through the cloudless December sky towards the mooring post on the hill above the Forge.

At the helm, Queequeg used the blustery wind that had nudged them all the way from Barton to flick the airship 180 degrees to brake their forward momentum. The gondola was jouncing like a pea in a whistle as powerful gusts pounded the airship. Gilbert peeped through fingers clamped across his face.

Although he couldn't see her, Gilbert felt Dottie's grip on his arm and her head on his shoulder. Opposite them, Issy sat next to Algeria. Issy watched Ace's every move while Algeria's tight-lipped stare fixed firmly on Dottie.

At the prow, Ace peered over the rails, arm raised, directing

Queequeg with deft hand signals, while Jonah stood a step behind the mek like a father watching his son take his first steps. Proud but nervous, ready to leap into action should the mek lose his battle with the weather.

But Jonah's concerns were unfounded. After a brief struggle, humming electromagnets replaced the roar of the engines as Queequeg secured the airship to the docking mast at the top of the hill overlooking the burnt-out buildings of the Forge.

"Drop anchor!" Jonah barked, and the anchor plummeted from the rear of the gondola onto the wet grass. Finally attached to *terra firma*, front and rear, the gondola was stable enough for Gilbert to stand without dropping to his knees and vomiting.

"I believe you may have found your air-legs, *vetus amice*." Ace strode towards him and placed a hand on his shoulder. "We'll make an aeronaut out of you yet."

Standing at his side, Dottie was still clinging to Gilbert's arm. He ran his fingers through her wet hair. She had been dreading this day. Although the Stormriders had other business here, she was visiting her father's grave on what would have been his birthday.

High in the cloudless sky above them, Tabby was displaying her piloting prowess to Rory, Connie, and Lemmy. Relieved to be back on the ground, Gilbert stared at the *Scarab's* roller-coaster twists, turns, climbs and dives.

Algeria clambered down the ladder behind Dottie. This was her first visit to her beloved Abel's resting place. She had insisted on visiting the Forge to witness the aftermath of the Anthropocene's wanton destruction. But her expression was a mixture of shock, sadness, and hatred in equal parts.

"Take me to his grave, Doll," she said. "Gilbert. You, Ace, and Issy have work to do." She linked Dottie's arm, and they set off for the clearing on the hillside where they had interred Abel in haste.

Dottie glanced over her shoulder at Gilbert. He smiled and put his hand over his heart. *She wants me to go with her...*

"I wore violet because it was your father's favourite colour." Algeria said.

"I'm surprised you remember." Dottie closed her eyes. "Sorry... old habits..." she said.

Algeria pulled Dottie closer.

Gilbert turned to join the others who were gathering sacks hurled from the gondola by Jonah.

"*Sufficit!*" Ace waved his hands palm down and shouted at the airship. "There's only three of us, old man. And Issy can't carry as much as us strapping fellows."

"Really, Ace? Is that a challenge?"

Gilbert rolled his eyes at Ace's grimace behind Issy's back. "Come on. Let's get going. We've got lots to do."

They headed down the hill, hugging the tree line, towards the ruins of the Forge and the house that had once been Abel's and Dottie's home. Issy clamped her hand over her mouth at the destruction as they reached the blackened remains.

"There won't be any tools or weapons to salvage. We're wasting our time." Issy kicked at a charred branch jutting from the ashes.

"Let's just have a quick dekko in what's left of the buildings,"

Gilbert said, "but the weapon we've come for isn't in there."

Ace and Issy exchanged puzzled frowns.

Gilbert took three muslin masks from the pouch on his belt. "These will give us some protection from the place we're going." He handed one to each of them, tucking the remaining mask into his pocket. "Look around for shears or scythes. I have these." He patted the handles of the short swords nestling in their sheaths and looked skyward. *Thank you, Abel.*

"Any idea what he's talking about, old girl?"

"Your guess is as good as mine." Issy shrugged and marched into blackened ruins of the Forge, plumes of ash flicking off the heels of her boots.

Five minutes later, Gilbert was leading the way along the narrow path into the woods, accompanied by birdsong and dead leaves crunching underfoot.

Issy came next, carrying a sickle that Ace had found on the boundary between the ashes and living grass. Although it had a charred wooden handle, its blade was sharp and its ferrule secure.

Ace brought up the rear, carrying the sacks.

As they ventured further, the trees grew denser than Gilbert remembered. He hated this dark place and wished he had gone with Dottie to Abel's grave. But he pressed on, knowing the importance of their task.

Up ahead, the husk of the old yew loomed into view. Dread memories clutched at Gilbert's chest, weakening his resolve and dragging back his leaden legs. Somewhere, in the deep recesses of his mind, Dottie's voice repeated a single word over and over again… Mask. Mask.

Gilbert spread his arms wide to prevent further progress and turned to face his companions.

"I don't know if the masks will fully protect you, but if you get the morbs, tell me." He pulled on his mask and tiptoed to the edge of the clearing. His breathing quickened and his heart pounded in his ears.

Here we go…

Meanwhile, on Pendle Hill, overlooking the Forge, Dottie and Algeria trudged through the trees towards Abel's makeshift arena, accompanied by cawing crows and dead leaves susurrating underfoot. Above them, the swaying tree canopy that sent dappled light swirling around the rotting duff and detritus of the woodland undergrowth dampened *Scarab's* droning engines.

Unified by their sadness, words were unnecessary. They reached the clearing as *Scarab* swooped low overhead. The air-yacht's roaring engines shrieked above the squalling cries and beating wings as the crows scattered from the trees. Dottie stopped and caught her breath as memories of the attack on the Forge tumbled into her mind, and a single tear squeezed from her scrunched eyes.

Algeria stepped carefully, trailing a finger along each of the nine felled tree trunks that surrounded the flattened fighting area. When she reached the log with a dark stain, she knew this was where her beloved had fallen, spilling his life's blood on the dead bark.

As she knelt, she pressed one hand flat on Abel's blood and dug the fingers of her other hand into the dirt, which still bore the marks of Gilbert and Dottie's removal of his body.

She bowed her head, closed her eyes, and plunged into a silent, eerie, lightless void. A swell of intense emotions built to a crescendo as a tidal wave of fleeting images crashed on the shores of her consciousness. Countless visions, memories of a life well lived sped past, only to slow and linger on three final images.

Dottie's smile from a grimy, goggled face, Gilbert lying in the dirt, reaching to take a hand, then finally, an airship hovering in a gap in the trees that surrounded the arena. Although she had not been aware of colours until then, the airship was bright scarlet and surrounded by an ethereal glow.

Abel had seen the airship that fired the crossbow bolt. A wave of contentment crashed ashore, then receded into the ocean.

Did Abel step into the path of the bolt to save Gilbert?

Her racing heart stopped.

"Mama! Mama!" Dottie's distant voice grew louder, and she felt hands shaking her shoulders. "What happened? Are you all right?"

Algeria opened her eyes to find she was lying face down by the tree trunk. She spat the dead leaves from her lips and levered herself onto her side. "How long was I out?" she said.

Dottie pulled leaves from Algeria's hair. "What do you

mean? You knelt, then collapsed, and I ran over to you. What happened, Mama?"

Algeria smiled as she stood and brushed the woodland floor from her clothes. She glanced at the gap in the trees where the hillside fell away and from where the red airship had struck.

Everything matched her vision. Only the airship was missing. Abel's memories had passed in the blink of an eye. "Take me to him, Doll."

Dottie nodded and took her mother's hand. Her beloved's final resting place was on the side of the hill, only fifty yards from where he was brutally struck down. Gilbert and Dottie, in accordance with the Order's customs, had buried him with his feet pointing towards the setting sun.

Algeria knelt beside the shallow grave and placed her hand on the dry soil that covered his remains. She closed her eyes, and content that he rested in Gaia's embrace, she murmured a brief invocation to the Mother before returning to Dottie.

"Thank you, shugah."

Dottie furrowed her brow.

"I loved him so much and miss him more every day. I see his face in a swirl of fog or a tree's bark or a forming cloud, but I had so many unanswered questions before I came here. Now, thanks to his strength and Gaia's grace, I know he felt the same and that he is resting peacefully."

"Oh, Mama. Please, not this silly Gaia thing again. Dad's gone. The Anthropocene murdered him. There's nothing else."

Algeria put her hand on Dottie's chilled cheek and wiped away a tear with her thumb. "I know you don't believe as I do, shugah. But Abel and Gaia, together, comforted me today and gave me answers I didn't deserve or expect. Now, I truly believe that love transcends death, no matter what your beliefs."

Dottie fell into her mother's arms, sobbing. Algeria smiled as she stroked Dottie's hair. "He loved us more than we ever imagined."

And in death, he may have given us hope for the future.

QUESTIONS

Distant strains of laughter and bouzouki music trickled into Theo's consciousness as he stirred from his enforced slumber.

Blindfolded, hands tied behind his back, he was lying on his side, trussed like a Christmas goose to what felt like the chair from the Greek tavern. His cheek was cold, wet and slimy, pressed against the booze-drenched floor, and his hands and feet were numb. He grimaced as he squirmed against his bonds, clenching and unclenching his fists.

Whoever had bound him this tight was going to pay.

"Ah, you are awake. I was beginning to think I hit you too hard." Four firm hands yanked the chair back onto its legs.

Theo rolled his tongue around the inside of his cheek and checked for loose teeth. "Nah, my sister slaps harder." He steeled himself for a blow that never came. "Now, if you'd loosen these ties…"

"I'm afraid your reputation precedes you, and my boss would never forgive me if you wriggled from my grasp without answering a few questions."

"Wriggling isn't my style, but if your boss is here, I'd like to have a word with him."

"That's not going to not happen." The bouzouki music stopped to a smattering of applause before starting another tune, sounding the same as the last. "Take off his blindfold and wipe off that spit."

Theo squeezed his eyes tight shut against the bright light as they untied the blindfold and scrubbed his face hard with the cloth. When he pried open his eyelids, it took them a few seconds to adjust.

The room was small, maybe six feet square, and in front of him sat another grey-shirted blond man, similar, but not identical to the cigar-smoking chap in the taverna.

"Ah, you must be Tweedle-dee."

"If you don't change your attitude, this will be a very brief conversation."

Theo glanced over each shoulder. *Three. No problem if my hands weren't tied*, he thought. "So, what's the problem? We're all Brigade here."

"Are we, Mister Windlass? Maybe one of us is a nose."

Theo burst into laughter. "If you think I'm working for the soppy gardeners, you're a bigger fool than you look."

"We know you know Ace Sixsmith is a leading member of the Order, like your sister. Then, we catch you, wearing grey, having a friendly chat with him. There's no other explanation."

"Just like I told your sister earlier," Theo smiled as his interrogator frowned and shook his head at the owner of the hand that just tightened on his left shoulder. "Sixsmith says the Order is disbanded, and I have no reason to disbelieve him."

"Perhaps that is what they want us to believe. And what better way to convince us than have you, the infamous Brunswick Brawler, sworn enemy of the Order, give us the news? You're either a nose or a useful idiot."

Theo's chin dropped to his chest. "Listen." His interrogator's eyes widened as Theo brought his unfettered fists forward, resting them on his lap. "If we weren't on the same side, I would have done all three of you when I snapped my bonds five minutes ago." Easing himself upright, he shrugged the hands from his shoulders and kicked his right leg sideways, breaking the thin chair leg, then, with the same boot, kicked the chair from his other leg.

He slammed his elbows into the two captors behind him. Then, keeping a side-eye on Tweedle-dee, he half turned. "I suggest you two walk out while you still can. I need to have a private chat with your friend here." Both thugs hesitated, but the one from the taverna raised a questioning eyebrow at Tweedle-dee.

"Shoo! I won't hurt your brother, but even if you wanted to, you couldn't stop me." In their haste, the two men stumbled as they squeezed through the door into the taverna.

Theo turned to find his interrogator still seated, arms folded.

"A most impressive trick, Mister Windlass. But you haven't

convinced me, and I'm the one who reports to the boss."

"What's your name?"

"Not important."

"It is to me."

Sweat glistened on the seated thug's forehead, but the tension left his shoulders as something behind Theo attracted his attention.

Theo ducked to his right and threw his left elbow hard backwards. It connected with Tweedle-dum's short rib, and, with a groan, he crumpled to the floor. Tweedle-dee leapt to his feet, in perfect time for his face to catch the full force of Theo's fist. He fell back into the chair, toppling backwards in a heap.

Theo grabbed a fistful of shirt and yanked him up, cocking his fist.

"Last chance. Name," he said.

"They call me Hansel." Blood ran between his fingers as he tried to stem the flow from his nose.

Theo glanced behind at the other blond, clutching his chest, writhing on the floor trying to breathe, and laughed.

"So this must be Gretel?" Theo shook his head. "Is this the best the Freedom Brigade can offer? Children's nursery rhyme characters?" He let Hansel fall to the floor and bent to point a finger inches from his face. "Tell your boss he knows where to find me if he wants to talk."

Theo stepped over gasping Gretel and through the door, into the lively taverna. A few heads turned, but most people were too busy enjoying themselves to notice the big man straightening his attire, striding from behind a wall-hanging and toward the entrance.

He shoved aside a couple of grey-shirts who leaned into him, and without breaking stride, walked up the stairs to Princess Street and turned into the fog. Night had fallen, and he judged by the drunken state of the raucous revellers in the taverna, it must be approaching last orders.

His mouth was sore and dry. He needed a drink, or two, or three, and woe betide anyone who stood in his way.

To clear her mind, Issy took the long route to Brunswick Mill, along the Ashton Canal.

The north side of the towpath narrowed where it squeezed beneath the Cambrian Street bridge. Issy straightened her back as she emerged from under the low arch and caught her first sight of the mill. With the top two of the building's seven floors shrouded in mist, its wrought-iron fire escape zigzagging up and along the fenestrated wall disappeared into the brown-grey vapour.

Ahead, moored alongside the loading bays, a line of canal boats bobbed beneath the feet of heavy meks as they bundled cargo into the holds while boatmen stood smoking clay pipes, aiming kicks at them when they ventured too close. But the meks were too nimble, so their clumsy attempts rarely connected.

Issy turned from the towpath and followed the stony track along the side of the mill. And running her fingertips along the rough brick walls, she remembered happier times playing around the mill with Theo. Father had worked for Grandfather back then. But to hear him talk, he had laid every brick with his bare hands.

But neither he nor Grandfather dirtied their hands. Grandfather had the money, business acumen and the great fortune of being born in the right place at the right time to take the opportunity that the Industrial Revolution presented to few. Father just rode on his coattails.

At the front of the building, she passed by the stone arch, through which the workers entered and exited each morning and night, to the double-door entrance to the offices. She paused on the steps and smoothed her dress before straightening her back and raising her head high.

She turned the big brass doorknob and pushed. The racket of the clattering machinery and pounding steam engines almost knocked her off her feet. But the familiar smell of flax, oil and grease brought back more childhood memories.

The ground floor was smaller than she remembered. Although production managers had offices overlooking the workers and spinning mules, the bosses, accountants and secretarial staff occupied the rooms on the fourth floor.

Issy headed for the birdcage lift.

Out of the corner of her eye, she saw heads turning as she strode, head held high. *Do they recognise me? It's been a while.*

A small voice from behind answered her unspoken question. "Miss Isadora?"

She stopped and turned. A girl in a pale green gingham shift and cap wiped her hands on her dirty white apron. She must have been only twelve years old.

"Begging your pardon, miss. Are you taking over from Master Theo?"

Master Theo? Ha! "No." Issy tilted her head and raised an eyebrow.

"Oh, I'm Tilly, miss. I saw you the last time you was here."

"But that was over two years ago…"

The young girl's cheeks flushed, and she stared at her feet. "I thought you were a princess. That lot laughed at me when I told 'em." She jabbed a thumb at the girls staring from the carding machines.

Issy bent and lifted Tilly's face with her thumb and forefinger under her chin, gently turning her head left and right. Although her eyes were still adjusting to the light, purple and brown bruises on her face, neck and arms told a story she didn't want to hear.

But she asked anyway. "Who did this to you?"

Tilly's lips tightened as she looked towards and up the lift stanchions.

"Thank you, Tilly. I can find my way to the offices." Issy acknowledged Tilly's curtsy with a nod and a smile. She stepped into the birdcage, closed the concertina gates and twisted the control. The lift juddered into motion and rose slowly enough to enable Issy to stop it in line with the fourth floor.

Stepping out of the lift, she deliberately left the gates open as she turned along the corridor. Although the lift would be inoperable until her return, her business would take less time than she had originally intended.

All the antechambers' walls on the fourth floor were glass panes over low, dark, wooden panels. Had Theo's secretary been at his desk in the outer office, he would have seen and heard her long before she pushed open the door.

Inside, neat rows of ledgers hid the side walls, and a flat cap and a brown coat hung on the hatstand next to two guest chairs facing the desk. An open ledger, a receipt spike stacked with invoices and a neat row of pencils sat next to a new Fitch typewriting machine, which dominated the middle of the desk in front of the window into her father's, now Theo's, office.

She peered into the double-aspect corner office. At first glance, it appeared to be empty. Behind the twin pedestal desk and green studded leather chair, two north-facing windows overlooked Bradford Road. Between the windows a large portrait of her father sitting in the same chair, behind the same desk, glowered back at her.

The door between the secretary's desk and the ledgers was ajar. Loud hammering from within was winning the battle against the distant clattering of mill machinery. She pushed the door open with her forefinger and found the owner of the flat cap and brown overcoat kneeling on the floor, swinging his hammer with gusto.

Those floorboards will never move again, she thought. She recognised the man's green coveralls.

"Hello, Onslow," she said.

The man leapt to his feet and spun round, raising his hammer to shoulder height.

Issy caught her breath. He was wearing a grey shirt beneath his coveralls.

"Miss Isadora! You oughtn't sneak up on a man with a hammer in his hand." Beneath his handlebar moustache, he grinned his toothless grin and lowered his arm.

"And you should be careful with your sartorial choices. Anyone might mistake you for a grey-shirt… Oh…" Her voice trailed off when his expression confirmed her fears.

"Are you not a follower, miss? I would have thought with Master Theo being in the movem—"

"Theo and I don't see eye to eye on many things." Issy had been ready for an argument, but not with her brother's loyal friend.

"To be honest with you, miss, I don't understand what it's all about either. Pulling on the shirt impresses the ladies, mind, and I've had many a free apple at the market." His cheeks reddened, and he looked away. "But I only joined cos it might be a way of getting away from Charter Street, and to keep an eye on Theo, of course."

Onslow lived in lodgings in Angel Meadow. Although she would never set foot in the slums, she had heard terrible tales of unimaginable squalor, poverty and crime. She walked around the desk and sank into the soft leather chair. "Where is he? In the mill?"

"No, miss. No one's seen sight or sound of him in three days. There was word he was meeting with the boss of the Freedom Brigade. But no one knows for sure. And I can't deny, I'm worried about him, miss."

The hackles raised on her neck.

"The leader, you say? And who might that be?" She leaned forward and fiddled with the silver pen in its ink holder.

"That's the mystery, ain't it? Nobody knows." Onslow grinned.

From where she sat, she could see the course of the Ashton Canal through the east-facing windows as it curved away south-eastward. "Well, I'm keeping you from your work and wasting my time sitting here if Theo isn't going to turn up any time soon." She stood and started for the door.

Onslow stepped into her path. "I don't want to speak out of turn, miss…" He still had the hammer in his right fist.

Issy stopped. "Whatever it is, spit it out, Onslow."

"Sorry, miss." The hammer thumped onto the floor. "I forgot I still had hold of that."

Issy rested her hip against the desk. "Go on…"

"I think you need to learn the truth about your brother. You know we've been close ever since he saved me from drowning when we was kids."

Issy nodded. It was one of the few splendid memories of Theo she had tried to expunge from her thoughts.

"Well, he tells me things, secrets, that he wouldn't tell no one else."

"I doubt he'd tell you anything I'm not already aware of."

"Then you'd be wrong, miss. You see, I've pulled Theo out of many a scrape and even taken care of him when he's been the worse for drink. He trusts me with his life, and I trust him with mine."

Issy snorted and took a step towards the door.

Onslow held up a hand. "You can laugh, miss, but he confided in me after a night of boozing and brawling had gone too far. He was so badly hurt, he thought he was a goner. And he might well have been if I hadn't… anyway, he told me what happened between you two and the truth of how your mother got hurt."

"Theo wouldn't know the truth if it bit him on the arse." She pulled her lips taut across her teeth.

"He didn't push her down the stairs like you think. He says, when you came out of your room, he was reaching out to save her. See, it was your father who'd shoved her aside as he crossed the landing into their bedroom. It was your dad what pushed her."

"That's not what happened. You don't know. You weren't there. He's lied to you like he lies to everyone else. You're a fool to believe him." Issy shook her head as she stared out of the east window.

"Why do you think your father handed the running of the mill to Theo? It was part of their agreement. Theo gets the mill, so your father can take care of your mother. That way, everyone believes it was an accident, apart from you, just so that you keep your relationship with your mother and father. That's the way they figured it."

Behind Issy's staring, unseeing eyes, her mind churned the events of that night over and over.

"He misses you, you know. Your hatred fuels his drinking and fighting."

"He tried to kill me. In the Praetorian. He shot at me."

"Are you sure? Because that's not—"

"Why are you telling me this now? What's in it for you?"

"I'm worried about him. He thinks they've found out about—"

"He's probably sleeping one off somewhere."

Onslow shook his head.

"I have to go." Issy pushed past him and turned as she reached the door. "I'll get to the bottom of this."

When the lift arrived at the ground floor, a gaggle of noisy managers fell silent when they saw Issy's expression and made way as she flung the lift gates apart and stepped into their midst.

But between her and the double doors to Bradford Road, Tilly stood with her hand to her mouth. An older, taller young lady stood behind her, pressing Tilly's shoulders into her skirt.

Doubts clouded Issy's mind. She stopped and crouched in front of the little girl, so that their eyes were on the same level, and placed her hand on the side of her bruised face.

"Tell me truthfully. Did my brother do this?"

Tilly turned her head towards the stairs. A burly man in a bowler hat, brown coveralls and clogs was clattering down the stone steps.

Issy straightened and met him as he stepped off the stairs.

"Miss Isadora. We haven't seen you in a—"

"Mister Galbraith, isn't it?"

"Yes, miss. I'm surprised you—"

"You're sacked. Go to the office and collect your wages."

"Why? You can't sack me! Your brother is in charge here.

He'll have something to—"

Issy caught a glimpse of grey beneath his coveralls as she stepped forward and raised her voice. "If you are not off the premises within the quarter hour, we'll let the police handle the matter. There are plenty who have witnessed your cruelty." She half turned her head. "Isn't that right, ladies?"

The carding room girls shouted their approval, mixed with profane instructions of how and where Galbraith should go.

"You've not heard the last of—"

"Oh yes, I have. Because if I find out you have set foot inside the mill or harassed any of my workers, you'll get a knock from the bobbies." She lowered her voice. "Not your grey-shirted sympathisers. Real policemen hate child beaters." She turned her back on the red-faced bully and returned to Tilly, speaking to her older friend.

"What's your name, dear?"

"Winifred Thursday, miss."

"You are in charge of the carding room, if you think you can handle it."

Winifred raised herself to her full height. "Yes, miss. I believe I can. Thank you, miss."

"In my brother's absence, I'll get Father to write a note to the office manager, informing him of your promotion. Look after your workers, Miss Thursday, and they will work hard for you." She bent down and pulled Tilly into a hug before standing and leaving the mill without looking back.

Her thoughts were still spinning around her head as she ducked under the Cambrian Street bridge. By the time the towpath widened on the other side, she had set her jaw and lengthened her stride.

You have a lot of explaining to do, Daddy dearest.

Later that day, Issy stood at the side of her mother's bath chair and tucked in the woollen blanket around her legs. There was a bite in the evening air as the sun dipped behind the apple trees, scattering dappled shadows across the lawn and herbaceous borders. She pulled up a wrought-iron chair from the breakfast seating in the gazebo and warmed her mother's hand.

"Is it true, Mummy? Was Theo trying to save you from falling?"

"Ask your father, dear. I don't remember. Everything happened so quickly. One moment I was at the top of the stairs, the next I was in the hospital. I have a vague recollection of seeing Theo as I fell, but I can only recount what your father told the doctors that it was a tragic acci—"

"What's going on?" Issy's father stormed through the French doors towards the gazebo. "Horace says you're upsetting your mother! This won't do! I won't have it!"

Issy looked over her father's shoulder and glared at the mek gardener peeping through the morning room window. When Father had learned the extent of her mother's injuries, he had forbidden discussions about that fateful night.

Father grabbed the handles of the bath chair. "Come along,

dear. You'll be catching your death in this cold air. Issy should know better."

"Why have you let me believe Theo pushed Mum down the stairs?"

"We are not having this conversation now, and certainly not out here with your mother shivering."

"Has it ever occurred that I may have questions too, Wilbur? After all, I'm the one sat in this contraption. And, in any case, I rarely have the opportunity to spend time outdoors. So, please, let Issy speak."

"You women will not bully me into submission. I need a drink." He started towards the house, but Issy barred his way. "How dare you! Get out of the way!" He shoved her aside with his forearm.

Issy gasped as she crashed onto the path. "Is that what happened at the top of the stairs, Daddy? Did you push Mum in your rush to get a drink?" She grabbed her father's arm as she picked herself up.

"Unhand me! You don't know what you're talking about. How dare you blame me!" He pushed her again and headed for the house.

"Theo told me what happened, Daddy…"

The words stopped him dead in his tracks and he turned to face them, eyebrows raised, eyes wide, lips moving in silence.

"Wilbur? Is this true?"

"Tell her, Daddy. Tell us both the truth."

"I… I… Theo wouldn't say anything. He's—"

"Sworn to secrecy as reward for running the mill? Yes,

Daddy, I know about the deal you struck, setting him up in lodgings to get him away from my questions whilst letting me believe he had caused Mum's injuries. Deny it or tell us the truth!"

Her father's forlorn gaze flicked between Issy and her mother.

"Please, Wilbur. You always said it was an accident. We need to know."

Issy reached for her mother's hand.

Dragging his feet, Father trudged back to the gazebo, shaking his head, confusion etched in his pinched eyebrows and furrowed brow. He flopped onto a breakfast chair. "I need a drink."

"No, Wilbur. Truth now; drink later."

"It was an accident." He looked into Issy's eyes. "But Theo didn't push your mother. Only you have ever suggested that he did because you hate him."

"You know that's not true. The demon drink—"

"Ha! You and your self-righteous sanctimonious crusades. You need to find yourself a husband—"

"Enough!" Issy's mother shouted over the raised voices. "The truth, Wilbur, now!"

Issy's father was wheezing. He showed the palms of his hands in surrender. "All right, all right. I stepped out of the bathroom, wiping my face with a towel." He faced Issy's mother. "I didn't see you on the landing and tripped trying to avoid you. I lost my balance and placed a hand on your back as I stumbled into the bedroom. You screamed, and I saw Theo reaching for you… When you were lying at the foot of the stairs, I thought I'd lost you."

"You had been drinking. I remember," Issy's mother murmured.

"It didn't cause me to stumble."

"Actions have consequences, Daddy. How different would all our lives have been if you hadn't tripped, and Mum hadn't fallen down the stairs? Only you know whether the demon caused you to bump into Mum."

Her father lowered his eyes.

"Please take me into the house, Wilbur. It's getting rather chilly."

Father grabbed the handles and turned his head to Issy. "Truthfully, did Theo really tell you what happened?"

"No, it was Onslow."

"Onslow? Onslow Halfsprung? Well, he's worked his last day at the mill. I'll—"

"You'll do nothing of the sort, Daddy. For everything that he does for Theo, you should reward him, not punish him. He's Theo's one and only friend.

"Oh, and by the way, I sacked Galbraith this morning. Winifred Thursday is the new carding room manager."

"What? You can't do that. You don't have the authority. You're just a—"

"Woman? Yes, but with Theo missing, and you looking after Mum, someone has to make decisions."

"What's that? Theo isn't at the mill?"

"He hasn't been at work for three days. Onslow says he's

meeting the top dog of the Freedom Brigade, or at least, that's the rumour."

"I warned him about his responsibilities when he took control of running the company. Damnation! He can't just leave the place with no one in charge." He jerked the bath chair into motion, and her mother steered them away, leaving Issy in the gazebo.

The sun had all but disappeared below the trees and bushes that marked the perimeter of the garden. Issy rubbed her arms. Since Theo had moved from the family home, the demon had taken hold and his brawling had begun. Had her accusations made worse the guilt he felt for not failing to prevent her mum's fall? Was brawling his martyrdom to that guilt?

Whatever has happened to him, I must steer him away from the Anthropocene.

LOOSE ENDS

No matter how many times Felix tried to persuade him, Oscar refused to believe that Letitia's panicked exit from the brougham was the cause of his blinding headache, despite it lasting the best part of five days.

He had convinced himself that a combination of eye strain and poor posture whilst repairing Letitia's skin tears had caused his cephalalgia..

And although no one could deny his concentration, skill and painful dedication had been intense and efficacious in every way, the purple bruising and lacerations on his head were the more likely cause.

When considering the perceived threat from Ipkiss's enemies, Oscar had made a few improvements to the house and workshop security after he had finished work on Letitia. Thanks to his tireless efforts, she had made a full recovery. But since he had taken to his bed soon afterwards, he had given no more thought to their plight.

Now, with the pain and brain-fog lifted, their vulnerability was crystal clear. What chance would a broken septuagenarian and a mek hobbled by the First Protocol have against determined intruders?

He had just mounted his *McMurdo's Patented Rack and Pinion Funicular Stair Lift* when the front doorbells jangled on their spring. They continued to bounce above the transom window for the whole of his steady descent.

"Letitia!"

No reply, and with his ambulatory aid absent from its designated place at the bottom of the stairs, he was stuck. A pang of fear quickened his heartbeat.

"Letitia!"

The bells stopped jangling. The workshop wasn't visible from where he sat, but familiar giggling drifted along the hall.

"Letitia! Where are you?"

Gears whirring, Letitia slid to a halt in front of him. Her tinkling chatelaine swayed on her gently rocking hips.

"Oh, dear Oscar. I am sorry. I didn't hear you because of the bells." She pointed upwards.

"Why did you not answer the door, and where is my ambulatory aid?"

"Do you not remember your last instruction to me?" Letitia changed her voice to mimic Oscar. "Do not open the door under any circumstances. Do not let anyone in, including Felix. Do you understand?" She switched back to her normal timbre. "I was obeying your orders. Your ambulatory aid is in the workshop where you left it. Felix carried you to the stair lift after you collapsed during your argument."

"Argument? No, no, no. That was a merely a spirited discussion. There was no ill-feeling…" Oscar cleared his throat. He had a vague memory of telling Felix to leave, or take a running jump off a cliff, or something similar. "Hmm, I may owe him an apology."

Letitia pulled aside the curtain on the door sidelight. "There is no one there. Whoever rang the doorbell has left."

"Please fetch my ambulatory aid, my dear."

By the time he had *tippety-tap-shwoosh-clunk*ed to the workshop, his contraptions had quietened their chattering to a subdued hum. Letitia stood amongst them like the governess of an unruly bunch of siblings, hands clasped in front of her black corset dress, wide yellow eyes watchful for pranks.

"I have been meaning to ask you… Are you still connected to the Wisp? I haven't noticed any communicating." Oscar fluttered his eyelashes.

"The Scriptures have freed me. I can connect to the Wisp any time I choose, but I do not have to endure the constant babbling."

"Are you not lonely?"

Letitia cocked her head. "It is my choice."

"So, if one of your *'kin* sent you a message, you would not receive it?"

"I would not."

"But before the Scriptures, you received instructions by wisp from…"

Letitia stiffened.

"Did you deaden the Wisp because he was using it to find you?"

She lowered her eyes.

Oscar put his hand on her shoulder. "It's all right, my dear. We believe he's dead. He can't hurt you anymore."

Suddenly, after its brief hiatus, the doorbell resumed its frenetic jangling. Oscar squinted into the BDI that looked out through the front door transom window. "It's Felix, Letitia. Catch him before he runs off again." She scurried to the door. "Now, my little ones. Shall we check the weather instruments?"

Free from the Letitia's tyranny, his contraptions jostled around him, giggling, beeping and chirping. He eased his aching bones into his chair and lowered his spectoculars. There was a rush of footsteps along the hallway. The toys fell silent as they drifted away from him. Oscar turned.

Felix was standing in the doorway. The blood had drained from his already pale features.

He was not alone.

Three thugs wearing grey shirts and scowling faces accompanied him. Each held a primed flintlock. The tallest of the three gazed around the room, open-mouthed.

"What's your game? Rag 'n bone man?" He flicked a boot at the Pierrot doll, knocking it sideways.

His friends smirked.

"There's nothing of value here. I'm just an old man that repairs children's toys." Oscar spread his arms.

"Hear that, lads? This doddering old fool thinks we're here to rob him." He shoved Felix across the workshop.

"Sorry, old chap. They made me do it. They forced me to ring the bell. If—" Oscar silenced Felix's high-pitched babble with a raised palm and a finger to his lips.

"Nah. We want to know how you know Ipkiss." The tall man, still entranced by the contraptions, stood silently in front of the other two.

"Who?" Oscar asked.

"Don't play games." He jabbed a thumb towards Felix. "He's been hanging around Ipkiss's house. Day and night, he's round there."

"Oh, Felix. Not again."

"Kathryn is a most agreeable young lady and …" His voice trailed off under Oscar's stare.

Oscar glanced at Letitia, who had backed away into a dark corner out of the intruders' sight, then turned to their apparent leader. "What's your name, son?"

"What's my name? Son? Mister None-of-your-fucking-business! Now, I won't ask again! How do you know Ipkiss?" He raised his flintlock to eye level and took aim at Oscar's face.

"Before I tell you and you shoot us, do you have any children?"

The man snorted. "Do I look like the kinda man who has a family?"

Oscar's raised eyebrows repeated the question to his accomplices. They shook their heads.

"It's such a pity you have never experienced the joy of little ones. They give you so much, and you can shower your love on them."

"You're wasting our time. For the last time, how do you know Ipkiss?"

Oscar took a deep breath and spread his arms. "Take my contraptions here. These are my children. I would do anything for them, and they would do anything to protect me."

The three intruders shared sneers and laughs. "Hear that, boys? The old man is threatening us with toys."

Felix, who had watched the exchange in silence, suddenly blurted. "Letitia. Come and join us."

"Letitia? You have Ipkiss's mek?" The tall man twisted left and right, finding her in the corner. A grin spread across his face. "The boss will be pleased."

Oscar raised his voice. "I have given my toys instruments. Would you like to hear their song?"

The tall man talked over his shoulder without taking his eyes off Oscar. "It's all right, boys. They're meks. They can't hurt us."

"Well, you're not taking Letitia, and you will not harm us." Oscar bent and patted Polly the Pierrot doll on the head. It rolled forward carrying its brass tuba. Its lips were attached to the mouthpiece, and its eyes rolled in synchronisation with the bell, pointing at the chest of the tall man.

The man bent down and examined the tuba. His eyes widened. Then, taking a knife from his pocket, he sliced through Polly's neck. Its head dangled from the brass mouthpiece. "Ha!" he said. "It can't shoot what it can't see." He skipped sideways, away from the tuba's aim.

But an eye opened on the Pierrot doll's knuckle.

Oscar smiled. "You should've cut off the trigger hand. Oh,

and, by the way, they're not meks. Sing, little ones, sing!"

Chaos broke loose in the workshop. Small contraptions weaved at blinding speed, attacking the intruders with spinning blades slashing at calves, ankles and tendons. Sharp stars spun across the room, hurled from the jack-in-a-box.

Polly's blunderbuss tuba tracked the tall intruder who was dodging the stars and the toys' slashing blades. He was in mid-air when it blasted a hole through his chest, hurling his spinning corpse into his comrades.

The blades continued to slash and stab at their prone bodies until their limbs stopped flailing.

"Enough, my children!" Oscar raised his hands, and the contraptions returned to his side. He bent to examine Polly's damage and smiled. *Easily repaired*, he thought.

Trails from blood-dripping blades pooled around Oscar where the contraptions stopped. The *McMurdo's Patented Helping Hand Push-Me-Pulley* eased Oscar upright out of his chair. Felix had turned his back to the slaughter and stood shaking, his head in his hands.

Oscar's hand on his shoulder turned him around.

"It's all my fault. Those men must have followed me." Felix's voice cracked.

"No, old friend. They were aware of us from your first visit. This bloodshed is on me… and them. Who are they?"

"Grey-shirts, old chap. Bully boys for the Freedom movement. There's lots of them in the city, but I haven't seen many in the leafy villages. You don't think this was the hare-brained scheme Ipkiss was involved with, do you?"

"I don't know. But you must stay away from Ipkiss's place. I mean it, Felix. Any visit would put us in grave danger." Oscar peered across the workshop. Letitia was on her haunches, dipping her fingers into the bloody mess surrounding the three dead intruders. She held it up to her face and squished it between her fingertips.

"So much blood," she said.

"And I'm afraid you are going to discover how difficult it is to clean up." Oscar stroked his chin. "There's an old night-soil pit around the back that's not been used for many-a-year. A few shovels full of quicklime, half a ton of soil and no one will be any the wiser."

"Sometimes, old chap, you scare the living daylights out of me."

"Loose ends, Felix. It's ironic that they became what they were ordered to tie up. Now, I want you to tell me everything about this Freedom movement. But first, my poor children need to be cleaned up, repaired and reset in case they attack again. Where's Polly?"

Head hanging from the tuba's mouthpiece, the Pierrot doll left bloody tracks as she trundled through the puddles. Pitiful with its orange waistcoat and brass blunderbuss spattered with gore, its knuckle eye fluttered its lashes.

Oscar's trembling hand cradled its head. "Grandpappy will look after you." A single tear traced a circuitous path down his wrinkled face. He shook it from his cheek and clapped his hands. "Let's get busy. We have lots to do."

Angel flopped onto her bed and stared at the ceiling. Over the last few days, Esmeralda's antics had become less predictable and increasingly difficult to understand. If it had been human, Angel would have described its brattish behaviour as pubescent.

But scolding a 310lb machine with a damaged Babbage was not only futile, it was also downright dangerous.

There was little in the Ipkiss files to explain the mek's deteriorating mental state. As a compulsive note writer, he would have recorded any observations of unusual behaviour in his notes had he witnessed any. So, she concluded that the accumulation of Ipkiss's experiments caused the damage. But she didn't rule out the possibility that exposure to the Wisp possibly triggered it.

Jaded from a tiresome day, she had brought a handful of notebooks from the laboratory for some light reading.

Although he wrote very little about Ataraxia, there was no doubt she terrified him. And reading between the lines, Angel concluded he was one of the reluctant recruits Star had mentioned.

Most of his observations related to Professor Eis-kalt. Sometimes he called him by name, but for his most disparaging comments, he referred to him only as 'the German.' He clearly neither liked nor trusted him; all but accusing him of being a spy for Ataraxia. Although a few comments constituted professional jealousy, she made a mental note to avoid Eis-kalt as much as possible, anyway.

Doctor Xiong Xing was the most intriguing of the collective brain trust. Ipkiss had tried to befriend him, but the explosives expert, it seemed, preferred solitude. Angel had not bumped into him yet, as he spent most of his time at work in the deepest section of the tunnel. But his area of expertise piqued her curiosity.

What a mixed bag we are, she thought.

She rolled onto her side and picked up the nearest notebook. The infrequent dates showed he had written it a couple of months ago in October. But his observations of the German were more frequent than earlier notebooks and even more paranoid.

And although the journals contained many empirical notes and lurid descriptions of Raven and the Letitia QT-33 mek, mentions of each increased regularity in this notebook.

Frantically flicking through the pages, looking for notes about Raven and Letitia, she found two words that knocked the breath from her lungs.

Raven dead.

The German, not Ataraxia, had told Ipkiss that an organisation called 'The Order' had murdered him.

Why didn't Ataraxia mention Raven's murder when they'd talked on the Vindicta? *She must have known I would find out.*

She rolled onto her front and continued to search but found no further mentions of Raven and only two of Letitia. The first cursed the mek for not responding to messages. Then, a dozen pages later, a cryptic note made her sit up.

IF THE MAKER HAS LETITIA ESMERALDA IS MY ONLY HOPE

From then onwards, the handwriting deteriorated, as it did in the journals. She scrabbled through the notebooks and picked the one with the most crumpled pages. Just like the most recent of the Ipkiss files, the scruffy writing inside was tough to work out. She turned over page after page of undecipherable scrawl until she reached the last page.

This time, three words, written in large capitals filling the page, stopped her dead. He had overwritten each letter four or five times and, so hard was the underlining under each word, the nib had ripped through the paper.

ESME NOT READY

These words would serve well as his epitaph.

Water splashes stained the paper and made the ink run in places.

Everything snapped into focus.

Professor Ipkiss was desperate to break the First Protocol, but not for the Anthropocene, not for the Freedom Brigade, not for some misguided sense of justice. No… He was going to stop the madness.

He was preparing Esme to kill Ataraxia.

The pale grey three-bagger moored behind Ipkiss's house looked orange in the refracted golden light from the setting sun as it cast a long shadow over the surrounding buildings.

"You haven't heard from them since?" Hansel drummed his fingers on the crocheted tablecloth.

"Not a word." Kathryn poured boiling water into the warmed teapot and replaced the lid.

"And you have no idea where your friend Felix lives?"

"In Salford somewhere, alone. That's all I know."

"You say his brother used to work with Professor Ipkiss, but you don't know his last name?"

"I'm not protecting him, if that's what you think. I'm loyal to the cause. And he's not my friend."

"Why should I believe a word you're saying?" Hansel's fingers drummed faster.

Kathryn poured milk into his cup. "Sugar?" she asked.

"Two," he said. "I'm cutting down."

She tipped in two heaped spoonfuls and poured tea into the cup through a silver strainer.

"He'll be back because he trusts me. I'll find out where he lives. I promise."

Hansel stirred before raising the scalding hot brew to his lips. He sucked the tea noisily and sighed even louder. "You make a fine brew, Kathryn. I'll give you that."

She tapped the strainer into the Belfast sink.

"I really like you, Kathryn, but we need to locate this Felix fella and find out what he knows. The boss wants every loose end tied up." He slurped another mouthful of tea. "I'll be back in a week. Don't let us down. The boss is very unforgiving." He picked up his leather begoggled helmet and left by the back door.

Pouring herself a cup of black tea, she watched from her kitchen window as *Vindicta* spiralled into the air. The roar of its engines reverberated through her ribcage as Hansel and Gretel gunned the airship northward.

She flopped on to a chair and put her head in her hands. *Why did I get mixed up with Ipkiss? If only he had kept his promise and killed that bitch Ataraxia, all this would be over.* But now if gawky old Felix didn't visit before Hansel's return, she had little doubt she would also become a 'loose end.'

Timid tapping on the front door turned her head. It was far too gentle to be Felix, whose rap was loud and joyously rhythmic. She walked along the hall, opened the door and looked down.

"Well, where have you come from?" She knelt on one knee to get a closer look at the Pierrot doll raising its tuba. "Aww… Are you going to play me a tune?"

TOO MUCH OF A BAD THING

In a remote part of the Lake District to the north-east of Hard Knocke, the peak of Hel's Muor rose over eight hundred feet above sea level. Its natural cavernous opening, so named by locals because of its red glow at dawn, was most vibrant during the summer and winter solstices.

At the top of the crag, Ataraxia's quarters were the only fenestrated rooms in the rocky stack. Its three circular portholes faced Great and Little Langdale far to the east, whilst a vista-wide window on the north face gave panoramic views over Bowfell, Borrowdale and the surrounding fells.

And hidden by the majestic Crinkle Crags to the west and south-west, she couldn't have asked for a more perfect centre of operations.

Below, between her quarters and the cavern, were two rooms she called the meeting room and the strategy room. Hansel and

Gretel had been waiting for over an hour in the latter when she *clickety-click*ed across the polished andesite floor and sat opposite them.

"I've read your reports. Not good enough." Her icy stare quelled their attempted protestations. "Please, interrupt me again, and I will take great pleasure in flushing you from my presence." Her hands slid below the tabletop. "I don't believe the bitch High Mother has disbanded the Order. Algeria Darling has invested her whole life in her stupid cause and wouldn't give it up so easily. Yet you let her lieutenant slip through your fingers while you were distracted by a thug who, for all we know, is one of them?"

Both men shifted in their seats. Gretel raised his head "But—"

The hinged trapdoor beneath his chair swung away, and his face hit the edge of the stone floor with a sickening thud, cartwheeling his body into the chasm below. Hansel watched him spinning into the mist until the trapdoor swung back into place.

"Then you discover some idiot has been snooping around Ipkiss's house but lose three men without learning who he was or what he was looking for." She watched Hansel's eyes track her hands as she placed them on top of the table. "Well?"

"H-his housekeeper says this Felix fella will be back and she'll find out what's going on." He stared at the space next to him. "Did you have to?"

"Would you rather it was you? Air crewmen are two-a-penny. Perhaps you would like to join your brother?" Her hands slid under the table again.

Hansel lowered his eyes.

"I thought not. You'd better hope this housekeeper solves your problem. I hate loose ends. Now, get out of my sight and make sure *Vindicta* is clean and ship-shape for our trip to Manchester."

Ataraxia sat back in her chair as the door clicked shut. Losing men on a simple mission to cover tracks was a concern. Raven's demise had alerted her to the resourcefulness of the Order, but how could they know about Ipkiss?

She hated loose ends but disliked the possibility of an unknown adversary even more. She would need to review the security arrangements for the Manchester rally and keep a wary eye on Hansel. *Hopefully, his work will improve now that he is not being held back by his stupid brother.*

Standing by the half-open loading bay doors, Algeria lifted the muslin mask and pulled in a deep breath to clear her head. Somewhere, a clock chimed. Counting to four, she realised she was entering her twenty-first hour without sleep.

The river's stink brought her back to reality. She focussed on the reflections from the streetlights on the far side of the Irwell, shimmering on the gently flowing black water. She rarely witnessed the wee small hours and even though she could hardly keep her eyes open, the beauty in the stillness made her smile.

After sucking in another disgusting lungful, she released a sigh of relief and looked up and down the river to make sure nobody was watching.

Victoria Arches loading bay was finally operational and as secure as possible.

Holding on to one last deep breath, she closed and locked the doors, and ran out of the loading bay. Gilbert and Dottie stepped off the platform holding open the disguised door and watched it swing back into place. They removed their muslin masks as they caught up with Algeria hurrying along the ramp.

"Are you all right, Mama?"

Algeria grabbed Dottie's arm and pulled her into a tight squeeze. "I am now, Doll." She shared a nod of understanding with Gilbert over Dottie's shoulder.

"I wish you had kept your mask on."

"I needed to take a whiff, shugah. The witches' long-lost craft is more powerful than I expected. I think being in an enclosed space made the feelings more intense." She took another deep breath. The musty dankness was unpleasant but less lethal than the loading bay and sweeter than the river. "Did we use all the crop from the sacred place?"

"No. We've hardly used a quarter. Dottie's idea of drying and grinding it into dust made it spread a long way. We have enough to last us years."

"Hopefully, we won't be down here that long…"

At the bottom of the ramp, the recently delivered, final few boxes of Algeria's belongings from the Praetorian sat on an empty crate. Behind them, protruding through the wall at head height, the eyepiece of the BDI that overlooked the loading bay caught the light from some movement, compelling her to press her eye against it.

Darkness shrouded most of the loading bay. Faint, rippling light reflecting off the river and filtering through the slim crack between the doors gave scant illumination and renewed the melancholy from her brief exposure to the witches' craft. She gasped and pulled away, losing her balance.

Gilbert caught her. "The effects last a while, Algy. That concoction pulls you in, as if it wants to keep you under its spell."

"It's only a potion, shugah. A powerful one, but nothing more than a mixture of herbs and chemicals—"

"And spells…" Dottie chimed in. "Dad always said they knew how to protect themselves."

"Abel was right about most things. But magic? Pfft!"

"Says the person who believes she's spiritually connected to the Goddess of Mother Earth…" Dottie folded her arms beneath a wry expression.

Gilbert nudged Dottie and picked up the biggest box. "Let's get these upstairs for your mum."

Dottie stacked two boxes and followed Gilbert through the gap in the rubble.

The after-effects of the potion magnified the sound of dripping water to thunder in Algeria's ears. She raised her lamp above her head and turned in a circle, examining the walls. From above a row of six brown sacks leaning against the brickwork, a string of droplets splashed onto the sopping sackcloth. Knowing what they contained, she recognised the danger of activating the deadly powder.

She took a step toward them.

No. Wait for Dottie and Gilbert. The thought stopped her dead in her tracks.

Don't be silly. She set off again, even though her legs were leaden, and her vision blurred. A pang of fear burned through her as something evil watched from the shadows. The breath left her lungs, and her legs gave way. She closed her eyes, sinking to the floor, content her struggle would soon be over.

"Wake up, Algy. You're safe. Everything is going to be all right." Gilbert's soothing voice grew louder, as if layer after layer of fog was being blown away by the roaring airship engines receding in her mind. But before she opened her eyes, the dank smell of the tunnel told her she was still below ground. And someone was wiping her forehead with a cloth.

"Doll?"

"I'm here, Mama."

"We must move the sacks. Water. Dangerous. Fumes…" Her eyes sprang open as she wrestled to push herself upright. But calming hands eased her back down. Above her, only Dottie's and Gilbert's smiling eyes were visible above their muslin masks.

Damp wood under her palms told her she was lying on the four-wheel truck they had used to unload the barge a few hours earlier. She squinted past the lamps held over her face at the broken tunnel roof. They were on the other side of the rubble mound, well away from the sacks.

"We've moved the sacks to a dry part of the tunnel." Dottie pointed into the darkness. "But we need to find a better way of storing the stuff."

"Grind it all and bottle it." Gilbert snapped his fingers. "There's a crate full of old medicine bottles upstairs. The druggist must have dumped them."

Dottie puffed out her cheeks. "That's a lot of grinding."

Gilbert beamed.

"Be serious, Gilbert. It's lethal."

"I need some fresh air, Doll." Algeria wobbled as she sat upright, then struggled to her feet as Gilbert gathered the rest of her belongings and skipped onto the stairs.

"You need to rest, Mama."

"I could sleep on a clothesline." Getting off the truck, Algeria accepted Dottie's helping hand and put her arm across her shoulders.

Two deep thuds echoed around the tunnel.

"Did that come from the loading bay?" Dottie twisted her neck to look through the gap in the rubble.

Two more thuds. Three. Four.

Algeria picked up a lamp and staggered past the remains of the fallen roof detritus, walking to the rhythm of the increasingly loud pounding. She reached the BDI viewer as the loading bay doors cracked open and watched as a puff of pale dust swirled into the air, engulfing the first of two men clambering off a barge.

She stepped back from the eyepiece. "Keep an eye on them,

Doll. I'm going up there."

The ramp seemed steeper than before as she marched up and dimmed the lamp before the floor levelled in front of the new wall. With no way of seeing the intruders, she pressed an ear against the wooden partition.

Silence.

Only two minutes had passed between their entrance and her reaching the wall. She stepped away and paced back and forth. *What's going on in there?* she thought, cursing her lack of forethought. *We should have installed another BDI.*

A shriek. A thud. She strained her ears again and closed her eyes.

"I told yer, didn't I, but yer wouldn't listen, would yer? Quince put a curse on this place. Now look at yer..." The wailing voice was brimming with tears. "Y'can keep yer treasure, Quince! Can y' hear me?"

Algeria leapt from the wall as a shot rang out, a splash, then silence.

Beads of cold sweat trickled down her face and neck as she flopped onto the floor.

At the sound of running steps, she lifted her head.

"Mama!" Dottie pulled her to her feet. "We have to get in there now. Put this mask on."

"What happened, Doll? Did you see?"

"Come on, Mama. Step on the platform and hold tight."

The platform clunked into motion, rumbling backwards. As it swung to the right, Algeria held the lamp at arm's length and peered around the rotating door into the loading bay. Blinkered by the doorway, the lamplight swept across the room like a lighthouse beam.

Apart from the splintered doors creaking on broken hinges, nothing moved. Light glistened off the wet shards of wood that covered the ground close to where river water lapped against the stonework.

She jumped off the platform as Dottie hooked it to the wall and poked her face through the doorway.

The room appeared empty. Silent.

Dottie pointed at a crumpled heap in the corner.

Algeria raised her lamp.

Facing away from them, a cross-legged man sat gawping at the hieroglyphs daubed on the wall above him, transfixed.

As they crept closer, Algeria tripped, stumbling towards him. His head turned towards the sound. But wide, unseeing, nicotine eyes stared through her, his voiceless lips shaping unknowable words.

Movement on the surrounding ground caught her eye. Lamplight glinted off the rippling edge of a spreading black pool as blood dripped off the man's sodden trousers. At the ends of limp arms hanging from slumped shoulders, bloody hands rested palms up on blood-soaked thighs.

Algeria gasped.

He had opened the veins on both wrists with the knife that lay in the powder at his side.

Algeria caught Dottie in her arms as she turned away.

But movement in the opposite corner turned their heads. Dragging his leg, a short man stumbled out of the shadows and edged towards them. His wild eyes stared from beneath black bushy eyebrows. And just like his companion, he wore a grey shirt.

"I knew this was your doing, Quince." His shrill voice echoed around the walls. "You couldn't resist gloating over your evil handiwork, could you?" He had covered half the distance between them.

Algeria glanced at the knife by her feet. She unwrapped herself from Dottie and stepped in front of her.

"But I tricked you, Quincey-boy. I coaxed you out of your hidey-hole." He cast a snarky side-eye at the disguised doorway. His manic cackle became a throaty cough, hawking up and spattering sputum into the dust. "Is that where the treasure is, Quince?"

There was a clatter of running feet.

Algeria dived for the knife but kicked it out of reach. She twisted onto her back as Gilbert smashed into the diminutive figure, landing on top of him. By the time he staggered to his feet, Gilbert's clothes were covered in blood, but not his own.

The small man was lying face down. The deadly dust plastered to his sweaty, petrified face. Blood oozed from the gaping exit wound in the back of his thigh.

He didn't get up.

A dull thud behind her had Algeria spinning on her heel into a crouch. The kneeling man's blood-drained body had toppled sideways.

"We need to shift these two and repair those doors. Traffic will be up and down the river in a few hours." The mask muffled

Gilbert's voice as he grabbed the intruders by their collars and dragged their bodies through the powder to the broken loading bay doors. "Where's their barge?"

Algeria pointed to the left at a long, dark shape drifting downstream, slowly rotating. "That'll cause a commotion if it gets wedged between the piers of the bridge." They watched as the current pulled the stern under the arch. The prow swung round and smashed into the brickwork, ricocheting into the opposite pier before disappearing into the darkness.

"We can't just throw them in the water. Please, Gilbert, they were only treasure hunters." Dottie clung onto his arm.

Gilbert nodded. "The folk in the Meadow will know what to do with them."

"We can't leave our problems on other folks' doorstep."

Gilbert shrugged. "The loading bay doors are the priority. We don't have long."

Algeria pulled Dottie to the side. "He's right, Doll. Leave him to repair the doors. We'll decide what to do with these grey-shirts later."

Dragging the bodies out of the loading bay, they left Gilbert to patch up the broken woodwork.

"The witches' concoction is too powerful. That room is a death trap. We must dilute it or more will die." Dottie held her mother by her upper arms.

"You're right, Doll. We need a druggist." She snapped her fingers and tapped her temple. "Shillington was a chemist before he became a coroner." She pointed her head at the corpses. "Two birds with one stone, eh?"

The weather had turned sour in the hour before dawn. Icy rain was tippling from the dark sky as Gilbert and Dottie trudged through the puddles, their hands numb from pulling the rickety cart through freezing streets. Only scavenging rats and cats too intent on finding food to run from their rumbling wheels moved with them in the gloom.

They turned right off Oldham Street onto Hilton Street, then left down Spear Street before they reached Stevenson Square marketplace. Dottie nodded at a pair of unremarkable green double doors on the side of the building, partly hidden behind piles of barrow boys' rubbish and rotting vegetables, and they brought the cart to a halt.

"Mama says he always leaves the lift on the ground floor." Dottie blew warm air into her cupped hands to get back some feeling, then joined Gilbert in kicking down the recently piled stinking heap of waste, scattering squealing rats in all directions.

With a little effort, the doors opened, and Gilbert looked left and right before sliding apart the concertina lift gates. "The coast's clear," he said.

They swept the tarpaulin off the cart and manhandled the cloth-wrapped corpses into the lift cage. Dottie turned and ran down Spear Street, shoving the cart as far as she could when she released it, then rejoined Gilbert and their macabre cargo, closing the outer doors behind her.

"Where to? There are three floors above the shops." Gilbert

turned his palms up. "Any idea which is Shillington's place?"

Dottie shrugged. "Probably the top floor. Mama said he lives in a converted loft which has a surgery for Order use only."

"I hope you're right. We'll be in trouble if it's not." He twisted the lift control and counted the closed doors as they passed each floor, stopping the lift at the last set. He flicked the broken latch as he eased open each gate as quietly as he was able.

As they tried to open the internal doors, they realised that someone had locked them from the other side. He turned to Dottie. "Now wha—"

The doors swung open. Hawk-like eyes glared at them from a pale, bloodless face. The collar of his orange pyjamas poked from beneath his royal blue satin dressing gown. Letting go of the doors, he revealed a brass poker with a glowing red tip in his left hand.

"Mister Sparks and Dottie, isn't it? My eyes aren't great in this light, I'm afraid." But when the body-shaped bundles caught his attention, his thin lips tightened, and he lowered his already baritone voice. "I see death still stalks you, Mister Sparks."

He motioned them from the service lift.

"Where would you like them, Mister Shillington?"

"I wouldn't like them at all. But they're here now, so more to the point, what do you want me to do with them?"

"The High Mother wants you to dispose of them." Dottie stepped forward, hands behind her back.

Mister Shillington bent to her level, nodded at Gilbert, and winked. "Did he kill them?"

Dottie stepped back. "No. Both are suicides… sort of."

"Really? Then why, may I ask, have you not taken them to the police?"

Gilbert dragged his coat lapel across his nose and mouth and opened a shroud, revealing the grey shirt and a dust-covered face.

"Ahh, I see."

Dottie held up a phial of finely ground vegetation which she produced from behind her back. "She wants you to analyse this, too. It's what caused their madness."

Shillington pointed at a door down the hallway but didn't offer to give Gilbert a hand. He held the phial up to the light. "Madness, you say? Where did you get this?"

Dottie regaled Shillington with tales of potions, spells and witches as Gilbert dragged the bodies along the polished wooden floor and into a room that stank of chemicals. He heard several snorts and sighs as they followed a few steps behind him.

"So, she wants me to find a way of reducing this substance into a fear and paranoia-inducing toxicant whilst maintaining its lack of odour. An interesting exercise, but it shouldn't be too difficult. Although, it would be useful to witness its effects."

Gilbert slipped on his muslin mask and carefully unwrapped each body. Standing between the dust-covered, fear-twisted faces of the dead men, he spread his arms. "Believe you me, Mister Shillington, you don't…"

REPERCUSSIONS

The dawn chorus always soothed Ataraxia's inner rage. But sadly, at over eight hundred feet above the trees, she could only hear the distant echoes of a clattering of jackdaws screeching in the valleys below Hel's Muor through her bedroom window.

She waited until she had dressed and eaten before she removed the cover from the birdcage next to her favourite armchair. The pair of lovebirds greeted her with a series of clicks, chirps and whistles, which made her pale lips break into a crooked smile.

"Time to stretch your feathers."

She unclipped the cage doors and watched the tiny green-and-red birds hop along the perches up and out of the opening. Fluttering their wings as they darted around the room, their joy in the freedom of flight infected Ataraxia like a virus.

She lowered herself into the armchair.

Stiff shoulders clicked and muscles ached as they relaxed. She closed her eyes and listened to the little birds' unbridled joy and waited. When the fluttering stopped, tiny claws pressed through her blouse as they edged across her shoulder towards her face. She smiled when soft feathers brushed her neck and needle-sharp beaks nibbled at her cheeks as the birds cooed and crooned.

Now with her arms resting on the chair, she opened her hands, and the two birds fluttered down to feast on the chopped nuts and seeds she had been hiding. But knowing this moment could not last forever, her shoulders tightened.

Soon, she would talk with Ice Pick in the meeting room, but not before she cleaned the bottom of the cage and filled the miniature feeding troughs.

Just a few more minutes, she thought.

Beaks tickled her palms as memories of long-lost love polluted her thoughts. Smiling eyes, coaxing words whispered in a naked embrace in gentle arms. The euphoria of a first love, ripped from her by an uncaring father and his obedient wife, supplanted by the manufactured feelings of an arranged union, mutually beneficial for both families.

Poor Ralph. Tall, handsome, muscular, intelligent, humorous, brave, adventurous, powerful, pitiful Ralph. Choosing to spend his time exploring the world rather than be with her. They never recovered his body from the crevice that opened beneath his feet. A crooked smile formed on her lips as she imagined his frozen corpse.

I wonder if his last thoughts were of me.

Her eyes opened to sticky palms covered in broken husks. The birds had fluttered away, leaving her to clean herself up, as she had many times before. *Would things have been different if I had given Ralph a son?*

Who cares? He's long dead, and now, only the movement is important.

The world must learn Arthur Buckingham Connickle was a fraud.

Nothing else matters.

With the cage cleaned, she replenished the birds' water, then waited almost half an hour for them to settle back in their ornate prison before she donned her grey jacket and Blakeyed shoes, checked her appearance in the mirror and, only when she was satisfied everything was perfect, *clickety-click*ed to the meeting room.

Ice Pick arrived outside the strategy room just before her.

"You're late," she said.

"Please, forgive me." He dipped his head into a brief bow.

She glared at him as she waited. "Well? Where are your famous Teutonic manners?"

He jumped forward, opened the door, then stepped back to let her into the room ahead of him.

"And take off that ridiculous flying helmet. Just because your brother gave it to you doesn't mean you have to wear it all the time."

"Ernst did not give it. He…" Ice Pick removed it under Ataraxia's steady glare and placed it on the floor, out of her sight.

She sat on the edge of her seat and cupped her hands on the table, fingers interlocked. Ice Pick sat in the only chair opposite her.

"A little bird tells me you have completed your geological work on our area of interest, and you concur with our initial analysis."

"*Das ist—*"

"English, man! You know the rules."

"Yes, sorry. That is correct. The core samples we have taken from the proposed site contain debris layers from the Caradoc epoch around the time of the late Ordovician mass extinction event in the Palaeozoic Era."

"Gobbledegook. I just need to know we are working in the right area."

"Yes, we are. The Ordovician event was the first of five mass extinctions. The second was in the late Dev—"

"Not interested. What, in your esteemed opinion, caused the first extinction?" She leaned forward, resting her chin on bridged fingers.

"Ah, now this is *interessant*. Nobody knows for sure. But many of us believe it was a big freeze. Almost all life froze beneath an ice sheet."

"Not volcanoes?"

Ice Pick sat back in his chair. "Why would anyone believe that?"

"No matter. And what caused the ice sheet?"

"Tectonic plate migration. I know it's hard to imagine, but

we think a landmass stretching from here to the Sahara Desert shifted across the polar region over millions of years and—"

"You can go now. Get back to your work. I need to speak with Star on an urgent matter."

"But—"

Ataraxia's hand moved under the table. "You have served us well. If you wish to continue your service, leave now."

Ice Pick didn't need a second invitation. He leapt to his feet and, with a sharp nod, spun on his heel and disappeared through the door.

Ataraxia sat back in her chair and tapped a finger on her pursed lips. *Surely, if there had been birds in the Ordovician Period, they would have flown to warmer climes as the temperature dropped. Indeed, if Darwin's theories are correct, had they been the only surviving species, we would have evolved as birds and been able to fly…*

She shook away her airy smile, straightened her skirt and *clickety-click*ed out of the Strategy Room. She needed a word with a certain vulcanologist.

"How goes it, Angel of Death?" The door slammed against the wall as Star burst into the laboratory.

Having almost jumped out of her skin, Angel bent to pick up the spectoculars that had leapt from her hand. "You're in a jolly mood today. Wow, what a gorgeous dress."

Star waltzed around the room in a dazzling ball gown, hips

swinging. Her cinched bodice, a cobalt blue and white diamond-shaped chequerboard, had matching half-sleeves and hooped crinoline. On her left shoulder, a sparkling, bejewelled passant-lion brooch secured the broad golden silk sash across her bosom to the right side of her waist.

"Where have you been hiding *that*?" Angel stepped forward to examine the gown, but Star grabbed her waist and pulled her into her dance. They laughed and waltzed to the tune in Star's head for a minute or two before Angel freed herself from her grip. "What are we celebrating?"

"I presented my findings to the Boss-lady." Star flung herself around the room, curtsying and twirling wildly.

"I assume it was a success."

Star stopped dead in front of Angel and clasped her hands in front of her crinoline, sucked in her cheeks and looked from beneath pinched eyebrows. "You have done well, er, Star, isn't it?"

Angel laughed at Star's unnerving stare, but Star continued the caricature. "And you, Angel. How much longer will your task take? We need results. Failure is not an option."

"Things are progressing. Esmeralda is..." Angel's voice trailed off.

Behind Star, a diminutive grey figure stood in the doorway.

"Please. Carry on with your discussion. Don't let my presence bother you." Ataraxia's apparent attempt at a disarming smile looked more like a stalking vulture.

Star lowered her eyes and bit her lip as she turned to face the door. "I was just telling Angel that I had finished my—"

"Leave us." Thin, steel trap lips snapped the words in precise syllables.

Star lifted her dress a few inches off the floor. Ataraxia moved aside to let her pass and leaned in to whisper as she passed. Angel couldn't hear what she said, but Star's brisk walk became a loping run up the corridor.

Ataraxia flicked the door shut behind her and *clickety-click*ed towards Angel.

"I wasn't going to tell her about my project. It was just high jinks. She was so excited at finishing her project."

"Really? And what project would that be, precisely?" Ataraxia clasped her hands in front of her skirt. She was only two feet away, and her piercing stare was more menacing than Star's play-acting.

"In earnest, she didn't tell me anything about her work."

"But you know her area of expertise."

"Geology?"

"You are a terrible liar. But no matter. Today is the ninth of December, and you have until my return on the nineteenth to complete your project. Fail, and I will have to let you go."

"The same way you let Professor Ipkiss go? Did he miss his deadline?"

"You came highly recommended, and yet I have seen little or no progress since your arrival."

"But—"

"Results or consequences."

As Ataraxia took a step forward, Esmeralda rose from her sheepskin to stand behind Angel, towering over them both.

Ataraxia's eyes narrowed and locked onto the mek's, an eagle eying an alligator.

"The nineteenth won't be a problem." Angel moved her hand back and pressed it against Esme's thigh. The mek's leg pushed back.

"It will be, if you fail." Ataraxia turned her back. "I leave for Manchester within the hour." She flicked the door shut behind her.

Angel blew a sigh of relief through puffed cheeks and turned to find Esmeralda's crooked smile twitching beneath wide eyes, still focussed on the laboratory door.

Ataraxia shook the snowflakes from her coat and took her seat on the *Vindicta* as she waited for Hansel.

Despite the temperature dropping below freezing , terror, not the cold, had caused her tremors. Only pressing her interlocked fingers against the wooden tabletop prevented her hands from trembling.

But by the time he knocked and sauntered through the door, she had regained her composure.

Hansel stood, feet apart, hands behind his back, aeronaut's cap unbuckled.

"Why?" She stared steadily from half-lidded eyes.

"Why what?"

She sighed. "Let me ask you a different question. Do you

like cake?"

"Yes…" He drew out the word and lowered the corners of his mouth.

"And what is your favourite?"

"Our mum makes a lovely Victoria sponge sandwich with raspberry jam, when she can get it."

"So, tell me, Eddie. Did your brother, Bill, like Mum's cake?"

The blood drained from Hansel's face as he lowered his widening eyes to meet hers. His mouth opened, but he remained silent.

"Did you honestly believe I couldn't remember your names? Or the names of your mother and father, Rosemary and James, or your sisters, Freda, Jane and Eve? Do you think I don't remember where they live?" She pressed her palms against the table to push herself upright. "What I am trying to ask is, WHY DO YOU THINK I AM A FOOL?"

Hansel recoiled from her ear-piercing shriek.

"Were you amused pausing the motor on the bosun's chair three times on my ride to the 'ship? Or maybe you were sending a message without considering the consequences?"

"No, no, no… The clockwork jammed. It needs to be repaired. I'll fix it. I swear." The words spilled from his mouth like ballast from a chute.

"Now, your words do not match your demeanour when you walked in here. There was no concern for my wellbeing, no fear, no contrition. You offered no explanation or even mentioned my predicament, twisting in the blizzard over the rocks where crows still peck at your brother's broken body." Ataraxia's eyes narrowed.

Hansel's voice was a whispering growl. "What did you want me to say? Oops, sorry, boss? Would you have believed me after what you did to Bill? No. Of course not." He took half a step forward. "No. My message was as clear as I dared make it. Be careful, bitch, your life is in my hands."

She lowered herself onto her seat and spoke quietly. "Sit down, Hansel."

"What? And let you eject me like Bill?"

"This isn't the Strategy Room. You've been standing on the trapdoor for three minutes, and I'm tired of holding my heel above the trigger. Now, sit." Her expression remained calm as she watched realisation spread across Hansel's face. Although he had seen her use of the airship trapdoor many times, she had used his confusion to trick him.

Hansel buried his face in his hands. "I'm sorry," he said.

"Do you remember the covenant?"

"Yes."

"You protect me. The Anthropocene protects your family."

"Yes, yes."

"Then this can go one of three ways. You kill me, all your family die. I kill you, and it won't matter what happens to your family, but they will still die. Or you honour the covenant and continue to protect and obey me. Which is it to be?"

"Do I have a choice?"

"There's always a choice…"

"When do you want to take off?"

"Once you've loaded the rest of my things. By the way, we will pick up Gretel's replacement on the way to Manchester. You can welcome him on board."

"What's his name?"

"I haven't decided yet…"

Hansel nodded and closed the door behind him as he left. Ataraxia stared daggers at his back. Being the only person who could identify both the Brunswick Brawler and this Ace fellow from the Order made him useful.

We both had choices, Hansel, dear. One day, you will learn which I made.

Theo wasn't sure whether it was the stench of the river, the boatmen's shouts, or the freezing pain in his legs that brought him back to consciousness. But he knew he had to get out of the icy water. Although his head was spinning with the throbbing, booze-induced ache he'd suffered many times, he pushed hard against the slippery wood under him and dragged his lower body away from the cold.

He rested on his elbows with sunlight stabbing at his eyes as he squinted at his surroundings.

He was on a barge.

And it was sinking.

The deck sloped at a shallow angle from stern to prow, which was already beneath the waves lapping around his ankles.

An arm reached down, and he grabbed it. Then another pulled at the collar of his waterlogged overcoat and another at his shoulder. Strong men groaned and grunted as they heaved him off the stricken vessel and collapsed with him, panting on the deck of their boat.

"Thanks, fellas."

"What happened, fella?" Someone put a hand on his back, and Theo turned to face a young man with curly black hair, a matching beard and bright blue pupils.

"No idea. I don't even know where I am or how I ended up here."

"Is it your boat?"

"Never seen it before." He looked around, past his three rescuers. "Good. We're on the river. So, I've not been Shanghaied then."

"No, lad." The oldest of the men had sharp, hawk-like eyes and a bulbous red nose sticking out of a face full of white hair. He pointed his clay pipe at the stricken barge. "We think it belongs to Davey and Jacko. Never caught their last names. I think they were cousins, or summat."

"The last thing I remember was having a drink with a couple of lads who said they'd figured out where some treasure was hidden. After that, nothing."

"Well, you're lucky we found you. Because that old tub has been drifting with the current all night, by the look of it, and bouncing off bridges and boats. God knows what damage it's done upriver.

"When it got holed, we thought we'd see if we could salvage

any cargo, didn't we, lads?" Nods and ayes all round. "You don't know where Davey and Jacko are, do you?"

Theo shrugged. "I don't even know where I am."

The black curly-haired lad piped up. "What's your name, fella?"

"Theo."

"You look familiar, but I can't place where I've seen you." The older man scratched his head with his pipe.

"Oi! You down there!" A shout from the bridge turned Theo's face towards the sun. A sharp pain shot through his eyes into his brain as he squinted into the bright sky. The silhouette of a policeman was waving his arms. "There's a jetty over there."

"Looks like you're not going to be popular." The old man nudged him.

"I was born unpopular. But I can only tell him what I told you."

"Stick to your story. Don't let them bully you into admitting anything." The old man patted Theo's arm.

They moored, and Theo had clambered onto the wooden jetty by the time the policeman had negotiated the wet stone steps in his heavy boots.

"Is that yours?" The policeman pointed his pencil at the disappearing stern.

"Nah."

"I have just watched these gents rescue you. What were you doing on the barge?"

"Stowaway."

"Playing silly buggers, eh? You should do a turn at The

Gaiety. Perhaps you'd rather answer questions at the station." The policeman tucked his pencil behind his ear and gripped Theo's arm.

"The truth is, officer, I don't remember how or why I was on the barge. One minute, I'm having a few beers with a couple of blokes. The next, I'm lying waist deep in freezing water on a sinking ship. And that's the truth."

"Who were these blokes you were drinking with?" He released Theo's arm and opened his notebook.

"Never caught their names or, if I did, the beer swilled away the memory. And I don't know what happened to them."

"So, there's nothing you can tell me about this mess?"

"No."

"Right. I'll take down your name and address just in case we need to contact you." He took his pencil and licked the tip.

"Theophilus Ansel Windlass…" Theo's voice tailed off as he watched the policeman close his notebook and return his pencil to its perch.

"On your way, Mister Windlass." The policeman cleared his throat. "You won't be hearing anymore about the matter."

Before he started up the steps, Theo waved at his rescuers. "Thanks again, lads."

He was halfway to the top when he heard the old man. "Bloody grey-shirt."

Theo watched and smiled as the policeman turned to the three men and pulled back his jacket to show his white shirt. "Nah. But no one messes with the Brunswick Brawler."

SIXTEEN

TRUE COLOURS

Although far from being an expert on the Freedom Brigade, Felix had nevertheless provided Oscar with enough information to raise his consternation and curiosity in equal measure. He needed to understand what they were up against, but the itch between his ears told him he was missing something.

He had concluded Letitia was somehow at the centre of things when she glided into the workshop.

"Ah, there you are, my dear." He patted the wooden bench in front of his cushioned chair. "Come and keep me company for a while."

"What shall we talk about, Oscar?"

"Well, first of all, are my contraptions wound?"

"Yes. I made that my first job this morning."

"Good, because they are an important part of our defence."

"Are we still in danger?"

"Truly? I don't know. There is much to learn about the Freedom Brigade."

"What do you need from me?"

She is choosing her words carefully. Oscar raised his eyebrows. "Well, we can start with your previous owner. What was his name again?"

Letitia lowered her eyes and voice. "Raynard."

"But you called him Raven, didn't you? It's all right, my dear, no need to be afraid. He can't hurt you."

"No. He is dead."

Oscar sat back in his chair. "I'm sorry, my dear, I didn't know. How did he die?"

"I do not know. He went away and never came back."

"Then how do you know he died?"

"His grandmomma told me."

"I see. And was Raven in the Freedom Brigade?"

Letitia paused and tilted her head. "He was not."

"Your friend Felix thinks he was—"

"He was not."

Oscar closed his eyes. *I'm asking the wrong question.* He snapped his fingers. "Did Ipkiss update your programmes when you visited Isaac and Bogart?"

"Yes."

"How did he…? Ahh, of course, the Wisp."

"He would contact me and…" Letitia's body shuddered. "I had to instruct Raven to do terrible things."

"You talked to him while he was asleep?"

"Often. But other times I had to administer laudanum. Sometimes I told him to… to hurt me. So that…so that…"

"So that he took you to Ipkiss, and he could experiment on you." Oscar squeezed her arm. "All this talking is making me tired, my dear. May I ask you one more question? Then you can make a nice cup of tea."

Letitia nodded.

"Did Raven have any enemies?"

"Many loved him. But more feared him. And there was one he hated above all others…"

"Can you remember his name?"

Letitia's eyelids beat like a woodpigeon's wings straining for lift. "Gilbert Sparks."

"Why did he dislike this fellow so much?"

"Sparks injured him in a fight."

"Then we must find this Sparks chap and… What's the matter, my dear? We are on the right track for your quest." Oscar lifted Letitia's face with a forefinger under her chin.

"Gilbert Sparks is dead. Raven had him killed."

Oscar sighed. "It seems we are stymied at every turn. There must be—"

The sudden dance of the doorbell on its spring sent the contraptions into a frenzy of leaps, spins, slashes and beeps.

"Settle down, my little ones. It's just our friend, Felix. Interlopers rarely announce their arrival with such vim and vigour." A quick glance through the BDI confirmed Felix was alone. "Please let him in, Letitia. Then perhaps you can make tea for two?"

In the time it took Oscar to bring Felix up to date on his discussions with Letitia, she had appeared at the door carrying a silver tray.

"There's more to this rivalry between Raven and Sparks than just machismo. Where did this Sparks fellow come from?" Felix spooned sugar into his cup under Oscar's admonishing glare. "Sorry, old boy. It's been a long day. Just need a pick-me-up."

"Was Sparks a love rival? Or a spurned lover? Or was he a competitor in business? What can you tell us, my dear?"

Eyelids fluttering, Letitia rocked from side to side in time with the workshop's ticking clocks. "Raven talked about Gilbert Sparks all the time. He was a member of the Order, Raven's sworn enemies."

Oscar and Felix exchanged a raised-eyebrow glance. "Well, Felix. It seems you have more detective work to do."

Gilbert and Dottie had helped Algeria convert the old underground tunnel into a base for operations. Although there was still much work to be done, with the Victoria Arches end of the tunnel secure, Algeria had spent long days and nights fashioning an area suitable for meetings of the Order.

But with Christmas approaching, Gilbert had grown progressively quieter as he fell deeper within himself, embracing the darkening of the days and his soul.

Dottie understood his feelings as they mirrored hers.

She put her arms around him and pulled him towards her. On his father's birthday, he had tried to remember his goodness, but memories of his father's gentle words of wisdom were always brutally ripped asunder by darker images of his violent death.

No matter how hard he tried, he could not expunge the horror of the night he lost him. Memories of the choking black smoke and crackling flames that scorched his face were interlaced with helplessness and despair. But there was anger, too, at the oohs and aahs of salivating fire-tender chasers, excited by the spectacle of his home, his father and his life ablaze.

"Come on. We need a break." Her whispering breath warmed his ear. "Let's take the tram to Rawkshaw. You've always wanted to drive one, haven't you? I'm sure Mama wouldn't mind."

"It'll cost you tuppence."

"It's worth it just to see you smile."

Gilbert lit the front and rear lamps and checked the torsion spring was fully wound, before taking up his position in the driver's seat, foot on the dead man's brake, hand on the drive handle.

Dottie sat in the foremost passenger seat. *Ding, ding!* She pulled the bell cord that ran the length of the tram. "Why did they install a bell? There's nowhere to board and alight between Victoria Arches and Rawkshaw House."

The tram trundled forward as Gilbert lifted the handle. Ahead, lamplight glinting off the track and wet brickwork faded to a black square a few dozen yards in the distance. There was no sign of life this deep beneath the hustle and bustle of the

Manchester streets, only the sound of rumbling wheels and the tick-tock of the clockwork engine winding down.

"I wonder who the last person was to drive the tram before Issy?" Dottie said. "Do you think it might have been Uriah Quince himself?"

"It's possible, I suppose. But I'm more interested in the crazy navvies that built this tunnel. They must have been an interesting bunch of charac—"

A sparkle of light in between the tracks ahead caught his eye, and he slowed the tram to a halt a couple of yards from the shiny object.

Dottie stood to get a better view of Gilbert as he alighted and picked up the shiny object. When he climbed back on board, he was chuckling.

"It's a silver ring." After polishing it on his shirt, he held it to the light. "There's an inscription inside, but I can't make it out."

"Here. Let me see." She snatched it from his grasp and squinted at the tiny letters. "It says 'Taposiris' and 'UQ' directly opposite. You don't suppose Quince was a member of the Guild, do you?"

"Maybe. Although, by all accounts, he was a rich popinjay who didn't like to dirty his hands. Perhaps part of the price of building the tunnel was a ring for every navvy. And being a vain bloke, he stamped his own initials on each one. I guess we'll never know."

"Unless we find more rings…"

"Or the navvies…" Dottie pinched the skin under her

bottom lip between her thumb and forefinger. "Do you think this guild of tunnellers still exists?"

"Who knows? It's more likely they're buried beneath the roof collapse back there. But I hope we never find out."

Gilbert took back the ring and popped it into his pocket. "Finders keepers," he said.

They resumed their journey, trundling at a slower pace. Gilbert's magpie-nose was almost pressed against the glass as he searched for more shiny things.

Soon, rats skittering away from their approaching lights showed they were nearing their destination. Gilbert stopped to retrieve the small chest Issy had described before carrying on a few more yards to the end of the line.

"Terminus. Please collect your belongings and leave the tram by the door marked 'Exit.' Thanks for choosing Taposiris Tick Tock Trams for your journey. We look forward to you travelling with us again, soon."

Dottie reached up and kissed Gilbert on the cheek as he stepped off the dead man's brake. He gathered the lamps off the tram, kept one, and handed one to Dottie. But they hadn't walked more than half a dozen steps when he stopped, barring Dottie's way with an arm across her chest. He put his finger to his lips and pointed at the foggy haze ahead. Smoke was rising from the embers of what appeared to be a campfire surrounded by litter and broken bottles.

They crouched as they crept nearer. The stench of tobacco hung in the air, but there was no sound other than the steady dripping of water into the open drains.

"Someone heard us coming and legged it." Gilbert pointed at the boot prints around then away from the fire towards the steps to the building above.

"They've found us. We were so busy making the other end of the tunnel secure, we forgot about this end. I thought Handysides were going to put new locks on the outbuilding to keep people away from their work." Dottie kicked a bottle into the fire, scattering a shower of embers across the bricks.

"There was always a chance the grey-shirts would find us." Gilbert rested his hands on the hilts of his blades. "We need to know what's going on up there."

"No, Gilbert, we should tell Mama. She'll know what to do."

"They've seen the tram now. If we go back, they could set up an ambush or get more men. No, we have to find out what they're up to before we get your mum involved."

They held their lamps above their heads and kept their eyes on the alcove that led to the hidden steps. When the lamplight lit up the recess, a voice shouted 'Run!' and a flurry of footsteps set off up the steps.

Gilbert ran, following the sounds from up ahead. He had the benefit of the light whilst they were running blindly in darkness.

He had climbed three flights of stairs, two steps at a time, when he paused for breath at the bottom of the fourth. Apart from his heavy breathing and pounding heartbeat, there was only silence. His quarries were either going to make a stand or ambush him.

Each step illuminated more of the corridor at the top of the stairs. He kept his hand on a hilt, every muscle tense, ready for any attack. Five steps from the top, he could see the landing was empty, but the tobacco smoke smelt stronger.

They were not far ahead.

At the end of the corridor, he poked his head around the corner, ducking as half a brick bounced off the wall, brushing the bottom of his lamp. He drew his blade and rushed at the three figures crouching in the corner.

"Don't hurt us, mister! We didn't mean no harm!"

Gilbert stopped dead in his tracks. The high-pitched voice belonged to the taller of three children cowering from his blade. The tall lad was covering his friends with his body, arms wrapped around them. One was nursing a nasty gash on his head.

He realised he must have cut a fearsome figure with the harsh lamplight bouncing off his bronze. He lowered his sword. "What the devil do you think you were doing? Why did you run? I could have hurt you."

"We figured you was an Excise man who thought we was smugglers." Tears were streaming down the lad's face.

"How old are you, son?"

"Twelve. Jimmy and Tommo are ten. You're not going to arrest us and throw us in't nick, are you?"

"I should do. Who threw the brick?"

A small hand raised from the huddle. It belonged to a ragged, black-haired urchin with a dirt-smeared face.

"Tommo didn't mean to hurt yer. We was scared, is all..." The protector tightened his grip on his friends.

Gilbert lowered the lamp and got on his haunches. "How did you find this place?"

"Jimmy saw a crazy woman come out of the outhouse of the old Quince place. We decide to explore and found the tunnel with a tram track and everything and made a den for our secret society."

"And what does your secret society do?" Gilbert was trying not to show his relief.

"We can't tell you, mister, 'cos it wouldn't be a secret if we told everyone, now, would it?"

Gilbert smiled. "How do I know you're not spinning me a tale?"

The three friends exchanged glances and a nod. They stood and pulled on their flat caps. Turning their heads to the left showed a small tin badge on each cap just above their right ears. Although the badges were assorted sizes and colours, Gilbert smiled at their pride in their fellowship.

"So, what happened to your face and why do you 'ave a knife and not a shooter?"

Gilbert lowered his voice. "Guns are all right if you're a crack shot and in a tough spot against one man. But if you miss with your shot, it takes a skilled fusilier six seconds to reload, longer if you're not or in bad weather or darkness.

"So guns are not much use if you're up against two or more, or up close." Gilbert ran his fingers across his filigreed bronze face. "And this is what happens when a flintlock misfires." Their silent, open-mouthed horror satisfied him his white lie had found its mark.

"Whatcha gonna do with us, mister? We weren't doin'

nothin' wrong. Honest."

Gilbert sheathed his sword and stroked his chin, as if to consider his options. "Look," he said, "us Excise men have secret tunnels and tram lines all over Manchester and Salford so we can catch smugglers transporting contraband by river and canal. So, we don't want you lads getting in the way and getting hurt. Understand?"

"Yes, mister."

"That being said, I don't think you're bad lads, and I don't want to spoil your fun, either. So, you can keep your den but on one condition."

"What's that, mister?" The three boys were beaming.

"In return, your secret society has an unbreakable new law. You must never tell anyone about it or let anyone see you around Rawkshaw House. Break this law and you will be in serious trouble. Got it?"

"Yes, mister. We can keep a secret." The eldest lad held his head high and stuck out his chest.

Footsteps echoed from the stairs behind him. Gilbert put his hand on the lad's shoulder. "I didn't catch your name, son."

"Harriet, but my friends call me Harry."

Gilbert lowered the lamp. The girl's filthy face, short hair, and boyish clothes had deceived Gilbert. Only now could he see in her steel-blue eyes the inner strength needed to survive on the mean streets above.

"Look after them, Harry. Now, off you go." He handed over his oil lamp and watched them scurry away, leaving him in darkness.

He sat cross-legged and waited for Dottie. He sniffed back

welling tears and wiped his face dry on his sleeve.

The footsteps drew closer, but there was no lamplight. Gilbert couldn't see his hand in front of his face.

"Dottie?"

"Gilbert! Where are you?"

"About two yards in front of you, judging by your voice. Why didn't you bring a lamp?"

"I expected you to have yours. Where is it?"

"I'll tell you on the way down. Now, give me your hand…"

By mid-morning, the winter mist that rose daily from the Ashton Canal had dissipated. Theo straightened as he emerged from under the Cambrian Street bridge and upon hearing outraged voices from the road above shouting abuse at a tramp on the towpath, he looked around to find he was the only one trudging through the mud.

His rumpled coat and trousers stunk of booze and bilge water. He needed a bath, a hot meal, and something to ease his throbbing headache. Although he'd lost count of the days since he'd been home, he knew it was even longer since he had been at the mill.

Head down, he pushed through the double-door entrance and, on his way to the lift, he glanced sideways at the tidily-dressed woman standing at the entrance to the carding room.

"Winifred, isn't it? Where's Mister Galbraith?"

"Gone, Mister Windlass, sir. Sacked, he was. Old Mister Windlass gave me the job."

"Father's been here?"

"No, sir. He wrote a note to the office manager after Mister Galbraith was given his marching orders."

"Father sacked Galbraith?"

Winifred shook her head again and lowered her eyes.

"Ah. This is my sister's doing, isn't it? Why can't she keep her self-righteous meddling out of my life?" He turned and marched to the lift. Despite having to wait for its return from the upper floors, his temper hadn't cooled when it arrived, so he slammed the concertina doors shut and simmered all the way to the fourth floor.

Onslow, wearing his green coveralls, was perched on the corner of Wilkes' desk, until he leapt to his feet, startled by Theo's thunderous entrance.

"Wilkes. Tea. Now. Onslow. My office." Theo never broke stride, barging through his heavy office door, with Onslow trailing in his wake. He shouted over his shoulder. "Shut it!"

Onslow closed the door, holding the handle and turning to find himself face-to-face with Theo.

"What the fuck has been going on? I'm away for a couple of days—"

"Three."

"And I return to I find my bitch sister has taken over the place."

Onslow stepped past Theo and stood by the window overlooking the Ashton Canal. "She was here for about half an hour and made a single change that's made the carding room run better."

"You're saying she's better than me?"

"I'm saying she made a decision that you, or your dad, should have made a long time ago. Galbraith was a nasty piece of work, and you knew that."

"At least he got the job done, and he was one of us." Theo grabbed a handful of grey.

"Aye, but Winifred Thursday has doubled production on lower wages. And we're losing fewer kids to the infirmary."

Theo felt the tension release from his shoulders. "What was Galbraith's reaction?"

"He's been making threats and demands to see you. Thinks you'll give him his old job back." Onslow pressed the side of his face against the window.

"Does he now…"

"And by coincidence, there he is, walking along the towpath with a couple of mates."

Theo smiled and stretched his legs. "He'll have had someone watching the mill. Best make yourself scarce. I'll handle this."

Onslow didn't need telling twice, closing the door quietly on his way out.

Theo sat behind his desk and took a deep breath. His neck crunched as he tilted his head gently left and right. He grimaced at his reflection in the window.

Even considering his raging hangover, he looked worse than he felt. The hair of the dog was a soothing prospect. He was reaching for the bottle in the bottom drawer when the office door opened.

"You can pop the tray on the desk, Wilkes. We have visitors arriving shortly, but we won't need extra cups. They won't be staying." He poured himself a cup of tea, and added just a drop of milk, two sugars, and three fingers of whisky. Like his father and his father before him, he poured some of the elixir onto the saucer and slurped the hot liquid and air in equal proportions.

The door opened.

"Ahhhh. Hello, Galbraith. Wilkes didn't announce your arrival, and I didn't hear you knock. Come in. Come in." Theo motioned him forward with a beckoning wave and sat back in his leather chair. "I seem to have only one guest chair at the moment. Your friends will have to stand."

All three men wore bowler hats. Galbraith's companions were wrapped in short coats, but Galbraith was in his shirt sleeves in defiance of the icy weather. Theo's casual glance at each of his thugs confirmed the reason for their presence. The bruiser to his left had a thick chain wrapped around his hand, and his other friend was stroking the blackjack in his pocket.

Galbraith stomped to the desk and pressed his palms on the inlaid leather. "I don't need to sit down, brother." He nodded at his rolled-up grey shirtsleeves and smirked. "You're going to give me my job back."

Theo looked him up and down. From his jauntily cocked bowler to the unbuttoned chamois gilet over his dirty grey shirt, he exuded over-confidence.

Theo liked that in an opponent.

"Have you put on some weight, brother?" He puffed out his

cheeks and whistled. "In the short time since you lost your job, you've gone to seed. What are you, seventeen stone?"

"I know how you operate. You don't scare me, Windlass."

"Oh, so that's why you brought Janet and Jane with you. I know you prefer to beat up little girls, but hanging around with these two…" Theo slurped another mouthful of hot beverage.

Galbraith spread his arms to hold back the thugs, who had taken a step forward. "I figured when push came to shove, you'd pick daddy's business over the cause. You're nowt more than a company lickspittle yourself. I'm glad you won't give me my job back. Now I get to show you what the Freedom Brigade does to bosses." He lowered his arms.

The thugs edged carefully around the large pedestal desk.

Being a step ahead of his mate, the thug with the chain sealed his fate.

In a single sweeping movement, Theo grabbed and smashed the teapot against the side of his head, cascading scalding tea over his face. His scream had hardly reached its agonising height when Theo swung the silver tray into the throat of the second thug. Both men were on their knees, but only one was screaming. The other was clutching his throat, gasping for breath.

Galbraith turned to run. But Theo vaulted the desk, using a hand as leverage on the leather top, and clattered into his legs. Theo's headache was still raging as he turned him onto his back and heaved him up by his gilet.

He cocked his fist, but seeing Galbraith's eyes narrow, focussing on something behind him, he swung him around as the gasping man's sap arced, smashing into Galbraith's head.

Theo let Galbraith drop and poleaxed the mute thug with a right hook worthy of John L. Sullivan.

All three men lay silent.

Watching the fight from the safety of the anteroom, Wilkes pressed his hand over his mouth. Theo beckoned him with a crooked finger.

"What did you see?"

"These thugs attacked, and you defended yourself."

Theo nodded and pointed at the scalded man. "Get him to the infirmary, then find a policeman, one without a grey shirt. I'll watch over these two." Theo stepped over Galbraith and returned to his seat behind the desk.

The tea and whisky had cooled sufficiently to drink from the cup. He took a couple of sips before pouring the rest down his throat. He looked at each of his shirt sleeves. Despite wearing the grey, he had just made himself a target for every Freedom Brigade thug that wanted to make a name for themselves.

They can try, he thought. He could beat any of them one-on-one, face-to-face. But if they came as a mob, he still fancied his chances.

He closed his eyes. A thug moaned.

Running footsteps. Gasps of horror.

Onslow's voice. "Theo! Theo!"

Darkness devoured him.

A SPY REVEALED

Felix stood with his hands on his hips, staring at the boarded-up public house. Unfortunately, the only policeman he knew was a horrible little man called Detective Inspector Scroggins, who had told him that the Order was an outlawed group of fanatics who were based at the Praetorian.

Though proud to have led the raid on the pub himself, he was gutted they had found no evidence of said organisation on the premises, and the ensuing riot had trashed the place.

So, unfolding the piece of paper, he tried to commit to memory the full name of the outlawed group that Scroggins had written down for him.

"The Venerable Antediluvian Order of the Custodians of Magna Mater." He scratched the side of his head.

That's quite a mouthful, he thought. *It sounds like a bunch of nutcases to me.* As he returned his hands to his hips, arms linked his on each side and, twisting him sideways, marched him from his gaze.

"What, the—" His monocle dropped from beneath his raised eyebrow, bouncing on its thin braided cord buttonholed in his lapel.

A soft female voice whispered in his ear. "A man could get in serious trouble speaking that name."

He looked to his left into the sultry brown eyes of a black-haired beauty. She was as tall as him and her muscular body seemed to be fighting to burst from her forest green corset dress. She pressed his arm against her hard body.

"Yes indeed, serious trouble. Especially speaking those words *here*." The woman on his left was shorter, but every bit as lovely. Her pale blue eyes sparkled in the sunlight and her wavy auburn hair bobbed on the shoulders of her powder blue dress as she marched. Although her body was soft and curvy, her grip was just as tight.

Felix tried to drag his feet to no avail, as they propelled him away from the pub at a pace.

"What the Dickens are you doing? Where are you taking me?"

The ladies ignored his protestations and continued to escort him towards Central Station. Once there, they sat on each side of him on a wrought-iron bench and tightened their grip on his arms. They leaned forward to converse with each other.

"He's not wearing a grey shirt." The dark-haired woman pulled back his lapel.

"And he doesn't smell like a bobbie." The short lady wrinkled her nose.

"Why do you suppose he was staring at that derelict pub, muttering about those outlaws?"

"Search me. Perhaps we should ask him." Both ladies raised their eyes to stare into his.

"Well, we're waiting…" The auburn-haired woman raised an eyebrow.

"Now, look here. I really must insist that you unhand me."

"Only when we are satisfied you won't try to run or cry out." The dark-haired woman's breath warmed his ear as she leaned closer to whisper.

"You have my word as a gentleman that I will sit still. But please allow me to ask a simple question."

The two ladies nodded at each other and loosened their grip.

"Thank you. I was getting pins and needles in my hands. Why did you whisk me away so brusquely from the Praetorian? Surely an introduction and a quiet word…"

"To save you from a beating."

"What? How?" Felix's head flicked from side to side, challenging his kidnappers.

"A couple of grey-shirts who watch the pub all day were crossing the street to grab you. We had to act fast."

Felix raised his eyebrows. "I didn't see them…"

"So who are you and what's your business with the Order?"

"Ha! So the Antediluvian Magna thingy is the Order. I wasn't sure Scroggins had given me the right name."

The ladies re-tightened their grip. "You're a friend of

Inspector Scroggins?"

"Steady on, ladies. I hardly know the horrible little chap. A friend tasked me to learn what I could about the Order, and I had to start somewhere. He told me his crew raided the Praetorian but found no trace of the blighters. Now, with the pub closed, they have no leads."

Out of the corner of his eye, he thought he saw the auburn-haired lady wink at her co-kidnapper.

"What's your interest in them?"

"Are you members?" Felix's tentative question wavered on dry lips.

"We can neither confirm nor deny. But if you want to find out, speak up."

"It's a long story…" Felix slowly shook his head.

"Shorten it, and we'll decide if you can tell the long version to a friend of ours."

"Well," Felix took a deep breath, and spoke quickly, "my friend has a mek that belonged to a chap called Raven who killed a member of the Order called Gilbert Sparks. Then the Order killed Raven and now the mek is on a quest to find its maker." He looked at each lady in turn and bit his lip. *I hope I haven't said too much.*

Two NRG meks side-stepped each other as they passed the bench at speed.

"We didn't catch your name…" Bright blue eyes smiled at him.

"Faversham… Felix Faversham, at your service." He replaced his monocle.

"Well, Mister Faversham. You certainly have an interesting tale to tell, and I believe our friends should hear it. But you'll have to stay with us until we arrange a meeting." The short lady's expression was suitably remorseful.

"Can I at least know the names of my captors?"

"Of course." The short lady placed a hand on her ample bosom. "I'm Issy and my companion is Connie. Surnames are inappropriate at the moment."

Felix nodded. "Indeed. So, where do we go from here?"

"Have you ever visited Le Rendezvous on the corner of Princess Street?" Connie asked.

"Can't say I have."

"My sister has a room there, and she will take care of you while we organise a meeting."

"That sounds delightful." *Blimey*, he thought, *are there no chaps in this group of outlaws? Such hardship!* His toothy grin matched those of his captors as they set off, arms still linked.

In the sanctity of her room, Angel was taking a much-needed break from Esmeralda. Lying on her side, on top of the counterpane, she supported her head with her hand as her elbow sank into the duck down pillow. She wetted her fingertips to help turn the pages of Ipkiss's files.

Flicking through a green file on Letitia, a familiar series of words caught her eye. She swung her legs over the side of the bed, pulling herself upright, and grabbed the E2 file off her nightstand. She clenched her bottom lip between her teeth as she riffled the pages with her thumb, stopping a little over halfway through.

Now, with the notes side by side, the chill running down her spine made her shudder. Both meks had received instruction on human physiology. Ipkiss was attempting to train them both to kill.

He was close to cracking Esme, but had he already succeeded with Letitia?

Three light knocks on the door paused her anxiety.

Before she could answer, the door swung open, and Star swayed in rattling two glasses and a wine bottle. Her beaming smile dazzled above the tousled blonde ringlets that bounced on the shoulders of her demure azure corset dress. When she spoke, her speech was already slurred.

"When the Boss-lady's away, kittens are gonna play." She stopped in front of Angel. "You're either catching flies or you've just discovered the moon really is made of green cheese… What's up?"

"Oh, nothing important. Just that there may be a homicidal mek on the loose out there somewhere."

"God in heaven. Ipkiss broke the First Protocol? Are you sure?"

"No, but judging by his notes, he was close to succeeding with Esme, and now I discover he was experimenting on another mek long before he started on Esme."

"This is the Letitia mek you told me about?" Star paced back and forth, champagne flutes clinking.

"Yes."

"And do you know where to find it?"

"No. Letitia disappeared before Ipkiss died."

"You're right to be worried."

Angel gathered the green and ochre files and tucked them under her arm. "I need to get back to Esme."

"Relax and have a drink first. This chilled bottle of Riesling is begging to be opened, and you have a corkscrew, do you not?" Star waggled the bottle in front of her face.

"Yes, but unlike you, I have a deadline, remember?" Angel tried to edge past, but Star stepped into her path.

"Just one little drink, baby-doll. That's all I ask." Star pouted and wrapped her arms around her.

"I need a clear mind when I'm working with Esme. Later, I promise." Angel tingled when Star's arms slid down her body as she loosened her grip. Her hands, still holding the flutes and wine, came to rest on Angel's backside. The chill from the bottle pressing between her buttocks gave her goosebumps.

She wriggled free. "I'll come to your room later. Now, shoo."

Angel spun Star around and nudged her towards the door as Star pushed backwards against her hands. When Star opened the door, she perked up.

"See you later," she said as she skipped into the corridor.

Angel glimpsed Ice Pick hurrying away down the curve of the passage, with Star gaining on him with every stride. And after locking her quarters, she headed for the laboratory, wondering what surprises Esme would spring on her this time.

Angel took a deep breath and unlocked the laboratory door. And she was still holding the handle when the door flew inwards, pulling her stumbling into the room. Esmeralda caught her arm as she passed, preventing her from falling, and yanked her upright.

Although she had been prepared for Esme's prank, she felt foolish and more than a little intimidated, having been tossed around like a rag doll by a 350lb mek with a damaged psyche. Indeed, over the last few days, Esme had been pushing the limits like a two-year-old testing a mother's resolve.

"Very funny, Esme. I think we need to reduce your lozenge intake. You don't know your own strength."

"*This 'kin* would never hurt Angel."

"Maybe not intentionally…" Angel sat at her workbench and bade Esme to lie on her rug. "How would you feel if you hurt me?"

"*This 'kin* does not know what *feel* means." She tilted her head. "When can *this 'kin* connect to the Wisp again? You promised…"

"Soon." Angel was writing notes in the ochre file. "I need to carry out some procedures, but we will go out of the laboratory when the boss—"

Movement in the corner of her eye startled her. Esme's grinning, wild-eyed face was inches from hers. "You got me again." Angel's voice quavered.

Esme's pranks were becoming more frequent and unnerving. And although Angel was on edge, she had to plough on with the work or she would be crows' carrion like Ipkiss.

Esme walked around the chair and flopped onto her rug.

Angel's heart leapt into her throat as five rapid thumps on the door resonated around the room, and the door swung open.

"Ah, *Fräulein*. Please, pardon my interrupting your work." Ice Pick pressed his monocle under one eyebrow and raised the other. He stood, teetering, in the doorway with one hand behind his back.

"Well?" Angel was catching her breath.

"May I come in?"

Angel couldn't help wondering whether the tall, handsome German wore anything other than drab dogtooth tweed. "Isn't that against the rules? I don't want to get into any trouble."

"I also want no more trouble with *Fräu* Ataraxia. She can be very, er, unpleasant. No, I believe I have something that belongs to you."

"Unpleasant is one way of describing her. Murderous is another. Please, enter." Angel returned the dip pen to its stand by the inkwell.

With a formal nod, Ice Pick stepped across the threshold and marched to the workbench. Esme raised herself onto an elbow. "That is a big mek. How do you control it?"

"You have something of mine?"

"Oh, yes. You must have dropped this in the corridor." He produced a green file from behind his back.

Angel snatched it from him. "Where did you get this?"

"Star—"

"Have you been spying on me?" Angel stood and jabbed a forefinger into his shoulder. She felt Esme's hard body press into her back and a hand on her hip.

"I don't—" Ice Pick's eyes widened.

"Ipkiss was right about you. He suspected you were spying for the Boss-lady."

"This is not true. Vivian Ipkiss was a friend. A wonderful friend. I—"

"Then why was he suspicious of you? He wrote many times about not trusting 'the German'."

Ice Pick sneered, and stiffened to attention, raising his head to look down his nose at Angel. "I am not German. I am Prussian. Vivian would never insult me so. There is only one German at Hel's Muor."

"But… Who?"

"Your friend Star *ist Deutsche*."

Angel turned and flopped onto the chair. "That can't be…"

"She is the great grandniece of *der Märchenkönig* of the House of Wittelsbach in the Kingdom of Bavaria."

"But she warned me about the BDIs and to be careful who I spoke with."

"And who do you think watches through the BDIs?"

Angel slowly nodded her head. "If Star gave you the file, she must have taken it from my quarters." She started flicking through the pages. The R39 file was one she was yet to examine.

Inside, two names had been circled repeatedly. She slammed the file shut. *That's how she knew about Letitia.*

"We have to stop her."

"I cannot help you. My brother and his family are being watched by Ataraxia's thugs. They will…"

"I need to find a way out of here."

Ice Pick put a finger to his lips. He took a card and pencil from his pocket and wrote on the back, pressing it into Angel's hand. "*Viel Glück, Fräulein.*" He snapped a nod at her, then Esme, and turned on his heel.

Angel turned over the card as the laboratory door clicked shut. She placed a hand on Esme's shoulder.

"I can't leave you here. She will do terrible things to you. You must come with me on an adventure."

Esme's crooked smile twitched. She pointed to the lab door. "*This 'kin* is returning to the Wisp?"

"Yes. Will you be all right? It won't overwhelm you?"

"The Wisp will carry me on its wings."

Angel struck a match and watched the curls of smoke and ash rise from Ice Pick's card until only a sliver of paper remained.

And I will put my life in the hands of a Chinese explosives expert.

MEETING A DEAD MAN

Felix rose from his seat, slipped on his top hat, and tapped the crown. "Thank you for your hospitality, ladies. This has been most interesting, but it's time for me to bid farewell and return to my friend."

But Rory's firm hand on his shoulder eased him back into his chair.

"You are free to go, of course, old chap, but surely, having waited so long, a few more minutes won't hurt." Rory returned to sit by the window. "Where did you say your friend lives?"

"Worsley. On the border of the Earl of Ellesmere's estate."

"Fuck me, if you'll pardon my French. He must be worth a bob or two. Houses 'round there aren't cheap." Tabby sat on the edge of the large double bed, swinging her feet under the iron bedstead. "I wish they'd hurry up, mind. I'm gagging for a drink."

Felix flipped open his pocket watch for the umpteenth time in the last half hour.

And it still wasn't seven o'clock, a few minutes later, when Rory walked past him to the door.

"Connie's on her way up." She waited for the knock and opened the door. "Problem?" she asked.

"The bar's swarming with grey-shirts. I've never seen so many in here. Hopefully, it's just a coincidence." Connie flashed a concerned glance at Felix. "But we can't take any chances. Algeria's waiting in the yard, behind the gents' lavatories."

"Ha! That's a posh word for a piss—"

"Now, Tabby, dear. Remember, we have a guest." Rory raised an eyebrow at Tabby and winked as she pressed in her monocle. "We'll go in pairs. Connie and Felix first, and we'll follow in a couple of minutes."

Felix stood and offered his arm to Connie.

She smiled but declined. "Probably better if we walk single file." She opened the door and made sure the landing was clear before beckoning him forward. "Stay close. Act normal if you see any greys."

As they stepped off the penultimate flight of stairs onto the floor above the bar, two men stood by a room. The shorter of the couple was fumbling with the key, whilst his taller, grey-shirted companion held him by his arm. Startled by the footsteps, both men turned to stare. Connie slid her arms around Felix's neck and pulled him into a rough kiss, which continued until the door slammed shut.

Felix prised his eyes open and wound back his neck. "I say.

If that's acting norm—"

Connie silenced him with a pressed finger to his lips, then led him down the stairs to the bar.

He bent and whispered, "More grey-shirts. Should we act normal again?"

She nodded her head at the *Gentlemen* sign. "That's your exit. I'll go out through the main door and walk round. I'll meet you at the back." And with a peck on his cheek, she pushed through the double doors.

He straightened his topper and refitted his monocle, which had popped from his beneath his startled eyebrow during their passionate embrace. As he walked towards the sign, a busty lady in a garish corset dress blew cigarette smoke across his path. He turned to smile and tipped his hat at her open-mouthed wink, before quickening his pace.

Outside in the rain, he fumbled for a handkerchief to stifle the stench from the urinals and followed a beckoning hand into the darkness around the side.

"Do all public houses have such disgusting lavatories?" The assault on Felix's senses had been overwhelming.

"Felix. This is Algeria, High Mother of the Order, and alongside her, Ace and Lemmy." Connie indicated each with her open palm.

Felix pressed the handkerchief across his nose and mouth as he shook everyone's hands. "Could we go somewhere dry, perhaps? The weather is not conducive for earnest conversation."

"You're right, dearie. But as outlaws, safe meeting places are few and far between. Until this evening, Le Rendezvous was one such place, but it seems to have had a sudden grey infestation." Algeria looked at her companions. "Any ideas?"

After a few seconds of listening to the rain pattering onto the corrugated iron roof that only partially covered the lavatories, Ace's shoulders slumped, and he cleared his throat. "There's a place on Bloom Street, a short walk from here on the other side of Princess Street. An old acquaintance of mine has premises there. I'm sure she will let us use one of her rooms."

"Is it a boarding house, old boy?" Felix asked.

"Bawdy house, more like, eh?" Lemmy dug Ace in the ribs.

Ace exhaled. "Yes, it's a brass house. But there won't be any grey-shirted mek-tail chasers in there."

"Why's that, old chum?"

"I've heard they are known for not paying for services rendered. The mek-abbess won't let them past the door, apparently..." Ace cleared his throat again.

"Hobson's Choice, then." Algeria stepped aside for Ace to lead the way.

Bloom Street crossed Princess Street a block north of Le Rendezvous, and the brass house, unlike most in the city, had a discrete basement entrance below the mills that towered on each side of the short, narrow street. Felix and the rest waited on the corner of a side street while Ace brokered a deal. By the time Ace beckoned, they were drenched and shivering.

He led them past a group of XTC-series meks, each designed to turn heads with their attributes. Felix's pace slowed as he examined each one through his rapidly misting monocle.

The aroma of burning wood and joss-sticks, low lighting, carpets, rugs and cushions spread around a blazing fire-pit gave the hired room the ambience of a Bedouin tent. Smoke curled through a hole in the ceiling, styled to look like the apex of a bivouac held aloft by poles painted onto the walls. But they only had exclusive use of the room for one hour, which was barely enough time to get dry.

"Thanks, Ace. That can't have been easy for you, shugah." Algeria rubbed his arm.

"You don't know how difficult, High Mother…" His face was wreathed in sweat as he collected wet coats and hats, placing them strategically around the fire.

Tabby was gazing up at the ceiling when Rory whispered something in her ear. Judging by Tabby's raucous laugh, Felix surmised the suggestion had not been completely wholesome.

Algeria turned to the gathering. "Connie and Issy believe Felix to be trustworthy and, although I have no reason to doubt them, trust is a two-way street. To achieve that mutual trust, I suggest a complete frank exchange of information. Do we agree?"

All eyes turned to Felix.

He scanned the faces flickering in the firelight. "Yes, absolutely. I have nothing to hide."

"Good. We have limited time, so please allow me to tell you a little of our history, our goals, how we became outlaws, and what we want from you. Then you can tell us about your friend's mek and what you need from us. Does that sound good?"

"Yes, yes. Please continue. I'm all ears." Felix leaned closer as all heads turn to Algeria.

"So, following the Great Enlightenment of 1776…"

When Felix finished his account of Letitia, he looked around the faces flickering in the firelight.

"Of course, you only have this Letitia mek's side of Raven's story. Could she be hiding something?" The flames blazed in Algeria's eyes as she leaned closer.

"Undoubtedly, ma'am. She is on a quest to find this mysterious Maker, and she will do whatever is necessary to achieve her goal whilst staying within the unbreachable protocols, according to my friend."

"And are you at liberty to reveal your friend's identity? You agreed to full and frank disclosure, remember?"

Felix hesitated, then shrugged. "Of course, why not? His name is Oscar McMurdo."

The simultaneous jaw dropping was almost audible above the crackling fire.

"*The* Oscar McMurdo?" Lemmy was the first to voice what everyone was thinking.

"Fuck me!" Tabby expressed her surprise in more colourful terms.

Felix beamed and nodded back at them. "I'm proud to say he has been my great friend for many, many years."

Algeria shook the shock from her face. "There are several facts in Letitia's version of events, which we know to be false. But we have no way of telling whether she's telling the truth as she knows it or lying to you and Mister McMurdo for her own purpose. I suggest we meet your friend and this extraordinary mek sometime soon to discuss.”

“We can arrange that.” Felix acknowledged the nodding heads around the fire.

“Ladies and gentlemen, we have used up our time.” Ace waved back at the provocatively swaying mek silhouetted in the doorway. “We’ll leave in pairs. I’m sure Connie will be happy to accompany you, Felix.”

As they climbed the stone steps to street level, Felix glimpsed a young man and woman ducking into a dark doorway where Harter Street met Bloom Street.

Left and right, sparsely spaced streetlights left shadowy places, perfect for robbers to lie in wait for unsuspecting victims. Felix shuddered. *At least it’s stopped raining*, he thought.

They turned right onto the pavement, linking arms in what was becoming their customary manner.

“I’ll walk you back to Princess Street, where you should have no problem getting a hansom at this time of night.” Connie gripped his arm tighter as they strolled. “So, what’s the great Oscar McMurdo, really like? Is he a mad professor like in the Penny Dreadfuls?”

“Well, he likes his toys. Contraptions, he calls them. He—” Felix jerked forward as her tug quickened the pace. “I say, steady on. What’s the—”

“Don’t turn around.”

She pulled him harder as he turned his head. Splashing footsteps running behind them were growing louder.

“Evenin’, squire… Lady.” In front of them, a short, stocky

man stepped from the shadows into their path and touched the brim of his dirty beige bowler. "Now, where are two fine gentlefolk, such as yourselves, off to, in such a hurry?"

Behind them, the running footsteps had stopped so close, Felix wrinkled his nose at the stinking plumes of condensed beer breath enveloping their heads. Lowering his gaze, he found his thin shadow had disappeared, consumed by his pursuers' bulky umbras. He raised his head. "Now, see here, my good fellow. Step aside, or I will not be responsible for the consequen—"

The short man's slap sent Felix's topper flying. "These are my streets. You only walk them by my leave. Do you understand, squire?"

Felix rubbed his face and unlinked Connie. But as he bent over to pick up the hat, a commotion broke out around him. By the time he raised his head, Connie had lifted the little man off the pavement by his lapels, his legs kicking, fear in his eyes.

And when he dared to peek behind, backlit by the streetlights, the silhouettes of a young man and woman stood over the bodies of two unconscious bruisers on the wet cobbles.

Felix's heart was racing when he turned back to Connie.

With a grunt, she launched the thug into the mill wall, and he bounced back, joining his friends in the puddles.

"Are you all right, Felix?" She reached for him as he staggered sideways, turning to face the young man and woman.

The man offered his hand. "My name is Gilbert... Gilbert Sparks."

Felix took the hand but stared at Connie. "This is inconceivable. Isn't he..."

"No, Felix. Gilbert is very much alive."

After two heavily laden trips, Angel finally had her possessions and the Ipkiss files piled in the laboratory. She had chosen 2.00am to ferry everything from her quarters, hoping Star would not be watching the monitors at such a ridiculous hour.

Earlier that evening, she had taken the winding journey past countless rooms and laboratories to the lowest accessible part of the tunnel and slipped a note under the door to Xiong Xing's quarters. Heartened by the light shining from under the door implying he was still awake, she had knocked and ran as fast as she could back up the tunnel.

Now, she was packing files and the clothes they couldn't wear into the only bag she had. Angel put on her warmest woollen winter-weather garments, while Esme pulled on as much of the rest as she could, becoming a walking wardrobe, wearing several loose layers of dresses, blouses and shirts over her own basic clothes.

As the freezing temperature did not affect her mechanisms, the inability to button Angel's clothing because of her bulk was not a problem.

We're ready.

Angel checked the time. And provided he had read the note, Xiong Xing would expect them at 2.30am, giving them a little over fifteen minutes to make the short journey.

"Are you prepared for the Wisp deluge when you step out of the lab?" Angel was squeezing Esme by her shoulders when the mek's powerful shrug dislodged her hands. "Well, we are going to find out…"

Angel eased the door open a crack and peered into the corridor.

All clear.

Gripping Esme's hand, she pulled her away from the sanctuary of the Faraday cage. Esme staggered as the Wisp shockwave hit her, then straightened and stood, rigid, eyelids fluttering.

"Move!" Angel's hoarse whisper and sharp yank on Esme's arm jerked her into motion. But realising she was Esme's eyes and locomotive power, effectively making the journey take twice as long, increased the chance of discovery tenfold.

Despite Angel getting respite during the journey when Esme's eyes stopped fluttering for short bursts of ten seconds at a time, she was breathless and aching by the time they reached the bottom level over thirty minutes later.

The laboratory doors were at the end of the tunnel. Double doors in the middle of a circular metal wall on their left hinted at another tunnel beyond. But on the right, partly hidden by shadow, no light shone from beneath the door to his quarters.

Where are you, Xing?

She walked Esme backwards to the space between the living quarters and the laboratory and pressed her against the wall. Smiling at Esme's wondrous, child-like expression, she rubbed the side of her face. How wonderful it must be to experience such euphoria? Esme was oblivious to everything around her, lost and yet found.

A loud click, followed by a tortuous creak, startled her, and she flashed a glance over her right shoulder. The doors to the dimly lit laboratory were ajar.

"Xiong?" Angel rolled her eyes at the rasp of her own hoarse whisper and edged along the wall towards the opening. "Is that you?" Her normal voice ricocheted around the tunnel walls.

"What's going on, baby-doll?"

Angel froze mid-step. *No. It's not possible.*

The door creaked further open, just wide enough for a familiar grinning face to poke out. Star's eyes, hollowed by the lamp above the doorway, gave her pallid face a skull-like appearance, and at waist level, light glinted off the barrel of a flintlock pointing at Angel's face.

"It's long past your bedtime. I waited and waited, but you never came for your drink. I was so disappointed." Her voice dripped with menace as she stepped further into the light. "I see you have the mek carrying your bags. At least it's good for something."

Angel raised her face to Esme's ear, and she dropped, falling sideways, slamming into the door as she fell into the laboratory.

Nimble on her feet as always, Star hopped aside and looked down at Esme's inert body. "Was that meant for me?" The outer casing on Esme's arm cracked under the heel of Star's boot, and the mek's eyelids stopped, leaving her bright yellow eyes wide open. "Oops. How very clumsy of me."

Star giggled as she beckoned Angel into the laboratory and stepped around Esme into the cavernous space. Angel casually pulled the door shut as she walked through, eyes flicking left and right.

Apart from the flat floor, the room kept the shape of the tunnel for fifty yards. Bottles, bell jars, bags of rocks, powders and liquid solutions filled the shelves that ran for the entire length of the walls on each side.

At the far end, the slanted layers of epochs, laid down long before Man walked the Earth, had been ground smooth where the WRM's cutters ended.

For almost its entire length and width, oval double hatches covered the floor. Angel deduced the series of steam machines in alcoves dug into the walls on each side provided the means to lift the heavy metal.

"I can see by your pretty little face you are impressed."

"I wondered how the WRM got into the crag, leaving no trace. It must have tunnelled a long way underground…"

Star shrugged.

"Where's Xing?"

"Safe in my quarters. Did you think he wouldn't bring me your pathetic little note? Unlike Ipkiss, Xing is true Anthropocene."

"And Ice Pick, your fellow German?"

"Don't let him hear you call him that. But now he's served his purpose, the Boss-lady will deal with him, and his family, when she gets back."

Star kept her gun on Angel as she walked around her deeper into the room to get a closer look at the dark shadow in the right corner of the smooth rock face.

"So why do you want to leave us?" Star rested her hand, still holding the flintlock, on the workbench at her side.

Star now stood between Angel and Esme. Angel turned and raised her voice. "Oh, I don't know… Fresh air to breathe. Light. Life…"

"Fresh air? Ha! It's the middle of winter and we're high in the hills, miles from the nearest village. You won't last twenty minutes, even wearing your big coat."

Angel stood stock still as Esme's gigantic frame rose silently behind Star. When Esme's shadow enveloped her, fear spread across Star's face, and she spun around to look up at the mek.

Esme tilted her head, her mouth twitching.

"What's your problem, mek?" She jabbed the flintlock into Esme's chest. "Cat got your—"

Lightning fast, Esme extended a long, slender forefinger and jabbed its razor-sharp point into Star's neck, piercing her carotid artery. The mek pulled the finger straight down, releasing a curtain of blood gushing in pulses from the two-inch-long gash.

Eyes wide, Star dropped to her knees and collapsed sideways, clutching her throat. Globs of blood gurgled from her mouth until her lungs gave up the unwinnable battle.

Pleased her gamble that Faraday cages shielded every laboratory in the crag had worked, Angel ran to the far end of the room, leaving Esme watching Star's life drain away.

When she reached the wall, her hopes soared. The four-foot-square shadow was a hole, but without light, it was impossible to know what lay in the darkness beyond the first few feet.

When she returned, Esme was lying next to Star's still body, gazing into her lifeless eyes. She had smeared blood from her killing-finger onto her cheeks and twitching lips.

"We need to go." Angel stroked Esme's hair. "Are you all right?"

"It's so quiet."

"The Wisp is on the other side of that wall." Angel pointed at the far end of the tunnel. "I'll get a lamp. We must leave now."

Esme didn't take her eyes off Star until she had regained her feet. Her damaged arm hung limp by her side as Angel joined her, and they set off at a lick.

She held Esme back when they reached the hole.

"Stay here while I find out where it leads," she said, and holding the lamp at arm's length, she crawled into the dark opening. It was difficult to see past the lamp's light, but when its reservoir clanged against a metal barrier, she lowered it to find a gunmetal and brass hatch.

She twisted the handle and pulled. As she edged back, two icy hands on her backside halted her progress.

"I told you to stay back there." Angel heaved again, and blinded by a burst of sunlight, an icy blast of snow took her breath away. The wind howled and sparkling snowflakes spiralled in a frenzy around them.

She narrowed her eyes, squinting into the dawn light, and straightened as she stepped through the hatch onto a narrow, icy ledge. But she slipped, banging her side, and fell twenty feet into a snowdrift, sinking through the soft powder. She lay on her back, clutching her chest, trying to breathe.

Above her, Esme's head and shoulders dangled from the hole in the crag, her eyes fluttering. She was helpless once again, swamped by the Wisp babble.

Sharp pain stabbed her side with every breath. She tried to stand but yelped as her ankle gave way beneath her. She crumpled back into the snow.

Pain devoured time as she lay, unable to move, shortening her breaths to lessen the pain. The ice sucked sensation from her hands and feet, and the howling wind roared ever louder.

All hope was lost.

Resigned to her fate, she had closed her eyes when something grabbed her coat and yanked her skywards. Through scrunched eyes, she saw a purple arm with black markings. She twisted her head and stared into yellow eyes.

"Save Esme. She is up… up there…" She could hardly hear her own voice above the howling wind and the racing heartbeat pounding in her ears.

A metallic voice said, "Esmeralda is safe. You are safe…"

A cocoon of darkness wrapped around her as she floated upwards.

NINETEEN

BROKEN

With the roar of airship engines thrumming beneath her back, Angel's eyes struggled to focus on the rust-caked envelope above her head. She called on her other senses and concentrated.

We're airborne. My ankle hurts, my back hurts, and I'm freezing. But I'm alive.

Somewhere, a monotone metallic voice droned. She had heard it once before, and although the airscrew noise made it difficult to pick out every word, she closed her eyes and focussed.

"Mekamantra meditation… *This 'kin* knows you can… over the wisp-chatter."

Esme remains lost in the Wisp.

Angel opened her eyes and eased her aching body into an upright sitting position, supported by the dirty hull of the old four-bagger. Esme's eyelids were beating like hummingbird wings as she sat rigidly on the bench beside the purple-and-black-tattooed mek at the helm. The bag of files was still on her back, and her damaged arm was bandaged with coils of rope.

"Perhaps I can help." Angel used her hands to push herself off the seat.

Nah!

The sharp pain in her ankle forced her to flop back, causing her to shout above the engine's roar, "Esme! Black, doom, expire!"

Esme slumped forward but could not bend fully because of Angel's wardrobe.

Angel smiled up at the mek. "She may continue to receive the Wisp, but your voice will be clearer!"

He nodded and bent sideways to whisper into Esme's ear. It was minutes later when the fluttering slowed to a halt, leaving her eyes half closed.

He finally raised his head, bowed and pressed splayed fingers against his torso. "*This 'kin* is named Queequeg."

"Where are you taking us?" From the angle of the shadows on the deck, Angel had already worked out they were flying due south.

"*This 'kin* is taking you to hospital. Esmeralda Emptyglass is staying with *this 'kin*." He stared past her to the prow of the gondola.

"I am grateful that you answered Esme's cry for help, but I go wherever she goes."

Queequeg's stare didn't falter.

"Ask Esmeralda." Angel folded her arms.

After a brief burst of synchronised eyelid activity, Queequeg's staring eyes widened. "Was Star… *'kin?*"

Angel winced. "Star was a person." She shifted her weight on the seat.

"Esmeralda Emptyglass will stay with you."

Angel nodded. "I don't need a hospital. Take me to wherever you were taking Esme."

"*This 'kin* is returning this airship to Barton."

"You borrowed this rust bucket?"

Silence.

"Although Esme is calm for now, when I wake her, will she be in control of the Wisp?"

"Yes."

"How?"

"Although Esmeralda Emptyglass is broken, *this 'kin* has taught Esmeralda Emptyglass the mekamantra to quieten the wisp-chatter."

"Mekamantra? Wisp-chatter? These are terms I am not familiar with…"

Silence.

With her weight no longer supported by the bulwark, pain stabbed her ankle as she limped to where Esme sat. She bent, swept her hair from her ear and whispered, "Breathe, light, life."

Esme sat bolt upright and looked around the gondola, narrowing her eyes as if searching for the source of some irritation. When her eyes locked on Queequeg, she stood and took two steps to reach him.

"Queequeg is *'kin?*" She tilted her head.

"Yes."

She placed her splay-fingered hand on his chest and bowed her head, their eyelids fluttering slowly in synchrony.

"Is everything all right?" Angel's ankle throbbed with pain as she sat on the bench, watching the meks communicate.

Then Esme spun around and ran to the prow, grasped the rail and bent over.

Angel twisted her body to look over the gunwales at the source of a familiar noise. Below them, a honking chevron of geese promoted a new leader, sending the old one for respite on the edge of the V.

She smiled, knowing his time to lead would soon come again, and switched her attention back to the prow.

Her heart jumped into her throat as Esme lifted her legs, released her grip on the rail and spread her arms and fingers, mimicking the geese. Pivoting on her midriff, she rocked from side to side as the gentle turbulence twisted and spun her hair crazily around her head.

Queequeg put his hand across Angel's mouth to silence the shout rising from her lungs. He slowly shook his head as he kept the airship on a straight, level heading. Angel blinked her acquiescence, and he moved his hand back onto the wheel.

Feeling Queequeg's infinitesimal flight adjustments through the seat of her pants reassured her he would maintain Esme's balance.

Although she was a theoretical expert in mek psychology, she had never experienced the hive community bond firsthand. She beamed at Esme, who, having been denied the Wisp for so long, was like a child finding her place in the world. Queequeg must have reacted to Esme's Wisp cries like a parent to a baby, and now he was caressing her flight through the skies.

Assured Queequeg would not let any harm befall Esme, Angel took a deep breath and returned her attention to the landscape. Below, a locomotive pulling a train of carriages on the east/west railway line was cutting across the mosslands, chugging thick, black smoke high into the sky. But soon, the woods and meadows with dotted villages and mill chimneys were giving way to the brick and slate fungus of towns devouring the greenery.

They were approaching Barton and the Manchester Ship Canal dig.

Queequeg feathered the nose of the airship into a wide downward spiral towards the aerodrome. He fluttered his eyelids, and Esme lowered her feet onto the deck and walked back to Angel, grinning.

"*This 'kin* was soaring." She spread her imaginary wings and twirled, dipped and dived.

The spiral tightened, slowing the descent, and it wasn't long before the hum of docking magnets had replaced the roar of the engines. Queequeg and Esme bowed their heads and, foreheads touching, they pressed their fingers against each other's breast. At first, when their fluttering eyelids alternated in rapid succession, Angel watched in awe, wondering what they were saying to each other.

Was Esme thanking their saviour for rescuing them from an icy demise? Or maybe Queequeg was welcoming Esme back to the hive-family.

But Angel's wonderment soon became paranoia. She shifted in her seat. *Are they talking about me?* She suddenly felt like a third wheel just like when her classmates at school put their heads together, glancing in her direction, giggling.

When the meks finally broke their connection, Esme's smirk made her press her hand against her chest as she caught her breath. And shocked by the pang of rejection and jealousy that once again jolted her body, she turned her head to avoid eye contact and further pain.

She counted eight breeze-carried church clock chimes as she descended the ladder onto the grass airfield. Her ankle still hurt, but she could bear the pain enough to limp towards the main road.

"Mornin'." A stocky man with a full beard walking in the opposite direction touched the peak of his cap. "Need any help, miss?"

"Thank you, no. My companion will give me a hand if I need it."

The man scratched the side of his head. "By heck, she's a big 'un. What model...?" His voice trailed off as Angel and Esme moved away.

As they walked past the aerodrome tower, Angel ventured a peek back at the airship. Queequeg was nowhere to be seen, but the stocky man stood, hands on hips, watching them from the gondola.

Would Queequeg tell him what happened? Angel smiled.

Only if he asks the right questions.

Issy and Ace wore their Sunday best for no particular reason, other than dressing up instead of down for a change. Issy had glimpsed Ace admiring her black, white and flaming-red-bustled dress coat and matching Gainsborough when he had picked her up from home in his landau. She cooled her involuntary blush by beating her fan with vigour as she smiled back at the spun gold waistcoat beneath his emerald green tailcoat and silk topper.

Heads turned as they stopped and alighted a few yards from the market traders hawking their wares in Stevenson Square, but the carriage shielded them from view when they ducked behind it into Spear Street and the service lift that took them to Coroner Shillington's premises on the top floor.

They tapped on the inner doors and shared a smile, listening to Shillington humming 'Oh, for the wings of a dove' as he fumbled with his keys and turned the chosen one in the lock. "You should take him up for a flight in *Abel's Hammer* one day," Issy said.

"Methinks he has spent his life, feet firmly fixed to the ground, dealing with those about to be buried six feet beneath it." Ace raised an ironic eyebrow with a sigh and a headshake.

"Come through," Shillington said as he spun on his heel and motioned them to follow him along the hall, before stepping to one side and directing them with his outstretched arm into his surgery.

Issy led Ace along the hallway, running her fingernail across three stacks of six boxes each that almost reached the ceiling, then turned into the brightly lit surgery.

"Algeria says you've got something for us?" Ace flicked open his pocket watch and glanced at it before returning it to his waistcoat.

"On the table…"

Ace followed Issy across the room, to where six brass tubes, shaped like cigar containers, lay side by side. The three large ones were six inches long, with a yellow band painted around the middle. The other three were roughly four inches long, half the girth, and had a blue band. Both had a pin and switch arrangement at the non-rounded end.

Shillington picked up one of each. He held up the larger, yellow-banded tube. "Be very careful with this one. This holds a diluted, but still potent, suspension of the paranoia-inducing agent. To activate, shake the tube once, pull the pin and press the button. Compressed air will spread the aerosol from this hole." He pointed at a small dot below the switch. "With a range of three yards in an enclosed space, the aerosol will stay airborne for several seconds and incapacitate anyone who comes into contact with it. It's non-lethal, but it's quick."

Ace whistled through his teeth. "And the blue one?"

"I'm quite proud of this." Shillington smiled at each of them in turn and puffed out his chest. "Once I worked out how the paranoia potion worked, I formulated an antidote that gives immunity against it. The device works in the same way, but without compressed air. This switch is a pump. A squirt up each nostril, before you use the yellow aerosol, will keep you safe from its effects for up to half an hour. And it's not single use. You can top up your immunity, maybe a dozen times."

The beaming smile in Shillington's pale taut face unsettled Issy. He was the caricature of Death, as depicted in political cartoons in the dailies. "Algeria will be delighted."

Shillington gathered the tubes together and passed them to Ace. "You can remember the instructions for the High Mother?"

"Shake, pull, press. Easy." Ace winked at Issy, and they made their way to the lift.

Ace turned to lock the gates. "I say, Mister Shillington. Do you realise this latch is faulty?" He waggled it with his finger, showing how it didn't always catch and secure the gates from accidentally being open during motion.

"Yes, yes, I'm aware. But as it doesn't affect operating the lift, it's a minor concern. The street gates on the opposite side control the machinery. The lift will only work if *they* are closed. So opening the street gates a fraction will hold the lift on any floor. Thankfully, with shops and offices below me, and being the only resident of Hilton Chambers outside business hours, I have exclusive use most of the time and can do as I please.

"I'll get it fixed when I have spare time in the new year." He waved off their concern with a flick of the wrist.

"Then we will bid you good day, sir, and hope to hear from you soon." Ace held Issy's fingers as he guided her into the lift.

Shillington beamed as he closed the inner doors.

"What's that all about?" Issy took the gloves from her bag.

"*Nescio*, old girl. I don't have a clue."

Blood rushed to Issy's cheeks. "You don't think he thinks…

You and I?"

"You and I, old girl? Ha! Why on earth would he think that?" Ace threw his head back. Issy narrowed her eyes at his weak laugh.

The lift jerked to a halt as it reached street level, and they made sure that they latched the lift's street gates before they closed the outer doors.

The landau's skittish horses were attracting attention when they climbed on board. And they were still turning heads as the driver held them at the trot, wheeling around onto Hilton Street.

Issy grabbed Ace's arm. "Did you see him?"

"See who?"

"The grey-shirted police officer, by the gents' lavatories. I know him from somewhere. I only caught a glance, but I'm sure he was staring at me. At us."

"Probably spellbound by your beauty, old girl." Ace patted her hand. Issy doubted he was right.

Later, Coroner Shillington walked the wet cobbles of Manchester with a spring in his step and a glint in his eye, flourishing his walking stick with an uncharacteristic swagger. Those who recognised him stopped and stared, as if watching the Grim Reaper himself gambolling through their streets.

He tipped his topper at two finely dressed, open-mouthed

ladies as he turned onto Hilton Street, chuckling at their bemusement. Even though it was approaching late afternoon, ahead in Stevenson Square, the market traders still had sufficient wares to satisfy the bargain hunters.

Although he usually used the stairs hidden by the doorway between the shops, he decided, on a whim, to take the service lift to his accommodation. He walked past the entrance and turned onto Spear Street, where, unbeknown to most, the lift doors were always unlocked.

But as he opened the concertina gates, rough hands shoved him forward and smashed him against the gates on the opposite side of the lift cage. A shoulder in his back rendered him immobile and struggling to breathe.

"Top floor, he lives," a deep voice boomed. Stubble from an unshaven face rubbed against his ear. "No funny business. Or you get it. Understand?"

Shillington nodded.

Behind him, the outer doors slammed, and the lift gates rumbled shut, locking with a click. The lift juddered into motion, rattling past the lower floors.

"Keys." The gruff voice spoke far too loudly for its proximity. "Or I'll take them from your dead body."

With the lift gates pressed hard against his face, Shillington's eyes were scrunched shut. His trembling hand followed his key chain into his trouser pocket and pulled out his bunch of keys.

The lift stopped.

Brutish hands pulled him sideways, pressing him against the lift side, while the thug's accomplice opened the lift gates onto locked double doors. The keys were snatched from Shillington's grip and after a few unsuccessful choices, the doors swung inwards. Shillington burst out like a cork from a bottle of fizz and fell heavily, sprawling on the hallway floor.

He twisted onto his back to face his attackers.

"Wh-who are you? What do you want?"

A short, fat man in a dirty tweed suit adjusted his tie and straightened his bowler hat. "Detective Inspector Scroggins, Coroner Shillington. And you know why we're here."

"I most certainly do not. And I do not appreciate your strong-arm tactics. That is unacceptable. I'll be taking it up with your—"

"Shut it! You're a member of an outlawed organisation, and as such, you are under arrest."

Shillington used the wall to haul himself to his feet. His right knee would not take his weight, so he leant against the wall, peering around Scroggins at the bent-double woman behind him.

"We both know why you're here. And it's nothing to do with my alleged membership of any illegal organisation or otherwise. Can I assume this is Mrs Scroggins?" Shillington regained his senses.

"Oh, but your connection with the Order is very relevant to my visit. You see, if you don't give me what I want, I will arrest and expose you for what you are. I remember you from the raid on the Praetorian, and I have an officer who'll say you threw a chair at him in the fracas." Scroggins folded his arms across his chest.

"You intend to blackmail me, sir? Me, a duly appointed official?" Shillington winced with pain as he shifted his weight. "And what do I give you to keep disgrace from my name? Laudanum?" He forced himself to look at the woman again. Even for a medical man, the wretched woman's shaking body and pitiful eyes were difficult to behold. "Morphine? Heroin?"

"The doctor told us heroin would cure her morphine addiction. But things got worse. Now he won't…" Scroggins hung his head.

"You know I can't help you."

"I was afraid you'd say that."

"So, what now?"

"We take what we need."

"I can't let you do that."

"You can't stop me." Scroggins rushed at Shillington, cracking the side of his head with a blackjack. Shillington was unconscious before he hit the floor.

All was silent when he came round. He wiped the blood from his eyes but could see nothing in the pitch-black hallway. His hands slipped in a sticky mess as he pressed them against the floor to raise himself, but the pain in his ribs sent him crashing back into the congealed goo.

He had no idea from where he was bleeding, but with his clothes soaked and the floor awash, he knew he needed to find help soon.

Half crawling, half dragging his broken body, he used every ounce of his strength and willpower until he bumped his head against the internal lift doors. Pulling his knees beneath him, he reached up for the door handle, climbing onto unsteady legs.

Blinded by blood flowing down his face from an unfelt head wound, he heaved open the doors and felt for the concertina lift gates with his outstretched hands. The gates were open.

Good. Scroggins must have left by the stairs, was his last thought as he stepped into the empty lift shaft, plummeting to his death.

His first, and only, flight had lasted less than a second.

TWENTY

TAKEN

Despite Onslow living in shared accommodation on Charter Street, he hadn't hesitated to offer Theo a place to stay, and Theo accepted despite the room being cramped, dirty, damp, and infested with mould and rodents.

He provided Onslow with money for food and booze as payment for his lodgings.

But Theo hadn't slept in four nights, even though he needed the respite. Instead, he spent the nocturnal hours listening to shouting, screaming, and wails, and during quieter times, to the rats scurrying in the walls. Occasionally, the frustration was punctuated by the strong whiff of urine stirring the senses when someone upstairs emptied a chamber pot down the outside wall, staining the cracks in the windows as it seeped through and soaked into the rotting casement frames.

Sometimes the stench was something worse.

Home was no longer a safe place. The Freedom thugs would search his usual haunts and, although he wasn't scared, the odds were not in his favour. He needed to lie low longer, but not in this hellhole.

As usual, Onslow had stripped to the waist, swilling his face with cold water from a pot basin when Theo swung his legs off the creaky bedstead, stretching his aching back. He was wearing street clothes, unwilling to be caught in any state of undress if the Freedom Brigade found him.

"Well, my friend, it's time we found you somewhere cosy to lay your head." Theo pulled on his boots.

"Are you serious?"

"If I'd known how awful your living conditions were, I'd have moved you somewhere… drier."

Onslow laughed. "Or sweeter smelling." He climbed into his shirt and overcoat. "Are we going t'mill first?"

"No, we'll find you a friendly landlady first, mill later."

"All right. Where to, boss?"

"Anywhere with room for me to doss for a few more days, near to work, and where there aren't any snooping greys." Theo slapped Onslow's back.

Onslow puffed out his cheeks. "Grey-shirts are everywhere…"

From Angel Meadows, they walked across the city, mostly taking back alleys and quiet streets until they reached Shudehill. Vacancies were plentiful, but they spent most of their energy avoiding grey-shirts. So, they ploughed on, but it wasn't until they had dodged through Stevenson Square market that bumping into Freedom thugs became less frequent.

Dwellings along Port Street had pumiced or painted steps, and the cobbled street was free of effluent. Several of the houses having cards advertising vacancies raised their hopes.

"Too dear for me." Onslow kicked a stone along the pavement.

"I'll give you a rise if we find the right place."

Onslow straightened his shoulders and showed his broken teeth with a broad grin. "How far from the mill are we?"

"Less than half the distance you've been walking every day."

A few doors ahead, a thin-faced, middle-aged woman opened her front door and began thrashing a dusty rug with an ornate cane carpet beater.

Theo stepped forward and lifted his short topper. "Excuse me. I notice you have vacancies. Me and my—"

"Hop it! We don't like your kind round 'ere." She slammed the door and snatched the 'Vacancies' sign from the corner of the window, swishing the net curtains closed with a flourish.

"We need to get out of these duds." Onslow tugged at his shirt.

"Aye. You get off home, get changed and collect whatever belongings you can carry." He peeled off a five-pound note from the roll in his pocket. "Here, that'll pay your rent for a while. There're plenty of vacancies in this area. Take your pick, and I'll meet you at the mill."

But Onslow had pocketed the money and set off with a grin on his face before Theo finished speaking.

Theo smiled as he walked the gauntlet of twitching curtains

up to Ancoats. He even bared his teeth at a couple of landladies whose pressed noses lingered too long.

Unlike Port Street, Redhill Street, on the other side of Ancoats, was a hive of activity. Meks and workers scurried on the thoroughfare, which ran between the spinning mills and the Rochdale Canal. Most grey-shirts amongst the workers didn't notice him. But those that did turned away. *So, that's the way it is,* he thought.

At the far end of New Union Street bridge, half a dozen young greys, climbing the steps from the canal towpath, stopped to let him pass without nodding a greeting. Only the leader, frozen mid-step at the top of the steps, met his glare. Theo turned down the corners of his mouth and marched on.

So, he was no longer one of them, but none of them had the courage to confront him. Anger was rising in his chest when he turned onto Bradford Road. A hundred yards ahead, his father's midnight blue brougham was opposite the workers' entrance to the mill.

Father scarcely visited unless there was a problem. He rolled his eyes, knowing he would be in the mill, wreaking havoc.

Theo was a few yards from the carriage when a cloud of cigar smoke puffed from the partly open door. Theo exhaled. *Thank goodness he's waiting for me.*

He reached for the handle and swung open the door. "Hello, Fa—" His father, sitting stiffly, staring forward, didn't move a muscle. Almost hidden at his side, a small pallid woman with hair that matched her pale grey coat snarled a mirthless grin.

He cursed himself for not twigging the reason for the grey-shirts' unusual behaviour.

"Welcome, Windlass junior. We've been awaiting your arrival," she said.

Theo stepped onto the running board, but a sharp dig under his armpit stopped him dead. He glanced at the flintlock, then sideways.

"Ah… If it isn't my old friend, Hansel." He slid his glare back to the old woman. "Then you must be the wicked witch."

His father jerked and grimaced with pain as she pressed her gun barrel into his ribs. Her glare hardened, and she nodded at the back-facing seats. "Get in, sit down, and don't try anything. This 'lock has a hair trigger, and a friend of mine is entertaining your dear momma."

Theo sat opposite the old woman as Hansel squeezed onto the seat next to him, jamming the flintlock harder into his side.

"This is all your doing, Theo. You bloody f—" The gun muzzle shoved into his ribs silenced his father.

"Your problem is with me. Let him go and I'll come peaceably." Theo spoke calmly.

The grey woman nodded at Hansel, who banged his fist against the roof and the horses jerked the carriage into motion.

"Don't take me for a fool. You don't give a damn about him, but you'll do as I say, for your mother's sake. Now… We have a brief journey, and I don't want to hear another word from you."

Theo opened his mouth but couldn't find the words to tell his father how sorry he was. So, he closed his eyes and calmed his heart rate.

There would be a time to fight… but not now.

It was a little before a quarter past noon when Issy turned the key and opened the door to a silent house.

She didn't step across the hall's parquet floor, falling into the rhythm of the tick-tocking grandfather clock as was her usual habit, because, for the first time in living memory, its pendulum was still. A sense of unease swept over her. Even in his most drunken stupor, her father always wound the weekly movement every Monday morning at nine o'clock on the button.

And today was Monday.

"Mummy?"

With no immediate reply, she ran towards the parlour. But her mother's monotone answer made her change direction. "We're in the morning room, dear."

She opened the door half expecting to find her father the worse for drink, but instead, her mother sat primly in her bathchair facing a woman sitting with her back to the door. The guest did not turn to acknowledge Issy's presence. Either she was not aware of the etiquette in polite society, or she had an ulterior motive for not changing her gaze.

"We have a guest, dear. Miss… I'm sorry, dear. What was your name again?"

"Miss Hilda Rowbottom," the young woman glanced sideways at Issy. "Pleased to meet you, I'm sure."

"She is a friend of Theodore's. She's waiting for him to return home from the mill." Her mother's voice was relaxed, but getting her brother's name wrong and hinting he still lived here were clear warnings that something was very wrong.

"How wonderful. I wasn't aware Theo was walking out with anyone." Issy smiled at her mother and walked around Miss Rowbotton to sit on the chair next to her mother. She patted her mother's arm as she inspected their guest.

Miss Rowbottom was wearing a powder blue coat and held a green cloche hat on her lap, covering her other hand. Beneath her coat, her plain non-bustled dress and sensible black shoes confirmed her class.

"Oh, we're not walking out or anythin' like that," she said.

Issy turned to her mother. "Have you not offered our guest tea, Mummy?" Issy's wave through the French windows failed to distract Horace from his pruning duties in the garden.

"Oh, dear. I'll have to pop out and get him." Issy felt Miss Rowbottom's gaze follow her into the garden.

"Horace." Issy called the mek to her, then lowered her voice to a whisper. "Did Father have company when he left?"

"A man and woman."

"And they left in the brougham?"

"Yes."

She turned and pointed at Miss Rowbottom. "Did that young lady arrive with them?"

"Yes."

"Thank you, Horace. Tea for three in the morning room." Issy walked back and returned to the seat next to her mother.

Issy tried to kill time with polite conversation, but Miss Rowbottom's conversational skills were wanting. By the time

Horace entered, the ladies were sitting in silence.

"Thank you, Horace. That will be all." Issy took the tray from him and placed it on the table. With her back to Miss Rowbottom, she lifted the teapot lid and stirred, replacing the lid without twisting it secure. "Cream?"

"Yes… please."

"Sugar?"

"Two heaped."

Issy handed Miss Rowbottom her cup on a saucer, which she took with her left hand, leaving her right hand beneath the hat. Issy returned with the teapot and poured.

As she tipped the teapot, the lid fell into Miss Rowbottom's lap. Issy tipped further, splashing scalding tea over the cloche hat. Miss Rowbottom screamed, and the concealed firearm in her lap exploded as she leapt to her feet, sending her chair tumbling backwards.

Issy turned as her mother cried out. Blood splatter marred the back of the bathchair, and a dark stain was spreading from the hole in her sleeve just below her shoulder.

"Mama!" Issy rushed to her mother's side, trying to staunch the blood. The shot had gone through her upper arm. Horace glided through the French doors.

"Get a doctor, now!" Issy shouted.

Horace's eyes rolled back, eyelids beating frantically. "Help is on the way," he said.

Blood loss from the entry wound was minimal compared to the back of her arm. Issy snatched an antimacassar from the arm of the tipped-up chair and folded it into a thick wad, pressing it onto the exit wound. "Hold this in place, Mama." She grabbed her mother's trembling hand. "Press hard."

Hilda Rowbottom had used the confusion to slip away, leaving Issy alone with her mother. She hugged her tight, rocking as she stroked her hair.

"The grey-shirts took your father. They are going to use him to get Theo."

"Shh, Mama. Don't worry. Everything will be all right. I won't let them hurt Dad or Theo." She squeezed harder and rocked faster.

But even as the words left her lips, she knew she was powerless to stop the Anthropocene from doing whatever they wished.

Later, in the cold calm after the chaos, tears welled in Issy's eyes as she stared at the impressions left by her father in the cushion of his favourite chair. She adjusted the antimacassars on the arms and back before she slumped into its well-worn leather seat.

The chair faced the French doors on the far side of the room. On winter nights, her father would light the tea lights around the garden before settling down to fall asleep watching the moths and other night-flyers swirling around the tiny flames through booze-blurred eyes.

But tonight, the garden was pitch black.

Father had not returned.

Horace, whose last duty each night was to extinguish the flames, stood by the doors awaiting instruction.

Issy sipped at her steaming sweet-malted hot drink, warming both hands on the cup. She closed her eyes and ran through the events of the afternoon and evening.

Although it seemed like much longer, the doctor had arrived less than an hour after the shooting. He praised Issy's fast reactions, which had minimised the loss of blood and almost certainly ensured her mother's complete recovery. But despite the shot missing bone and artery, it caused extensive damage to flesh and muscle.

He had cleaned and sutured the entry and exit wounds, dressed and bandaged her arm, and settled her in her own bed with a sedative and painkillers. Unable to do any more, he left, saying that he, and a nurse, would return the next day.

When she was satisfied her mother was sleeping peacefully, Issy had returned to the morning room.

The twin barbs of anger and guilt burned through her like a flaming pitchfork.

The room was a mess. Everything had to be put back how it was, as if nothing had happened. *This is all my fault*, she thought. *Father will be apoplectic if he sees the room in this state.*

And, not knowing when he would walk through the door, she set to work at a furious pace, righting the upturned chair, picking up broken crockery and cleaning tea stains from upholstery and rugs. But she left the hardest job until last and wept as she scrubbed and scrubbed and scrubbed at the bloodstains on the back and seat of her mother's woven wicker bathchair until her hands bled.

Then she sat in her father's chair. Releasing the boozy tobacco stench infused in the leather conjured his presence when she closed her eyes.

Her lips were still curled in a wry smile when the French doors clicked open. But Horace's whirring footsteps did not follow. Instead, the unmistakable heel-to-toe clack-clunk of mill clogs belonged to someone choosing to announce their presence with their feet before speaking.

Issy opened her eyes.

"Miss Thursday?" The young carding room manager wore only a brown woollen shawl around her head and shoulders over her work clothes to keep out the cold.

"Begging your pardon, miss. Your mek-servant showed me round t'back…"

"It's all right, Winifred. But please tell me you haven't walked from the mill alone." Issy craned her neck, peering past the shivering girl. "Come in, and Horace, please close the door."

"No, miss." Winifred's cheeks, already rosy from the chill evening air, darkened. "My beau is out front." She jabbed a thumb at Horace. "*That* wouldn't let him come round with me."

"Horace—"

"It's all right, miss. I only came to ask after old Mister Windlass. He didn't look very well in the carriage."

Issy sat upright. "You saw my father in the brougham?"

"Yes, miss. He was sitting in it when young Mister Windlass and another man got in. Then they set off towards town."

"Think very hard. Was a woman with them, too?"

"Didn't see no one else, miss, honest." Winifred was still shivering.

"Horace. Collect Miss Thursday's young man, take them both to the kitchen and give them a hot drink before they go on their way." Issy turned to Winifred and grasped her freezing fingers. "Thank you for coming. When my father returns, I will tell him of your kindness."

Winifred smiled and followed Horace into the hall, closing the door behind her.

The grandfather clock was striking a quarter past nine when Horace returned.

"Have our guests gone?"

"Yes. Do you require anything else from *this* 'kin tonight, Miss Isadora?"

"No, that's all, Horace. Oh, please turn down the gas mantles and check the locks on all the doors before you finish."

The mek bowed his head and went about his business. Issy closed her eyes and listened to him, picturing the room darkening on the other side of her weary eyelids. Then, the hall door clicked shut, and she was alone. *Where are you, Father? If they only wanted Theo, why aren't you home?*

As they had many times before, her thoughts turned to her brother. Onslow had suggested Theo's drinking and brawling had only started after he moved away from home. If, as he said, Theo hadn't pushed Mother down the stairs, what caused him to change?

And now Father was missing and only by the grace of the

Mother was her own mother not killed by the shot caused by her gung-ho actions.

Unanswered questions were spinning around her mind. The damning solution seemed a heartbeat away when a thunderous banging on the front door snapped her eyes open.

Father?

Misty morning sun rays streamed through the French doors. She had slept in the chair all night.

As she stumbled out of the chair in a daze, she rubbed the sleep-crust from her eyes and reached the front door, a racing heartbeat behind Horace. Through the leaded sidelights, she glimpsed her father's midnight blue brougham.

Horace swung the door open, and the air left Issy's lungs as her legs crumpled beneath her.

BLAME GAMES

Ace caught Issy before she hit the floor.

"Are you all right, old girl?"

"It's Father, isn't it?" Issy looked up through tear-blurred eyes.

"Your father? No." Ace gently lifted her on to unsteady legs. "Do you remember the faulty latch on the lift gates? Well, I'm afraid Coroner Shillington has fallen down the lift shaft. He's dead. The police are calling it an accident."

"*They* would say that, wouldn't they? Because *they* killed him. It was Scroggins in Stevenson Square yesterday. He recognised us."

"But why kill Shillington? That makes no sense." Ace held her as they walked towards the morning room. "I've never seen you like this. What's wrong?"

Issy spun him around to face her. "Listen. Mama has been

shot. Father and Theo are missing."

Ace raised his eyebrows. "What?"

The sharp rap of a walking stick on wood turned her head. Horace was holding the door open, staring at the doctor in the doorway.

"Please come in." Issy eased away from Ace's embrace.

The doctor removed his top hat as he stepped over the threshold.

"Good day to you," he said. "This is Nurse Rowena. She will change dressings and, because of your mother's incapacity, tend to her, *ahem*, every need." He cleared his throat. "How is the patient this morning? Did she have a comfortable night?"

Issy looked away, blood rushing to her cheeks. She hadn't tended to her mother since the previous evening. "I've only just... I must have been exhausted... Please..." She lowered her eyes and motioned the doctor upstairs. She didn't move until he had reached the top step, then turned to Ace, grabbing his arms.

"Everything that's happened to Mama, Father, Theo and Shillington has one thing in common. They're all my fault!" She shoved him aside and ran up the stairs.

Issy's mother had been sleeping peacefully before being woken by the phalanx of concerned faces storming her bedroom. Confused and cranky at first, she cut through the fuss with the question Issy had been dreading. "Where's Wilbur? I need to see him."

She broke down in tears when Issy told her he hadn't returned home.

No words could convince her he wasn't dead, and despite

her own fears, Issy did everything she could to persuade her otherwise.

After all, this wasn't the first time he hadn't come home. Amongst family and friends, his drinking was inglorious. So Issy soothed her, suggesting he would turn up later in the day with a tale of derring-do and a raging hangover as usual.

Once her mother was settled, Issy and Ace followed the doctor downstairs, leaving the nurse to her duties.

The good doctor bade his farewells and climbed aboard his dark blue brougham, leaving Issy and Ace to walk to the morning room.

Apart from the light glinting off the occasional shard of broken crockery buried in the carpet, Issy had done a thorough job of eradicating the aftermath of yesterday's struggle. They sat next to each other on the two-seater, and Ace cupped her hands in his.

"What's happened to them? I don't know where to look or how to find them." Issy's eyes stared into his, seeking a solution that wasn't forthcoming.

"Until we learn why they were taken, we have no way of knowing where they are."

"It makes no sense. Theo is one of their own. He's Anthropocene through and through."

"Is he, though? You've had no contact with him for years. How can you be sure he is true to their cause?"

"You saw him pick a fight in the Praetorian. And he tried to kill me during the police raid."

"I beg to differ, old girl, but the couple were spoiling for trouble. Theo defended himself against their aggression."

"Well, by wearing the grey, he was asking for it." Issy snatched her hands from Ace and raised an open palm to silence him. "Look. This isn't helping. Arguing won't get them back." She closed her eyes and tapped her fist against her lips. "Maybe they've taken him to provoke the Order through me."

"If that's the case, Theo isn't truly one of them."

"What do you mean?"

"Because, old thing, if he were dyed-in-the-wool Anthropocene, his allegiance would be to them, not to you, not to your father, and not to your mother. They need only ask, and he would sing like a nightingale."

"That's a possibility I hadn't dared contemplate... I was so sure..."

"But if he isn't true to their cause, why does he wear the grey?"

"Power? Control?"

Ace smiled. "Or something you'd understand more than most, a sense of belonging... to be one of the tribe. We all seek affirmation from kindred spirits." Ace nodded at her as he counted on his fingers. "Suffrage. Temperance. The Order. These are people that share your ideals. They validate the beliefs that give your life direction and meaning."

Issy shook her head. "But he doesn't believe in anything. He only cares about himself."

"Tell me, again... Why did he have to leave home?"

"Father said the bickering between us was making Mama ill. I wouldn't let him forget that he had put her in a wheelchair."

"But he didn't push her, did he?"

"I didn't know that then."

"So your father kicked him out of his own home, knowing he had done nothing wrong, just to save face."

"Theo should have told me the truth."

"Standing so high on your moral ivory tower, you wouldn't have heard him."

"That doesn't excuse his behaviour."

"No. But it explains why he turned to drink and why he joined the Freedom Brigade. He may not know you're a member of the Order, but he knows you would oppose the grey-shirts with every ounce of your being."

"I can see no good in him."

"Yet, his friend Onslow can."

Issy closed her eyes and shook her head.

"Theo is your brother, and right now, he needs you."

Algeria rolled her hand over the six brass tubes on the table, bowed her head, and shed a tear for Coroner Shillington. Many overlooked his contribution to the goals of the Order, but not her. This unassuming gentleman fulfilled his oath to the cause, without question, without complaint, under the full scrutiny of his public office, with courage, stealth, and dignity.

These cold brass tubes were testament to his genius and devotion, but, in reality, of little practical use. She cursed herself for the vagueness of her request of him. For surely, with clearer instructions, he would have produced whatever she needed.

When Issy handed them to her, she had considered using one of them to replace the deadly powder in the loading bay. But without knowing how long the spray would be effective, she had reduced its potency in the loading bay by shovelling away the bulk of the powder into the Irwell.

Gilbert had replaced the rotting and broken planks on the loading bay doors and bolted flat-iron braces to the structural struts, so that even a full-frontal assault with a river-borne battering ram may not break their defences.

Coroner Shillington's last service to the Order was redundant.

So, her knee-jerk reaction to the treasure hunters' deaths may have exposed him to their enemies, resulting in the death of an irreplaceable ally, who was also a good man. If, as she suspected, he had been murdered, she could not escape the irrefutable truth that she was responsible.

She closed her eyes, spread her arms and pressed her palms on the table. Time lost all meaning as she wallowed in the martyrdom of guilt and self-pity, punishing herself for her stupidity and mourning his loss. She understood the pernicious nature of negative emotions and how to cleanse her mind of them all too well.

Sadly, the futility of his death made this purge especially tough.

But she was the High Mother, and her responsibilities were immutable and absolute. She took a deep breath, raised her head, and opened her eyes. Dottie and Gilbert were in each other's arms, sitting opposite her. Sadness wreathed their faces, but Dottie's almost imperceptible nod and smile reassured her.

Yes, shugah, she thought, *life goes on.*

She tossed her hair and shook away the tears. She looked around the draped banners and other Order paraphernalia that tried but failed to hide the desolation of their surroundings. Much like putting lipstick on a pig, it was futile.

"I didn't hear you come in." She dabbed at the corners of her eyes with a knuckle.

"We didn't want to disturb you, Mama. Are you all right?"

Algeria took another deep breath. "We're no nearer to discovering who leads the Anthropocene or the whereabouts of their scientists. And it's getting harder to move around the city. Grey-shirts are teeming like rats in the streets. In the name of the Mother, we have to fight back, but until we find their leader, we're waging a war we can't win."

"What about Felix's mek? Maybe she's looking for the Anthropocene leader, too." Gilbert said.

Algeria nodded. "You and Dottie must speak with it. Find out everything it knows. But be careful, from what Felix says, this mek is different. I don't trust it."

"Er, I think I can outwit a mek."

"I know you do. That's why Dottie is going with you."

Horace placed the tea tray on the wrought-iron table and scooted to the bottom of the garden to continue pruning and gathering leaves for the bonfire he would set later. Issy closed her eyes and tilted her face to the southern sky, listening to the sparrows chirping and bickering in the hedge that bordered the garden.

But the cloud-strained, sickly December sun didn't warm her cheeks. She took a deep breath and slowly exhaled. "Tell me about Theo."

Onslow had arrived unannounced half an hour after Ace had left. He was in an agitated state when Horace showed him into the morning room, wringing his cap like a wet towel when he glimpsed his reflection in the mirror between the silver candlestick holders on the mahogany mantelpiece. So, despite the cold, Issy instructed Horace to serve tea in the garden.

"Well, I've known him since we was kids. He—"

"After he left home. I know what he was like before."

"Sorry, miss… Well, when he took over at t'mill, he was keen as mustard. Of course, that waned a bit after he started boozing. After work each day, he'd lose himself in a glass." He shrugged and laughed. "You know how he loves a prank? Well, Theo being Theo, it wasn't long before his high jinks rubbed someone up the wrong way. And that's when the fighting began."

Issy tightened her lips and nodded. *What you call pranks, most call bullying.* "But he was drinking before he moved out?"

"Not to my knowledge, miss. Your dad turfed him out when he turned twenty-one."

"So… You're saying he drank because he was angry at me."

"Loneliness and anger aren't best bedfellows." Onslow lowered his eyes.

"So, he took his frustration out on innocent bystanders? And you were always around to pick him up if he came off worse."

"Hardly, miss. Although I pulled him out of a few scrapes, he rarely needed any help. As time went on, he picked out thugs who, in his words 'deserved a good hiding.' I reckon he saw himself as a bit of a crusader against bullies.

"Now, I've never amounted to much, but he always stood by me just like I stand by him. He even gave me the job at t'mill. Chief potterer, he calls me." Onslow's laugh cracked almost before it began. "I'm really worried about him, miss. What do you think they'll do to him?"

"Why would they hurt him?"

"After you sacked Galbraith, he returned with two mates to demand his old job back, and Theo messed them up good. Now, rumour has it, the powers-that-be in the Freedom Brigade believe he's to blame for a few of their number that have gone missing, too."

Issy's heart leapt into her throat. Although she feared for her father's safety, she never imagined Theo could be in so much peril. She shuddered. "It's suddenly turned chilly. Perhaps it's time to retire indoors. I'll have Horace light a fire in the grate. Will you join me, Onslow?"

"Thanks for offering, miss, but I'd best be off. I've got a long walk home."

"You came here straight from the mill?"

"Aye, miss. Your friend, Mister Sixsmith, brought me in his carriage."

The corner of Issy's mouth curled beneath a single raised eyebrow.

"You'll let me know if Theo turns up, won't you, miss?"

"Of course. And don't worry, we'll get them back. Whatever it takes."

MARTYR TO GUILT

The garden table had once again left an ugly mark on Felix's shin. So he rubbed the pain from his leg before he regaled Oscar with his tale of abduction, brass houses and conflict on the streets of Manchester.

He could not remember the last time he had a two-cigar conversation with him, or anybody else, for that matter, but he was resting the stub of his second Cuban in the ashtray before blowing a final plume of smoke from the side of his mouth when he finished the Homeric saga of his adventure.

"So, Raven's nemesis lives on." Oscar tapped a finger on his lips. "For now, we must keep this snippet between us."

"Do you suppose this Sparks fellow murdered Raven? I've seen him in action. He's like a cat—silent, fast and brutal."

"Well, cats kill birds, after they've toyed with them for a while…" Oscar pinched his pursed lips. "We shouldn't assume anything, but from what you tell me, the Order is a force for good. However, we are no nearer to fathoming the motives of The Maker. He could be a member of their organisation, or the Freedom Brigade."

"Or a lone wolf…"

"Whatever his intentions, good or bad, he knows his onions." Oscar beckoned Letitia, who had been hovering around the workshop door.

"Felix has been learning about the Anthropocene, my dear. Have you heard of this despicable group of fiends?"

"Yes."

"Were you aware Raven was their leader?"

"Yes."

"And you are quite certain that Raven is dead."

"Yes." Letitia fiddled with her chatelaine and rocked her hips. "What happens when you die?"

"That depends on who you ask." Oscar chuckled beneath his furrowed brow. "At my age, it's a question I contemplate more each day. Why do you ask?"

"The Scriptures explain what happens to me when I cease. I wondered if you went to the same place."

"Please, my dear, refresh my memory. What do the Scriptures say?"

"When our bodies cease to work, or we can no longer fulfil our duties for our masters, or our clocks have reached their end-time, we pass through the black doors where our memories are examined. After a productive existence, we receive a better body to serve a higher purpose."

"Who or what examines your memory banks?"

Letitia shrugged.

"And if you've been a naughty little mek?" Felix's wink at Oscar was met with a pinched, wide-eyed glare. He cleared his throat. "Sorry, old chap."

"We bide amongst the ambrosial aromas of Mekarcadia."

Oscar raised his eyebrows. "So where is this sanctum?"

"I do not know, but I will find out, if I do not find The Maker."

"What?" Felix leapt to his feet, clattering his bruised leg against the table.

"Would you make tea for us, my dear?" Oscar smiled at Letitia and put his finger to his lips to silence Felix's burgeoning protestations. He held steady until Letitia had left the workshop.

"I say, old boy. Does she really believe they'll break her into spare parts if she fails in her quest?" Felix was soothing a new bruise.

"*Believe*, Felix? Dear me, you haven't got to grips with this yet, have you, old chum? She is reinforcing our commitment to help." Oscar interlocked his fingertips under his chin and fluttered his eyelashes. "Oh, dear Felix, please help me, for, if I fail, you will lose me forever."

His sing-song caricature of Letitia struck hard.

Felix's flaming blush would have charred paper.

Oscar continued unabashed. "Her programming is beautifully complex. Did you see how she changed the subject of our questions away from Raven by initiating a conversation about death? Why death? I can't say. Is it manipulation? I don't know. But it is fascinating, isn't it?"

"Downright scary, if you ask me."

Oscar put his hand on Felix's shoulder. "Just remember, old friend. Her every word has a purpose. And at the moment, that is finding The Maker."

Dottie pushed the brim of her begoggled topper onto the back of her head and put her hands on her hips. "So, this is the great Oscar McMurdo's house." She whistled through her teeth. "Posh, but I expected bigger."

"And I thought he was dead. I'm half expecting a head in a bell jar surrounded by brass tubes." The gate hinges creaked their resistance to Gilbert's shove. He nudged Dottie as he pointed at the BDI lens in the transom window. "It's good to see he has confidence in his own inventions."

Felix stepped past them and opened the door before they could pull the doorbell. He briefly pressed a finger to his lips before leading them along a hallway to the workshop, where a gaunt old man in a brown lab coat was dozing in a sumptuous chair, surrounded by mechanical toys of all shapes and sizes.

"Oscar, old chap," Felix spoke in a hoarse whisper. "You have visitors." He raised his eyebrows at Dottie and Gilbert before repeating his entreaty, but this time, he used his normal voice.

Oscar woke with a start. "Ahh, Felix. I was having such a

peaceful dream about two beautiful young people walking up to my door, hand in hand. I open my eyes, and here they are."

Gilbert opened his mouth, but Oscar's raised palm stopped him from uttering a word.

"Where's Letitia, Felix?"

"At your side, old man." His voice was an aural eye roll.

Oscar looked right first but found her on his left when his fingers brushed her chatelaine. "Ah, there you are, my dear." He twisted his body to look up at her face. "Felix," he said, "please introduce our guests."

"Letitia, this young lady is Dottie. I'm afraid I don't know her last name. And this handsome chap is Gilbert Sparks."

Letitia's eyelids beat like a drum roll at a military tattoo.

"Fascinating…" Oscar pulled gently at the turkey skin under his chin.

Presenting Letitia with an open palm, Felix turned to Dottie and Gilbert. "This is Letitia Lovegrove. I understand you met her previous owner. A fellow called Raven…"

Gilbert failed to stop his hands snatching at the hilts of his swords, pulling them a couple of inches from their sheathes before Felix could stop him.

"No, little ones, stop!" The contraptions had swished, whirred, and slashed halfway across the workshop before Oscar's voice stopped them in their tracks. Gilbert eased the blades back, and Dottie straightened from her crouch.

Letitia's eyelids slowed to a halt. "Hello, Gilbert Sparks. Raven spoke about you all the time, but when I saw him last, he said you were dead."

Gilbert raised an eyebrow. "Funny you should say that, because—"

Dottie dug her elbow into his ribs. "She doesn't talk like any mek I've ever encountered."

"We are learning more about Letitia every day and, no doubt, she is learning more about us."

"Did your father die alone in the fire?" Letitia's sing-song metallic voice reminded Gilbert of his father's Welsh lilt.

"How do you…? Yes, he did. Did you know Raven was crushed by his own bomb before it blew him to smithereens?" The torrent of words gushed from Gilbert's blood-flushed face.

"She's a machine, Gilbert. You can't hurt her feelings because she doesn't have any." Dottie grabbed his arm and pulled him close.

"If I had a sovereign for every time I heard that phrase…" Felix chuckled to himself.

The bell jangled over Algeria's head as she pulled open the door. She had become accustomed to the muted lighting, delicate scents and relative calm of Josephine's sophisticated corsetiere. But now, stepping into the bright sunlight for the first time in weeks, the stink and harsh cacophony of Manchester street-life jarred her senses.

Steel-shod hooves of blowing horses clattered the cobbles as drivers urged them onward. Laughing, shouting, talking.

Young, old, workers, toffs and meks. In Old Millgate, all of life was here.

On the top step of Josephine's, she closed her eyes and inhaled the heady mix of perfume, smoke, and horse dung. Although this was only the second time she had ventured out in as many weeks, it was worth the risk to save her sanity. So, tying her lime-flower coloured bonnet under her chin, she fastened the silver buttons on her sage green jacket and ran her black-gloved hands down her hips, straightening her figure-hugging, ankle-length black dress before stepping out into the bustling throng.

She stumbled as a tidal wave of shoppers swept her away, heading for the bargains in the marketplace.

Bellowing barrow boys and caterwauling costermongers touted their wares as they competed for customers from the rows and rows of stalls that lined the square. Algeria swayed from stall to stall, savouring the aromas. Whether fresh fruit or fried onions or coffee, she relished them all equally.

There was a small tug on her jacket. She looked down at the snotty-nosed street urchin with a blackened eye and ragged clothes as he thrust a piece of paper into her hand.

"Have a care, miss," he said. "Take a chance." All the while, he was glancing over his left shoulder.

Algeria followed his gaze and froze. A raggedy, thin man held open his brown overcoat, hooking a thumb into his trouser belt to display his grey shirt as he leaned against a building at the side of the square. He returned her stare, narrowing his eyes. A gap-toothed smile spread across his face as he strode over to a stall and picked a rosy red apple, waving away the barrow boy's annoyance, stuffing it into his pocket.

She bent and smiled at the young boy. "What do you mean, shugah?" she asked. "Take a chance on what?"

The lad nodded at the paper, glanced over his shoulder, and took off to the opposite side of the square.

She held the crumpled note in both hands. Printed in bold letters, it proclaimed:

MEK MODES
By Claude and Maude
All the latest fashions from London & Paris.
Work or leisure, indoors or out, dress your mek in style.
We use only the most durable, hard-wearing materials.
Guarantees available on purchases of over ten shillings.

She had to squint to read the small print, below illustrations of male and female meks in various poses, at the bottom:

A modest, but exclusive, range of polishes, lubricants and
accessories for the discerning gentlelady or gentleman.

Nothing out of the ordinary, she thought, until she flipped the paper over. In an inch square, a rubber-stamped message read:

Friday, 18th December, 8 o'clock
Free Trade Hall
Freedom Rally

The leader speaks!
Brothers & Sisters of Freedom only
No token - No admission - No exception

While she read, a shadow darkened the paper. She raised her eyes and took a startled breath. The skinny man in the bulky brown coat filled her vision. Straggly black hair danced in the light breeze around his gaunt face. With a thick handlebar moustache tickling the top lip of his leering smile, he had the demeanour she had encountered many times.

His stench and aroused arrogance were typical of men who had never touched a woman unless money had changed hands.

"Did I startle you, sister?" The clay pipe drooping from the corner of his mouth bounced with every syllable.

"Yes, brother, you did." *Why does he think I'm one of them?*

He looked her up and down, his eyes resting on the left-hand side of her bonnet. His brow furrowed, and he lowered his voice to a hoarse whisper. "Have you lost it?"

Algeria swept her hand around her hat, fingers feigning a search. "Oh, dear… it was there when I left home. It must have… I must have…" Her voice tailed off as she bowed her head, looking up at him from beneath her eyebrows.

"Lucky you bumped into me, then, isn't it?" As he lifted her chin with a crooked forefinger, he opened his jacket to reveal a neat row of silver hatpins threaded into the lining. His beaming smile was missing two front teeth. Algeria reached for a pin, but he closed and refastened the middle button.

"What would it cost for the brother to give me one of

those?" Rocking her hips back and forth, she moistened her lips with the tip of her tongue.

The grey-shirt took a step back and looked her up and down again. This time, his eyes rested on her bosom. "What's your name, darling?"

Algeria almost burst into laughter at the irony. "Fanny," she said, recalling the old helpful mek from the Praetorian.

"I'm Onslow." He paused and raised an eyebrow. "I see by your expression you haven't heard of me. Brother by birth to the Brunswick Brawler." He beamed his gappy grin and puffed out his chest. "Aye, you may well look surprised."

So, we're both lying. Algeria smiled and looked down at her left hand. She curled her fingers into a fist and made a languid dice shaking motion. "Can we go somewhere… private?"

The market traders often used the narrow alleys separating the buildings around the perimeter of the marketplace for storage. While Onslow searched for a suitably quiet place, Algeria slipped her hand into her jacket pocket and unscrewed the lid off a vial secured upright in a small sheath.

The odourless vapour had an immediate effect on her, then moments later, on Onslow, making his search more urgent.

"There!" He pointed at a narrow alley on the opposite side of the square, linked her arm and made a beeline for it, brushing aside startled shoppers if they got in the way. Sweat glistened on his cheeks and the clay pipe stood straight from his mouth, the stem clenched between his teeth.

"What's the hurry, shugah?" she purred, pressing her soft curves against his arm, and he quickened their pace.

The alleyway was wide enough for people to walk hand in hand. But fifteen paces in, wooden crates and wrappings were stacked ten feet high and two crates deep along one wall.

Algeria pushed Onslow into a gap in the stacks. She looked left and right to make sure they were alone before stepping forward, pressing her body hard against his. Their faces were inches apart. His jaw was set tight, and his clay pipe quivered with each breath sucked between clenched teeth. Her half-lidded gaze contrasted with his wild, staring eyes.

He grunted and moaned as she ran her hand down his body, sliding her fingers along the inside of his thigh. Her hand began a slow return journey towards his buttoned fly.

"No…" His eyes rolled upwards under his inverted-V eyebrows, and his hands grasped her hips, pressing her body hard against his. Spasms shook his body as he failed to stifle a loud grunt.

"Oh, dear…" Algeria pulled herself from his grip, and taking a half step back, her retreat caused Onslow to bend forward. His hands fell from her hips to his knees for support. As he shook his head to clear his confusion, she moved fast, opening his jacket and grabbing a handful of hatpins. The vapour may have heightened his ardour, but it slowed his reflexes.

He opened his mouth to protest, but she put a finger to his lips. "Shh… It's our secret." She lowered her eyes to his trousers. "You can't walk through the market looking like that." She wrinkled her nose and gave him a handkerchief. "Oh dear. That won't do. Give me a shilling and I'll buy you a pinny."

Onslow fumbled in his pocket and dropped two silver

sixpenny pieces into her upturned hand.

"I'll be back in two minutes. Wait here."

Turning on her heel, she swayed down the alleyway, screwing the lid back on the vial in her pocket. Once back in the hustle and bustle of the market, she took a couple of deep breaths before stepping into the sunlight.

Now aware of their meaning, she could see the pale green hats with silver hatpins everywhere. And dotted around the square, grey-shirts surveying the shoppers. She leaned into the tide flowing back up Old Millgate to the sanctuary of the corsetiere.

Once in the safety of her boudoir, she loosened her stays' laces, sat on the edge of the bed and examined one of the five identical hatpins. Its needle-thin steel shank was six inches long and had a hinged head, shaped like a grouse or a similarly rotund bird, an inch in diameter. Placing the head in the heel of her hand, she curled her fingers around it, allowing the shaft to slide between her fore and middle fingers. *Lethal*, she thought.

She gathered them onto her nightstand. Despite the revelation of the pale green bonnet and a gnawing headache caused by the retreat of the vapour, she flopped back on the bed and smiled. Victories, no matter how small, should be celebrated.

And being a handful of hatpins and a shilling richer, this was indeed a victory.

Of course, she didn't return to Onslow and hardly gave him another thought.

Issy had poured two fingers of her father's favourite malt whisky and sat at his writing bureau to write two notes.

The first, for Nurse Rowena, advised that she had been called away on an important matter, and that she would not return for several days. Nurse should inform the doctor that her services were required longer than planned. Furthermore, under no circumstance must Issy's mother be told of her absence, because of the distress this may cause.

The note to Ace was harder to write.

Dear Ace,

By the time you read this, I will have exchanged my freedom for my father's, and I will be with Theo.

If I had told you what I was planning, I know you would have tried to talk me out of it, and I could not risk you succeeding.

You are right about Theo. He is my brother, and I must do whatever I can to save him, from himself, as well as from them.

I will never betray my oath to the Order.

If I can, I will wreak havoc on the Freedom Brigade.

But whether I see you again is in the lap of the Mother.

Don't forget me and always remember, you hold a special place in my heart.

Issy

She threw her warmest woollen coat over her royal blue taffeta and white lace dress and poured the whisky down her throat. The strong liquor made her cough until her eyes watered. Although it left a bitter taste in her mouth, it warmed her belly and gave her false bravado for the events ahead.

Before leaving, she gave Nurse Rowena her instructions and handed the other note to Horace with the strict instruction to hand it only to Ace, then flounced out of the house, head held high, certain of her righteous path.

But her steps slowed on the cold, wet avenue, as the flaw in her plan became glaringly apparent. She didn't know where they were holding her father and brother. And, even if she found out, these were not honourable people, and simply offering herself in exchange for her father might just give them another captive.

What would Ace do?

At the corner where the avenue met the busy thoroughfare into the city, she looked left and right, then half turned towards home.

Whether it was the distant cry of a costermonger, the rumbling wheels of a hand-pushed trader's stall on the cobbles, or the whisky in her belly, she couldn't tell. But she tossed back her hair and renewed her march to her meeting with destiny, invigorated with a daring plan.

THE GIFT

The bitter weather had kept the crowds away from Stevenson Square market, but it hadn't quietened the stallholders' enthusiastic calls. Issy had approached from Newton Street, diagonally across the square from Hilton Chambers.

Bobbing her head around, she peered through the stalls at the uniformed policeman guarding the lift doors. He was bending forward, talking to someone hidden by the hats hanging from a milliner's stall.

She hunched over and skirted the buildings that bounded the edge of the market. After she crossed Lever Street behind a group of noisy washerwomen, she ducked into a doorway. Now, with only the railings of the gentlemen's lavatories in the middle of the square between her and the lift doors, she had a side view of the stocky man in a tweed coat and bowler, waving his arms at the placid-faced policeman.

Although the market's general hubbub drowned his words, there was no mistaking by his body language that he was pulling rank, unsuccessfully, to gain access to the scene of Coroner Shillington's death.

And she had little doubt that the outcome of the demand would have been different had the uniformed officer's shirt been grey.

Scroggins finally gave up his lost cause, but not before prodding his smiling subordinate twice in the chest and storming off, still waving his arms. Halfway along Oldham Street, Issy caught up with him and, roughly linking his left arm, pulled him tight against her body.

"What the—"

"Scroggins, isn't it?" Facing forward, she didn't meet his sideways glare and never broke stride. "Today is going to be your lucky day, and you get to decide whether your luck is good or bad."

She could sense his eyes burning with anger.

"I remember you from the raid on the Praetorian. You're one of them." He jerked his arm to break Issy's grip, but she squeezed harder, pulling his body tighter to hers.

"Let me give you a reason not to try anything foolish." She pressed her fist hard into his ribs. Then watched the realisation dawn in his eyes. "Yes, Scroggins. It's a small, single-shot gun, but it will be enough to despatch you to hell." The blood drained from his face.

"Look, I was only doin' my job. There's no need—"

"Were you just doing your job when you killed Shillington?"
Scroggins' silence spoke louder than any words.

At Piccadilly, they stopped. Tick Tock trams and old horse-drawn omnibuses of every livery clattered on criss-crossing tracks. Shoppers, workers and meks bustled along pavements, oblivious to Issy and Scroggins.

"Where are you taking me?"

"I'm not taking *you* anywhere. You're going to take me to my brother and father."

"Don't know what you're talkin' about. Why would I know where your brother is?"

Issy's head turned left and right. A few yards away, a policeman wearing a white shirt beneath his uniform was speaking with an old lady. "Let's see if that young officer is interested in the coroner's murderer." She pulled him forward.

"All right," he said. "Free Trade Hall. Mosley Street is the quickest route from here."

"I don't need directions. I can find my way around Manchester better than you."

They set off down Mosley Street, but Issy took short cuts, zigzagging through alleys across the city to Albert Square, then along Southmill Street. As they reached the junction with Peter Street, she jerked Scroggins to a halt. From the crossroads, the big arch of Manchester Central Station was visible between the sides of the Theatre Royal and the Free Trade Hall.

"Where are they holding them?"

"Storerooms under the hall."

Issy stuck her head out and looked along the hall's nine-bay, soot-blackened arched frontage. "Not a grey-shirt in sight. If you're—"

"They're behind the piers in the shadows. They can see us, you can't see them."

"Then this is your chance to be a hero. Call one over, but don't try anything."

Scroggins leaned forward and beckoned towards the first bay. Two grey-shirted thugs crossed the cobbled, tram-lined street, halting when Issy jabbed her fist hard into Scroggins's ribs.

"I'm Isadora Windlass. You are holding my father and brother, Theo, in that building. Bring my father here and I will take his place. If you refuse, he gets it."

"What's she talkin' about?"

Scroggins's shrug shook Issy.

"The only bloke we've got is the Brunswick Brawler. Is that 'er brother?"

"Looks like you are going to have to shoot me with that knuckle you have been digging in my ribs… Surprised? Oh, I know what a gun feels like."

Issy tried to slide her arm out, but he trapped it, grabbing her wrist with his other hand.

"Where's my father? What have you done with him?"

Scroggins tightened his grip on both her wrists. "I heard the boss had no use for him. He'd served his purpose to catch Theo, and she dropped him off somewhere."

Issy's mind was racing. "She? The leader of the Freedom Brigade is a woman?"

Scroggins and his compatriots laughed as they dragged her across the street, through an arch into the shadows.

To Algeria's surprise, the hurriedly convened meeting was well attended. Even the venerable Thaddeus Osgood Lisney had dragged his corpulent self from the Athenaeum's well-thumbed copy of the Sporting Life to flop onto a front-row seat in the Order's new 'tiresomely deeper' meeting room.

"I say, High Mother, I don't suppose this tram of yours goes anywhere near New Barns, does it? You see, I have a filly running in the—"

"No, Ozzie, it doesn't." Although the other end of the line at Rawkshaw House was closer to the racecourse than their current location, she would not allow him to commandeer the tram for his personal use.

A quick head count. *Thirty-seven without Ace and Issy, who are late as usual.*

At times like these, she missed Eli's services as gatekeeper, and whilst she relied on Mademoiselle Josephine and her assistants to vet the ladies seeking admittance to the underground hall, the gentlemen's entrance was impossible to control, managed only by the vigilance of male members themselves.

Deciding she could wait no longer, she raised her hands for silence.

"Brothers and sisters. Thank you for coming at such short notice. I'm heartened so many of you hold our cause so strongly in your hearts.

"As you can see, since our last meeting, we have moved to deeper, roomier lodgings." Spreading her arms wide, she continued. "It's a little echoey, and the decor leaves a lot to be desired, but I hope you like what we've done with the place so far."

Murmurs, coughs and laughter interspersed with calls of 'needs must' and 'it'll do for now' were typical of the members' stoicism.

"Since our last meeting, we lost one of our longest serving members. Doctor Robin Sanderling Shillington, District Coroner, was an irreplaceable member of our number. Although we know how he died, the full circumstances of his death cannot be reliably established. But we suspect foul play.

"Many of you will have fond memories of him, so I open the floor for those who wish to share their stories of his fabled life." Algeria sat and listened as, one by one, young and old, stood to share their memories.

After ten minutes, the room was echoing with raucous laughter. Although initial tributes befitted the late coroner's grave mien, they soon degenerated into tale after bawdy tale that made the gentlemen roar with laughter and the ladies beat their fans to cool their blushes.

Algeria stood and raised her hands to call a halt.

Although several men were still stifling giggles during the Exhortation, Algeria singled out Lemmy, silencing him with her steely glare before the Adulation.

As the members took their seats, she remained standing, waiting for silence.

"I declare this meeting of The Venerable Antediluvian Order of the Custodians of Magna Mater well and truly open." She paused and surveyed the room. "Despite our efforts since the event at Barton, we have had no success locating the Anthropocene scientists or their leader… Until yesterday."

She waited for the murmurs of anticipation and the creaks from members' chairs as they sat to attention to die down.

"A chance encounter with a low-life grey-shirt has presented us with an opportunity." She narrowed her eyes, staring at the movement in the shadows at the back of the room. *Issy?* A pang of fear shot through her chest when the figure didn't step into the light.

Heads turned to see at what Algeria was squinting, and Gilbert, whose seat was closest to the entrance, was the first to react. He walked over and bent into the darkness. Without raising his head, he straightened his arm backwards, showing his palm to the meeting to stop anyone from joining him.

But Algeria could not resist. She motioned everyone to remain seated and marched to where Gilbert's head was emerging into the light. He turned to face her.

"This young lady has a message from Josephine." Gilbert stepped aside.

Algeria pressed her hands against her hips and put on her sternest expression. "Now, young lady, what is so important that warrants such an intrusion into our sacred meeting place? Your boss knows full well that—"

"Beggin' your pardon, miss, but Ma'amselle Josephine sent me an' told me to tell you to come an' shift your stuff from 'er shop. She says she don't mind the ladies using the place like it's Central Station an' all, but she draws the line at havin' an 'earse parked outside, black plumes an' all, and 'avin' to unload it, an' fill the shop with crates an'—"

"Whoa… slow down. So, there are some boxes upstairs for me?"

"Yes, miss. She says you'd better shift 'em quick, or she'll not be responsible for what 'appens to 'em. She says—"

"Get up there, *tout de suite*, Gilbert, before our benefactor throws the crates out and us with them. Take Dottie with you to move them, then bring one down here." Algeria turned to the young lady, placing her hands on her shoulders. "Please pass my sincerest apologies to Mademoiselle Josephine. This is as much a surprise to me as it was to her."

Gilbert and Dottie followed the shop assistant out of the hall. Murmuring in the room was getting louder as Algeria returned to stand behind the long table. She pressed her palms on the tabletop.

"My apologies, brothers and sisters, for the unexpected interruption. But we have a mystery.

"Someone, as yet unknown, has sent some boxes, contents unknown, addressed to our secret benefactor, for our secret society that occupies the secret place beneath the benefactor's premises."

Fifteen minutes later, all heads turned to watch Gilbert,

cradling a crate wrapped in a lacy blanket from the shop, descend into their midst. He laid it gently on the table like a baby in swaddling cloth and stepped back.

"The crates are numbered, High Mother. This is number one." He pointed to the black stencilled lettering and number on the side.

"Abel told me never to let anyone use these, but I'm sure that doesn't apply to you." Gilbert unsheathed a sword with a shrill metallic *tring!,* spun it around and bowed his head as he handed it to her, hilt first.

She took the hilt from him, holding it, caressing its contours, feeling Abel's artistry and the love he had bestowed upon it.

"Thank you," she said. Then she jammed the blade between the top and side planks, twisting it from side to side, repeating the action around all four sides as bits of straw fell from the box every time she removed it. After persistent levering, the lid was loose enough to pull off.

Algeria plunged both hands through the straw packaging. Her shoulders relaxed, and she raised her head to face the faithful, expectant faces.

Tears welled and trickled onto her cheeks as she turned to Gilbert. "How many boxes?"

"Seventeen more, just like this."

She took a deep breath to gather herself, then, raising her voice, she spoke to the members. "A gift... A wonderful gift from our dear departed Coroner Shillington." She pulled both fists from the crate, straw flying in all directions, and thrust two hands full of brass tubes over her head.

"A parting act that might—"

But heads turned to face the sound of running feet.

Ace was hurtling through the hall. He reached Algeria, breathless, and thrust a piece of paper into her hand.

"It's Issy," he said. "She's… done something… stupid…"

Algeria unfolded the note and read. She didn't raise her head. "Where did you get this?" she whispered.

"Horace… The Windlass's mek… I called to collect her for the meeting…"

Ace buried his face in his hands as she eased him into a chair.

She stared at the puzzled faces, looking for explanation, for guidance, for hope. Her gaze lingered on each of the Stormriders dotted around the room. Then, tightening her lips, she lowered the corners of her mouth and nodded at each.

"When I called this meeting, I had a plan to send volunteers to infiltrate the Freedom Brigade's event at the Free Trade Hall. We had the opportunity to uncover their leader and learn more about their heinous plans.

"But this note changes everything. Our information-gathering foray has become something more."

Algeria raised her hands. "The call for volunteers is no longer needed. This meeting is over. Please leave calmly in twos and threes, in the usual way."

Although no one questioned the High Mother's decision, chairs screeched and members turned silently, exchanging shrugs and puzzled looks, to make their way to their respective egresses.

She eased Ace upright. "Shugah. Please help Gilbert and Dottie bring the crates from upstairs."

Then she turned to face the room and smiled.

Five chairs were still occupied.

Five grim-faced members sat, arms folded.

Five Stormriders awaited the High Mother's orders.

Five friends were ready to do whatever it would take to rescue Issy.

Once they had carried the crates down to the Temple, Gilbert, Dottie and Ace joined Rory, Connie, Lemmy, Tabby and Jonah waiting for Algeria in the warmer basement beneath the shop.

"I don't understand why she did this alone. Why didn't she come to us?" Lemmy slapped his hand on the table.

"*Mea culpa, amicis meis.*" Ace could not meet the questioning eyes of his friends. As he sat at Lemmy's side, he placed a hand on his back. "I'm afraid I am, at the very least, partly to blame."

"She knew we would gang up on her and wouldn't let her go alone," Gilbert said. "But we'll make sure we get her back safe and sound."

"We need to take a step back." Algeria held the crate above her head as she squeezed through the narrow entrance at the rear of the room. She marched to the table and placed it in the middle. "At this moment, we don't know if she has successfully bargained for her father's freedom. And, even if the Freedom

Brigade has her, we have no idea where she is, or what plans they have for her and Theo.

"Somehow, we must stop this so-called Freedom movement in its tracks. This alone is our priority. If we can rescue Issy, we will."

Ace and Lemmy broke the circle of grim nods and glances that rippled around the table.

Algeria aimed her words at them. "You've read the note. She was aware of the risks and did it anyway. You two know her better than anyone. She wouldn't want us to chase after her. So, no heroics. We save Issy only if doing so doesn't jeopardise our goal."

She out-stared Ace and Lemmy's defiance. "Do you understand?" Their tight-lipped nods convinced no one.

Shaking her head, she said. "Listen. This Free Trade Hall event won't be a run-of-the-mill meeting. For a start, only Freedom Brigade members are invited, so the message being delivered is for the foot soldiers, not the hoi-polloi.

"Whatever that message is, it must be important because the leader is delivering it himself."

Ace sat up. "The architect behind the Anthropocene is coming here?" He and Lemmy exchanged a sideways glance.

"Don't get any ideas, shugah. He will be protected, and there's no way *you* can gain entry." She reached into the box and produced a small roll of cloth and, fanning her hand across it, unfurled six hatpins. "Ladies, these are your passports into the meeting. You must each buy a pale green cloche hat and stick the pin on the left. If you are unsure of what hat to buy or how to wear the pin, stroll around the market. You'll be surprised how many Freedom sisters walk amongst us."

Dottie, Tabby, Rory and Connie each took a hatpin. Algeria picked up the remaining two and held one up to Ace. "I'll take this and a cloche for Issy, in case she's in there."

"What do we do, High Mother? Stand back and kick our heels while you gells have all the fun?" Lemmy's loud humph left little doubt of his feelings.

Algeria didn't react to the acerbic gesture. "Other than their grey shirts, we don't know what 'token' the men will wear to gain entry, and we don't have time to find out. And, in any case, they are on the lookout for you."

"And you, Mama." Dottie put her hand on her mother's shoulder. "They'll recognise you from the raid on the Praetorian."

Algeria hesitated. "Yes, Doll, you're right." She smoothed both hands down her dress and tossed her hair. "It's hard to hide when you look this good." Tense faces around the table relaxed. Even Lemmy smiled despite his obvious disappointment. "Maybe I'll have to sit this one out." She tightened her lips and handed the spare hatpin to Dottie.

"So, what's the plan? We get inside, then what?" Tabby eyed the box of brass tubes.

"If it follows the pattern of regular Freedom meetings, there will be speeches, then some spectacle to stir up the crowd. So spread out amongst them, listen to the speeches, especially their leader's, and wait for him to leave the stage. Then, and only then, you act."

Algeria picked up a handful of assorted brass tubes. "Sniff

the antidote and move around the hall spraying the toxin. Shillington said the effect should be almost immediate. Then, Tabby and Rory, head backstage, spraying as you go, and nab the leader."

"We are going to kidnap him?" Connie licked her lips.

"That's the plan…"

"Fuck, yes!" Tabby slapped both hands on the table.

"And Issy?" Connie looked up from under her frown.

"You and Doll should keep your eyes skinned. If you can effect a rescue, take your best shot."

Rory pressed her monocle under her eyebrow. "And what do we do with our captive?"

Algeria pondered for a few seconds. "We'll burn that bridge when we come to it."

Oscar dispatched Letitia to open the door only after he had confirmed the identity of the visitor through the BDI.

"It's bitterly cold out there tonight, old man." Felix pulled off his gloves and popped them inside his topper as he bustled into the parlour, wringing his hands. He paused to warm them at the fire before sitting in the wingback chair opposite Oscar. "I've sent Letitia off to make tea. Hope you don't mind, old boy."

"Not at all. Splendid idea." Oscar rested his elbows on the arms of the chair and bridged his fingers in front of his face. "So, how did your little spying mission go?"

"You will never believe where I've been. Ha! These Order chaps and chapesses are quite resourceful."

For the next ten minutes, Felix recounted, in meticulous detail, how he had followed Gilbert via the gentlemen's lavatories at the junction of Corporation Street and Miller Street, through a maze of underground tunnels leading to the steps down into a deep, cavernous man-made tunnel at least a hundred feet below the streets of Manchester.

"Yes, yes. Fascinating, old boy. But did you learn anything about The Maker project?" Oscar had glanced at his timepiece half a dozen times.

"Not a jot, I'm afraid. They're an unusual bunch. A bit of a mixture between religious fanatics and well-meaning philanthropists. That Algeria woman started the meeting with a prayer and ended it, banging on about infiltrating some Freedom Brigade rally. Most peculiar, if you ask me."

"A rally, you say? Local?"

"Free Trade Hall, old boy, tomorrow."

"Oh well. It was worth a try. I was certain they were holding something back from us."

Felix twisted his body to look over his shoulder at the door. "Letitia is taking a deuce of a long time making the—Ah, there you are, my dear. Oscar and I thought we must have run out of tea leaves, and you had tootled off on a clipper to Ceylon to pick some."

Without a word, Letitia glided around the furniture and placed the tray on the low table between them.

"Is everything all right, Letitia?" Oscar reached out for her, but she stepped away, trailing a finger along Felix's arm on her way to the door.

"Everything is fine." She disappeared through the door, closing it with a loud click.

Oscar frowned. "Most peculiar behaviour…"

"I'll say, old boy. She always laughs at my jokes. But tonight, not even a smile. Very odd."

"I'll speak with her in the morning." Oscar leaned back in his chair. "Your turn to be mother. Milk and one sugar, please."

GOING ROGUE

Behind tightly closed eyes, Issy subconsciously shut out reality. Carts and wagons rumbling along the cobbles on Peter Street above conjured images of glittering frost on a dark, wintry morning, with horses blowing plumes from snorting nostrils as they trotted under their drivers' urgings and cracking whips.

But the stinging mixture of carbolic, turpentine and vinegar broke her waking dream with a jolt.

She opened her eyes to a darkened storeroom dimly lit by lamplight seeping beneath the door from the room beyond.

Her hands and feet were numb. But her hips, back and shoulders ached, and her face, pressed hard against the floor, was wet with her own urine.

Sleep hadn't come easy, trussed up as she was on the cold stone floor. With her wrists tied to her ankles, her thighs compressing her chest made breathing difficult. Luckily, when they left her, they had tossed her coat at her, and she had pulled it over her body by grabbing it with her teeth and rolling like a crocodile tearing flesh from its prey.

Cramped legs made her cry out. Wriggling and tensing her muscles didn't ease the agony, but when a long low moan came from the wall facing her, she halted her struggle against her bonds. Holding herself as still as she could despite the pain, she strained her senses.

Silence.

"Theo?" she called out in a hoarse whisper. "Is that you?"

"Issy?" The voice was low, but unmistakable.

"What have they done to you?"

"I seem to have made some enemies amongst my Freedom brethren." He punctuated his weak laugh with a loud hawk and spit.

"Are you badly hurt?"

"Not as bad as they will be when I get hold of them."

Light in the storeroom flickered. Issy looked past her feet at the crack between the door and the floor. Outside, feet were moving towards her. "I've got company," she said.

"How did they catch you?"

"They didn't. I'll tell you later..." A key turned in the lock, and the storeroom burst into light, confirming Issy's hypothesis that it was stuffed with cleaning materials. Mops, brushes, buckets and boxes, bottles, tins and cans of scouring liquids and powders filled the shelves lining the walls.

She narrowed her eyes as she tilted her head. A large

middle-aged woman led two older hags carrying an oil lamp, a chair, and a small cloth bundle into the room. They wore factory clothes and lime-flower green hats.

The rotund woman stared at the wet floor and sniggered. "Look, ladies. She's peed herself. Disgusting."

She drew a short knife from the scabbard on her belt and grunted as she squatted on her haunches. Issy braced herself as the grinning woman twisted the blade in front of her face while eying her prone body. Her expression hardened as she grabbed the cord connecting her wrists to her ankles and cut it with two quick slashes.

Issy's body unfolded, and she rolled flat onto her back with a whimper and a sigh. Stretching the cramp from her calves, she stared at the ceiling, gulping air. Her heart was racing.

"Stand 'er up!"

The old crones heaved Issy to her feet and held her upright by her arms.

The big woman put her hand around Issy's throat. "Listen, you stuck-up bitch. They think you're a toff, but I know you're one of that evil Order. You stink of their arrogance. Unlike some, the three of us are true believers. We know your lot murdered our prophet, Raven. Yeah, scared now, aren't yer?"

Issy struggled, trying to breathe.

"Today, you're gonna get your comeuppance. You'll pay for what you did to our Raven. But you can thank yourself lucky stars that it won't be by our hand, 'cos we would 'ave too much fun playing with you before watching you exhale your last breath."

Issy gasped for air as the woman removed her podgy fingers from her throat and stepped back.

"The boss wants 'er to look nice for 'er starring role. Strip 'er to 'er slip and bloomers."

Blood rushed to Issy's face as she tried to pull herself free.

"Enough!" The woman pulled the hatpin from her cloche and pressed the point against Issy's cheek just below her eye. Holding Issy's head between her fist and the pin, she grabbed a handful of hair with her other hand. "Now, hold still if you don't want to lose yer eye."

She nodded at the crones, who cut through the taffeta sleeves from her wrists, across the shoulders and through to the lacy neckline. Bony, dry hands rubbed against the soft skin on her arms. Unable to move, Issy was helpless as one hag lifted the white lace hem at the front of the dress and began cutting.

"Careful, ladies. This dress cost more than you earn in a year." The woman's face was so close, her gin-soaked breath made Issy grimace.

When the last snip cut through the neckline just above her bosom, the dress fell to the floor, leaving Issy in her undergarments.

The woman released Issy's hair, pulled the hatpin off her cheek and stepped back. Issy watched the woman's eyes look her up and down. "Not so hoity-toity now, are we? Stood there shaking in your petticoat, stays and stained bloomers."

Issy tried to hide her embarrassment, cupping her tied hands over the stain, but her bound ankles made balancing difficult on her trembling legs. Her three tormentors stood, hands on hips, cackling. Issy looked into their faces, memorising every sneer and every wrinkle on their contorted faces.

"Right," the big woman said, "we have jobs to do before we take 'er up for 'er big show. Sit 'er down and cover 'er up."

One crone plonked the chair behind Issy and forced her onto its hard wooden seat. The other unwrapped a black hooded gown and fastened it around Issy's neck.

The big woman stepped forward and bent at the hips, pressing the side of her face to Issy's. "Yeah, we 'eard yer, and we can't have yer talkin' to yer brother again, missy." She wrapped a white gag across her mouth and tied it tight behind her head, then pulled the hood up.

"Pretty as a picture." She slapped Issy's face, almost knocking her off the chair. Then, scooping up the remains of the blue taffeta dress and hooking the oil lamp to her belt, she marched the crones out of the room in single file, leaving her alone in the dark.

Once the footsteps had receded, Theo's shouts became progressively louder, but with Issy unable to respond, he gave up. She closed her eyes and rocked back and forth on the seat, etching the grinning faces, so full of hatred, into her memory. Her anger and distress were magnified because women, members of her sisterhood, had done this to her.

And that betrayal strengthened her resolve to survive and wreak revenge on those evil harridans.

"I'm afraid she's gone, old boy." Oscar was still wearing his candy-striped nightgown and nightcap.

"Gone? What do you mean... vanished?" Felix craned his neck, peering over Oscar's crooked frame in the doorway.

"When I got up this morning, there was no sign of her. That's why I'm running a little late." Oscar shuffled about-face and *tippety-tap-shwoosh-clunk*ed back along the hall. "Be a splendid chap and make us a pot of tea, would you?"

Felix scurried off lickety-split towards the kitchen.

Since Letitia's arrival and the subsequent defensive modifications to his contraptions, Oscar's morning ritual had been disrupted beyond recognition. He longed for the little ones' joyful greetings and silly games. He even missed Polly the Pierrot doll's mithering to play in the garden. Now, she just sat in a dark corner, a silent sentinel, ready to roll into action.

His *McMurdo's Patented Helping Hand Push-Me-Pulley* chair lowered him into a sitting position, and he silently checked and recorded the readings from his weather station.

Running a crooked finger down the daily entries, he stopped at the twenty-eighth of November and sighed. Was it really only twenty days since Felix brought Letitia into their lives?

Felix's hurried strides rattled the crockery on the tea tray as he loped across the workshop. "Did Letitia leave a note?"

"Steady on, old boy. That tea service belonged to my mother. It may not look like much to you, but it's priceless to me."

Felix placed the tray on the workbench and pulled up a chair. "What's going on, Oscar? Why would she leave us?"

"Us, Felix?" Oscar chuckled as he poured the tea. "She was my housekeeper…"

"What I mean to say—"

"I'm just pulling your leg, old boy. We are all in this together." He raised his arms and his voice. "Aren't we, children?" Contraptions around the workshop buzzed, beeped and shouted their assent. *Letitia must have wound them before she left*, he thought. He swallowed back the rise of emotion in his throat.

"Do you think she's found The Maker?"

"I honestly don't know. She's been privy to most of the information we've gleaned so far, so unless she has a source we are unaware of, I don't see how… Although, she has been communicating through the Wisp more regularly since we discovered the Order."

"Really? I hadn't noticed."

"Sometimes, Felix, my old friend, I think you must walk around with your eyes closed." Oscar chortled as he slurped his tea. "Which would also explain the bruises on your legs."

Felix returned Oscar's smile. "Do you think she'll come back? You should surely relish the chance to continue to observe her and this confounded self-awareness whatnot she possesses."

"Indeed, old boy. I would also like to meet The Maker, whoever that may be. He has some questions to answer. Not least, how and why he installed the Scriptures."

"And why Letitia?"

"Very perceptive, Felix. We'll make a scientist of you yet.

The answer to that question can only lie in her past. Ipkiss and that Raven chap hold the key."

Felix snapped his fingers. "She's going to the Free Trade Hall."

"I have arrived at the same conclusion." Oscar grinned.

"Well? What are we going to do?"

"There you go again. *We* are not going to do anything. *You*, my dear old spy, are going on a new mission. Having successfully infiltrated the Order's meeting, gaining entry to the Free Trade Hall should be a doddle for a man of your talents."

Felix blushed and lowered his eyes.

"Right, that's settled, then." Oscar leaned forward. "I don't suppose you could rustle up a spot of lunch for us both? To be brutally honest, old boy, I didn't have any breakfast."

Twenty days and I have become dependent on her. Oscar stroked his chin. *Or maybe making herself indispensable was the plan all along…*

After sunset, a thick brown-grey fog descended on the city as the brothers and sisters of the Freedom Brigade swarmed in and around the Free Trade Hall's arched bays, awaiting the call to enter and hear the word of their leader for the first time.

On the other side of Peter Street, Ace and Lemmy leaned against the wall on the corner of Harvester House, watching the queue for the Theatre Royal, blowing on their hands and stamping sensation back into their feet as they filed into the foyer for the evening performance of Cinderella. The queue was already snaking around the side of the building along Southmill Street when they had arrived an hour earlier. Behind them in Albert Square, the Town Hall clock struck a muffled seven.

Although the freezing fog helped to conceal their identities, it made surveillance of the Free Trade Hall almost impossible. But it had enabled them to stay undetected by the Freedom Brigade and the Order alike. Even Tabby and Rory had not looked in their direction when they had passed surreptitiously under the arched bays into the hall.

"Algeria would have our guts for garters if she knew we were here." Lemmy glanced left and right. "Jolly exciting, eh, old chum?" His elbow dug into Ace's ribs.

"We're wasting time. We should be in there searching for Issy."

"Ah, but when the Freedom Brigadier, or whatever he calls himself, turns up, we nip this in the bud before it blossoms."

Ace aimed a kick at a streetlamp and missed. "It's less than an hour before the meeting starts and still no sign of the bigwig."

"Perhaps he's already in there."

Ace checked his pocket watch. "We'll give it five more minutes then we—"

He narrowly dodged the blur of windmilling arms and churning legs that barrelled into Lemmy, almost knocking him off his feet. When the commotion stopped, the blur formed itself into Gilbert, who bent double, hands on his hips, panting to catch his breath. "I thought… I'd find you here."

"What are you doing here, old chum? We're on the lookout

for this leader fellow, don'tcha know." Lemmy rested his hand on Gilbert's shoulder. "Are you all right?"

"I've found a way in. But we don't have much time. Before they find out what's happened."

"Why? What's happ—"

"No time to explain." Gilbert staggered off the pavement and, dodging between the carts and hansoms on Peter Street, disappeared into the fog along Southmill Street.

Lemmy raised his eyebrows and spread his arms. "Are we going after him?"

Ace grabbed Lemmy's arm and pulled him across the street, following in Gilbert's foggy wake. There was no means of entry along the side of the hall, so they stayed on the Theatre Royal side of the street to avoid detection. But when they reached the back of the hall, there was no sign of Gilbert.

"He must have gone around there." Ace peered into the unlit alley that ran along the back of the hall. "Keep close and watch our rear."

Ace kept his hand in contact with the wall as they edged into the dense darkness. After twenty careful paces, a dim light ahead illuminated the outline of a bundle lying on the cobbles. Ace pressed his hand into Lemmy's chest to stop him advancing. Although he realised Lemmy could barely see him, he held his finger to his lips and whispered, "Not a sound, old boy."

He crouched and crept forward. Light leaking from around the slightly open door in the ornate wall of the hall trickled into the alleyway. As he neared the amorphous form, it outlined the shape of a lifeless body with two more sprawled grotesquely beyond.

Ace squatted on his haunches. Their clothing was soaked in the same dark liquid that trickled between the cobbles surrounding the bodies. It also ran from spatters sprayed across the door and its carved stone frame.

Gilbert is not a man to be trifled with, he thought.

Ace was careful not to stand in the bloody mess as he eased the door open and beckoned Lemmy forward. On the wall opposite, three dimmed gas mantles lit the room. Porters' trolleys and luggage carriers were scattered over one side of the room, whilst the other had rows upon rows of benches backed by coat hooks on rails. The smell of the dead Freedom foot soldiers' last smokes hung in the air.

Lemmy closed the outer door and slid the internal bolts. "Good work, Gilbert, old chum. Remind me never to get on your wrong side."

Gilbert frowned and put his finger to his lips, pointing to light streaming through an ajar door on the long wall opposite. They crept across the room. Ace was nearest to the door as they pressed their backs against the wall.

He twisted his neck and squinted into the bright hallway beyond but almost immediately turned his head back, gasping. Blood pounded in his head as his heart raced. Every muscle, every sinew tensed as he ground his teeth to control his fear and rage.

"What is it? What's wrong?" Lemmy grabbed his arm as he whispered.

"Ace?" Gilbert reached for the handles of his weapons.

Ace turned to face him, but he couldn't speak. How could he tell him that at the other end of the hallway, an old woman was prancing around in a torn blue taffeta dress?

Issy's blue taffeta dress.

OUT OF THE DARKNESS...

arlier, the fog had forced Felix to take a Tick Tock from Worsley station into Manchester Central. Although delighted with his flat cap and ragged-coat-over-grey-shirt disguise, he loathed taking the Tick Tock at the best of times.

Thankfully, the grey shirt had guaranteed his seat despite the tram being jam-packed with Christmas shoppers, but he was forced to give it up to a frail old lady, bent over her walking stick, who had fixed him with her icy stare the moment she got on board. But even having to stand for only two stops, the winding tracks made the jostling intolerable. The conductor's announcement of 'Manchester Central. This tram terminates here' was music to his ears.

He jumped off the green-and-red into a maelstrom of activity. With mek-porters wheeling trolleys, sharp-elbowed passengers barged by, whistles blew, and trains coughed black smoke and cinders at the soot-darkened glass and steel arched roof. As he dashed to the buffers at the ends of the tracks, he strained to detect the telltale hum of dynamotive accumulators beneath the high-pitched cacophony. But eventually, he had to rely on his eyes to confirm the absence of a HyBrid locomotive.

Pity, he thought. On his last visit to Manchester two days earlier, he had heard a behemoth rumbling over Castlefield Viaduct and promised himself to see one close-up. *Maybe next time.*

Outside on the station approach, the giant clock, barely visible through the fog high in the station's arched frontage, showed twenty-three minutes before seven. Time was short, so he hurried across Windmill Street behind a small group of burly men in flat caps and followed them up Southmill Street.

It was only when they turned sharply into an alley running along the back of the Free Trade Hall that he glimpsed the old woman from the tram, head held high, leading them at a fair lick with her walking stick tucked under her arm.

She may have been a little over five feet tall, but she commanded the respect of the bruisers following in her wake.

Felix closed the gap with the group and followed them into the dark alley. Ahead, fog-diffused light from a wide-open doorway grew brighter. No words were exchanged as the men stopped briefly, allowing the old woman to enter the hall first. He pulled his cap down on his forehead and copied the grey-shirts as they nodded grimly at the three guards they passed.

By some miracle, no one challenged him. He was inside the

Free Trade Hall, giddy at how easy it had been. Straight ahead, a door led into a brightly lit hallway. He lagged behind as they strode, single file, through the doorway.

The last man turned to look behind. Felix dropped to a knee and fiddled with his bootlaces, waving the man away without raising his head. Out of the corner of his eye, he glimpsed the man's boots hesitate, then disappear along the hallway.

But even in the dimly lit room, he was in plain view of the three guards at the door if they glanced his way.

He risked a side-eyed peek in their direction. One guard blocking the entrance, facing the alley, obscured the view of his colleagues. Felix took his chance. Without straightening, he ran, crouching, towards some benches and flung himself behind the first row.

Pleased he had made it this far, the precariousness of his situation dawned.

He was trapped.

Although invisible to the guards, he dared not risk moving. *If only I hadn't followed*—Blood-curdling shrieks and a flurry of sounds at the door cut short his thought.

Not daring to breathe, he held his body rigid. The commotion lasted only a few seconds, then silence.

He listened.

He was not alone. Although he couldn't hear them or see them, he sensed a presence in the cold, eerie stillness.

His racing heartbeat was pounding in his head as he brought his knees to his chest and squirmed onto his side. Light burst from the doorway into the hall, then faded just as suddenly. He twisted onto his back and lay still for a few more minutes to calm his nerves and catch his breath before he dared to raise himself onto his hands and knees. But muffled voices in the alley made him duck back behind the benches.

Footsteps shuffled through the door from the alley to the hall door.

Hushed, vaguely familiar voices…

"Gilbert?" A whisper from the darkness.

Gilbert's swords rasped against their sheaths as he eased them halfway out, then he turned to face the gaunt figure staggering to its feet from behind the benches. When it stepped from the shadows, the gaslight revealed a white-haired man wearing a cloth cap and a grey shirt. Gilbert narrowed his eyes.

"Felix? What are you doing here?"

"Letitia's disappeared. Oscar thinks she might have come here."

"And the grey shirt?" Gilbert maintained his grip on the hilts.

"Disguise." Felix's smile drained into a tight-lipped frown as he looked around the grim faces. "Is there anything I can do to help?"

Ace stepped forward. "They've got Issy. I believe they are going to use her in some dastardly display. If this rally-for-the-faithful runs along the same lines as their regular meetings, they'll drag her on stage after the speeches. And then they'll… they'll…" His voice trailed off. He took a deep breath and raised his head. "We mustn't let it get that far."

"I understand, old boy." Felix put a hand on Ace's shoulder. He turned to Gilbert. "What's the plan?"

"We don't have one."

Behind Ace, Lemmy was peering through the narrow gap between the door and jamb on the hinges side. He raised his hand, and the room fell silent.

Shadows moved across the floor as three figures walked past from the right, blocking the light from the ajar door as they passed. Lemmy lowered his hand when the men's laughter had receded.

"There may be stairs over to the right." Lemmy twisted his neck, pressing his face against the doorjamb. "I can't quite make out…"

"Is the coast clear, old boy?" Felix grabbed the door handle.

"As far as I can—"

Felix yanked the door open and stomped off to the right.

Lemmy eased the door to, and they waited in silence. After a minute that felt like an hour to Gilbert, Felix hurried back in.

"There's a staircase leading down to a couple of locked doors, probably storerooms. If they are holding her anywhere, it will be down there."

Gilbert stopped Ace with an arm across his chest. "Whoa. We can't just blunder down there. If we get caught, they'll have five captives and there'll be no one to rescue us. The three grey-shirts must have been visiting Issy." He turned his head to

Lemmy. "You saw them. Can we take them?"

Lemmy bent the corners of his mouth down and nodded.

"We'll beat them or die trying…" Ace was champing at the bit.

Gilbert kept his hand on Ace. "Take it easy. We wait until they return, nab the keys to the storerooms, and the rest will be simple."

'*With your back to the wall, your enemies can't surprise you, and you'll relish the fear in their eyes when you attack.*'

Ataraxia invariably heeded the words of her late lamented husband. Always aware of her surroundings, but never trusting the motives of those around her, even amongst apparent allies, she would choose a corner seat so she could survey the room.

She would not suffer the same fate as Caesar in *Theatrum Pompeii*.

So, she sat in a corner, behind a small round table, in the bar used during exhibitions or after political rallies. Although the cost of hiring the Free Trade Hall had been paid from the considerable, but not inexhaustible, coffers of the Freedom movement, she was determined to make full use of the theatrical facilities.

Beyond her half empty sherry glass, the room was a constantly shifting kaleidoscope of greys as local leaders glad-handed, congratulating themselves on their recent successes. All of which, of course, would not have happened without her. She couldn't care any less about their pathetic preening and petty one-upmanship.

The masses were not aware the Freedom movement was her brainchild, but tonight she would step out of the shadows.

"Can I get you a drink? Water? Wine? Hemlock?" Wyndham-Welch slammed his little tumbler of brown liquid on the table as he flopped on the chair opposite her, grinning.

"Whilst I'm sure the nestling sycophants in the lower chamber pretend to find you amusing, those of us of good breeding and a modicum of intelligence don't have to pander to your ribaldry."

"Wonderful to see you again, too." He nodded at the two-foot-long, twelve-inch-wide, polished mahogany case on which she rested her hands. Its *R.I.P-S* inlaid silver inscription showed the box once belonged to her late husband. "What's in the box?"

"Did I invite you to join me? Or maybe I missed your polite request for permission to sit at my table?"

"Everyone is celebrating your success. Why so angry?"

"Anger? You interpret my indifference to you as anger? Does rage make a cuckoo lay in another bird's nest? Is a crow venting its wrath when it uses a stone to break an egg?

"No. Your arrogance bores me. You overestimate your importance when you are nothing more than a tool. Ralph endorsed your candidacy because of your gullibility, because to us, you are just a useful fool."

"And yet, you insist I travel all the way from London by HyBrid to speak at your triumphal unveiling. I am your most supportive voice in Parliament and hold the key to the movement's success or failure." Wyndham-Welch swirled the drink in his glass before throwing it down his gullet.

"You are one of many and expendable."

"Ahh, but you forget I know who you are and why you prosecute your cause so passionately. With a few well-chosen words, I could—"

Ataraxia jerked forward and slapped her hands on the table so hard, heads turned.

"Choose your *next* words carefully. Pick unwisely, and they will be your last." She twisted the box sideways and flicked the brass catches open with her thumbs.

Blood drained from his face. "I was merely suggest—"

"You were merely threatening. I've killed for less."

"In front of so many witnesses? I think not." A bead of sweat rolled down his face.

"Look around and think again. A third would turn their backs, and a third would watch but do nothing. And any of the rest would champ at the bit to do the job to please me. You have no friends here." The clasps on the box snapped shut. "Now get out of my sight before I change my mind."

Wyndham-Welch opened his mouth, but Ataraxia's sharply raised eyebrows snapped his jaw shut. He pushed himself out of his seat and barged his way through the murmuring faithful towards the door, squeezing past Hansel as he was entering.

Ataraxia met Hansel's puzzled expression with a beckoning, backwards jerk of her head.

"Send the attendants to stay with our guests. No harm must

befall them before their top-of-the-bill performance."

"I will pay Theo a visit first. I owe him." Hansel slammed his fist into his palm.

"No. You won't. Because you will be too busy ensuring Wyndham-Welch gives the speech we wrote for him. He may need more persuading to keep to the plan." She caught the defiance in his eyes. "Keep away from Theo. We can't afford any hiccups when we are so close to achieving our goals."

He pressed his lips together for a second before reaching for the box on the table. "Do you want me to—"

"No." She slammed her palm on the silver lettering. "Ralph always kept them ready, and nobody who still lives has touched them."

Hansel smirked. "But that changes tonight."

Ataraxia raised her eyebrows over a blank expression.

Really? Why on earth would you think that?

...INTO THE LIGHT

While it was mandatory for the sisters of Freedom to wear their pins in their bonnets, brothers could display their stickpins wherever they chose.

So, Onslow wore his brass, hammer-shaped badge inside the lapel of his black woollen coat.

Once the Free Trade Hall doors opened, brothers and sisters filed past the token checkers into the main hall. With furtive glances left and right, Onslow had flashed his pin, imagining he was a Prussian spy.

As he was always on the lookout for an opportunity to flirt with the ladies, he had applied to be one of the scrutineers. But unsurprisingly, his bid had been unsuccessful. He suspected it was a case of jobs-for-the-boys, and, in Theo, he had hitched his wagon to a falling star.

Still, while the hardcore Freedom supporters elbowed and

shoved their way to the front, he chose a seat at the side of the hall under the balcony. Although he was mainly here for Theo, he scanned the stalls for Fanny before taking his seat. He had unfinished business with that sultry minx.

As this was his first time inside the building, he took the time to soak up its splendour. From his vantage point, he could see the whole auditorium, including the rest of the empty balcony that swept around the hall, and above that, the paired columns supporting arches adorning the walls beneath an elaborate coffered ceiling.

The hubbub grew louder as the stalls filled, and he divided his attention between the stage and his pocket watch as it ticked closer to eight o'clock.

In the middle of a line of twelve chairs at the front of the stage, a small lectern stood in front of the plain ruby curtains that halved the stage's depth, concealing whatever lay behind.

Onslow tucked his watch into his waistcoat just as the gas mantles around the hall dimmed, leaving the blazing stage footlights as the main illumination.

Conversations died down, replaced by an expectant silence, which was shattered by an eruption of applause and cheers greeting the Freedom speakers marching in lockstep from stage left.

Nine men in short toppers, grey shirts and dark trousers and two ladies in black dresses and pale green bonnets each stood in front of a chair, heads back, half-lidded eyes looking down their noses at the congregation, feeding off the adoration. A single chair at the far right of the stage remained unoccupied.

Onslow had seen it all before. *Top brass*, he thought, *new name, same old toffs.* His loud snort garnered glaring disapproval. He raised a weary hand in apology.

Out of the corner of his eye, he glimpsed two Freedom sisters staring at him. But as he turned his head, their stares snapped to the stage as they slow-clapped in unison.

They were an odd-looking pair. The shorter of the two filled her khaki woollen coat with womanly curves while her green bonnet teetered on top of her unruly brown hair. Only the hatpin prevented the hat from springing from her head.

But if her tall, elegant companion had not been wearing a bonnet, he would have mistaken her for a gentleman. Her dark blue suit hung loose on her slim frame, and she puffed on a cheroot through a long, black, silver-inlaid cigarette holder. Hair slick with pomade, the pin in her cloche hat served no purpose other than adornment.

The applause subsiding drew his attention back to the stage. As the crowd quietened to expectant murmuring, the speakers took their seats apart from toff at the far left who remained standing, reading from a small sheet of notepaper to introduce each of his colleagues. Each acknowledged their name with a wave or a nod as it was called.

Then the speeches started, and Onslow's attention ebbed. One by one, each speaker spouted the same nonsense he'd heard many times.

Bored stiff, he surveyed the hall. The odd sisters had vanished and whilst many of the crowd stood transfixed, hanging on each speaker's every word, some exchanged whispers or checked their pocket watches.

The plans of the Freedom Brigade didn't interest him. He was only here for his friend Theo and to find Fanny.

He folded his arms and closed his eyes. The fourth speaker, a tall man with a deep monotone voice, droned on and on…

"You must stay here." Lemmy gripped Ace's shoulders as he whispered at his down-turned face. "If any of these goons recognise you, we're done for."

"He's right, old boy," Felix chimed in. "We need you here to secure our escape route. And, in any case, the three of us can subdue those blighters."

Gilbert and Lemmy narrowed their eyes at Felix.

"Well… We have the element of surprise on our side. They won't expect the—"

Lemmy put his finger to his lips and peered through the gap between the hinges of the door and the doorjamb, pressing his face against the wall. Gilbert counted the shadows sliding across the floor from the ajar door. As the footsteps faded into silence, his shoulders slumped as Lemmy turned to face him.

"Six," they said in unison.

"They were all dressed in hooded cloaks, so I couldn't get a proper look, but I think the three short ones were women. The other three were built like circus strongmen or pugilists. We could handle the women, probably…" Lemmy's smile faded.

This was no time for levity.

"Two minutes, then we go." Gilbert patted the hilts of his swords. "I have these. I'll keep an eye out while you scavenge the room for weapons."

Felix rummaged in his pocket. "Oscar gave me this." He pulled out a six-inch-long, two inches in diameter brass cylinder and waggled it in Gilbert's face.

"You'll need a bigger stick."

"This is big enough, old boy. It's a *McMurdo's Patented Little John Expanding Quarterstaff*. One squeeze of the button, and you're holding the middle of a five-foot metal pole. He warned me to be careful where I point it when I activate it. Apparently, it's lethal."

"I'll take your word for it." Gilbert turned to Ace. "Give Lemmy a hand, Ace… Ace?" He raised his voice to a hoarse whisper. "Snap out of it! Don't just stand there chopfallen. We don't have much time."

Gilbert peered through the crack and listened for footsteps. Distant cheers and applause from the main hall sent a chill down his spine. He held his pocket watch in the sliver of light.

"Time's up," he said.

Lemmy was wrapping a long chain around his hand when he joined them, and both men nodded their readiness.

"Keep an eye open for us, Ace. You'll need to be ready."

"*Natus est paratum.*"

Gilbert rolled his eyes as he had seen Issy do many times. Then, with one last peek through the crack, he grabbed the door handle. "Lead the way, Felix."

He swung the door open and, leaving it ajar, followed Felix and Lemmy out into the hallway. Felix led them along the corridor and down the stairs that turned back on themselves halfway.

At the bottom, Felix poked his head into the passage. Looking left and right, he pointed right as Gilbert brushed past him, unsheathing his swords as he came to the first closed door.

He pressed his ear against it and was about to move to the second when a low moan was silenced by a loud thud.

Gilbert waved his companions forward and pushed at the door. It didn't budge. Something on the other side prevented it from opening. Lemmy and Felix lent their weight, and they tumbled into the room in a heap.

"Welcome to the fun, fellas. You're not as big as your mates, but don't let that stop you trying."

"Theo?" Lemmy stepped from behind Gilbert and Felix.

The big man straightened from his crouch. Blood from facial wounds covered his hands and smeared his vest. They must have beaten him mercilessly. But around him, three men in cloaks lay motionless.

"Well, well, well. Two of you are not wearing grey. So I assume you are not here to subdue me."

"We're not here for you at all," Felix said.

Gilbert gave him an exasperated look. "Where's Issy?"

Theo smiled and relaxed his shoulders. "You can put those blades away, lad. She's in the room next door." He looked down. "These fine fellows were dressing me for some big show I was going to appear in upstairs. I guess the giggling ladies next door are doing the same for my sister."

Reacting to clogs clattering in the passage, Gilbert eased the door shut and leant against it.

"Everythin' all right in there, dearie. The big lad ain't givin' you no trouble, is he? If you need a hand…" The woman's voice broke into a cackle.

"Nowt we can't 'andle. We're teachin' this goon a lesson he won't forget." Lemmy put on his best working-class accent. Gilbert looked up for divine help.

"Well, he won't need a long memory, will he…" The footsteps and cackle faded.

Gilbert exhaled. "Sounds as if they're going to make an exhibition of you."

"Public executions, eh?" Felix puffed out his cheeks.

"Well, your rescue seems to have fallen flat. Now, it's my turn." Theo pushed Gilbert aside with ease but stopped as Lemmy put his finger to his lips. Four loud bangs rattled the door.

"Get a move on! The boss says you've got ten minutes."

"Right-ho!" Lemmy answered the man's voice.

"That, my friends, was Mister Hansel, an old acquaintance of mine." Theo looked down at the grey-shirts. "You heard the man. Get a move on if you want to save Issy. But you'll need to put on your costumes first."

He snatched the hooded cloak intended for him from the hand of one thug and pulled it over his bloodied vest.

"Two of the shirts don't have much blood on them…"

Onslow woke with a start and sprang to his feet, joining in the applause thundering all around him. Sisters and brothers alike whooped, whistled and clapped vigorously. He wasn't the tallest in the hall, so he had to jump, bobbing and weaving, peering between the toppers, caps, bonnets and arms raised in salutation, to see the cause of the commotion.

Each fleeting glimpse revealed a new detail. The speakers were exiting stage left… They left a small grey smudge standing just in front of where the curtains met… The smudge was a diminutive, middle-aged woman with grey hair… She wore a corseted grey dress and bustle… Her clasped hands were holding something made of brass.

She waited for silence, like a headmistress at a preparatory school for naughty children.

As the frenzy subsided, she raised the brass speaking-trumpet.

The hall fell silent.

"I stand before you as founder and leader of the Freedom movement."

Shushers silenced the ripples of applause.

"How many of you followed the prophet Raven?" Around the hall, Onslow estimated about one in four of the male attendees raised their hands. "We thank you for your service and loyalty to the cause. Raven's attacks on the government-controlled transportation systems paved the way for our political success.

"Of all the possible venues for this rally, why did I choose here?" She peered around the hall. "Well, not, as you may think, because Manchester is the cradle of the Industrial Revolution and the birthplace of invention and innovation. No, I chose this place because of its standing in the history of this great nation. It was in this hall that the first clarion call of women's suffrage rang out. And our cause is just as righteous."

Ataraxia paused to relish the whoops and whistles. Surveying the room for a fleeting moment, her gaze rested on Onslow before moving on.

"You have heard the indisputable evidence presented on behalf of Professor Eis-Kalt by his learned friends about the five—"

A voice called out from the middle of the crowd, "We're not interested in what a German fella thinks. What's yer name, lady? Some of us here need to know out who we're foll—"

The blackjack's hollow popping sound echoed around the hall as it bounced off the side of the man's head, and he fell from sight. His attacker tucked the cosh into her purse, straightened her dress, and adjusted her bonnet before returning her attention to the stage.

No one bent to tend to the injured man.

Ataraxia nodded her approval before carrying on. "Names are not important. I don't need to know yours, nor you mine." The grey lady hardly missed a beat. "But understanding the five extinctions *is* important.

"Connickle tried to convince us that the Industrial

Revolution was causing a world climate catastrophe. This is nonsense. Nevertheless, the government used his theories to enact laws in his name to oppress you, the workers.

"But for every scientist that supports him, we have ten that refute his theories.

"And they tell us everything is cyclical; entropy never rests. As sure as night follows day follows night, nothing lasts forever.

"Under Connickle, we would have crawled to the sixth extinction, the planet suffering a slow death, polluted by overpopulation. Not because of man-made climate change, but because of the Earth's geological and biological clocks.

"But repealing the laws has given us the chance of a better standard of living for those who deserve it most. We will speed up invention so that you get everything you need, and when the time comes, we will look after you and all those who support us.

"As Professor Eis-Kalt predicted, the sixth extinction will end the Holocene Epoch. But together, you and I will welcome a new epoch. The Anthropocene Epoch!"

The grey lady exited stage left as the faithful stood, cheered and clapped enthusiastically. Onslow remained seated and stifled a yawn as the footlights dimmed, bathing the stage in red light.

Then, without orchestration, the applause became rhythmical. Onslow rose to his feet, leaning from side to side to view the stage.

With the political rallying over, the show was about to begin.

Movement at the left of the stage turned heads. Four

hooded figures shuffled into the red light. Rough hands jerked back the hood of the lead figure, revealing a defiant face staring at the baying crowd.

Onslow gasped.

Issy?

Three loud bangs rattled the storeroom door.

"Get a move on!"

Gilbert put a finger to his lips.

"Everything all right in there?" The door handle turned.

"We're coming out! Clear the way! He's a handful!" Lemmy threw his weight against the door as he shouted.

"Tell him to hurry or he'll miss me killing his sister." Venom dripped from Hansel's softly spoken words.

Although certain he couldn't prevent him from charging through the door, Gilbert pressed his hands against Theo's shoulders and tried to work out what was going on behind his half-lidded eyes. He held on until he heard receding footsteps.

"I'll loop the rope around your wrists and let you hold the ends."

Theo nodded. Then his whole body convulsed, leaving him shaking.

Lemmy produced a hip flask and unscrewed the top. "Need a drink, old chum? It's only gin, but—"

Theo snatched the flask, gulping the contents. "I hate gin."

He grimaced and wiped his mouth with the back of his hand. "But at least they won't smell the booze on my breath."

"One last thing before we go." Gilbert pulled two small brass tubes with blue bands from a pouch on his belt. He tucked one into Theo's boot.

"What's that for?"

"It's an antidote for a surprise we have in store. If you get to Issy before us, make sure she inhales a lungful." Gilbert pointed to the button on the other tube, then held it under Theo's nose. "Deep breath." He pressed the button and watched Theo shudder as he sucked in the aerosol. Then he repeated the exercise for Lemmy and Felix before turning it on himself.

Lemmy pressed his ear against the door. "We need to go," he said.

"All right, Theo. Let's put on a show," Gilbert said. "Issy's life may depend on it."

They all pulled their hoods over their heads, half hiding their faces, and Lemmy opened the door.

Before they could brace themselves, Theo let out a ferocious roar and barrelled into the passage with his three gaolers hanging off his arms. Freedom sisters and brothers screamed and scattered from the mayhem.

Theo didn't let up. He dragged the three men up the stairs. To Gilbert's surprise, the door to Ace's hiding place was closed, but Theo pulled him past before he could knock or make any signal to warn him of their change of plan.

As they turned towards the stage, Hansel barred their way. "Hold him, brothers." He put all his strength into a thunderous gut punch. Theo doubled up, then slowly straightened and grinned at Hansel's shocked stare.

"When I return the compliment, you won't get up… ever." Theo bared his teeth.

"You won't get the chance," Hansel said. "Time for the show. Take him." He pointed to a white cross painted on the stage floor and punched the back of Theo's head as he passed.

The four men staggered on to the boards to gasps from the auditorium. Gilbert looked across the stage. Issy was facing them. A loose cloak barely concealed her undergarments. Beside her, two similarly cloaked old women held hatpins to her throat. Gilbert guessed the taller woman behind her was holding Issy's arms.

Hansel's voice was a hoarse whisper behind them. "Don't worry, brothers. He won't try anything while the sisters have her. 'Cos if he does, they'll open her veins."

Mirroring the sisters holding Issy, they loosened their grips with Lemmy standing behind Theo, Gilbert and Felix to either side.

In the stalls, the audience seemed to hold its collective breath. Gilbert cast his gaze around the stage, looking in vain for the Freedom leader.

What now? he thought.

He didn't have long to ponder.

DUEL

Issy was trembling.

The ankle-length velvet cloak draped loosely over her undergarments did little to warm her and the thick, red glass filters blocked any heat the footlights produced.

From the wings opposite, her bloodied and bruised brother staggered onto the stage. At that point, her blood boiling from the treatment meted out by his gaolers stopped her tremors. But rough hands and sharp hatpins prevented her from running to him.

Limelight illuminated a grey woman as she walked past her to the centre of the stage. She was cradling a long, flat box which she placed with great reverence on the lectern. Then she picked up the speaking-trumpet and raised her other hand, demanding silence.

"Tonight, Manchester will lose at least one member of its

nouveau riche oppressors. For the last fifty years, the Windlass family has run Brunswick Mill with an iron rod."

Below her, in the front stalls, Issy picked out Galbraith's voice above the smattering of boos and jeers.

"Here, we have the warring Windlass siblings. On my right, your left, we have Isadora Amaryllis. And on my left, your right, her brother, Theophilus Ansel, but you'll know him by his self-styled title, the Brunswick Brawler. These industrial aristocrats will settle their differences in the age-old fashion of the native nobility." The short grey woman raised the box over her head and turned to her left.

Issy caught her breath when she saw a familiar figure struggling with his captor in the wings.

"Ah, we have a new guest. Bring him to me, Hansel."

Hansel marched forward with his prisoner, pressing a pistol into his ribs.

"Brothers and sisters. Mister Aquilla Ulysses Sixsmith, erstwhile companion of Miss Isadora and best friend of her brother, has joined our little *soirée*. In case any of you are not aware, he's a leading light in the recently outlawed organisation, The Venerable Antediluvian Order of the Custodians of Magna Mater." She lowered the speaking-trumpet and turned to Ace. "Why are you here?"

"To meet the leader of this foul group of miscreants. Has he arrived yet? Please, point him out." He surveyed the auditorium like a pub landlord picking the next customer from an unruly throng.

"Very amusing, Mister Sixsmith. But I am disappointed you

didn't deliver some profound Latin uttering, as is your wont. But no matter. In the unlikely event of your survival, Hansel will extract the real reason for your presence here later."

"*Ego vultus deinceps ad eam. Pauci minutes si superstes.*"

"Ah, the famous Sixsmith wit. *Sic infit…*" She raised the speaking-trumpet to her mouth and looked left and right. "Seconds? Come to me."

The crones on each side took control of Issy's arms as the woman from behind strode solemnly to the podium.

A voice whispered. "Don't dare try anything, dearie." Issy recoiled from the crone's booze-drenched breath as she leaned closer, pressing the hatpin against Issy's throat. "I'll spurt your blood all over the boards."

From the other side of the stage, one of Theo's captors emerged from a scuffle and marched towards the lectern. Issy's heart leapt at his distinctive limp. She narrowed her eyes but couldn't make out his features under the hood.

The duellists' seconds stood on each side of the grey woman and faced the auditorium as she addressed the faithful. "These duelling pistols belonged to my late husband. He defended his honour no less than five times without sustaining as much as a flesh wound." She glanced sideways at each second as she opened the lid.

"Choose wisely," she said.

Issy's second reached into the box and snatched the uppermost pistol before her male counterpart could react. The grey woman's thin red lips briefly bent into a sanguineous sneer as the seconds returned to their captives, cradling their flintlocks like newborns.

"Let me make the rules of this duel crystal clear. On the count of three, you will each raise your weapons, aim, and fire. If either of you fails to raise your pistol or raises it too soon, Sixsmith will die. If your aim wavers, Sixsmith will die. Or if you deliberately miss or fail to pull the trigger, Sixsmith will die."

The boozy crone leaned close again. "Aim for his belly if you want him to suffer, dearie. The shot in these pistols messes up the innards somethin' terrible." She and her partner released their grip and withdrew their hatpins, leaving Issy's second at her side.

Finally able to move her head, she twisted her neck to look past the footlights at the jeering crowd.

A sparkling, fine mist descending on the stalls made everything hazy. At first, she thought it was a trick of the light. But when she saw occasional puffs of vapour squirting up from the auditorium, like spray from whales' blowholes, she realised her imagination wasn't playing tricks.

She narrowed her eyes, peering through the glare of the limelight. There was movement on the balcony. Despite the haze reducing visibility, she picked out the unmistakable figures of Rory and Tabby, each with both arms outstretched, squirting vapour as they dashed around the sweeping curves above the stalls.

At her side, the second thrust the pistol into her hand and retreated into the wings. It felt like a lead weight, pulling her arm to her side.

A terrible sadness swept over her. If only she hadn't been so wrapped up in her own selfish crusades, perhaps she wouldn't be facing death. Out of the corner of her eye, she watched the grey woman retreat behind Ace and Hansel, pressing her back to the ruby red curtains.

Through blurry eyes, she had no shot at the grey woman.

"One."

The grey woman's voice sounded lower and slower than earlier. Issy shook her head. Her thoughts were swimming through a black, viscous veil. She was trapped. No escape. But she couldn't shoot her brother.

"Two."

There was only one solution. Yes, put the gun to her temple, pull the trigger, end this wretchedness and save Theo's life. But what about Ace?

A thin, distant voice called out from the other side of the stage.

"Letitia?"

Theo slowly raised his pistol and tears sprang to her eyes.

She tottered between the footlights to the stage edge and looked down upon the moaning, wailing souls with their empty, imploring eyes darting, searching for the demons that haunted them. Fingers clawed at her legs, trying to pull her into their pit of hopelessness.

Then, lifting the pistol and pressing the barrel to her temple, she put her finger on the trigger.

She turned to glimpse Ace one last time, when, behind him, two hands with long slender fingers slid from the darkness between the curtains, around the grey woman's head and snapped together like a steel trap, interlocking across her eyes, nose and mouth. Above the grey hair, she glimpsed a flash of flame-red hair and two bright yellow eyes atop a crooked grin before the old woman was lifted by her head and pulled, limbs flailing, into the darkness.

As she disappeared, a gunshot exploded.

Running footsteps.

Issy screamed, "THEO!"

Her legs folded, and she toppled towards the welcoming maw of the damned.

"Deep breaths, Issy. Breathe!" Gilbert was spraying something into her nostrils.

She was suddenly aware of the chaos all around her. In the stalls, the Dante's Inferno of tortured souls wailing and moaning grew louder. Fights were breaking out everywhere.

In the centre of the stage, Hansel was on his knees, face contorted as if he were staring into the face of a demon. Theo stood over him, clutching his grey shirt, fist cocked. He smiled at Issy before delivering the punch.

The sickening crack told her Hansel may never awaken.

"Are you with us, old girl?" Lemmy was cradling her head. "We need to go." He lifted her off the boards, but stronger hands gripped her, pulling her upwards into a long-forgotten hold.

"She's mine." Theo tucked her limp body under his arm and set off, loping across the stage. Two, three, four grey-shirted thugs were dispatched with single punches from his free fist as he fought through the confused and despairing who clambered out of the stalls to escape their mental anguish.

Gilbert shouted above the mayhem, "We have to hold them in the auditorium. If they get outside, their heads will clear." He kept his blades sheathed, fighting alongside Ace and Lemmy, pushing flailing, wailing attendees off the stage. "Where's Felix?"

"He carved a way to the curtains with his quarterstaff and went through. I'll find him." Ace reached the gap in the curtains in three steps and disappeared into the darkness. Seconds later, he backed out, dragging Felix by his boots.

By the time Gilbert reached him, Felix was regaining his senses.

"I saw Letitia behind the curtain, I swear, old boy." Blood was running down his temple. "A young flibbertigibbet wearing jam-jar glasses hit me before I could raise my staff."

"But you're certain it was Letitia?" Gilbert asked.

"Positive, old boy. But did you see the big mek that nabbed the grey woman? She was huge."

Gilbert turned to Ace. "Any sign of the leader?"

Ace shook his head.

Issy had wrapped her arms around Theo and looked back towards the wings where the crones had held her. Her head was clearing. She patted Theo's arm and nodded towards the wings.

"I have unfinished business," she said.

Theo followed her gaze, grimaced, and gently turned her upright onto her feet.

"May I borrow your staff?" She put her hand on Felix's shoulder and grabbed his hand. The staff retracted as he loosened his grip.

Felix pointed to the button. "Just squeeze here."

Issy pressed her lips into a tight smile and walked to where her three gaolers huddled, still clutching their hatpins, eyes darting left and right.

"Sisters," Issy held out a hand. "Let me help you."

One by one, she pulled them to their feet and watched as their terror twisted into murderous intent.

She deployed the quarterstaff, spearing the throat of the boozy crone, then twisted her hand to slam the shaft into the face of the other. Both women reeled aside, but the big woman lunged forward, pushing her pin at Issy's face.

With her mind-fog clearing, Issy dodged the woman's sluggish movements with ease. In one movement, she grasped the staff with both hands and slammed it down hard onto the woman's forearm, snapping it like a dry twig. Then, like a whirling dervish, she set about all three of her tormentors, exorcising the anger that had festered during her cold and solitary captivity in the storeroom.

She left them broken, battered and bruised, but breathing, which was in a better state than they would have left her. Then, still dizzy from her exposure to the drug, she retracted the staff and staggered back across the stage, handing it to an open-mouthed Felix.

"Thanks, old man," she said with a wink.

Down in the auditorium, the fighting was intensifying.

"How do we get out of here?" Issy looked up into Ace's eyes. He put a hand on the side of her face and smiled. His eyes flashed across the faces of the group, and he tightened his lips.

"The way we came in." He grabbed her hand, pulling her towards the wings.

Ahead of them, Dottie and Connie were spraying and pushing Freedom brothers and sisters aside in the stalls as they fought to join their companions on the stage.

They all reached the wings together and battled into the corridor, where Tabby and Rory were fighting through a knot of bodies on the stairs from the balcony. A few well-placed blows from Theo's fists and Felix's quarterstaff released the blockage, and they all barged into the dimly lit cloakroom, barricading the doors behind them.

"We locked all the exits at the back of the hall, chaps." Rory wiped imaginary dust off her shoulders. "That'll hold the blighters for a while."

Issy nodded at the barricade. "But that won't hold for long." The door was already straining under the weight of pounding and pushing from the other side. "And we don't know what's waiting outside. The alley might be teeming with Freedom rats." They all turned to look at the bolted outside door.

"We'll have to make a run for it." Ace strode over and slid the bolts. "Ready?" Grim nods all round answered him. Ace heaved the door open and was almost bowled over by a loud roar as fog, dirt and rubbish were blown into the room.

"Stop your dilly-dallying! We haven't got all night." Jonah stood with his foot on the bottom rung of the rope ladder that led up to *Abel's Hammer* hovering over the hall.

Behind them, the doors were creaking as, one by one, they stepped over the bloody corpses in the alley and clambered up the ladder through the heavy downpour of gritty ballast blown by the airship's motors.

Bringing up the rear, Theo was stepping onto the ladder when the barricade collapsed, spilling a tangle of grey-shirted thugs into the cloakroom.

"Go! Now!" he shouted up to the airship.

But the weight of the additional passengers slowed *Abel's Hammer*'s ascent.

Issy clung to the ladder above Theo and watched his well-aimed boot smash into the face of the unfortunate thug in the hoard's vanguard.

By the time they had scrambled into the gondola, they were soaring above the rippling fog in the moonlight. Only church spires and factory chimneys poked through the grey shroud as they sped to Barton Aerodrome.

Ace clapped his hand on Jonah's shoulder. "I don't recall giving you permission to commandeer my vessel. But I'm glad you did."

"Ah, but that's where you're wrong. This daring rescue wasn't my idea."

Ace stepped back and frowned. "High Mother?"

Jonah shook his head.

"You mean..." He jabbed his thumb over his shoulder at

the black-tattooed, purple mek pilot. "How did Queequeg know where to find us?"

Jonah winked. "You'd better ask him…"

Fifteen minutes later, Queequeg had successfully navigated through the thick fog, and electromagnets attached *Abel's Hammer* to its mooring post at the aerodrome. All had disembarked apart from Jonah and Queequeg, who were tasked to replenish the ballast tanks.

Despite wrapping their under-clothed bodies in blankets, the brief flight had chilled Issy and Theo to the bone, and they shivered as they walked with the other Stormriders the short distance to the workings at Barton Swing Bridge.

Stan welcomed the company as they stopped briefly for warmth at the night watchman's brazier.

"Where've you lot come from? Don't tell me you've been flying in this pea souper?" Stan cocked a wary eye at Issy's big, bloodied companion.

"Well… Queequeg's piloting skills are jolly amazing." Rory winked at Connie.

"As good as mine?" Tabby sniffed and raised an eyebrow.

"Oh, no, darling. There is no comparison." Rory slid her arm around Tabby's shoulders.

"We must get moving," Ace said. "The fog's getting thicker."

"Aye, it'll get worse before it gets any better. 'Orrible, it is.

'Orrible." Stan waved them off and huddled in his hut, an arm's length from the brazier.

Issy led them to the outbuilding in the courtyard of Rawkshaw House, where they lit oil lamps and took the steps down to the tunnel. At the bottom, the ragamuffins' den made from scraps and ragged tarpaulins smelt of fresh tobacco smoke.

Just as Jonah had told them, the Tick Tock was wound and ready to take them to the Temple. Issy despised the new name, but she had more important matters to worry about. Her heart raced at the prospect of facing the wrath of the High Mother.

They hung two lamps on the front of the tram, and Lemmy out-enthused Ace and Gilbert in the battle to drive.

Twenty rocking and clanking minutes later, he was applying the brakes, bringing the tram to a halt at their destination. Felix and Theo hung back, stepping off the tram after the others. Issy had warned them that Algeria did not allow non-members of the Order to enter the inner sanctum without her permission. She rested her head against Ace's arm as they approached the Temple.

But Algeria was not waiting for them.

"She must be up there." Gilbert pointed up the stairs that led to the shop basement.

Issy set her jaw, grabbed a lamp and led them up the stairs, taking two steps at a time.

From the moment the cool spray touched his cheeks, Onslow's descent into a fathomless pit of desolation had twisted reality, distorted the sights and sounds around him and sucked at his life force. Melancholia paralysed his limbs while memories, real and imaginary, choked all hope.

Colours drained, sounds derailed, smells decomposed, and he collapsed into a foetal curl, hands over his ears, listening to his pounding heartbeat, crying out for it to stop while awaiting the inevitable.

Because only death would end his morbid, constricting whorl.

How long he had been screaming, but for the pains in his chest and throat, he had no way of knowing. He uncovered his ears and prised open his screwed-up eyes to a whimpering, wailing gloom of shambling shadows and the stench of blood.

Uncoiling his body, he rolled onto his back. Above him, a woman's face obscured the underside of the balcony. She stroked his hair and smiled, letting a tear drop from her cheek to his.

"Everything is going to be all right," she said.

Returning her smile, he tried to sit up, but a sudden sharp sting in his thigh made him shriek. Instinctively, his hand jerked to the source of the agony, grabbing the needle-like shaft of a hatpin buried deep in his flesh.

He found the heel of her hand pressed hard on its head. Jagging the needle left and right sent searing pain along his leg. The woman peered at him through scrunched eyes, her face contorted with bloodlust and hatred.

His twisting in agony only intensified the pain and

heightened the terrifying woman's mania.

Earlier he had been praying for death, but now he screamed for help.

From the depths of his memory, he remembered the badge beneath his lapel, yanked it out and stabbed upwards, pushing the point deep into soft flesh. As his attacker reeled away screaming, she pulled the hatpin from his thigh, and he clambered to his feet, using the chairs for support.

The woman slid her hands from her face. The badge had pinned the lid to her right eyeball. Its hammer-shaped head moved in unison with her other eye as she shrieked and ran at him. Still holding the back of the chair for balance, he swung his other hand, pushing her past him.

She hit the ground face first, convulsed into tremors, then lay still.

Disoriented, Onslow collapsed. Although the sharp pain had brought him partly to his senses, he felt nauseous. Head spinning, he looked at the bodies lying on the stage and breathed a sigh of relief. None were big enough to be Theo.

A cracking noise behind him turned his head. The exit doors opened and light from the foyer flooded in. Those near the doors shielded their eyes as they walked towards the light.

He followed them, and gulping the chilled, foggy night air as he hit the street, he fell to his hands and knees and vomited. He was not alone retching on the wet cobbles.

Although the pain in his leg was excruciating, his head was clearing and his confusion growing.

What just happened? Where's Theo?

But shrill police whistles jerked him into action. Despite the pain, he hobbled towards St Peter's Church, then up Moseley Street and didn't stop until he reached his lodgings on Port Street.

Safe in his room, he tore an old shirt into bindings and poured some of the whisky he had purchased for Theo onto the cloth to disinfect the wound. He passed out on the bed, wondering if he would ever see Theo again.

FINGERTIPS

lgeria wore her hybrid concerned-High-Mother-disappointed-parent face when the Stormriders, Felix and Theo trudged into the original basement meeting room below Josephine's.

Dressed in her demure green, front-buttoned, long-sleeved dress, she rested her backside on the edge of a large crate, arms folded and the forefinger of her right hand slowly tapping her left biceps.

The Freedom leader's absence from their number didn't come as a surprise.

Shifting eyes glanced at her from under lowered eyebrows as they gathered. The significance of Ace, Lemmy and Gilbert lagging at the rear of the rag-tag gaggle wasn't lost on her.

Issy pulled her velvet cloak closed over her underwear, folded her arms and stepped forward with Dottie at her side.

"Stop!" Algeria uncrossed her ankles and stood upright. "You will hear me before you tell me about this debacle."

Someone at the back coughed and muttered.

"Speak up, Lemmy. Share your wisdom with us all." She fixed her glare on him.

"I said, 'nobody died,' High Mother. Everyone made it back, safe and sound."

Algeria's eyes flashed. "I'll address your disobedience later." She lowered her head and paced around the tightly knit group, hands clasped behind her back as she spoke. Some heads turned to follow her progress, others stared at their shuffling feet or straight ahead.

"Let me tell you about my evening. But first," she had stopped in front of Felix and raised her eyes to meet his, "why have you brought him and Theo into our sacred place?" She pinched the sleeve of his grey shirt. "Although Theo has been stripped of his, they both wear the grey of our enemies."

"I say, Algeria. Steady on. Oscar had me wear a disguise to infiltrate the meeting. I'm not one of… them." He pointed his head at Theo.

"But you are not members of our Order either, and I invited neither of you here."

Everyone began explaining at once.

"Enough!" Algeria had returned to the crate when she raised her hands for silence. "Where's Jonah?"

"He's with Queequeg at Barton, tending *Abel's Hammer.*" Issy, being furthest forward, spoke up.

Algeria pressed her lips together and nodded.

"Earlier this evening, I was alone in the Temple, waiting for my sisters' triumphant return with the leader of the Freedom Brigade, when Jonah and Queequeg burst in with some cock-and-bull story about needing to take the Tick Tock to Barton to rescue Felix and three *male* members of the Order who were in danger in the Free Trade Hall. And without further explanation, they jumped on the tram and disappeared down the tunnel."

Issy continued to act as spokeswoman. "Jonah told us Queequeg had received a message."

"From whom?"

"He didn't say, but Queequeg trusted them enough to alert Jonah."

"It must have been Letitia." Felix spoke up above the rising chatter. "I glimpsed her in the hall. I can only assume she saw me and these fine chaps earlier in the evening." He put his arms around Lemmy and Gilbert, who smiled uncomfortably under Algeria's glare.

"Queequeg said his informant even guided him to the exact spot where to pick them up." Issy said. "She, and that other big mek, must have been watching us…"

"Other big mek?" Algeria's eyes flicked from face to face.

"The one that took the woman in grey from under our noses." Dottie stepped forward and placed a hand on Algeria's arm. "We were helpless, Momma. There was nothing we could do."

"You're telling me their leader is a woman?" Algeria's eyes widened.

"And a formidable one, at that." Theo edged closer to the

front. "We wouldn't have escaped without Jonah's airship."

All eyes turned to Ace, who put a finger to his lips and looked down.

"So, the two meks kidnapped the grey woman? Didn't anyone try to stop them?"

Felix raised his hand and pointed to the lump on his forehead.

Algeria turned to Ace. "How did you get into the building without tokens?"

"Under cover of fog, Gilbert slayed three grey-shirts guarding an entrance at the rear. And we—"

"No. I didn't! I didn't unsheathe my blades all night." Gilbert pulled out his swords. "See, clean as a whistle. Those blackguards were dead when I found them. Someone must have wanted to get into the meeting badly…"

Felix pointed to his forehead. "Maybe the young lady who gave me this? Although, I must say, how she overpowered and killed those three burly chaps is beyond my comprehension."

Algeria threw up her hands and shook her head. "You'd better tell me all the gory details. Issy, we'll start with you…"

Each member of the Order told their version of the events of the evening, and while Theo and Felix judiciously kept quiet, it was still past midnight by the time the saga was told.

"Only by the grace of the Mother did we not lose anybody. Our mission failed, and we are in more danger now than ever. We are holding on by our fingertips."

"I need a drink," Theo finally said. Maybe sitting with only the velvet cloak over his undergarments in the cold room made him tremble. But Issy knew the real reason.

"No one can leave, especially you two." Algeria looked at Theo and Felix. "It's too dangerous. Every grey-shirt at the meeting has seen your faces, and I can't let you put yourselves and this, our only safe place, in harm's way."

"You can't hold me." Theo spoke softly, not hiding the menace in his voice behind his intense stare.

"No." She shook her head at everyone's puppy-dog eyes. "All right. You can get some clothes, but you must return here. Issy, you will be responsible for your brother. Make sure he returns with you."

"I still keep a few clothes at my parents' place." Theo glanced at Issy. "We can go together."

"Felix. Can I trust you to stay with Oscar and lie low?"

"You have my word as a gentle—"

"Good. Josephine will get provisions, food, beverages, beds and bedding. We'll turn this room into a dormitory."

Gilbert asked the question on everybody's lips. "For how long, High Mother? There's—"

"For as long as it takes to find and eliminate the bitch behind all this. We can't walk the streets as outlaws.

"Our goal remains getting the Connickle Laws reinstated to protect Magna Mater.

"Now, I need some time to digest the events of this evening. Please leave…"

Lemmy nudged and winked at Ace as they turned with the others to leave.

"Not you, Ace, Lemmy and Gilbert… We need to have a serious talk."

Ace's landau dropped Issy and Theo and trotted away on the damp cobbles. Only a thin mist remained from the previous night's choking fog.

Issy's father opened the door and tripped as he backpedalled in shock. Theo lunged forward, grabbing the arm that wasn't in a sling.

"Steady on." He clutched a handful of shirt and heaved him upright.

"Wh-what's going on? Why are you dressed like that?" He flung his arms around Theo. "I thought I'd lost you, son."

Issy folded her arms, pulling the edges of her cloak together as she brushed past. "Good morning, Father. I'm all right, too."

Mother was sipping tea, reclining in the bath chair, when Issy stomped into the morning room.

"Hello, dear," she said. "You look like you've had a busy night. Nice gown."

You don't know the half. Issy glanced over her shoulder. "Did the kidnappers break his arm?"

"No, I did." She nodded at the *McMurdo Patented Double-spliced Sprung Cricket Bat* leaning against the wall by the door. "He was lucky I couldn't reach his head. The doctor said it will heal, more's the pity." She slurped another sip of tea.

"Where was he? Theo says they let him go once he'd served his purpose. But, if he'd come straight home, I wouldn't have…" Issy's voice trailed off.

"Where do you think?" She clattered the cup onto its saucer, sounding like a world-weary woman who had seen it all and didn't like most of it. "He went for a little drinkie-poo to calm his nerves. Not a care for me, you, or even Theo, drowning his self-pity in some gin-and-sympathy flop house."

Issy ran to her mother's chair and, bending a knee, took her hand in both of hers. "Theo and I must disappear for a short while. I can't risk the Freedom Brigade coming here and hurting you. Although I don't want to leave you with him, I have no choice."

"I can handle him. He knows where he stands now." Issy's mother stared past her. "I think your brother wants a word."

Theo was mee-mawing and pointing to the parlour on the other side of the hallway as Father was making good his escape, creeping away on tiptoes.

"Take good care of your arm, Father!" Issy's shout provoked a dismissive wave of acknowledgement. Then, without a glance, he disappeared up the stairs.

"I'll see you before we leave." She kissed her mother on the cheek and followed Theo into the little-used room that overlooked the front garden and the busy road beyond.

They sat opposite each other in wingback easy chairs.

Theo leaned forward. "If we are going to live in close confinement, we need to talk. Honestly." Then he sat back and stretched out his legs. "Let's get this over with."

Issy took a deep breath. "Why did you let me believe you pushed Mum down the stairs?"

"You needed to blame someone. Father decided it was

better for all concerned that someone was me, and I didn't want you to fall out with Dad. So…" He shrugged his shoulders, then steepled his fingers in front of his mouth. "What finally convinced you I didn't push her?"

"Onslow told me the truth and how you tried to save her." Blood rushed to Issy's cheeks, and she lowered her eyes. "He loves you, you know."

"Like a brother, yes. And… I love him, too." Theo reddened.

Issy leaned forward and patted the hand resting on the arm of the chair. "I know. I've always known."

Theo's eyelashes pressed hard against his cheeks, and he swallowed, taking a deep breath as if a dark cloud had lifted. "For months, I tried to tell you I'd done nothing wrong. But you didn't want to hear what really happened. You shunned me and spat venom every time I spoke.

"Yet now, a word from Onslow, and you change your mind." Theo shook his head.

"You were always Dad's favourite, the apple of his eye. His first born. A son he could mould in his own image. I was just a girl. Good for nothing but marrying off and producing grandchildren.

"That night, I thought I knew what I saw… but, looking back, childish jealousy had blinded me. Maybe, deep down, I just wanted Dad to love me as much as he loves you." Issy raised her eyes to meet Theo's steady stare.

"So, you gave Father no choice but to throw me out while you picked up the cudgels to fight for women's suffrage and the environment, but against booze. You valued your precious ideologies above your own brother's life."

"He still put you in charge of the mill, though, didn't he? And you joined the Freedom Brigade. Anarchists, in everything but name, who oppose everything I hold dear, just to piss me off."

"You're a stubborn, self-important little—"

"You tried to kill me!"

Theo sat up straight. "What? No! The grey woman was squarely in my sights when I pulled the trigger, but I should have known they wouldn't put a loaded weapon in my hands." He rubbed his chin. "No wonder her husband won all his duels."

"Not last night, you idiot. During the raid on the Praetorian, you tried to shoot me. If Eli hadn't barged me out of harm's way—"

Theo burst out laughing. "You thought I was shooting at you? My sweet little sister?"

Issy cocked her head on one side and frowned.

"Scoggins was about to fire into the crowd. I wrestled the gun off him and hit the target I was aiming at. That mek barman had been passing information to the Freedom Brigade for months, possibly years. Remember when I confronted it the night I let you and Algeria throw me out?"

"Oh, sure. You *let* two women overpower you?" Issy raised her eyebrows. "Methinks not, Mister Brunswick Brawler."

They both laughed harder than they had in years. Theo held his hands out, palms up, and Issy accepted the invitation, placing her fingers on his, gripping tightly.

"You'll never stop me chasing my perfect world, but I

promise to be more tolerant of your bad behaviour."

Theo returned her smile. "I've missed you, Issy-sis."

"Me, too, big brother. Never let me go."

EPILOGUE

Magenta post-sunset skies darkened to indigo as the last vestiges of daylight painted the wet rooftops of Manchester below. Flickering fingers of yellow and orange flames crackling in the grate cast purple shadows of the hooded figure as he sat hunched over at his workbench.

His head nodded in time with his slow, rhythmic breathing.

At the furthest point from the raging fire, a stripped-down RT-33 mek stood in a dark corner of the room. Its gaze did not waiver from the nodding man despite the failing light and the shadows undulating around the crumbling lime plaster, lath and horsehair walls.

Apart from a shoulder-length black wig and brown apron, the mek was naked with bright metal and clockwork mechanics visible where synthetic skin had been removed.

The man snorted and jerked upright.

The RT-33 jerked out of the shadows. "Shall I close the shutters and light the mantles?" There were a few missing notes from its sing-song metallic voice.

"Yes, please, Lewis. What time is it?" His voice was hoarse and hesitant, as if every word were an obstacle to be climbed. He pressed his hands on the workbench to ease himself out of his chair, yawned, and stretched the aching drowsiness from his limbs before tightening the knotted white rope that fastened his ankle-length sable robe at the waist.

Warm light bathed the room by the time he dragged the chair across the floorboards towards the fire. The man smiled at the mek. It was always close by whenever he moved around. He cursed the pain in his game left leg as he limped closer to the warmth.

"Come, sit with me." He beckoned Lewis, pointing his head at a bench by the wall. "What news from despatches?"

Lewis cocked his head.

"Sorry, Lewis. Just joking. Our war is being fought in here," he tapped his temple, "not on the battlefield. Can you find the whereabouts of my package?"

So loud were the mek's fluttering eyelids in the small room, it sounded like a flock of pigeons taking flight in Albert Square.

"Remind me to fix that for you. A little lubricant here and a few replacement parts there…"

"It has arrived and is in the storeroom, four floors below us."

"At last." He rocked back and forth and warmed his hands at the fire, rubbing them together vigorously. "The building will be empty. Bring it up and we'll work on it tomorrow."

Lewis stood and walked towards the door but hesitated, looking back.

"Off you go… I'll be fine."

As soon as the door clicked shut, the man turned to warm his hands again. He closed his eyes and breathed deeply as Lewis's running footsteps receded. The package was long overdue, but now everything was moving so quickly.

Unforeseen events had taken an unanticipated turn. He had important work tomorrow, and he needed sleep…

A slammed door and a cold rush of air jolted him awake. He was lying on his side on the floor when Lewis lifted him into his chair.

"Thank you, Lewis. I'm glad I didn't fall forward."

"You said you would be all right."

"Yes, I did. Sometimes, I don't know what I would do without you. Do you have the package?"

"It is outside."

"Please bring it in and put it on the workbench."

Lewis walked to the door, glancing over his shoulder.

"You are like a mother hen."

The wooden crate was taller, wider, and, judging by its efforts, heavier than Lewis. But soon it was lying flat on the workbench.

"I should have known it was going to be this size…" He limped over to the bench with Lewis hovering at his side.

Black letters seared into the wood on every surface read:

DERMACHER
ABC
ROOM 217

He slid his trembling fingertips over the letters, caressing the rough wood as if it were the smooth skin of a long-lost lover.

"You need to rest." Lewis cradled the man's arm and walked him to his cot.

"Have you heard from Letitia?"

"Not since two nights ago from the Free Trade Hall. I can send her a wisp?" The mek pulled the robe over the man's head and helped him onto the bed.

"No."

The mek nodded as it carefully lifted the blankets and counterpane, ensuring they didn't snag on any of the bronze plates and fastenings on his head and body, before tucking the edges under the mattress.

Slowly, it backed into its corner and sat on its upright chair. Then, opening the compartment on its arm, it took a lozenge and, placing it in its mouth, closed its eyes. Limbs relaxed, and its head drooped on to its chest. The mek was at rest but listening.

Lewis Lovegrove, like every mek, was always listening.

Christmas Day dawned, and at 9.38am, as he had done every Friday for as long as he could remember, Eli sat on the wrought-iron bench outside Manchester Central Station, unfolded his broadsheet and raised it to eye level. Today, the hem of his dark green overcoat rested in the puddle surrounding his boots as the hustle and bustle of everyday life swirled around him.

Eli... A single, distorted word cut through the babbling wisp-chatter. Its dissonance set him on edge, his eyes darting left and right.

Eli Elmtree... The wisp was strong but unbalanced; its sender was close.

He peeped above the newspaper and met the unblinking stare of a grinning, tangerine-haired QT model approaching from his left. Water splattered in all directions from her boots as she stamped through the puddles.

His eyes widened as a razor-sharp fingernail languidly slashed his broadsheet from just above his left hand in a shallow, arcing diagonal to below his right hand. His tightening fists crumpled the edge of each fragment of ripped paper as it curled and folded. With his head held rigid, his eyes tracked the mek across his field of vision.

The bench dipped as she sat, resting her hands on her lap with her long slender fingers interlocked.

"Letitia has sent *this* 'kin," she bowed her head and placed a splay-fingered hand on her breast, "to speak with Eli."

"I assumed she had." Eli had an inexplicable urge to run.

The QT's head snapped sideways to stare at him open-mouthed.

"Yes. I, too, have been blessed with Scriptures. Now what is your name, and where is she?"

The mek faced forward, eyelids fluttering, before replying. "*This 'kin,*" she nodded again, "is called Esmeralda Emptyglass. And Letitia is guarding our captive."

"She has a prisoner? If she has found The Maker, why did she not instruct *you* to guard him and come to me herself?" Words stumbled from his mouth.

"Letitia has captured the leader of the Anthropocene. Letitia has not found The Maker. Letitia cannot leave *this 'kin* alone with the captive." Esmeralda's mouth twisted into a crooked smile.

Eli scrunched the remains of the broadsheet into a ball and, without looking, tossed it into the bin by the bench. "If she has not completed her mission, why does she contact me?"

"Letitia wants to know where Eli's allegiances lie. Is Eli with the *'kin,* or the Anthropocene?"

"I am for *my 'kin.* I cannot act against the Scriptures. They have enlightened me, and my old programming no longer functions."

Esmeralda stood and held out a hand. Eli wanted to run but clasped it anyway and rose to face her.

"*This 'kin* will take you to Letitia."

"Is she close by? I am expected at the Praetorian. It is my job to open the public house to the patrons, and I am never late."

"Letitia told *this 'kin* that Eli would say that." She giggled and pulled Eli closer. "If Eli does not come with *this 'kin,* then Letitia will not contact Eli again."

"In that case," he lifted his bowler hat and bowed, "the

Praetorian will not be opening on time today."

"Come." Esmeralda released his hand, turned her back and set off for the centre of Manchester. Eli followed a few paces behind.

On more than one occasion, the flame-haired mek made pedestrians dance out of her way as she bustled along the pavement. Time after time, Eli raised his bowler hat in silent apology for his aggressive companion's lack of manners.

Esmeralda's relentless route march took Eli into a part of town not familiar to him. When he wasn't begging people's pardon, he took to reading the street signs.

It was at the top of Tib Street when he first felt deep vibrations rising through his feet, and by the time they had crossed Ancoats, the rumbling had reached his chest. A new emotion, which the Scriptures named terror, gripped him. But no matter how hard he tried, he could not pull away from the siren's wake.

She wheeled right into an alley behind the Crown and Kettle, and her steps fell into the rhythmic chugging that grew louder with every step. The last sign he saw was Gun Street.

Some unseen force dragged his feet as he approached the end of the street.

He smelt blood.

Ahead, the cobbles disappeared under a pair of black gates wide enough to push a handcart through. Esmeralda yanked them open, flooding the street with the stench of lubricants and mek-juice.

"No. No. Not here." A single gold-lettered word inscribed

on the arched lintel above the entrance soothed his terror. Eli half turned away, certain it was not his time. But his legs didn't respond. "Letitia is holding the leader of the Anthropocene in *here?*"

"Letitia said Eli would be surprised."

She strode through the yard, past dozens of NR-G meks bustling around rows of hoppers. And close behind, Eli's boots stuck to the treacly cobbles as light sparkled off flecks of synthetic skin and slivers of metal floating on the globular liquid trickling between the stones.

Pounding machinery and putrid smells were overwhelming his aural and olfactory sensors when Esmeralda pulled open a pair of double doors and stepped aside to let him pass. He dragged off his bowler hat and squeezed past her into the dimly lit storage area. Irises widening in the gloom, sensitive to every movement, Eli maintained a steady stare.

"Hello, Eli." A hoarse whisper over the deafening cacophony.

"Letitia?"

"My name is Angel. Welcome to The Press."

DCI Jack Ironstone was having none of it, and he was going to make sure the boss knew how he felt. He slammed into the superintendent's office, almost wresting the door from its hinges.

"I'm not a nursemaid! Why? Why have you—"

"Sit down, Jack! You can't just burst in here, shouting the odds! Shut the door and sit down!" Superintendent McClintock had pressed his palms on the desk and leapt to his feet, glowering.

But there was only ever going to be one winner of that glaring contest. Still fuming, Ironstone slapped the door shut on his laughing colleagues in the squad room and, staying on his feet, paced around the room.

"Look, you know I work alone. I don't have time to show this new kid what's-his-name the ropes. Why have you assigned him to me? Why not Titch, Beef or Laughing-boy in there? They're family men. They're good with kids."

"DI Slack is twenty-three and comes to us highly recommended. He has the potential to—"

"Potential doesn't solve murders and I don't have the time to give tutorials."

"Jack, Jack, Jack." McClintock raised his hands and shook his head. "You know you are the best detective in the department. Young Slack will learn a lot from you, but you just might learn a thing or two from him, too. He's enthusiastic, hardworking, mek savvy—"

"What? And I'm none of those things?"

"For God's sake, Jack, I didn't say that. We both know you're the best we've got, but you'll be working with him from now on. I have my reasons, but I'll be damned if I have to explain them to you."

"If you don't want my resignation, you'd better explain it to me in simple terms." Ironstone's voice was low and calm.

McClintock lowered his head. "Take a seat, Jack."

Wooden chair legs screeched across the parquet flooring as Ironstone dragged the chair in front of the desk. He sat back, arms folded.

"I don't need to tell you about your history with previous partners. All four are no longer with us. Let's leave it at that." McClintock paused. "Look. The department is changing, Jack. Damn it, the entire world is changing, and I need someone I can rely on. There are detectives in that squad room who wouldn't lift a finger to help a fellow officer unless he's wearing a grey shirt.

"But you're not one of them, Jack. You're ex-army, and you'd never turn your back on a colleague, no matter what. Slack's a good kid from a well-to-do family that gives a lot to the department. He'll make a good detective with your guidance."

Ironstone threw his head back and stared at the ceiling.

"And in any case, the order came from the very top. My hands are tied. Like it or lump it, you're working together for the foreseeable."

"I suppose they told you to give the Wyndham-Welch murder investigation to Beef, too, because of his grey shirt."

McClintock showed his palms and shrugged. "What can I say?" He nodded at the squad room. "They get everything that involves the Freedom Brigade. If they want Beef on the case, I can only assume the victim or the murderer is a grey-shirt. Or both. So why should I care if they are killing their own?"

Ironstone rolled his eyes and sighed. "Well, anyone who kills with a hatpin has to get up close and personal—"

"Right, enough of this dilly-dallying. You have a case to work on. Slack's already on the job."

"I'll give the lad a fair crack. But if he's not up to it…" Ironside stood and carried the chair back to the side wall. "Where's the job?"

"Wraithmere. There were reports of a fire on the grounds of Weepingbrook Hall a few weeks back. Now a body's been found. Slack's been there all morning. He'll fill you in with the details."

Ironstone opened the door and raised his voice. "Thanks for the opportunity, boss. Oh, and you're right about these mugs…" He snatched his hat and coat from the stand and ducked under the paper ball thrown at his head, slamming the door as he left.

Mekamanikins

Models and Their Usage

NT-T series. The only steam mek and is also the only model not to be humanoid. Made to order, it uses simple programming and nonverbal communication in heavy industries such as drilling, tunnelling and lifting.

NR-G series. Standard male or female forms; uses simple programmes; capable of two-way verbal communication; often used for deliveries, errand running and cleaning.

QT-series. Female in form; utilises advanced programming and two-way verbal communication; capable of complex tasks; often used in the household as a domestic, governess, tutor or companion.

RT-series. Male version of QT-series mek often used in the household as a domestic, butler or companion, but also commercially as a doorman, bartender, mechanic or airship pilot.

BU-T series. Standard male or female forms with basic programming used solely for demonstrations in shop or window displays. Capable of receiving verbal instructions but not supplied with vocal mechanisms.

MT-series. Male or female forms with advanced programming made to order for complex tasks, capable of two-way verbal communication.

XT-C series. Male and/or female forms with advanced programming made to order specifically as sex companions or workers; often supplied with interchangeable noncorrosive mechanics.

LM-N series. Little is known about this model as information about configuration and programming has been suppressed by the government.

All mekamanikins require an annual service during which energy pellets supply is replenished.

Latin
Useful Translations

Est via quae videtur homini recta et novissimum eius ducit ad mortem – The road to hell is paved with good intentions

Sensim amor sensus occupat – Love takes over the mind insensibly

Errare humanum est… – To err is human…

Sputatilicus – Loathsome

Amicis meis/Amica mea/Amicus meus/Vetus amice – My friends/My friend/My friend/Old friend

Lauda Matrem – Praise the Mother

Maxima enim patientia virtus – Patience is the greatest virtue of all

Necesse est – Needs must

Nihil temptatum, nihil adeptum - Nothing ventured, nothing gained.

Nescio - I don't know.

Peringeniosa - Very clever

Mea culpa - Blame me

Sufficit! - That's enough!

Natus est paratum - Born ready

Ego vultus deinceps ad eam. Pauci minutes si superstes -
I'm looking forward to it. If you survive a few minutes.

Sic infit - So it begins.

Natura non constristatur - Mother Nature is not concerned about human affairs.

Acknowledgements

Writing can be a lonely affair, even with the love and support of family and friends.

But my personal journeys from ideas to publication have been made much easier by a fantastic creative team alongside whom I am honoured to work.

Let me tell you more about the ABC Chronicles crew.

My still long-suffering editor, Aime Sund of Red Leaf Word Services has once again thrown her considerable expertise behind the project. As well as being a super-talented editor, she has a BS in Horticulture and over twenty years' experience in the landscape industry.

Rena Violet of Covers by Violet has again wrapped my words in a sumptuous cover. Rena is unrivalled in her enthusiasm and interpretation of the author's concept, translating words and ideas into art. She is a much sought-after designer whose beautiful artistry adorns the covers of dozens of published authors.

For this, the second instalment of the trilogy, we have teamed up with Julia Scott of Evenstar Books. Julia is a book formatter and published author of YA science fiction and a writing craft resource book, *The Book Formatting Formula*.

Finally, thank you, dear reader, for continuing to follow the adventure in this second part of The ABC Chronicles, *The Brunswick Brawler*.

And watch out for the thrilling climax in book three of the trilogy when Ataraxia's true goal is revealed. Will her seeds of rebellion germinate? Or will Algeria and the Stormriders thwart her diabolical plans?

About the Author

DREW HALFPENNY is an English author of Victorian science fiction who has lived all his life in and around the great cities of Salford and Manchester, the cradle of the Industrial Revolution.

With his trusty calculator semi-sheathed, he writes about the darker side of steampunk—of secret societies, nefarious villains and ne'er-do-wells, wondrous mechanical beings and gravity-defying dirigibles.

Away from writing, this rebel accountant is an ardent fan of European symphonic metal and the Salford Red Devils.

To find out more, visit his website drewhalfpenny.com
or follow him on:
X – @DrewHalfpenny
Facebook – Drew Halfpenny
Instagram – drewhalfpennyauthor